P9-CRG-558

Praise for Isabel Cooper's

Highland Dragons

"The mix of hardheaded realism and fantasy in this novel is enchanting... Victorian mores and melodrama are cast in sharp relief when dragons and fantastical quests are thrown into the plot."

—Eloisa James for Barnes and Noble,
for *Legend of the Highland Dragon*

"An outstanding read! A fast-paced, smartly written plot— fraught with danger and brimming with surprises—makes it impossible to put down."

—*RT Book Reviews* Top Pick, 4.5 Stars for
Legend of the Highland Dragon

"Mesmerizing, ingenious, slyly humorous, and wonderfully romantic, this unusual charmer is a winner for fans of paranormals. A Highland dragon? How can it miss?"

—*Library Journal* Starred Review for
Legend of the Highland Dragon

"With a well-developed plot and rich language, Cooper's tale is rooted in romantic suspense and aligned with fantasy, making for an excellent crossover."

—*Booklist* for *The Highland Dragon's Lady*

"The fantasy, interesting characters, mystery, danger, sensuality, romance, and love will keep readers intrigued right up to the very satisfying ending."

—*Romance Junkies* for *The Highland Dragon's Lady*

"Another incredible, unique romance from the ingenious Cooper. Smartly written, fast-paced, and brimming over with magic and surprises, this is exactly what readers crave and what Cooper continues to deliver."

—*RT Book Reviews* Top Pick, 4.5 Stars
for *Night of the Highland Dragon*

"An imaginative historical fantasy... I can only hope that there will be more stories about these fascinating shape-shifters."

—*Night Owl Reviews* for *Night of the Highland Dragon*

Also by Isabel Cooper

Dark Powers
No Proper Lady
Lessons After Dark

Highland Dragons
Legend of the Highland Dragon
The Highland Dragon's Lady
Night of the Highland Dragon

Dawn of the Highland Dragon
Highland Dragon Warrior
Highland Dragon Rebel

HIGHLAND DRAGON REBEL

ISABEL COOPER

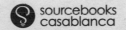

sourcebooks
casablanca

Copyright © 2017 by Isabel Cooper
Cover and internal design © 2017 by Sourcebooks, Inc.
Cover art by Craig White

Sourcebooks and the colophon are registered trademarks of
Sourcebooks, Inc.

All rights reserved. No part of this book may be reproduced in any form
or by any electronic or mechanical means including information storage
and retrieval systems—except in the case of brief quotations embodied
in critical articles or reviews—without permission in writing from its
publisher, Sourcebooks, Inc.

The characters and events portrayed in this book are fictitious or are
used fictitiously. Any similarity to real persons, living or dead, is
purely coincidental and not intended by the author.

Published by Sourcebooks Casablanca, an imprint of Sourcebooks, Inc.
P.O. Box 4410, Naperville, Illinois 60567-4410
(630) 961-3900
Fax: (630) 961-2168
sourcebooks.com

Printed and bound in the United States of America.
OPM 10 9 8 7 6 5 4 3 2 1

PROLOGUE

1320

MOST MEN CALLED FOR SOMEONE AT THE END. *MOTHER* WAS popular. God, Christ, the Virgin, and various saints all received their share of pleas. Occasionally, dying lips shaped themselves to a specific name: a lover, a child, a sibling.

Moiread had never heard a man ask for the one who'd led him into battle.

In the minds of the dying, she'd done enough.

The field far below her was sodden red, good growing land churned into dirt by hundreds of desperate feet. It would recover eventually and bear all the richer for the day's work. Blood improved the earth—her grandfather had made sacrifices along those lines in his day—and most of this blood came from Englishmen, which lessened any loss she might have felt.

Fee, fau, fum, she thought as she flew high above the carnage, remembering giants in children's tales. Giants and monsters: all took a great deal of effort to kill, and the English hadn't had a Jack with them that day.

For her, the battle had gone well. Oh, she'd taken a slash to her belly that stung like the devil, and an arrow had nicked the tip of her right wing, but both wounds had come from normal steel. A good night's sleep would heal them. She'd dodged the few glowing crossbow bolts that would have done her more lasting damage, and her fiery breaths had hit the English armies hard in return. It was rarely practical for the MacAlasdairs to take dragon shape in battle, but when they could manage it, they generally left a mark.

She folded her wings and dropped, landing near the back of the army. In the second before she changed back to human form, with its less acute senses, the stench of burnt flesh was almost overpowering.

Then she was herself. The smell wasn't so bad. The screaming was worse. When she was human, it was easier to understand the words.

"M'lady," said Angus, her second-in-command, meeting her as she walked out into the camp proper, "'tis good to have you back."

"Our count?"

"Ten dead, six as good as, twelve injured." That was only among the hundred or so of Loch Arach's men-at-arms. Two other lords and their men had fought with Moiread against the English, there by a stream whose name she couldn't call to mind right then. "Young Lord Murray got a poleax to the back of the head. His priest's with him. He'll last a few hours yet."

A man was crying nearby. His sobbing sounded faint and twisted, but not wet the way it would have been from an arrow to the lungs. *Gut wound*, Moiread thought. "The English?"

"Mostly fled. Fifty hale prisoners, twice that wounded. Lord Fraser's for killing them all...says the English aren't likely to pay any ransom, considering."

"That they aren't," said Moiread slowly.

Slaughtering prisoners was poor form. It wouldn't be the first battle since Berwick where it had been done, nor other acts that Moiread preferred not to think about. Men drunk on victory and rage were unpleasant creatures, and hard to rule. The MacAlasdairs, not being entirely mortal, had an easier time keeping their soldiers in line, but there was always a struggle.

She flexed her hands. "I'd rather not spill more blood today. I'll see what I can do. First, I'll see Murray."

The young lord had been a pleasant companion, decent at dice and fair of voice. He'd taken both her feminine nature and her draconic one in stride after the first shock. Even if none of that had been true, he was a lord. Rank meant standing at each other's deathbed.

He was likely the lone dying man, out of the hundreds on the field—out of the thousands over the course of the whole bloody war—for whom Moiread's presence would make any difference at all.

ONE

Scotland, 1328

HOME.

"Praise God!" said Angus, and although Moiread didn't share his vocal devotion, her silent thanks were equally heartfelt. She could have kissed the dark walls of MacAlasdair Castle like a sailor returning to land. She settled for an ear-to-ear grin and a yell that made the guards at the gate straighten up in alarm before they saw her face.

It wasn't just that she'd been away for more than twenty years. It wasn't just that she was coming home victorious. The damn sky had opened for the last two days of her journey back. Her cloak had struggled valiantly before giving up and now hung like a giant sponge across her shoulders and down her back. Her mail would need hours of polishing, and the damp leather beneath the chain had been chafing her for the last ten miles. Her boots were squashy, and the fat, elderly plow horse she rode was up to her fat, elderly hocks in mud.

Even if Moiread wanted to abandon her men, she couldn't have flown in that weather. Between the gusts of wind and not being able to see more than a foot in front of her face, she'd probably have ended up in Rome. And while dragon blood meant that cold and wet wouldn't harm her like they would mortals, it didn't make them more pleasant.

But up ahead were stone walls to keep out the rain, a roast turning on a roaring fire, and her room, full of clean, dry clothing, another fire, and—praise Christ and all the saints in heaven—a *bed*.

She grinned at the bowing guards as she passed them—too slowly for her tastes, but the horse had served her well and she didn't want to strain it—waved to the servants in the great courtyard, and practically jumped out of the saddle with more spirit than she'd had since midway through Yorkshire.

"Have her rubbed down well and give her a hot mash," she told the stableboy, a lanky redhead who'd probably been toddling when she left. "We've been a long time traveling."

"Aye, Lady…Moiread?"

Clearly he'd picked up the name from the older grooms talking around him. Or he'd seen the soggy banner her men carried and realized there was only one MacAlasdair woman likely to ride in at the head of a company. Moiread laughed. "That's the one, lad," she said, and extracted a coin from her belt pouch. "Don't worry,,, You'll have a chance to get used to me this time."

Now free of the horse, she made good speed to the inner door. A number of smells filled the staircase beyond, but the castle was clean, and food odors were the strongest: bread and meat. It was just past lambing season, Moiread remembered, and her stomach growled at the notion, sounding nearly as loud as her own roar could be in her other shape.

"Lady Moiread!"

One of the maids rushed up to her and dipped into a curtsy, the top of her blond head coming briefly to Moiread's waist. It didn't rise above her chest when the girl stood either. She was a short one, and Moiread was taller than most men.

"Aye," she said, trying to remember how to talk to servants who weren't also fighting men. The maid was a few years older than the stableboy, Moiread thought, but nonetheless young—nobody she'd have known ten years ago, and that visit had been a short one. "I'll want a fire in my room and a bath."

God's wounds, but it was a relief to make such requests freely, knowing that she wasn't condemning a brace of footmen to sudden and intense labor. At most of the places where she'd been quartered, from farmhouse to castle, baths meant dragging tin tubs up a flight or two of stairs, then heating buckets of water and carrying them as well. For the MacAlasdairs, sorcery made those matters considerably easier.

"Yes, m'lady. Your father's given orders for both already."

"Did he? Good man." Her scouts would have given Artair warning, even without divination, but Moiread's father was always busy and not always prompt about passing his knowledge on to the housekeeper. This time the dice seemed to have come up in Moiread's favor.

The maid nodded. "Only he says to tell you, m'lady, that you're to dine in the hall tonight."

"Oh."

Moiread shoved a splotch of wet hair off her forehead and thought less charitable, less filial things. *I just got home!* was one, and *I hope he doesn't expect three coherent words out of me* another.

"There are guests, m'lady, from Wales."

"And Artair doesn't think he can entertain them by himself? The world may be ending." The maid kept tactful silence on that. Moiread couldn't blame her. "Very well. Tell the laird my father that I am, of course, at his service. I'll even try to look civilized for the occasion, though I can't promise not to fall asleep in my soup if it goes too late."

"My lady," the maid said and curtsied again before nipping off to tell Lord Artair a most likely *heavily* altered version of Moiread's sentiments.

Artair would probably translate them back into the original adeptly enough. Being family for more than two centuries provided them with a private master language of their own.

Dripping her way up two flights of stairs, Moiread wondered idly what Welshmen were so important that Artair had demanded her company for the occasion. Her mother's people had ties to the country, but Wales had been under English rule for decades, having lost to the same bastard excuse for a king who'd tried to take Moiread's own country.

Longshanks must have spun in his grave when his stripling grandson signed the treaty with Scotland. The idea still made Moiread smile, the better part of a year later.

No, the prospect of a formal dinner couldn't lower her mood, not with that memory fresh to take out and polish. She'd have that story to dine on, and she'd eat better than she had in months. Meanwhile, the fire in her hearth already warmed the room, a metal tub of water stood steaming in front of it, and two maids were waiting nearby.

Quickly, they plucked Moiread clean of cloak, belt, and boots. The mail gave them a moment of trouble—they were used to waiting on ladies, not soldiers—but they took instruction well and Moiread wore her hair short to some purpose. In little time, she was naked, ignoring the way the girls stared at her scars, and easing herself into the hot water.

"Welcome back, lady," said one of the maids.

Moiread sighed with pleasure. Odd how being surrounded by water was so vile when it was cold and near bliss when it was hot. She flexed her toes against the end of the tub and leaned her head back on the other rim. "I am never leaving again."

MacAlasdair Castle hadn't changed a great deal in twenty years.

A few of the tapestries in the great hall had been replaced; a hunting scene now hung where Madoc remembered the martyrdom of Saint Sebastian. Outside was rainy late spring rather than snowy early spring, with brave buds beginning to show themselves on the trees, but that was due to the time of year rather than the years gone past.

The long, dark-walled hall with its high ceiling was the same, of course, as were the heavy tables lining it. Those probably hadn't changed in generations, let alone mere decades. A fire roared in the hearth, necessary for most of Scotland's year. The people also looked the same: mostly small and dark, a few outliers, brisk and busy and talking quickly in Gaelic the whole time.

Most dressed in the *léine*—a long shirt—and trews, with plaid cloaks pinned around their necks. Except for the reds and blues of the plaids themselves, their clothing was dark or undyed wool. On the dais beside Madoc, Artair and Douglas were brighter figures, their layers of robes and the fur at the neck and wrists proclaiming their wealth, but their clothing was as it might have been for half a century, without the changes Madoc had heard about from the French court.

Well that might be. The MacAlasdairs' blood had mingled with that of a dragon's far in the past, and fifty years could be a blink of an eye even to Douglas. It certainly was to his sire. Madoc didn't remember a time when he hadn't heard of Artair and his brood, and he himself aged slower than most men, though without the MacAlasdairs' other gifts.

Artair—immense, gaunt, and white-topped, like a mountain taken human shape—was a change. He'd not been present in person on Madoc's last visit and now sat at the head of the table, rarely speaking but nonetheless holding all eyes either on him or ready to glance his way at a moment's notice. His younger son, Cathal, and the woman Cathal had taken to wife were absent, off in France, as was the lady Douglas had taken hostage during the first and least successful bout of their war with England.

In almost all other respects, the castle was as it had been, and Madoc was glad of it. Change was as inevitable and as obvious as a spring flood almost everywhere else, and while he bent to it, he welcomed the chance to linger in a steadier place.

"Oh yes," he replied to Douglas, drawing himself back from memory and picking up their conversation again. "It's been that wet the last few summers. We've had a struggle getting any sort of stores in, and the crops themselves have been poorly. My father's for clearing more of the forest. He says that way we can maybe sell the wood, and the land opened up may be richer."

"Could be," said Douglas, "but forest land is a tricky sort, even without the trees. Here it's half rocks, best kept for pigs and deer."

Neither he nor Artair said so, but Madoc suspected it also gave them concealment. Men like Artair wouldn't want their villeins seeing all they did—or all they were.

Even without those considerations, he'd have preferred to believe Douglas. Lord Rhys, Madoc's father, was probably right. Opening the forest to more fields was the practical thing to do and best for their people...and yet Madoc had too many memories of playing in the forest as a child or hunting in it as a young man. He loved its twisting pathways, the shadows beneath the trees, and he could never quite be easy with the idea of diminishing them, however slightly.

But this is no easy world, is it?

He sighed and distracted himself by spearing a slice of pork as the platter came by. The MacAlasdairs hadn't stinted on their hospitality during his last visit, in the middle of war and soon after winter, and the changes since had been for the better.

Madoc was about to say as much, phrased more diplomatically, when movement from the lower tables caught his eye. Those seated were turning, a few nudging their neighbors to take their attention from food or conversation, all looking toward a tall, slim figure striding up the hall toward the dais. Thus alerted, his companions on the dais turned as well, and Artair smiled. "Ah, good."

Paternal affection suited his predator's face oddly, but it was also unmistakable.

Just as unmistakably, the woman approaching was of his line. She almost had Madoc's height. He thought they would see eye to eye, or nearly, and he was a tall man for any people but the MacAlasdairs. For a woman, she was broad-shouldered, with full breasts and slim hips, and she carried herself like one used to bearing the weight of armor. Just then, she wore only linen and wool: a blue-gray kirtle and a rich, blue overgown embroidered with white flowers. Above the fabric, her skin was winter pale but with shades of olive, her hair glossy dark brown and short as a page's, curling slightly below her ears.

"My younger daughter," said Artair, rising as the

woman reached the dais and curtsied. "Moiread, lass, 'tis well to have you back home."

He gave her a quick embrace, kissing each cheek. Douglas, farther away, stood and bowed, smiling warmly.

"It's good to be back, Father." She had a pleasant, smooth soprano voice. She also had Artair's ice-blue eyes, but her gaze was both amused and weary. "Douglas, you're looking well. And my lord"—she curtsied to Madoc—"I take it you're the reason I'm keeping myself awake for a few hours."

"Madoc, heir to Avondos," said Artair, while Madoc was trying to decide whether Moiread had meant to be suggestive. If she hadn't spoken so straightforwardly, and if her father and her brother hadn't been so close at hand, his thoughts could well have gone along those lines in a more decided fashion.

Hastily, he made his bow to her. "And honored to be your father's guest, Lady Moiread, and to have the pleasure of meeting you as well."

"Aye," she said, and a cynical smile spread across her strong-boned face. "You honor us with your presence. But…" She sat down and began to pile food onto her trencher, speaking at the same time. "Fine company as I'm certain you are, I misdoubt my father called me to this dinner only for that, not when I've barely had a moment to wash the dust from my boots and the blood from my hands."

"You've grown no less prone to exaggeration, I see," said Douglas.

"God's not so pleased with you as that," Moiread replied easily. "And so, I pray you, one of you reveal the purpose of this meeting before I recall how weary I am."

TWO

BLUNTNESS FROM MOIREAD SURPRISED NONE OF HER FAMILY. Cathal might have teased her about it, were he there, and Agnes might have expressed her disapproval in any number of ways, but Artair and Douglas only smiled. The stranger, the Welsh lordling, blinked eyes a shade darker and closer to gray than her own, but otherwise kept the same pleasant smile he'd had when he'd greeted Moiread.

"We've won a great victory," Artair said calmly. "You most actively among us, most of all at the end."

"The Bruce won a great victory. Our men and I helped. Sent enough of the English bastards to hell to make a difference, I hope."

"Take the edge off that anger soon, Daughter. We may need them in a hundred years." Artair spoke as coolly as usual, a man advising builders on the best place for a stone or telling his child to lower her arm when she drew her bow.

"Mmph," said Moiread. She was old enough to check the protest that rose from her heart to her throat—that she'd call on the devil himself for aid before she turned to the kings of England and their men. She was too tired to say anything gracious in its place. "You didn't summon me to the hall to tell me *that*."

"No. The English, I think, will not be long content with the truce." Artair paused as the wine cup came around the table, raised it to his lips, and then handed it on. "We have won ourselves a space to breathe, to act, and to make alliances—particularly with those who have their own reasons not to love the men of the south."

He gestured to Madoc with one huge callused hand.

"Without, however, involving ourselves in another war so soon," Douglas said, forestalling Madoc's question with exactly the same tone their father had used. He truly was turning into Artair's mirror, though his hair was red and his face far less wrinkled. "Particularly one which, alas, I misdoubt we could help to win this time."

"You'll have no quarrel with me on the matter," Madoc said. "I'd never dispute your men's strength, and it's certain all the legends of your own are as honest as the day is long, but even that would not take the English rule from my land, I think. Not now."

Madoc smiled, speaking with gentle regret but no bitterness. Either he was more serene of mind than most priests Moiread had encountered or he'd learned diplomacy well. She was inclined to think the latter. For certes, his pretty face would make negotiation more pleasant.

It *was* a pretty face, and sharp and thin-lipped enough not to be feminine either. His slate gray eyes were big and his lashes long and black, like the faintly curling hair of his head, and when he smiled, it was slow and charming. He had a lean but strong body of Moiread's own height and a smooth baritone voice. The whole combination probably had parted thighs from Cardiff to Dover, dairymaid to at least minor nobility.

She sat cleaned and well-dressed, but no more than that, pinched and rough-skinned from hard travel and probably with shadows like the pits of hell under her eyes.

Oh well. I wouldn't have the strength for bedroom sport now if Adonis himself fell at my feet.

Moiread took a bite of pork. Food, properly cooked food—not half-roasted bits of squirrel on sticks—was considerable consolation and added greatly to her store of patience. And yet the more she ate, the harder it would be to stay awake.

"No," Madoc went on. "I have in mind not rebellion but preservation, the concealment of our treasures and the strengthening of old ties"—he hesitated and glanced at each of the MacAlasdairs in turn—"as I believe and hope that such things may aid us in years to come."

That pause bothered Moiread until she looked at her father. Artair *was* good at reading people. He'd dealt in matters near and far for six hundred years and more, and *his* father had survived a youth in the snake pit that had been Imperial Rome at its end. When Artair met her eyes and smiled reassurance, Moiread calmed and reclassified Madoc's hesitation from *hiding something* to *doesn't want to explain all the details right now*.

God love you for that, stranger, she thought. *Whatever you need me for, pray be as quick about it.*

"Mystically speaking," said Douglas, once the servants had moved off and the sounds of the hall covered his lowered voice. "Aye?"

"That it is. It's never a journey I would attempt while we were at war. Neither is it one I'd make were the English not still recovering themselves and thus distracted, for which I owe you all my thanks."

"Glad to be of assistance," said Moiread, helping herself to a share of purple-red boiled beets.

"And yet," Artair said, "our victory has made the journey more necessary. Aye?"

"I'd not say that so definitely," Madoc replied with another of those diplomatic smiles. "It may well be that the English would seek to tighten their grasp on us no matter what. Conquerors are as they are, and ever shall be."

"World without end, amen," said Moiread. "How does your wandering keep them off your people's necks?"

As Douglas had, Madoc made certain his words wouldn't carry, then said, "The world contains places of power. Each has qualities of its own: independence here, say, and defense. Should I succeed in performing certain ceremonies at four of these sites, with the united efforts of their rulers, it will not free my country, but turn away the more harmful of England's impulses, the more destructive whims of its lords. It will make my people as safe as they will ever be under such a rule. If I complete the journey before England acts, that is."

As a plan, it seemed sensible—but nowhere in it did Moiread see the importance of *her* presence. "Are you here for one of those ceremonies?" she asked.

"Yes," said Madoc, "but we'd concluded that before you arrived, though I'm certain you would have enhanced it."

Unlikely.

She wasn't as inept with magic as her brother Cathal—how that one had managed to win himself an alchemist's favor twenty years back was one of God's greater mysteries—but she wasn't as skilled as her father or her other siblings either. She certainly wasn't a virgin, which was the only other mystical role she could think of where she would have made any difference, unless she'd been married to one of the participants or his lover.

Quickly she glanced at Artair again, and this time saw nothing on his face. Marriage seemed unlikely. Dragon-blooded females couldn't breed with human men, and Madoc appeared human enough. Besides, with Cathal gone to France twenty years before and Artair's years advancing, she was of more use on the battlefield than in the marriage bed.

Coupling during a few rites was helpful, Moiread knew, and essential for others—spring and fertility and whatnot. She'd never heard of it aiding defensive magic, however. Besides, the ceremony at Loch Arach was over, so it seemed unlikely that was her intended purpose. What in God's name were they planning?

Madoc went on. "I came here first. When I leave here, I must go to three other places. I'd not be a braggart," he added, "but there are men who'd say I have no small skill at arms, mounted or afoot. I *could* make the journey alone, if there's need."

"But," Artair said, "one man is still one man. We have powers you lack, as you have skills we haven't mastered. Best when men can shield the backs of their companions. And alliance wears better on many points. So—"

He gestured to Moiread.

"Oh," she said, startled into further bluntness. "I'm to be his *guard*?"

"And why not?" Artair asked, while Madoc tried to weave a response. Moiread's open dismay touched both his pride and his guilt at once. He believed himself no bad companion, nor his quest so loathsome, but he didn't want anyone forced into his service, least of all a woman of noble blood. Unencumbered by such considerations, Artair leaned forward and pressed his daughter on the subject, emphasizing each point by thumping a forefinger on the table.

"His folk have long been friends of ours. I'm too old to go wandering the country. Douglas needs to assume command here. Cathal's in France, and his ties are there now. Agnes is married wi' bairns. I've already told Sir Madoc how you led our men against the English, if you hadn't made that clear, so there's no doubt of your skill. You're the most suited to do it."

"I'm also," Moiread shot back, "scarcely out of the saddle." She turned to Madoc, the tips of her hair swinging against her cheek. "How soon would you need to leave?"

"There's no definite time to it. It's best that I move quickly, as I said, so as not to give the English the chance to regroup."

Moiread nodded slowly, then held up a hand. "Very well. As a military asset," she said, stressing each word, "I'll need at least a night of good rest and three full meals before I'm in any real shape for fighting. Double that if I'm to keep watch for assassins and brigands and Christ knows what else. It's no gift to send me at half strength."

Slowly, with a low noise of consideration, Artair nodded. "That'd have you leaving the morning after next. It sounds within reason to me, if you're amenable," he added, suddenly turning to Madoc.

"Of course."

"Why do I think now that I should have started with a week?" Moiread asked her brother.

"I'm sure I couldn't say." Douglas grinned, then winced; Madoc suspected the surreptitious application of either elbow or foot.

"Now eat," Artair commanded both his children. He might have included Madoc as well; he had that sort of voice. "We will discuss specifics afterward, in a place better protected from any sort of intrusion."

That place was a small room high in the western tower, with a small well in one corner, a five-sided table in the

middle showing Loch Arach and the lands bordering it, and
no chairs at all. Madoc wasn't surprised. He'd been in the
room twice before—most recently to seal his bloodline's
bonds to the MacAlasdairs', and twenty years before, when
he'd played apprentice to Douglas's master magician and
cast the spell that let Cathal MacAlasdair save his lady.
Anyone who'd done much magic could sense the layers of
spells around the room, and many were protections. It was
the natural place for a private conference.

Moiread took a place by the wall as soon as they entered
and leaned her weight against it, careless of what the rough
granite would likely do to her clothing.

"I'll need my gear cleaned and mended," she said, eyes
half shut and voice slurred, "and we'll need to find a fresh
horse that'll carry me. Unless—" She opened her eyes and
looked at Madoc. "You know what we are. If I flew you
there, it'd be a damn sight quicker."

"And more obvious," said Douglas.

"Not possible, I fear," said Madoc. He could have told
them about the lines of force and the connection between
mortals and the land, but he observed Moiread's face and
merely said, "The journey by land is part of the rite itself.
It's also why I cannot do this with those we know in France
or Ireland."

Moiread laughed shortly. "Naturally," she said. "Where
will we ride, then?"

"First to Hallfield, in the southeast, and then along the
coast to Lancashire."

"England?" Spurred to alertness again, Moiread stared
at him. "Hell and damnation, no wonder you want a guard.
But you're never trusting them with anything, are you?"

Madoc shook his head. "An Englishman's duty is to his
king, and I'd not risk that. In Lancashire lies the entrance

to another land, and I wish to have dealings with the folk there. They can add a great deal of magical power to the spell, and their disconnection from this world will help. You understand me?"

Even with all he knew of magic and the unseen world—or perhaps because of it—he wouldn't name the Fair Folk if he had a choice in the matter. He caught Moiread's eyes instead and held them for a minute, marveling at their bright winter-lake color even when they were hazy with sleep. He couldn't let his thoughts run for long; she comprehended and nodded swiftly.

"And then," Madoc went on, "back to Wales, and one of my mother's uncles. Llanasef Fechan, that'll be, in the mountains. Up there will be the center of the spell, the anchor of place and country."

"You'll be on familiar ground there," said Douglas.

"I think I can picture it, though you'll need to show me a map when I've slept. Will I need to do aught, other than watch your back?"

"You shouldn't, no," said Madoc.

"Good. Then one other thing." She straightened up and fixed her gaze on him, suddenly alert and taking in every word, every shift of his expression. "Have you been in any danger yet? I'll go with you if you say aye or nay— England's not a place to risk alone—but it's best to know."

Madoc sighed. "Yes," he said slowly. "Or, I think so. There was a broken saddle band on the way here—or perhaps that was chance—and an arrow when I was riding. It missed, I ran, and it could have been brigands, but..." He splayed his hands.

"Be suspicious," said Moiread. "It's hard to go wrong that way. If that's all for now," she added, with a glance at her father that was equal parts sardonic and affectionate,

"I'm off to seek my bed. Try not to think of any urgent missions for me in the middle of the night, mmm?"

She bowed as she left the room. The masculine gesture looked odd coming from her—particularly in her gown—but charming in a way.

"She'll give less trouble once you're on the road," Douglas advised. "She really is verra skilled."

"I don't doubt it," said Madoc, seeing again the way she'd marched down the center of the hall.

THREE

MADOC DIDN'T SEE MOIREAD AGAIN UNTIL AFTER NOON THE next day. The rain having stopped, he and Douglas had found their way outside and over to the practice yard. A short man with gray hair was yelling orders to a motley assortment of young men with spears, while another older collection of men shot at straw targets. He and Douglas found an unobtrusive corner and watched.

"They're quite a promising lot, to my way of seeing it," said Madoc after a few minutes of companionable silence. He recognized one or two of the pikemen as the guards who'd challenged him when he'd ridden up to the gate. They were polite lads, if young.

"Aye, more promise than fact just now," said Douglas. "But the mountains are our best defense. It's rare that an enemy gets this far...one with men and horses, that is." A memory shadowed his face briefly, one that Madoc didn't want to ask about. "The real soldiers will have just gotten back, having been out in the field with my sister. Speak of the devil," he added, and raised a hand in greeting as Moiread wandered up to the yard.

She wore men's dress, plain in cut but not in color: emerald-green breeches and a knee-length tunic in a plaid that mingled the same green with dark blue and bright yellow. A belt around her waist held a long dagger, but on her shoulder she carried a sheathed sword nearly as long as she was tall.

"Slander," she said amiably. "If I'd known, I wouldn't have raided the kitchens for you." Reaching into the pouch at her belt, she tossed a withered apple to Douglas, then one to Madoc, and grabbed a third for herself. "Seems we'll miss the fruit in season this year. We can always raid the English pantries, mayhap."

The apple was sweet, though shriveled. Madoc swallowed a few bites. "And I've ample funds to pay," he pointed out. "We'll stay in as much luxury as we can. I give you my word on it."

"Oh, I've coin as well. Raiding's better sport. But I'll behave," she said in answer to a glance from Douglas. Then she eyed Madoc and smiled ruefully. "And I should ask your pardon for last night, my lord. I've spent too much time among men-at-arms, and just then I'd spent too little in bed. Nor had I known anything of these plans."

"When could we have told you?" Douglas asked. "The messengers canna' find you if you don't stay in one place."

"We *had* been going on the double the last few days. And I know the air-sprites don't do well in rain." Having made these concessions, Moiread looked back to Madoc. "So I apologize, then, and I give you *my* word I'll try to be more pleasant company."

"You've no need of my pardon, lady," said Madoc. She did look better: no shadows under her eyes nor haze in them, more expression in her face, and a neat precision in her motions that had faltered the night before. Despite male attire and what he thought was some skillful binding, she looked female, and he hesitated, doubting—and then doubting how to voice his doubts. "Ah... Had you thought to travel...in this manner?"

"More or less," Moiread said, taking his meaning so quickly that Madoc worried she'd caught his glance at her breasts. She frowned, though not at him. "Men don't take it greatly amiss in the field."

"Not when you're commanding, no, and not our men," Douglas said.

Moiread grimaced. "Aye. There were a few who raised a fuss when the fighting was done. Times have changed, and in some ways not for the better." She made another face, then shrugged away philosophy. "Illusion before we leave, then, if you or Father would be helpful. The question is which way."

"Which way?" Madoc asked.

"Aye. They can enspell me to be more manly to the eye, though I do pass as is half the time." She laughed at his carefully blank expression. "You knew already. And it's a bonny bright day here, with me not in a cloak or half covered in mud. But a touch of magic can help. Or I can dress as a fair maiden, wi' *you* escorting *me* to all eyes, and the illusion can cover my sword. Only one, though, aye?"

"Unless Father's found some clever art he's not told me of," said Douglas.

"So. Being a maiden could make me more of a surprise, should any think to attack us. I couldna' avoid the skirts, though, and they'd be an encumbrance for certain. But two men might put folks' backs up where one and a girl might not. So," she said again, and her eyes glinted with humor. "Am I your manservant, or are you my guardian?"

Either suggested images, stories that men passed between themselves when drunk. Madoc suspected that this time the suggestion was intentional, even if only for the mirth of it. He felt a brief sting of lust and fought to keep his gaze from sliding down Moiread's body again.

Most likely she was joking. She'd been at war, and soldiers' humor was not gentle. It meant nothing, Madoc decided, and fortunately her brother's presence kept him from feeling anything stronger than that momentary shift in awareness.

It would be good to keep his mind away from that path, good to keep thinking of Moiread as a comrade in arms.

"Best we see which is more valuable, isn't it?" he asked and tapped the hilt of his own sword where it hung at his waist. "Do you care for a bout?"

There was room enough in the yard for a pair to spar, even with the men training. Moiread had managed it often enough in her younger days. She vaulted the fence— Douglas mouthed something that sounded suspiciously like *show-off*, but she chose to ignore him—and drew her sword, getting her feet settled. The ground was a wee bit squashy, but not bad. Certainly it was a damned improvement over an actual battle.

Practice bouts always were. Moiread had time to adjust her weight and take in her surroundings. She wasn't slamming sideways into her own men or having to keep an eye on her opponent's fifty friends. And the place didn't reek of death. Absent the bloodlust, which had its flaws but also its merits, the whole business was to be preferred.

Certainly there was more skill in a practice bout, and Madoc, it soon became clear, did not lack for skill. He fought with a long dagger in his off hand, all the better against a foe with the sort of large weapon she wielded. She was quicker with a long sword than most. In human form, she was stronger enough than mortals to make up a bit for the difference in weight with her opponent. Still, Madoc evaded her as they moved around the practice ring, ducking sideways from one blow and stepping back from another, only to dart in with a stab that forced Moiread to react fast and set her off balance.

Flat of the blade, they'd agreed, and to five touches or

one killing blow. Madoc had the first touch, a grazing slap to the back of Moiread's leg that would have barely missed cutting the tendon.

Out of pride, Moiread might have wished to blame the point on her travels, to think that weariness and stiff muscles had slowed her reflexes. She knew otherwise. Her people recovered fast. She'd had ten hours of good sleep and two full meals, almost enough for her to heal most minor wounds, let alone simple exhaustion. She was as well fit to fight as she ever had been, and Madoc was good.

Besides, it was exciting to realize the loss. It had been a long time since she'd fought a single opponent who was a true challenge. It had been a long time since she'd sparred for the enjoyment and the skill of it. The last occasion might have been ten years before, with Douglas, and she knew his tactics too well. Madoc was new.

She grinned acknowledgment of the touch and pressed on, delighting in the weight of the sword, the stretch of her muscles, and even the lingering smart on her calf. The spring air was fresh and cool in her lungs. Madoc was coming around her side, slim legs bunching as he began to lunge. Moiread sidestepped, thrust, and caught him in the shoulder, pulling the blow instinctively.

Another pass. This time he blocked her at close range. They stared at each other across locked blades. Madoc's face was flushed, with beads of sweat at his temples, just as Moiread could feel them at hers. His chest heaved as he caught his breath.

There were other aspects of a sparring partner who wasn't a relative. Moiread felt her heart speed up in a way that had little to do with pure exertion.

That happened. The physical was the physical, and it was easy enough for sensation to transfer. Many a camp follower had made herself a comfortable living on that account. Moiread ignored it. Or mostly she ignored it. The man was near at hand and damned attractive, and there was no harm in looking.

She didn't stare long enough or intently enough to miss him going for her ribs with the dagger, at least, so all was well.

Then it was back into the fray, and she drowned attraction in the need to concentrate, anticipate, and finally move at the right moment and with the right amount of force.

In the end, Moiread won. It was a close thing. Madoc had four touches to her two when he misjudged her timing. She pulled her swing, changed the angle, and caught him clean across the gut, careful to use almost no force. Even blunt impact could be deadly there, with so many organs lying vulnerable. She'd seen that more than a few times before.

Madoc stepped back and bowed. "That finished me, didn't it? You're remarkably good, Lady Moiread."

"I've advantages. Time's not the least of them." Moiread sheathed her sword and leaned against the fence. "I'm guessing you haven't put a century into learning. Have you a verdict?"

"Male dress, I should think," he said. "If we seem less formidable, we'll be all the more likely targets for it, and I'd rather not add to whatever foes we have. Unless you've any objection to it, of course."

"None at all. Makes riding easier, and God knows I could always use the help there."

FOUR

THE NEXT MORNING DURING THEIR LEAVE-TAKING, MADOC DIS-
covered what Moiread had meant by that statement. His tall
chestnut mare stood saddled, ready, and looking sideways
at a fat, black gelding that must have been at least fifteen
years old. At first Madoc wondered if they'd be taking a
packhorse along, but he saw quickly enough that the beast
was saddled.

When Moiread came out of the stables, he begun to
understand. Rhuddem was no plodding nag, but neither was
she fractious nor given to nerves—Madoc had ridden her
to hunting often enough. Even so, she snorted at Moiread
and edged sideways. Madoc's presence on her back and
his hands on the reins kept her calm, but without them, he
knew she'd have sought greener pastures.

The black horse swung its head around to eye Moiread
with no affection, yet it stood and let her mount, which
she did aptly enough once she'd embraced her father and
her brother.

"If we don't get killed, I expect I'll be back in a year or
so," were her parting words. "God keep you both."

She looked like a woman until they'd ridden out of the
castle gates, across the drawbridge, and down the start of
the winding road, which led away from Loch Arach. Then
she reached up to her neck, where a cloudy white stone
hung from a silver chain, and spoke a word too quietly for
Madoc to hear.

Then a young man rode beside Madoc. He seemed

more youth than man, that age between eighteen and twenty that was mostly limbs and awkwardness. There was no suggestion of womanly shape beneath the plaid cloak Moiread wore.

"There," she said. "No point confusing the villagers, aye?"

"Fair," said Madoc, who'd been expecting a gruffer voice and more stubble on the chin, to say the least. "Will you be my squire, then?"

"It's as good a story as not. You can call me Michael, if you need to address me. At least it starts the same."

"It's a clever sort of a token, that."

He pointed, but only briefly. Rhuddem was picking her way along with more nerves than usual, and Madoc thought it best to keep both hands on the reins.

Observing as much, Moiread sighed. "That," she said, "is one of the minor curses of my family. Even when we're in human shape, we dinna' smell quite human, at least not to horses. And they're not fond of it. She'll calm a bit as we go along."

"But you couldn't ride her?" Madoc guessed.

Moiread shook her head. "I could maybe stay on her back," she said, "but it'd no' be worth my while, save in dire straits indeed. With the younger ones, or the worse-tempered, the best I can do is stay on their back when they bolt. Maybe. Our beasts are more used to us, but even they're nervous." She paused, took a glance around to make sure they were alone, and then added, "And should I ever have to change form around you, don't be on horseback if you can help it. It's a damned rare beast who won't panic *then*."

"All beasts?"

"The beasts of the field, at any rate. Dogs are a bit better. My sister keeps terriers. And cats don't seem to care one way or the other, or not so far as I've noticed." She grinned, an expression that was no less engaging in her male disguise. "I had an old, gray moggy that followed me about when I was a girl, and never minded what form I was in. Probably thought dragons would give him better scraps."

"And your brother does keep falcons," Madoc said, remembering the tour he'd taken of the mews.

Moiread laughed. "Aye. One hunter keeps company well enough with the others, mayhap? One of my uncles fancies himself a man of natural philosophy, and he spent three years writing about how our flight compared to the hawks'. Took apart their wings, as I recall, when the wee birds died."

"What did he find?"

"Oh, you'd have to ask him for most of it, and he's off in Turkey or the like now." She furrowed her brow and gazed into the distance, thinking. "Different sorts of bones. Though both are hollow, which I suppose must happen by magic. Devil knows where the rest of it goes when we change. Same place the scales and all that come from, I suppose."

Madoc nodded. "I've only seen your brother in his… other form…once, and that from a distance. Cathal, that was, not Douglas. And that was twenty years ago now."

"Oh?"

"I came here with Douglas. It wasn't of much note, I suspect, especially since your brother was breaking curses and falling in love and so forth at the time."

"Ah. Aye," Moiread said with a wry twist of her lips. "I wasn't here, and the accounts I heard… Aye, Cathal rather overshadowed you, I fear. And in *his* telling, his Sophia was the brightest star in the firmament. I do recall a mention or two, now that you remind me."

The clear morning air and the gray mountain walls sent Madoc's laughter back to him. "It's this I'll remember," he said, "when I start feeling prideful."

"Ah, well," Moiread said. "The priests do say humility becomes a man. But if it's any consolation, we'll often not see each other for ten or a dozen years at a stretch. Cathal and I in particular, neither of us being very settled. Or he never *was*."

"And you still aren't?"

"I've not had the chance to consider it much, not for thirty years or more." Frowning, she corrected herself, "Though I was holding the castle for the first few years of that. One of us had to stay behind, and Father's only started feeling his age."

"How old is he?" Madoc asked.

Moiread shrugged. "The figuring gets less important as we go on. He'd seen nigh half a century when the era turned, I know that."

Not for the first time in his life, Madoc thought of the difference between knowing and *knowing*. He'd heard stories and even some verified accounts from Douglas. He'd heard of and met other long-lived folk, but they were different, less human. Moiread looked and talked like any young man off to make his fortune, right up until she referred casually to centuries going by, and Artair hadn't…

Well, to think of it, there *had* been a feeling of age about the MacAlasdair sire. It simply hadn't been age as Madoc thought of it, of which white hair and wrinkles were minor manifestations. Instead, the man had the aura of a mountain.

"Ah," he said.

At his side, Moiread's lips twitched. "If you're wondering," she said, "I've a little more than three hundred years.

And I doubt I'll see Father's age. The blood thins, aye, unless we breed back with our own kind as my sister did, and as Father did not. Not with our mother… We've some half-siblings elsewhere, I hear, but far away."

"I have a few of those myself," said Madoc. "My father married again a dozen years back, and his wife has borne five living children. Pleasant enough youths."

"They generally are," said Moiread cheerfully.

They rode on, talking quietly and falling silent by turns, as the road took them down out of the mountains. It was a pleasant day for it: clear and bright, in the middle of spring, not warm enough to make riding uncomfortable nor yet with the cold wetness of the previous few days. Trees budded around them, with the hazel and alder sprouting long catkins like yellow-green cats' tails, and birds called to each other, making a counterpoint to the sound of hoof-beats. It was yet too early for the heather to flower, but the plants spread green over the hillsides.

For the better part of the day, they went alone on the road. Just as Madoc had seen when he approached, leaving Loch Arach meant leaving all other human presence. The road echoed that. Well-maintained up near the keep, it became pitted and rocky shortly after they stopped at noon for cheese and bread. The horses picked their way across gingerly. A few times they had to cross fallen branches, blown down by a past storm.

"I'll have to send messages back," Moiread said after the second such incident. "This isna' rightly our land, but Douglas or Father will be able to talk with Laird…" She pursed her lips. "Congilton, I think. Have some men from each clan see to the clearing, once the planting and the lambing are done."

"Did you not come this way before?" Madoc asked.

"Aye, but I wasna' paying much attention to the road then. Lucky thing my neck's still whole, is it not?"

"I'm certainly glad of it."

Despite such delays, they made decent time. By twilight, while they remained in the mountains, they'd started to see signs of human habitation once again. Forests beside the road had given way to plowed fields and flocks of sheep, and to an occasional stone or turf cottage or a larger house with a barn beside it. Men in plaids drove beasts through the fields with plows behind them or herded sheep with large dogs at their sides. They looked over at Moiread and Madoc from time to time, but took no more than a momentary interest.

As the sky darkened, Moiread gestured toward one of the larger houses that was roofed with heather and had walls of solid stone, rather than the stone-and-turf patches Madoc had seen on cottages. Smoke curled out from the center of the roof and into the red sky.

"There's the best we'll do for the night," Moiread said. "We'll likely have to share quarters wi' the children, but hopefully not wi' the pigs, thanks be to God."

They were more fortunate even than that. The man who came to the gate to greet them was middle-aged, his wife likewise, and their children either married or apprenticed save for a babe small enough to sleep next to his parents' bed. That bed was indeed in a separate room, for the house was large for its kind and solid. Madoc guessed that being so near the road was a handy way to come by extra coin.

Moiread provided coin casually, at least pretending not to notice when the man's eyes widened. "My lords," he said, and bowed deeply. "Shall I take your horses to the barn?"

"I'll do it," said Madoc, catching Moiread's eye. She nodded. They both remembered the broken saddle band.

"They're nervous creatures, and I'm the only one who can generally see them settled for the night, more so in strange country."

The barn held an extremely elderly donkey and a small flock of chickens. It was dark and close and smelled of its occupants, but Madoc had been in worse—had slept in worse, on journeys that had taken him far from civilized lands—and the time he spent unsaddling and brushing the horses was no hardship. It was calming, rather: familiar action even if the place and the company were both strange.

When he came back to the house, the woman was handing around thick clay bowls, ladling their contents out of the cauldron on the hearth. "Only potage, my lords," she said, ducking her head, "but if you bide a while, I can kill one of the hens and roast that."

"This will be fine," said Madoc quickly.

At home he might have asked for meat, particularly with the coin, but he didn't know these people, nor their lord. It was best not to risk taking advantage or giving cause for complaint. The potage looked good, too—thick, with onions and turnips, and with the faint smell of meat about it. Likely they'd put a bone into the pot to boil as well.

"Aye," said Moiread, "this is most hospitable."

They ate, speaking in generalities of weather and spring planting, until near the end of the meal when the man added, "…and wi' the war over, you'll not be the last guests we have." He glanced at Madoc, the question clear on his face, but he didn't voice it.

"Did you have people in it?" Moiread asked as a distraction.

"My brother, God rest him."

"I'm sorry," said Madoc.

The man shrugged. "He fell bravely, m'lord, or so they told me. It's a comfort. And we beat the bastards, did we no'?"

"That we did." Moiread flashed a grin then, despite obviously trying to prevent it, and yawned. "Beg pardon. It's been a long day riding."

It had been. With food settling into his stomach and the fire heating his toes, Madoc felt all the hours on the road coming home to him.

Still, when he stepped into the bedroom with Moiread and the door closed behind him, he wasn't too tired to feel the awkwardness of it.

Men traveling together nearly always shared a bed, unless they were wealthier than Madoc. Even strangers bedded down together at times, in small inns where there was little space. Ladies of rank generally didn't share beds with men other than their husbands.

Moiread had taken off her boots, but not her illusion. She sat on the bed, examining her sword in the dim candlelight. "We made good time today," she said, pitching her voice low enough that their hosts wouldn't overhear. "You'll let me know, aye, if you get to thinking we need to ride through the night or the like?"

"I will," said Madoc, "but we shouldn't need to. I think you've bought us a while before those measures are worth the cost to use."

Moiread tested the sword's edge with her thumb, nodded either agreement with Madoc or approval of what she felt, or both, and re-sheathed the blade. "What happens," she asked, "if we fail?"

"Nothing certain," he said as he'd done in all his explanations before. The line between persuasive argument and false prophecy was an important one. "I don't see the future. I only know what the English are likely to do and guess what's likely to happen as a result. For the first, taxes the people and the land cannot support, suspicion beyond all reason and the devil's own torments for the lightest offense, and lords of people with anger to spare. You know how men act in defeat."

"Aye," said Moiread, with a twist of her mouth.

Madoc stared into the shadows, seeing again the horrible patterns that all his information and his lines of reasoning had drawn. "We've survived English rule, but what's to come, unless I act... They'll press us until we snap, and when we do, we'll be unprepared and desperate. *That* fight will make the wars here seem like a market-day brawl. I don't know how such a war will end, or if it will." *Or how many of my people might survive it.*

Wales couldn't afford to rebel the way Scotland had—not now. Perhaps not ever. All that was left to them was to defend themselves as best they could. Madoc aimed to see his country had the best shield he could manage.

Although the light was dim, Moiread's pupils didn't narrow as she studied his face, and she seemed able to see him quite well. After that moment's scrutiny, she said, "I'd have my arse on horseback too, in your place. Father knows what he's doing. Again."

The weary affection in her voice drew a quiet laugh from Madoc.

Moiread stood and reached for her belt, then frowned. "I don't *think* we need to keep watch here," she said. "The doors and walls are thick, and I'd wake were a man to come sneaking about the house."

"You hear well, then?"

"We all do. And if I'm no' fresh from a battlefield, it's not been a verra long time either." Unbuckling the belt, she placed it and the weapons it held by the side of the bed, near at hand, then crawled under the blankets. "Christ, it's good to lie down."

It was, Madoc discovered when he stretched himself out beside her, but it wasn't the same as sharing a bed with another man. Moiread's illusion covered sight and sound well enough, but not scent. Even from a respectful distance, Madoc could smell heather from her hair, and from her body a smoky, musky scent that was not quite human but definitely female.

He was glad the day had been so long and tiring. The night would have been very long otherwise, and not at all comfortable.

FIVE

THE NEXT NIGHT BROUGHT THEM OUT OF THE MOUNTAINS AND
into a village that was almost a town, although Moiread
didn't know its name. It had a church and a blacksmith's
shop and, most important, an inn with a decently drawn
sign outside its door: a wolfish dog baying at the moon.

"Poetic, after a fashion," Madoc said.

"Aye." Moiread laughed. "Are we meant to be the dog,
do you think? And the ale the moon?"

"I'd bay loud enough for a cup, I confess," said Madoc,
but cheerfully enough to belie the words. "Though I'll
wager our coin will speak loudly enough."

He dismounted easily and, once Moiread was on the
ground, took the reins of both horses, leading them toward
the small enclosure that this inn had instead of a stable.

For all that, the inn wasn't bad, with two stories and an
actual chimney. Here, where the people were half heathen
and the king hadn't been in a way to endow abbeys for some
years, secular travelers sought shelter, and those who provided it prospered—more so if they also gave the local folk
a place to sit and have an ale in the evenings.

A few of those good people were already gathered around
the fire or at crude, heavy tables against the walls when
Moiread walked in. She guessed that more would arrive as
darkness fell and they put their labors aside and their stock in
pens. One or two of the drinkers turned and looked at her—
curious, as they'd be for any new arrival, and respectful, as
befit a man dressed in her clothes and carrying a sword.

"Good sir." The innkeeper—a short, bald man with a sparse blond beard—bowed to her. "How may I serve you this evening?"

"Lodging for myself and my master, if you have it," Moiread said. She handed him a silver penny.

"Aye, and welcome. There's a room upstairs if you care to spend a bit more."

"In front of the fire will be fine," said Moiread.

In truth, she wouldn't have minded a bed, but sleeping in the front room meant one of them would likely wake up if one of their fellow guests snuck off to cut straps on their gear or simply rifle through their saddlebags. They were nearer the main road now. That had its flaws as well as its merits.

She sniffed the air and liked what she smelled. A joint of meat was roasting in the fire, with a thin adolescent boy turning the spit regularly. It was lamb from the odor, common enough at this time in the spring, when the shepherds would be ridding themselves of the males. "A meal for two, as well," she added, "and ale."

By the time Madoc entered, she'd found a table near the fire and stretched her legs out underneath, relishing warm toes and a seat that didn't move.

"All settled?"

"And easily at that," Madoc replied. "They were as happy to stop as we were, and they're enjoying the new grass, if I'm not mistaken."

"You get along well with them."

"I do. They're simple beasts when there's nothing spooking them." Here, his eyes glinted briefly and his smile turned teasing before he fell back into the slow, thoughtful rhythm of his speech. "It's a change to be around creatures who don't think through everything, not just once but over and over again, and then think about how they're thinking it."

Moiread laughed quietly. "Aye, I know that well enough. There's a relief that way to the fight...and the hunt."

Anyone overhearing would think she spoke of horses and hounds. She and Madoc both knew otherwise, and that shared secret was like a shield wall around the table, giving a surprisingly good feeling.

"Among other things," Madoc said.

The curve of his grin was slow and meaningful, not an invitation—as it couldn't be here in this crowded inn with Moiread posing as a man—but a suggestion, a touch of bawdy humor not unlike her own. From him, it made her pulse leap, and her nipples hardened inside her tunic.

Easy, my girl. You've a long way to travel with this one yet, and it was *only a joke.*

"Aye," she said and flashed him a smile in return, as she would have to any of her men when they spoke of wenching. "But the hunt's less trouble the next morning. Generally."

"Generally," Madoc agreed. He held out one sleekly muscular arm, turning it over and splaying out his hand. "I broke this going over brush when I was but a boy. They said I had the saints' own fortune that it healed as clean as it did. It only aches for snow."

"Not *always* a wizard with horses?"

"Even a wizard can press his luck too far. I was asking for what I got and more, back then—as my father said. It was only the arm that saved me from the strap, I'd say. That and my horse being wise enough to take no harm of the thing."

"Valuable creature, I take it," said Moiread.

"Not so much in coin, but we've never been ones to use our horses ill. They figure greatly in our legends—Pryderi, a hero of ours, was raised in a stable for the first few years of his life, for instance."

"Must have been hard on his mother," Moiread said.

Madoc shook his head. "No. Well, yes, but not the way you're thinking it. I've dropped you into the middle of the tale, you see."

Moiread leaned back, tipping the chair onto two legs, and folded her arms comfortably across her chest. "Oh? Then you should tell it from the beginning."

"If you'd like to hear it."

"I would. I told you stories all day." Although that had been fun, remembering all the tales of her childhood and hearing them new as Madoc took them in. "I may as well have some return."

By his smile, it was no hardship. "Well, then, once there was a prince of Dyfed…"

For a little while, Moiread listened to the story: the prince Pwyll going to meet with either harm or wonder and encountering a beautiful lady in gold riding a white horse, and how Pwyll and his men couldn't catch her, though they rode as fast as they could and her horse only walked. Moiread was waiting to hear what happened next when a plump woman in a green dress set their ale down in front of them, and a younger woman followed with food.

It smelled wonderful. Madoc apparently thought so too, because he reached for his knife. Moiread stepped on his foot, lightly but firmly enough to get his attention.

"Wait," she said, "until I let you know. Act like you're eating, toy with the food, but don't eat or drink yet. We're not all eating from one pot here."

"Ah," he said, embarrassed. "I hadn't thought of poison."

"Neither had I until now," she said and was glad Madoc didn't look disturbed at that confession. God knew it disturbed *her* plenty.

"It'll be the same here about the food, yes, or even more so?" Madoc asked the next night as they managed to find seats in the crowded front room of a larger inn. The town, Erskine, lay at the junction of two roads, and while Madoc was sure it was nothing compared to London or even Edinburgh, to his country-bred eyes it was busy enough.

Moiread nodded. It had been a day of rain and wind, and both of them more silent than otherwise because it was difficult to talk with their hoods up. Companionable silence, for the most part, though Madoc feared Moiread was thinking about a place before the fire in her father's castle and resenting him more with every raindrop.

Yet once they were settled at the table, she seemed in good humor, and all the more so when she started in on her stew. "I came this way the first time I left home," she said, shaking her head slowly. "Seemed a terrible big place back then, full of all varieties of folk. And me swaggering in as if I owned the lot, for I thought that'd be the best disguise for my gawping. Saints preserve us, but I was *young* then."

Well able to imagine it, Madoc laughed. "You were the sort to take dares, weren't you?"

"Always! And give them too, but I soothe my conscience and think I was never cruel in it."

"Would your brothers say the same?"

"Not Cathal, probably," she said after a moment of consideration. "On my deathbed, or his, he'll bring up the time he had to sing in front of the hall."

"Bad voice, has he?"

"No, a lovely one. For a boy his age, that may have been worse." She tilted her head and touched a slim finger to her lips, thinking. Even when she looked masculine, the gesture caught the eye. "Agnes had me climb out one of the windows. Douglas wasna' pleased. He's a good deal older than the rest of us, and he's taken things seriously as long as I've been alive. Tries to be more like Father than Father. I wouldn't wonder… Wait."

Moiread stopped. Very carefully, very precisely, she put her spoon back into her bowl. She closed her eyes.

All was not well. Madoc knew that much and suspected the precise type of wrong even before he saw Moiread's tongue flick out, probing at her lips. He held still. Speech would hurt her concentration, produce errors in judgment. He held still, but he rested one hand on the hilt of his sword.

When she stood up and bolted for the kitchen, he was at her side.

There were two people beyond the door: the innkeeper himself, who doubled as a cook from the flour on his hands, and a half-grown girl slicing turnips. At Moiread and Madoc's entrance, the girl cringed. The man swung around, ready to bluster until he saw their faces, their dress, or both. Then he too shrank in on himself.

"My lords?"

"Who had charge of our food?" Madoc demanded.

"I, m'lord. I… Is there…"

"Belladonna, I think," said Moiread. Her voice was calm, quiet, and completely toneless. "I could be wrong. I havena' vast experience with the stuff. But I think so. They call it deadly nightshade here."

Both faces went white at that. If Madoc was any judge of human nature, neither the innkeeper nor the girl had been the one whose hand held poison, but he didn't truly care in that moment. The word had pierced him with shock as well. He turned to Moiread. "You… Should I get the priest?"

"No," she said, and her eyes shone pale blue in the fire-light. "I'll live. But I'll not be useful for much longer. Is there any chance I'll need to be?"

Madoc glanced around the kitchen and saw nothing out of the ordinary. "Does anyone else come in here?"

"A beggar, sir," said the girl. She was barely looking at him. She was watching Moiread, and her lips were trembling. "Getting warm by the fire. He left a little while back. Before you'd have gotten your food."

"He could doubtless work out which bowls were ours," Madoc said.

"And," said Moiread, "there'll be no catching him now. Damn the luck." She put a hand against the wall, steadying herself. "We'll need that room you offered. For a few days. If you're a wise man, you'll ask no payment."

"No," said the innkeeper. "Of course not. My lord, I am... I had no idea..."

"I believe you," said Madoc, and he didn't intend it to sound like a threat, but he suspected it did. He couldn't be bothered otherwise.

As tall as Moiread was, and as well-muscled, she still fit into his arms easily when he picked her up. Madoc suspected that she was being helpful, balancing her weight as best she could. He also suspected that he'd have enjoyed the experience considerably under other circumstances. She was a warm and pleasant weight against his chest. As it was, she looked like a young man, her eyes were already unfocused, and Madoc took the first few stairs with desperate speed while muttering the Ave Maria.

"Do you want me to fetch anyone?" he asked when they were alone and nearing one of the private rooms.

"No. No. Poison... Only silver and wizardry can truly kill us, or great wounds to the spine or the heart. I think.

And if it was poison, it'd take more than this." She shook her head. Her hair fell into her face, and when she raised a hand to bat it away, the gesture had none of her usual precision. "No," she said again. "The next few days willna' be pleasant, but I'll live, wi' no real damage done. I should. I think."

"You think," he repeated.

"It's the first time I've been poisoned," Moiread said. "Go easy on a lass, will ye no'?"

She managed an approximation of a smile. It somehow made everything worse.

SIX

"Go," Moiread said. Madoc didn't seem to have heard her. It was hard to tell. His face was blurred, and his whole body kept fading in and out. She propped herself up on her elbows. She'd regret that later. "*Go*. Downstairs."

"Lie back down," he said. He bent down. Moiread heard a thud. It puzzled her briefly; then she felt the air against her feet.

Right. He'd taken her boots off. Nice man. No priorities. She shook her head, which she regretted immediately and profanely. "I'll hold on. Lying down. Boots off. You talk to the girl. While she remembers."

Having said her piece, and with her arms rapidly turning to wax, she let herself slump down against the pillows again.

Madoc made an uncertain sound. "I don't know how long that might take, and you—"

"I'll be fine." That was a lie. She didn't think she'd die. She'd had belladonna a few times before as a treatment for pain, which generally hadn't worked on her, but never enough to make reality melt this way.

She was fairly sure she wouldn't die.

Dying wasn't her main concern.

"I'll be here. I'll manage the rest. Talk to her. You have to go down anyhow. I'll need water. And meat. Lots of both. I'll pay."

"That you will not," said Madoc, all clipped anger.

"Then—" She gestured, and the hand she used sank into the coverlet. It belonged to her arm, but that arm grew longer, falling down and down into nothing. Moiread bit her lip. "Sooner you go, the better I'll hold on."

That swayed him. Even in delirium, Moiread could sense the shift in his thinking. "I'll return before long," he said.

Do. Please. She didn't say it. Couldn't, after trying so hard to convince him, knowing it was necessary. But the room felt empty when he was gone, and the shadows began to crawl with shapes: not frightening in themselves, not to her, but very much so in what they portended.

Tasks would help. Focus would help. Moiread lifted one heavy hand, willed it to compliance, and started to undo the lacing on her breeches.

About a year later, she'd managed to strip down to her shift and taken the illusion off. It didn't draw much power from her normally, but Moiread suspected she'd need every particle—and nobody who didn't know her would get close enough to make out her true sex unless something went wrong.

Unless something *else* went wrong.

With the slow clumsiness of a badly wounded animal seeking shelter, she crawled under the blankets, curled on her side, and shut her eyes.

A door opened. Moiread didn't know what door at first. That it *was* a door and not a tent flap meant she wasn't at war, but otherwise she was lost. She made a questioning noise.

"I've brought food," said a voice—male, Welsh, pleasant. Madoc. Memory came back. Her vision focused a little too.

"The girl?" she managed.

"She said the man was thin, shorter than me but taller than the innkeeper, unshaven but not bearded. Dark hair.

She thought dark eyes as well, but he was wearing a robe with a hood. He'd a chain around his neck too."

"Could be half the men in town."

"That he could," Madoc said, his words echoing and distorting. "I doubt the man has lingered about the place either. In his shoes, I'd have had a horse waiting for me and been a good mile out of town by the time we realized there was anything amiss."

"Unless..." Moiread said, and then stopped. There'd been an objection. She'd been thinking of it. Now it was gone. "Damn."

"Oh, he may have waited to see if his plan worked. It's possible. But I doubt he lingered. Drink." His wavering hand set metal to Moiread's lips. She opened her mouth. The ocean washed in, drowning what Madoc said next.

Men in plate were marching—*clank, clank, clank*—and she had to go and meet them, the English, keep them from her home. Why was she lying in bed? Her men would be waiting. She went to rise, and a hand on her shoulder pushed her back down.

"No, not for a while yet," said Madoc, and his voice cleared her head. He held meat to her mouth. Moiread chewed and realized that the clanking sound from before had been knife against platter. "It's working fast, the poison."

Moiread swallowed and nodded. "Everything's fast for us. Save age. I never understood that."

"And it's likely no time for either of us to try. Meat and water... Shall I keep bringing those, or will you need other things?" He fed her as he talked, but paused to let her answer.

"Those will do." She stretched her mouth into a smile, pulling the muscles out and up in each direction. "It's a siege, aye? You lay in supplies, and then you wait for it to pass."

Madoc had seen people poisoned before — not often, and often not intentionally — but easing pain was a tricky matter, and one sort of berry frequently resembled another. He'd seen the confusion, the blurred vision, the sight and sound of things that weren't there. When Moiread's limbs shook, or when she lay with flushed face and glassy eyes, Madoc worried, but he felt himself on familiar ground.

Other things were not familiar at all.

On the second day, helping her drink another goblet of water, he felt heat coming off her when his hand was inches from her skin. Carefully, Madoc pushed back Moiread's tangled hair and touched fingertips to her forehead. Her skin was like a fresh warming pan — not hot enough to blister him or set fire to the sheets, but far hotter than any fever, even a deadly one, would explain.

He called on the saints in a whisper, crossed himself, then picked up the goblet again.

Madoc ate his own meals rarely, grabbing slices of bread and meat when he went to the kitchen after Moiread's food. Gradually he trusted the girl, Jillian, to guard the room for short intervals, but never more than a few minutes. He never had her bring food, and he slept, uneasily, in a chair beside Moiread's bed.

Her hand on his bicep wakened him from one such doze. Everything was dark around them — it must have been after midnight — but her eyes glowed like a cat's. The pupils were round, though, and huge, almost swallowing the witch light of her irises. Her hand was hot iron. "You. Madoc. Please."

At once he stood and moved to her side. Her hand slid down his arm to his wrist, and her fingers grasped tightly. "What is it? What can I do?"

His first and deepest fear was that she'd been wrong, that she was dying after all, but her voice was strong and lower than he was used to.

"Talk."

"Pardon?"

Her pupils *had* been too large a moment ago; belladonna did that. Suddenly they were far thinner, though just as long. Madoc thought of snakes. The blue-white glow from her eyes was far brighter than before. "The body fights. Old tactics. Doesn't understand why not. Not *now*. Not *here*. It doesn't know."

Sharp pain lanced through his wrist. Madoc looked down. He'd never noticed Moiread's fingernails, but he vaguely remembered them as short, sensible, as fit a woman with plenty to do and most of it physical.

Now silver-gray claws pierced his shirt and his skin. As he watched, they blurred and went away, and it was a woman's hand clutching him.

"Give me words," she said, her eyes still glowing. There was a blurring all around her, a sense of potential. "Keep me human."

Understanding brought with it another sort of fear, and so, as Madoc nodded, he began with the first words that came to his mind: "*Pater noster qui es in caelis, sanctificetur nomen tuum...*" He stopped. "Will Latin be all right?"

"Will be fine." She chuckled like a rusty blade coming from its sheath. "I speak a few tongues. Any will do."

And so he prayed, and then spoke of his father's priest when he was growing up, and how the man had been known for his temper but patient enough with a lad who'd constantly asked questions and wanted to hear stories of saints and miracles. That led into the story of Saint David, and how a hill had risen up under him while he was preaching,

and the festivals in Wales on his day. By the time Madoc
had exhausted himself on that subject, Moiread had fallen
back into an uneasy sleep. With her eyes closed, it was
harder to tell, but the sense of impending change had gone.
She looked like any other woman on a sickbed.

That night was the first of many such incidents. Madoc
bandaged his own wrist, pulled his sleeves tight to cover
it, and told Moiread about Branwen and the "Dream of
Rhonabwy," recited poems, and sang songs he'd heard
from his mother or troubadours or drunken guards. Once a
forked tongue flicked out of her mouth while she listened;
another time, silver scales appeared across the bridge of her
sharp nose, like unearthly freckles on her pale skin.

"If you need to change…" he said during one of those
moments. "If it'll help, I can perhaps get you far enough
outside the village—"

"No." When she opened her mouth, her teeth were
pointed. "You couldn't. Not wi' so much motion, so many
smells. And…" She hissed in a breath. Her hands clenched
on the bedsheets, and the fangs disappeared. "If I change
when I'm ill, it'll be easier to get lost to instinct. To…
Well, I'll no' do it around so many people."

Her meaning was impossible to miss. Madoc didn't
raise the subject again.

None of the later trials was as bad as that first night,
perhaps because both he and Moiread were better prepared
or perhaps because the poison, and her body's defenses,
had peaked in those dark hours. Gradually the shifting
stopped, but Madoc kept up the stories and the songs.
Moiread seemed to rest easier with them, and he felt as if
he was doing something when he spoke, even if it was only
distracting her.

He wished he knew more of physicking. Bleeding

might help, or herbs, but he'd no training in such matters even where humans were concerned, and Moiread wasn't. Madoc watched the too-shallow rise and fall of her chest as she slept, put cool cloths on her forehead, fed her, and made himself eat.

The body fights, Moiread had told him. In the night, as she slept or muttered rambling commands to phantom armies, Madoc wondered if hers had given up, if remaining in human shape was a sign that she'd surrendered to the poison.

Those thoughts made sleeping even harder and left food sticking in his throat.

On the afternoon of the fourth day, with no preamble, Moiread opened clear eyes, shook her head, and sat up with no apparent trouble. "God's teeth, but I'm glad *that's* done with. Worse than childbed, or so I hear." She looked at Madoc, who sat staring at her, and put her hand on his shoulder. "I'm in your debt, sir."

"No, for it's my fault," he managed.

"I'm sure someone would have tried to poison me on my own merits one of these days," Moiread said. "You stayed. And you helped. It speaks well of you." She climbed out of bed, a touch clumsily and weakly for her, but not at all what Madoc would have expected from an invalid. "And now, I suggest you sleep. I'm going to go see if there's any chance of a bath."

SEVEN

THEY LEFT TWO DAYS LATER, EARLY IN THE MORNING, ONCE Madoc had gotten a chance to sleep and they'd both been able to make inquiries in town about the "beggar." Surprising neither of them, they got few answers. One man, who sold chickens close to the tavern, said that he'd found a robe wadded up and shoved under his stall. By the time he spoke to Madoc and Moiread, he'd long since sold it to the ragman.

"But we can assume," Madoc said, "that they or their master are magicians."

Moiread blinked. "Can we?"

They traveled a main road now, wider than those that had taken them from Loch Arach, and so as they talked, they both kept an eye out for anybody who might overhear. Just then, they were the sole travelers in sight, but they kept their voices low in case—as much as that was possible when talking on horseback.

"The beggar was only present the one night. He had the poison ready, and he didn't act long after we came in." Madoc reined his horse right at a fork in the road, then went on. "Now, I suppose he may have been watching all the taverns, in various guises, but that doesn't seem likely. Nor do I think that my enemies had a man at each inn: a rather frightening prospect, if the case."

"Aye."

"So then. Either the man knew well in advance where we'd be and when, or he'd followed us from Loch Arach to Erskine without either of us sensing him. I won't say I'm such a woodsman as to make that impossible, but between the two of us, I would believe we'd have spotted any man without unearthly assistance."

"I like to think so," said Moiread dryly. She stared off into the hazy blue sky, thinking while she enjoyed the sun on her face and the fact that the world stayed steady and real in front of her. Few things beat illness for bringing life into focus, though she'd not advise belladonna as an experience.

"We can tell the future a bit," she finally said, "but only in the castle, in that room you saw, and then it's weather or land or illness. Large things, and not with their own will. To foretell the actions of two people...I've never heard of that done."

Madoc nodded. Riding in the sunlight, with the wind ruffling his short black hair, he gave a fair impression of a hero in a tapestry, or mayhap a saint on a stained-glass window. His face had that sharp ascetic's appearance, particularly when he frowned in thought. "With people, the future is never certain, or so my few studies in the area have taught me. You can find a likely moment at best, and the more specific, the more likely it is to go wrong. Our enemies may have taken that chance. Or"—he looked around them, then over his shoulder—"they may have trusted in human eyes, only hidden them from us."

"If they'd entered the castle so, we'd have known it. But they may have suspected as much. There are stories."

"I know." Madoc smiled quickly. "One day at our leisure, perhaps you'll tell me which among them are true."

"A few more days like these, and I'll have nothing left to tell you," said Moiread, laughing. Then, reluctantly, she turned back to serious matters. "They'd have waited outside the castle, then, until we left. Could be done. And I could almost pity the poor bastards doing it, had they been on a less murderous errand."

"I have heard of such enchantments," Madoc said, "though I know no spell to counter them."

"I might be able to see the magic, if not the men. But I can't manage it through the illusion"—Moiread gestured to her artificially flat chest—"nor can I do it on horseback. And meanwhile I'll be no good in a fight."

"Could you teach me the way of it?" Madoc asked.

"Aye, I think so. Or at least I know no reason why you couldn't learn it, save that I've never taught anyone magic before, and I doubt I'll do it well. It's a spell, though, not a gift of my blood, so any man *could* try."

"You could do it when we stop for a meal, if there's nobody else around us. Until then, I'd lay odds we'll be safe. The man behind all this may know by now that I live, and he *may* have set men on our trail again, but it must take them some time to catch up. Unless they had a band waiting in Erskine."

"Or he truly *can* see the future and set wee clumps of assassins all along our path. Although then he'd have seen in advance that the first one wouldn't work, and why bother with him then?" Moiread shook her head. She was glad for many reasons that seeing the future didn't often work. Not least of those was that trying to reason it out gave her a headache.

"And my thought is that they'd have tried to strike by now in the first case, and it will hardly matter in the second. Indeed, if my foe is a man powerful enough to see so far and so finely into the future, and wealthy enough to hire many killers, it says that my quest is either hopeless or very important indeed."

"Nothing says it can't be both, you know," said Moiread.

"I do." Madoc looked off into the distance, watching the gray-green hills on the horizon. The metal of his mail shirt and the hilt of his sword glinted as he rode. His tunic was red as garnets or heart's blood, and he sat his horse with gracious ease, though they'd been many hours in the saddle already. Quietly, he said, "I had believed that if I went without a troop of men or much state, I would pass unnoticed, or no man would know my task well enough to want it stopped. I had hoped."

"Aye," said Moiread. She recognized the tone of his voice. She'd heard it from her father, those few times when his plans had been baffled, and from her captains after ambushes gone awry. She'd used it herself often in the long months between Falkirk and Bannockburn. "And now—"

"Now I have all the more reason not to turn away," Madoc said. "But if you say I've dragged you into danger unwarned, I'll not blame you."

"I agreed to guard you, and I assumed those I was to guard you *from* had a bit of skill at their craft. And I've spent a year or twenty at war, aye, and risking my neck more than I've done as yet."

Madoc smiled. "Then I thank you again, and I promise I'll be as apt a student as I can."

"You'll only have to do this the first time," Moiread said. She sat tailor-fashion on a flattish stone. The brook at her side rushed loudly, swollen with the spring rains. "After, it'll just be a matter of saying the words. It's a compact you're making, like most spells, though I've not heard of anything coming in person to agree. Too minor."

"It's rare that they do," Madoc agreed, "or at least rare that they show themselves for it."

Magic, or most magic, was a matter of talking directly to the forces of the world: the spirits of those forces in the oldest tales, the demons or angels governing their spheres in more modern lore. All spells invoked, most indirectly. Madoc had never been present for an actual summoning. When he was thinking sensibly, he was glad of that. Everything he'd learned said that even the holy ones would frighten the bravest man.

"Good," said Moiread, evidently sharing his thoughts. "Here."

She held out a twig of yew, dark needles and bright-red berries attached. In the last village they'd passed through, Moiread had taken them by a churchyard and stopped long enough to break the twig off the tree, which, as in many villages, grew by the gate.

"Now," she went on, when Madoc had taken the twig, "hold it up and repeat after me."

Slowly Moiread began, in Latin as good as any priest's. "In the names of Gabriel, Amariel, Nargeron, and Almighty God, I call upon you, O powers of the worlds. I invoke you, and by invoking, I command you to grant me sight of the union of the spheres. Part the veil that blinds mortal eyes and give me to see the subtle workings of the world, now and whensoever I should invoke it again."

As Madoc followed her lead, he felt power gathering. It wasn't much—as Moiread had said, this was a minor spell— but the earth and the air both shifted, as if he could feel them being drawn slightly toward the yew twig. The twig itself began to feel both heavier and less present. Madoc was half worried that his fingers would go through it. In the sun at midday, it was hard to see, but he also thought it glowed.

Moiread nodded. "Now crush the berries. Close your eyes, and smear them on your lids."

The sliminess Madoc had expected lasted barely a moment. Then it turned to a cool tingling across his closed eyelids and, in another heartbeat, vanished. His skin felt untouched.

"And open."

Madoc did, and caught his breath. He was no stranger to magic, but never had he been able to see the whole world through such entirely different eyes.

A faint haze hung above the grass and trees, a paler shadow of their natural green. The rocks and road looked normal, though their colors were deeper than they had been a moment ago. Madoc looked to the horses, peacefully cropping new grass a few feet away, and saw that each of them glowed a shade of brown: the steady darkness of wheat bread for Moiread's horse and a slightly lighter color for Rhuddem.

Madoc raised a hand in front of his face. His fingers shone red, shot through with streaks of silver. He flexed them, and the colors shifted accordingly.

"By God," he said. "This is truly a lovely art you've shown me."

"Useful, at times. But aye," Moiread said admittedly, "rather beautiful too, in its way."

She was beautiful. The spell stripped her of her illusion. Her hair lengthened slightly, her figure swelled and narrowed, and her face became a shade more delicate, so that a young-looking woman in men's clothing sat facing him. In the world of the spell, a pattern of dancing lights played across her body, like diamonds set onto the crisp blue that washed over her skin.

In this world, her shadow was nothing remotely human. Two vast wings stretched out behind her, the brook running through their shade. When she tilted her head to watch him, the shape of an immense head, on a serpentine neck, separated itself from the larger shadow and turned toward Madoc. The same pattern of lights glittered in the shadow.

Mayhap it would have been sensible for Madoc to fear her then, but he wished only that he had more time to sit and watch her.

"A bit revealing, aye?" Moiread asked, clearly aware of where he was looking. To his relief, she sounded amused. "That is why we don't generally teach the spell. We didn't come up with it, but we've enough luck that not many know it."

"Do you care so greatly for concealment?"

She shrugged a shoulder. "It's no great peril, in my view of things, to be found out. There are already those who know what we are and speak of it with varying degrees of truth. Once more knew, or we were more willing to admit it, or both."

"What happened?"

"To us? Time and duty. The world gets fuller. A clan turns from hunting to farming, and it's no' such great use for its laird to spend his days flying in dragon shape. Less use still in court, and we must go there to be part of the greater world, to lead a clan rather than a tribe in a cave. Our sires have other duties, and we as well. Our foes have magic of their own. Dragon shape is no sure victory."

"I have heard that," said Madoc, "and seen a little too. Only ran into one sorcerer myself."

"We've not fought them often, no' directly. The English magic turns more toward enchanted weapons"—she rubbed her calf, wincing in memory—"or strengthening castles. Crafty spells."

"Like the one I'm doing?" Madoc asked, speaking the words that courtesy would have Moiread avoid.

"No shame in taking a weapon from your foe," said Moiread. "We may have fought the people we learned this from"—she gestured around her, indicating the world revealed—"or we may fight them in the years to come. I'm still glad to have it."

"So am I."

EIGHT

MOIREAD LEANED BACK ON HER HANDS AND WATCHED MADOC adjust to the new landscape the spell showed him. She'd learned the *visio dei* young, renewed it every seven years, and grown to take it for granted. Seeing the wonder on Madoc's face brought back her own memories—and it pleased her to give him that moment of joy, after he'd spoken so grimly earlier.

And it could be that she was not so bad a teacher. Doubtless the student made the difference. From all Moiread had heard and seen, Madoc was more familiar with most forms of magic, and the theory of it, than was she, who'd always felt it required too many details and too much standing still.

"Do you think you could tell if there was anyone nearby using magic to stay hidden?" she asked.

"That would depend on what sort of magic, I think, but I believe I could. At least, if I spend enough time seeing the world like this, I'll quickly grow to know what it looks like *without* other magic, and that may help."

"Aye," Moiread said.

Birds sang in the trees above her. By her head, the brook ran merrily past, and further out she could hear the quiet sounds of the horses as they chewed grass and flicked their tails at insects. The rock was warm beneath Moiread's palms and arse. She did not want to rise.

And yet time waits not.

She sighed and opened her eyes. "Dismissing the sight

is easier," she said, and spoke the words for it. "And *visio dei*, to call it back, from now on."

"Vision of God?" Madoc asked, lifting dark eyebrows. "Or vision of *a* god?"

"Either, as far as I can tell. I didn't make it up. The spell's at least as old as my grandfather. But it makes a bit of sense, does it not?"

"It does that. At least, I suppose it does. I wouldn't presume to know if it's an *accurate* description."

Moiread pushed herself to her feet. It was an unfolding sort of task, getting her limbs all lined up in the proper manner. "If you were God, or even the sort of creature they used to *call* a god, I don't think you'd have need of a guard."

"Need, perhaps not." They'd been sitting closer than Moiread had noticed, or a trick of footing had brought Madoc closer to her when he rose. She found herself staring into his eyes, no more than a hand's length away from him. "But it could be that even the divine want company, might it not?"

"It might. I'm hardly a priest, to say with authority." There were horses to mount and miles to cover. The first step would be a step away from the brook, and from where she and Madoc stood. Moiread stayed in place.

Madoc smiled, cocking his head so that he looked aslant at her through long, dark lashes. "And there are many myths about the old gods seeking out mortals, you know," he said more softly. "To test them, for example."

That was far from the only reason, or the main one. Even Moiread knew that. Her body tightened; she slid her tongue over suddenly dry lips. "I'm not mortal," she said. "But I do wonder if I'd pass such a test."

"I'm no god," Madoc said. He stepped forward

slightly. They didn't quite touch, but Moiread could feel his breath against her face when he spoke again. "Yet I'm sure you would."

She thought of half a dozen jokes then: he said that to all the girls, she was waiting for the lightning strike, she'd be rather annoyed if she had to fight a Minotaur before she slept, on and on. None of them made it past her throat.

Looking up at Madoc, she saw that the breeze had disarranged his hair. Not falling in his face, it nonetheless hung over one eye. Slowly Moiread reached up and brushed it back. It was like heavy silk beneath her fingertips.

"I do value your confidence," she said.

"It seems the least I can offer." Madoc's voice had fallen to a murmur, the kind that invited her to lean in closer. She shifted her weight, not taking her hand from Madoc's face.

Off at the other end of the clearing, the gelding snorted and then neighed in protest. Madoc and Moiread both spun around, each grabbing for weapons, and then both relaxed when they saw the cause—a minor territorial dispute over a good patch of grass, settled when Rhuddem nipped her companion sharply on the shoulder.

The sound had broken the moment, though, scattered the water before a vision could emerge, and that might have been well. They were alone and outdoors, with a destination yet some way ahead and probably men abroad who wanted to kill them.

"We should be off," she said, and hoped she hid both the arousal and the disappointment in her voice.

"Wise," said Madoc.

He spoke briefly. That was well. Otherwise, Moiread might have spent more time trying to determine what *his* voice held, and what he might be concealing.

Late in the afternoon, as the sun was touching the tips of the mountains and turning the stone to gold, Moiread asked, "What is it you *want* to happen?"

They were riding through gentler hills, forest and stone giving way to field and orchard and more villages than they'd passed before. Madoc had been watching the landscape change and letting his thoughts drift. At Moiread's question, he turned to her with a briefly blank mind.

Sunset suited her. The light gilded her skin as it had the mountains and called crimson glints forth from her dark hair. She rode with straight back and square shoulders. The sleeves of her brown tunic, falling from beneath her mail shirt to ruffle in the breeze, were the only part of her that didn't look straight and still, honed so that there was almost nothing left to spare. She seemed at home on the empty road, her shadow—human now—her lone necessary companion.

In response to Madoc's temporary silence, she shrugged and explained, "What you want to stop is a horror, aye. But there's more than stopping matters from getting worse. You said you didn't want rebellion now, that your people would be unprepared. Are you planning for ten years gone?"

"I am, and then I am not," Madoc said.

"Is that a way of telling me to be about my own business?" she asked with good humor in the question as far as Madoc could tell. "Right enough if so."

"No," he said quickly, "no. It's only that the rest of it takes longer to explain, and I want to put it into words rightly. I'm not sure I quite managed at home." His father had understood; his father was also aging and had reason to want to believe his heir wise and sensible. His mother had been more skeptical.

With that memory closer to hand than he'd like, Madoc began. "Any rising of my people is likely to be more than ten years in coming, if it ever does. It may not be in my lifetime, or my children's—or your children's, for that matter. It may be that we'll not ever be our own nation again."

"You're a sight calmer about *that* prospect than I would be," she said.

"It's been a while now for us," Madoc replied. "Two generations more or less, and longer in places. After a time, men stop thinking of what might have been and turn their thoughts instead to what is, and how to live within it."

"And do you think that's as it should be?"

"At times," he said. "Not at others. To accept ill use merely out of habit, to let the familiar keep you from striving for better...that is wrong. Yet to spend all your strength, and your people's, in fighting when there's no hope or use to the cause may be as bad."

"I know that you pick your moment, and you choose your fight. 'A time for war and a time for peace,' as the priests have it. Only..." She shook her head. "When the damned English ruled us, I hated them. I wanted to fight, though I knew we couldna' manage it then. But then, I wasna' born into the conquest."

Madoc nodded. "Then too," he said, "the Romans reached only a little way into Scotland, and not for very long."

"My grandfather was a Roman," Moiread said, and then chuckled. "But I don't think he was acting for the empire when he settled at Loch Arach. He just fancied a local lass and a quiet country life, or so he always told us. What have the Romans to do with the matter?"

"We were occupicd, were subjects, for a few hundred years. Not such a great length of time for you, I understand," he couldn't resist adding teasingly, "but more than a few generations of man. We fought, yes, sometimes, and other times we made peace and bent to their rule, and we remained ourselves. And then the empire fell and its legions departed, and there we were. Our own people once more."

"Huh," Moiread said.

They crossed a bridge, the horses' hooves clattering loudly over the timbers and the river rushing past the dark rocks beneath them, fast and full enough for the spray to wet Madoc's face.

On the other side, once the noise had receded enough, Moiread said, "You speak of endurance."

"When I must. And I've not the authority to speak at all, truly. My father lives, and when he doesn't, I'll be only a lord, one among many. Nor am I so certain that my people would care greatly who rules them in the end. Kings are distant creatures to a man whose longest journey is to market thrice a year, and what does it matter whose face is on the coins when you see few of them?"

Her face darkened. "There's a shade more to it than that, you know."

"As a man, yes, I do," Madoc said. "I'd have fought and gladly, had I been a man in our wars. If it comes to another war, I'll go. If there comes a time when war will do us more good than harm, then so I'll counsel. Until then, I gain nothing from bitterness, and as my father's heir, I must think of my people before my pride."

Moiread fell silent again. "It was different for us, you know," she started and then shrugged, her armor clinking and creaking with the motion. "But then, it was different for you twenty years back, aye. I take your meaning." She didn't sound like she agreed, or not entirely, but neither did she sound angry. "My father and his father said similar.

That it's the way of men and nations to seek conquest. You fight when you can and bend the knee when you have to, but there's no more faulting them for it than there is faulting a hawk for stooping on a pigeon."

"I'm not so certain about that last," Madoc said slowly and then impulsively added, "and while your father and your grandfather are *honorable* company, I'd rather you didn't think of me in the same light."

Laughter crinkled the corners of Moiread's eyes. "I promise," she said, holding up a hand, "I never have before, and I doubt I will again."

"I'll do my best to prevent it," Madoc said.

The implications of their teasing came to mind then, combined with the moment by the brook earlier, and he shifted uneasily in the saddle, all the more so when Moiread bit her lower lip. She looked away from him—at the road ahead—and cleared her throat. "If you're not planning for rebellion..." she said in a forcibly casual voice that became genuinely curious as she went on. "What *do* you have in mind?"

"I think that an occupied people should have places to go, or powers to call on, that their rulers neither know of nor control." Madoc spread his hands. "What I do now may help us fight the English in ten years, or a hundred. It may help us fight another foe entirely, should one arise. Or these ties, these bonds may simply help us do as we did with the Romans: preserve enough of ourselves to *remain* ourselves, no matter what land claims us as its own."

He stopped and rubbed at the back of his neck, then added, "And then, it's also what's within my power to do. I'm fond of the old customs and treasures for themselves. I'd not see them perish whether the foe was England or simply time and change."

"Endurance again," Moiread said thoughtfully. "Things never remain quite as they are, but trying to carry the vital parts forward... Aye. I think I understand."

NINE

ALTHOUGH SHE HADN'T SPENT MUCH TIME THERE, HALLFIELD was passingly familiar to Moiread, and the Colquhouns — Calhouns, now — who ruled there more so. She'd passed through a few times during the wars, and before that when she'd been young. Four days' ride wasn't so distant, particularly not when she'd been able to fly most of the way and transform in a convenient bit of forest.

"Will you want to go in undisguised?" Madoc asked when he heard.

"No, it'd confuse folk. And I've not properly visited the castle in years." She glanced at the fields they passed: wet, brown earth fresh plowed from spring planting, strips neatly divided to go with the neat cottages that lined the road ahead of them. "There's not nearly as much convenient forest as there once was."

Everything had been wilder in her youth. It still was, in her mind, and she felt the difference. The growth of fields and houses made her feel not only exposed but old.

Still, the castle was mostly as she remembered: a round wooden tower at the top of a hill and a small castellum below it, all surrounded by a wide moat and a thick wall. Two men stood on each end of the bridge, carrying spears and watching Moiread and Madoc as they approached. The wars hadn't been over long, and they'd gone harder here than in the north.

Out of habit, Moiread noted both the men's alertness

and their posture with approval, caught herself nodding satisfaction, and chuckled quietly.

"Hmm?" Madoc asked.

She grinned at him. "A bit used to command. And a bit slow to realize what's not my problem any longer. Is there any baggage you'd keep with us, by the way?" she asked, slowing her horse slightly as she thought of the question. "We'll likely not be able to put the beasts up ourselves here."

"One bag," he said. "Treasures of my people, and a few other items I'd as soon keep by my side."

"I'll take that, unless you'll need it here."

"No, that's unlikely."

They halted in front of the bridge. "Who comes?" asked one of the guards. He and his companion stood in the center. Their comrades behind them fanned out to the sides of the bridge, where each had a good line of sight if he needed to throw his spear.

"Madoc of Avondos, and my squire, Michael. I sent word to the Calhoun of my visit."

"Aye, my lord," said the head guard. "Enter and be welcome."

He and his fellow stood aside. The way in was only wide enough for one to ride, so Moiread took the front, reflecting briefly that the portcullis was left raised for the first time in years, as far as she could recall: another sign of peace.

The buildings inside the round castellum were the same as Moiread remembered, and much the same as in the courtyards at Loch Arach: kitchens, chapel, smithy, storehouses, and the stables, where she and Madoc surrendered the horses into the care of two youths and a grizzled man with a limp, and most of the baggage to a small assortment of pages, to whom Moiread tossed small coins.

It never hurt to gain favor, particularly with the people who'd have their eyes on her mount and her gear.

Following behind Madoc took getting used to. Even such short experience as she had at being a bodyguard suggested strongly that she take the lead, wary for ambushes and traps. *Calm yourself, girl*, she said silently. *You're on friendly territory now*. It didn't help much. She managed to follow Madoc up the stairs to the keep at a proper remove, and to keep her free hand from her sword while she did it, but it was a conscious effort and a struggle against her reflexes.

Near the top of the stairs, a small crowd came out to meet them. The Calhoun was tall and red-blond this generation, with a beard a small mammal could get lost in. His wife, Glynis, was short and dark, and their three daughters looked like they'd end up with various interesting combinations, though it was too soon to say anything for certain. They were all in that vague stage somewhere between walking and marriage.

All looked better than they had when Moiread last passed through. She'd come then in rain-soaked darkness, which hadn't helped, but the change was more than sunlight. The Calhoun—Eachann, Moiread thought his name was—had lost the grim cast to his face. His wife was smiling, and the children were watching the strangers with unmixed excitement, not waiting to overhear bad news.

"My lord Madoc of Avondos," Moiread said, belatedly remembering what she'd seen men do in her place and bowing before the assembly.

Then she stepped out of the way, letting Madoc and the Calhoun take hands and exchange greetings. Behind the younger members of the family, she spotted a late arrival: Uisdean, who'd been the chief of Hallfield the last time she'd stayed there as a noble guest rather than a soldier. His hair and beard had gone from brown to pure white, and the hair was considerably thinner. So was the man. When the crowd moved toward the keep doors, she saw that he'd lost perhaps half his flesh. His brown eyes were cloudy too, and Moiread saw him squint as he peered from her to Madoc.

That infirmity would aid in her disguise, yet she couldn't be glad of it.

"Here, lad," said one of the guards, putting a comradely hand on Moiread's shoulder. "Och, but you're a nervous one," he added, as Moiread tensed, not quite reaching for her sword. "The war's over, isn't it?"

"It's been a long trip," she said, making herself relax. The man's broad face was good-natured and honest. She put little faith in that, but he *was* one of the Calhoun's guards, and not the lowest ranked at that. She remembered playing dice with him when she and her men had camped before the inner walls. "Your pardon, sir."

"Easy enough granted. Come along wi' me. Your gear's under a bunk already, and I'd wager you're hungry. Might as well feed ourselves while our lords go through their paces, do ye no' think?"

Briefly, Moiread watched the crowd bear Madoc away toward the great doors of the keep. He walked by Glynis's side, as was proper for a guest. The two talked quietly and with cheerful faces, looking back at Eachann frequently as he spoke. Uisdean followed with the children, a tall figure yet among them.

"I've heard considerably worse ideas," Moiread said.

"Truth to tell, I know little of these matters," said Eachann Calhoun as they came out of the castle's chapel into the evening air. "It was my aunt who'd made any sort of study, ye ken, and I've only the tales she told me, nor have I ever tried to use the knowledge."

Eachann wasn't just trying to warn Madoc of his ignorance; his uneasy backward glance at the chapel said as much. He'd worn a brief but poorly concealed expression of relief when Madoc had come with him to vespers, but his guest's ability to step over the church threshold and say the Lord's Prayer without incurring a bolt of lightning clearly only went so far toward reassurance.

It was a pity Sunday was so far off. Communion might have put the man more at ease.

"Oh, that won't be any trouble at all," said Madoc. "I'll do everything that requires study." The man's own half-conscious evasion was a useful one. He spoke again, trying to sound reassuring rather than desperate. If Eachann was having second thoughts now that Madoc was there, it was a bad sign, and Madoc didn't have many days to be persuasive. "Your part will only be to accept. It's mostly an oath, truly."

Here it was mostly an oath. Here at Hallfield, all the magic would come from the beings Madoc called on to witness the pact, the spells he had cast at the beginning of his journey, and the momentum of the journey itself, with the tracks of foot or hoof a tie between the two lands. At his two remaining destinations, matters would be different: as showy as the rite at Loch Arach had been, or more.

"Good," said Eachann. "If it'll give me or my son or my grandson the upper hand, should the English get greedy once more, there's not much I'll not welcome, and gladly." This time his look toward the chapel was almost defiant, and all the briefer for it. "But I'm glad I'll not have to fumble my way through."

"You don't strike me as a man who fumbles much," said Madoc, smiling with relief and trying to pass it off as amusement.

"That's because I stick to what I know, life allowing."

Madoc, who thought that sounded like a dull way to live, but who knew that Eachann could have easily said *I'm glad I'll not have to meddle with unearthly things and put my soul in jeopardy*, or decided he *didn't* have to do that, made a gesture of assent and changed the subject. "I didn't know you had a son."

"Adair." The bearded face split with a proud smile. "Sixteen and already my height. He did himself right well in the war too. He's been gone as a squire for the last two years. A shame he's not here now, or he and your lad might have a bit to talk about between them."

"That they would," said Madoc, laughing both because it was expected and because it felt strange to be discussing Moiread in such a manner. "And I can only pray that Michael's accounts would all be good, and that the word *tyrant* got used but rarely."

He would have liked to be a fly on the wall during such a conversation, even knowing Moiread's end of it to be more than half falsehood.

"He's not given you trouble, I hope?"

"No," said Madoc. "He's quite promising."

"And handsome with it." Eachann snorted. "There's at least one of my girls making cow eyes over him already, and her not yet twelve. D'ye ken his family at all?"

"Ah," said Madoc, not having anticipated quite this turn of questioning. "Only a little. My father knows more of them. A...Seymour, I think?"

"An English name, that."

"Yes, but his mother's family is Scottish, and they've

had the raising of him since his father died." Madoc silently noted all the details and hoped he'd have a chance to pass them along to Moiread before she had to answer any such questions herself. "A bit of bad blood there, actually, I'm hearing."

The Calhoun nodded. "And so there would be, I'd think. Well—" He rubbed his chin idly. "Many a young man's come from humbler stock."

"So they have," Madoc agreed. They climbed the steps toward the keep side by side. The view near the top wasn't as dramatic as that from the high windows of Castle MacAlasdair, but it had a beauty to it: blue-violet sky over peaceful fields and stars beginning to shine. "They seem pleasant children, your daughters."

"Oh, mostly, though Gara, the middle one, has the devil's own temper when she's vexed." Eachann hesitated, resting a hand on the stone ledge, and then added, "Seonag, my eldest, she knew my aunt well. She's taken an interest—not that I've much I can teach her, but there are a few records."

"Ah," said Madoc. "If you think she might be of assistance tomorrow, I'd welcome her."

"Well, it comes to mind that, even if 'tis but a vow, I'll not only be taking it for myself." Eachann said. "No man lives forever. Best that my children know who they can call on—and who can call on them. Adair's far from here. And he's no more given to these arts than I am, truly."

Again Madoc heard the words beneath the words, the ones that the Calhoun was too much the host—and too polite in general—to speak aloud. Magic might do well enough for women, sometimes, under the right circumstances, if it stayed firmly on the side of the angels. Men had better, more honest ways of addressing the world, or should. His guest, both man and magician, was an exception, of course.

Present company excepted. Mostly because it's present, and company.

A man did as well as he could with what he'd learned and who he was. Madoc smiled honestly back at his host. "I'd say that was wise of you, sir."

TEN

Lacking magic to heat water and start fires, the accommodations at Hallfield weren't quite as luxurious as those in Castle MacAlasdair, yet they were a blessed improvement after a week on the road. Madoc came to dinner freshly washed and with the smell of fresh meat and bread reaching him even before he entered the great hall.

As he passed the lower tables, he spotted Moiread immediately among the men-at-arms. She sat at one end, laughing as an older man told a story with demonstration by way of knife and trencher. Her clear skin was flushed with laughter and the heat of the hall. Catching Madoc's eye, she gave him a quick, graceful bow from her seat.

She too had changed from the journey, Madoc noticed. She'd cleaned herself and replaced her brown tunic with a fine linen one of pale yellow, almost white, with a dark green surcoat over it. She wore both belted loosely, no doubt so that the illusion would have less work to do, but left no doubt of her height or her strength.

Others had noticed as well, including, obviously, Seonag. Calhoun's daughter made a proper curtsy to Madoc and greeted him in a well-bred, friendly manner, but turned her great brown eyes back in Moiread's direction as soon as she thought nobody noticed her.

Madoc kept his laughter silent. There would have been a lesson in that for any lord grown over-proud of his wealth and rank. To eleven, apparently twenty was enough older to entrance, while twenty-five, no matter how finely dressed, was nothing less than ancient.

That was as well. As they sat listening to the harper after dinner, when the children and the elderly priest alike had departed for bed, the Calhoun leaned over to Madoc and quietly asked, "Does your squire know...ah..." He waggled a hand in the air.

"No, not really," said Madoc. "That is, he knows what I'm doing, but he couldn't do it himself."

He thought that was true enough. He hadn't considered including Moiread as part of the ritual, lest the bonds he'd already strengthened with the MacAlasdairs become tangled up with those he forged with the Calhouns, and out of worry that either the illusion she wore or the power of her bloodline would complicate the spell. When he answered the Calhoun, Madoc thought that he would prevent any expectations of "Michael's" involvement. He hadn't expected the slow nod Eachann gave him.

Ah. Oh dear.

Madoc hadn't expected a squire, and one of unfamiliar blood, to attract any lord's eye. He also hadn't taken war into account. The benches where Moiread and the rest of the men-at-arms sat weren't as crowded as he would have expected, and many of her companions sported fresh scars or missing limbs. Men of rank might have fared a little better, generally facing ransom more often than hanging; they were also better targets.

He wondered how many lords, both in Scotland and England, were looking at their unmarried daughters and adjusting their aspirations downward, wondered how many convents would gain a profusion of novices as men tried to buy divine favor when earthly alliances proved lacking. He wondered whether the same situation had held true in

Wales in the years before his birth. Madoc's aunt had taken the veil. He'd always thought it was a calling, when he'd thought of it at all.

He hadn't, really, thought of it at all.

Speaking as casually as he could, he added, "I doubt he's had the chance to learn. Youngest son, you see. He'd have gone for the church, but it was the second son who felt that urge."

"Ah," said Eachann, more resigned and less speculative than he had been. At worst, he'd likely decide to wait a few years and see how the boy did for himself, thus letting Madoc and Moiread get out of the castle without many more awkward conversations.

Madoc cleared his throat and looked to the corner where Uisdean sat with his eyes half closed, listening to the music. "Your father does well, it seems."

"He does, by the grace of God," said Eachann, "but the last few years have been hard on him."

"The war?"

"Aye, that's troubled all of us, but it's Father's eyes that vex him particularly. He's still sharp as anything." So Madoc had seen at dinner, when the older man had taken a swift and lively part in the conversation, asking questions, making jokes, and telling stories of his own. "And still hale enough for his age. His sight, though... That started to fail a half-dozen years ago. Now he can get around on his own and feed himself, but that's all. He can't tell one face from another, much less read, and he was always a learned man."

"A pity it is," said Madoc.

Eachann nodded. "I've not had a physician in who's been able to help. 'Tis age, they say, and in truth he's had more than his threescore and ten. There's none can change that."

At the end, his voice rose slightly, suggesting a question that he didn't actually come out and ask.

Madoc shook his head. "None that I know. I've met men who could heal blindness from illness or injury or curse, and I'll send them in your direction if you'd wish, but"—he sighed—"I've seen no spell yet that could make a man young again."

He'd heard of a man *keeping* himself young, or middle-aged. That had been Albert de Percy, who'd styled himself "Valerius" and threatened the MacAlasdairs. De Percy had been the blackest of sorcerers. His powers had come from a pact with hell itself, and Madoc suspected that de Percy's extended life had been part of that bargain. Otherwise, the span of a man's years seemed a matter of blood and the effects of those years.

"A saint *might* help, or a relic," he said cautiously, never having tried either himself and knowing how many false relics men sold.

"I'd thought perhaps a pilgrimage to Saint Denis," the Calhoun replied. "Now that the war is over, we may be able to do it. I'll wait through this winter, make sure the harvest is safely in."

Again the unspoken words: *and make sure the peace is going to last this time.*

No truce lasted forever, but a man could hope for room to breathe: a few years to gather in crops, to let sons come to manhood, to visit shrines, to do all the work of peacetime that built against wars to come and made them less devastating when they did.

Madoc wished he'd thought to say those things before, when he and Moiread had been talking. As Eachann poured himself more wine, Madoc took the moment to look off toward the rest of the hall, seeking her face in the crowd.

"Don't fret," said Clyde, a man-at-arms at Hallfield and Moiread's self-appointed guide. "If your lord wants you, he'll send a page to call you up. Plenty of the lads running around."

"Aye? Glad to hear it," said Moiread, turning her gaze away from the high table. She'd had only a moment to meet Madoc's gaze before Clyde intervened, but it was of little import. Madoc looked content, though thoughtful, and certainly suited to the lord's dais.

And what Clyde said was true, in its own way. Had Madoc any pressing business with her, it would have been easy enough to call her up and speak under the pretext of setting tasks for her.

You're only jumpy, Moiread told herself again. This business of being a man's only guard was taxing on the mind. She might have preferred war, where she merely needed to watch her own back and mind her men's in a tactical sense.

Clyde handed her the wineskin and the dice.

"Good man, is he?"

"Very," Moiread said and rolled, thinking that her duty did have its advantages. There were wine and dice in the camps, of course, but not often with a sturdy roof overhead or a fire nearby. The wine was never as good, and men were more apt to turn murderous over the dice. "Easy service, so far."

"Would be, wouldn't it?" said another of the castle guards. "Away from the wars and all."

"I was in the wars," Moiread shot back, responding almost instinctively to the accusation in the man's tone. Silently she swore, and shrugged as the men looked dubious. "I've come to his service lately, and I was a page with the armies when I was young."

"'When I was young,' he says." Clyde laughed, trying to soothe the troubled waters. "Hark at the graybeard."

"But your lord wasn't," said the other man.

"Well, no," said a fourth. "I've heard the man speak, and he's not from any bit of Scotland I know."

"Welsh," said Moiread. "So no. Hardly his fault, is it?"

"English, then." It was the first guard, a dark-haired man with a scar pulling his upper lip up on one side. "Or as near as."

From around them came an intake of breath. "No," Moiread said again. She set the dice on the table with a *clack* of bone on wood and leaned forward. "No, and be damned to you for saying it."

"Be damned yourself," the scarred man replied. His face was flushed in the firelight. "The English king rules them, does he not? And they fight in his wars."

"Now, Grant," said Clyde, holding up a hand.

Moiread snorted. "Losing a war doesn't make a people, you dolt, else we'd have been English ourselves twenty years gone."

"Aye, and we were men enough to rise up again, weren't we? Which I don't see your lord doing," Grant spat back.

Everything Madoc had said came back to Moiread: the need to bide time before an overwhelming force, to pick battles and save what could be saved, what was worth saving. She thought too of her own military understanding, the difference in borders and ground and troops. And she knew that none of those arguments would aid her against this man. She knew what was expected of her.

Moiread rose from the bench. "I'm a guest in your lord's hall," she said, "and I'll not disgrace him or my lord by brawling here. If you'd care to step outside, we can settle any questions of manhood you have in mind."

"I'll teach you manners and gladly, boy," said Grant.

Various murmurs rose around them. Clyde was saying a few things, trying to calm the situation, but he would know as well as Moiread that it wouldn't do any good. Once certain words took the air, all that would cage them again were fists. The best he could do was keep it to a brawl.

Madoc was watching her from the dais. Moiread gave him a quick bow and saw him start to stand. Eachann put a hand on his shoulder and spoke, low and amused. *Young blood*, it could have been, or *let the boy prove himself*. Whatever it was, Madoc sank back down, though he didn't look happy about it.

Neither was Moiread happy, leaving the warm hall and the music for the windy courtyard. The light wasn't wonderful, and it had been a few years since she'd been in a fight without weapons. She sighed as she walked out the doors and around the corner.

Only Grant and Clyde went with her, the others having more sense than to leave comfort in order to watch a fistfight.

"Will neither of you give over?" Clyde asked as he stepped out of the way.

"Can't," said Moiread. "Sorry."

"I spoke but the truth," said Grant, slurring his words more than a bit, "and I'd say it again. Your lord's maybe a spy and most likely a coward."

He might have gone on, but then Moiread punched him in the jaw.

Pulling the blow was always the hard part. In human form, she was no stronger than a hefty mortal man, but that was considerable force, and men did die in tavern brawls. Killing this one, even by accident, would have gone badly.

So she struck more lightly than she could have—a solid

hit, but not enough to put a man out, especially a drunk one. Grant staggered backward, righted himself, and threw a punch in return. He had a good arm on him, and his eye was keen. Still, Moiread ducked it easily.

Enough of this foolishness.

She jabbed a fist quickly into Grant's stomach. He doubled over. She pulled back, swung, and hit him in the nose with a satisfying *crack*. Still she pulled her blows, but it didn't matter. Speed was as good as strength for an advantage once a fight was underway, and less likely to be accidentally lethal.

"Can we have done with this now?" she asked, stepping back but keeping her guard up.

Grant was clutching his nose, blood flowing freely through his fingers. To give what little credit he deserved, he wasn't yelling with pain, only making a low noise in the back of his throat.

Moiread pressed on. "Will you keep a civil tongue about my lord in the future?"

Hesitation, then a jerky nod, gave her the answer.

"Aye," said Clyde, "go find the leech and get that seen to. Your snoring's bad enough as it is. He's a decent man, in his way," he added after Grant had departed. "But he took the war hard. Plenty do, in that way or another. You're maybe too young to have seen it."

"Ah," said Moiread.

Thinking she was embarrassed about admitting it, Clyde clapped her on the shoulder. "Youth's an ailment we all recover from, lad, and sooner than we'd like. Come back inside, and we'll finish the wine."

She went. Wine sounded good right then.

ELEVEN

"You've made a name for yourself, rather, in a short time," said Madoc.

"By how badly I've lost at dice? I promise I've not cast us into poverty," Moiread replied. They followed a curving path up a hill, riding behind the Calhoun, his daughter, and their priest toward the ring of stones at the top. Three men-at-arms followed at a distance, one of them Clyde. "And whatever the blond kitchen girl says, *I* wasn't the one with her last night."

Madoc lifted his eyebrows and shook his head, but laughingly, and there was good humor in his voice when he spoke again. "I'd not heard of those exploits. I was thinking rather of your skill with your fists, or what I'd heard of it."

"Oh, that." Grant was *not* accompanying them. He'd caused no further trouble, and kept himself away and silent when Moiread was present. She shrugged. "Only defending your honor, my lord."

"Were you, now? And you left him alive and able to go about his duties, I hear. That was kind of you."

"Your honor doesn't need much defending," Moiread said, flashing him a grin.

Madoc wrinkled his brow, then shook his head again. "I was attempting to picture you striking someone with a gauntlet on my behalf," he said. "It doesn't quite work."

"Try getting on the bad side of a man of rank, and I'll see what I can manage," said Moiread. "If he gives voice to his feelings when I'm there and you're not, that is, and that could be difficult to arrange."

"Slightly."

A short distance from the hilltop, the party separated. Moiread and the men-at-arms stayed behind, not witnessing but guarding. Even in peacetime, there were bandits, not to mention wolves and wild boar. The others moved out and upward. Against the gray sky and the dull brown hill, their clothing made spots of brightness, save for the priest's black cassock.

Moiread watched them go.

Around her, the horses stamped and blew. "Damned restless beasts," said Clyde.

"'Tis the weather," said Kinnon, one of the other guards. "Likely a storm coming up."

"No, they've been out many a time in worse," said a third man, "and never been so skittish. It's this place."

"Don't be foolish," said Kinnon, as Moiread surreptitiously relaxed.

"I'm not. We all know yon ring of stones"—the guard gestured—"is uncanny, and why would they choose the spot else?"

"Can't be too uncanny," said Clyde uneasily. "They've Father Parlan with them."

Having no ready response to that, the guard made a skeptical noise in the back of his throat and fell silent.

"He's young," Moiread said, seizing her opportunity to get away from dangerous lines of discussion. "For a priest, that is."

Kinnon nodded. "And a good change, that. The man we had before him was old as the hills and slept through mass half the time by the end. Died during the war, and it took the best part of a year before we got Parlan. Things were that disarranged."

"Pious folk had to ride half a day to be shriven and confessed," Clyde added. "I was with my lord in the battles, and we had priests with us, else I'd have had a hard time tending to my own soul. It's quite a way to go when a man has duties."

Moiread made what she hoped was an appropriately sympathetic noise. Her concern about her immortal soul had always been haphazard at best. Between having a grandfather who'd done equal reverence to Jupiter in his day and knowing that most of the Church would think their ancestry damned regardless of deeds or faith, none of the MacAlasdairs had ever quite managed devotion. Men gave such matters more thought. Moiread was mortal enough to consider it on occasion, usually during a wakeful night, and to go to confession and mass when she thought of it. She was enough her father's daughter to keep her tongue still and act understanding otherwise.

Thinking out what to say next, she heard Madoc's voice. It was extremely faint; Moiread couldn't have heard it at all if she'd been human. Even she couldn't make out words, but from the cadence it was likely the start of the ritual. When the hairs on her arms and the back of her neck stood on end, she knew for sure.

"He's earnest, aye, and scholarly," said Kinnon, watching the hill. "Not like old Ervin. Remember when—"

He turned to Clyde, starting on a story from their youth that had them both laughing at the memory before Kinnon was more than a few sentences in. Moiread listened and laughed herself—in the right places and often genuinely amused—but she had to make an effort to concentrate.

There'd been magic in the war. Moiread had faced most of it, because most of her men couldn't. It was never a light matter, nor one to ignore. Even when the spells cast came from her own side, she'd learned to take them as a signal to prepare herself and her troops. Magic had a way of making things happen.

Now there was no preparation to do. She could stand and wait. She'd learned to do that well too—but a part of her was ever thinking of what happened up the hill.

They made an odd group, Madoc thought. The Calhoun stood opposite him in the middle of the stone circle, stiff-shouldered and thin-lipped in the way of a man who was trying desperately not to fidget or wince or finger the rosary at his belt too hard. Father Parlan, standing in the east, actually looked more comfortable with the whole process, while tiny Seonag, in the west, was clearly fascinated.

She hadn't looked down the hill once since they'd arrived. Evidently the prospect of the ritual had overcome her infatuation with "Michael"—an impressive feat to Madoc, who remembered his own heart at that age.

He raised his hands skyward and began, speaking the Latin slowly and deliberately, but at the top of his lungs. Every word was important in a spell, every syllable, just as every gesture and every moment of mental activity. Get any of them wrong, and failure was the best possible outcome.

"I, Madoc, heir of Avondos, son of Rhys, son of Aberthol, a servant of God, now do in the eyes of Christ and the saints, and of the angels Michael and Zeruch, pledge my aid and friendship, and that of my line and land, to the Calhouns of Hallfield."

The spell began to work. Madoc felt it at first as a tingling in his palms, heat despite the day's chill wind. As he spoke, he pulled that warmth down into his body and through him to the land beneath him, joining his spirit to the power and then both to the earth.

"Be it known to those present and to come," he went on, "to those visible and invisible, terrestrial and celestial alike, that I promise strength, counsel, and refuge to the Calhouns and their liege men. I pledge to always conceal and never reveal that which they bring to me in secrecy, to lend my spirit and the spirit of my land to their defense should there be need, to always give good counsel and never to work against them, whether by word or by deed."

Going down on one knee, he put the palm of that hand flat against the earth. The soil was cold, damp, and gritty against his skin, the pale ends of the grass barely showing through the dirt. For the moment, the layers of tunic and hose kept Madoc's knee from the wet ground, but he suspected moisture would get through by the time he was done. He had taken part in ceremonies with more dignity.

Yet he felt the power, warm beneath the chill ground and warm inside his body, humming in threads of sensation he barely had the skill to part and manipulate. Madoc sensed them going further than him, just as they went deeper than the ground. The magic reached out to his siblings, then forward to those who would come after, tying them all into the spell. He saw no presence, heard no celestial music, but felt witnesses beyond the human all the same, as a hunter knew the unseen life in the forest around him.

Slowly the Calhoun knelt, mirroring Madoc's pose. He reached out a hand and Madoc took it, so that an irreverent observer might have thought of men arm-wrestling with no table to be seen. "I, Eachann Calhoun," he began, speaking even slower and considerably less surely than Madoc had done, "son of Uisdean, son of Eachann, a servant of God…"

As he went on, the tendrils of magic wrapped around him too, entering his soul and through him that of the daughter nearby. Madoc felt the connection and sent his own power out to strengthen it, making a deeper channel between the two families and the two lands. They could draw on each other's strength magically now, and if any of their blood was in need near the other's domain, each would be drawn to the other, even if they didn't know why. Through him, the land's power would also flow into the shield when he cast it. It would bring in the mortal aspects of England's enemies, men more ordinary that the MacAlasdairs and more civilized as well.

Eachann came to the end of his oath and drew breath again, not to speak further but in clear relief at having gotten through the speech without disaster. Facing him, Madoc felt the magic solidify like fired clay. One with force or skill could break it, but left to itself, it would last.

"It is done," he said with the sudden weariness that always followed major spells. While the magic was tied to him and his blood, it was part of him no longer, nor he of it. The departure left him drained and hungry. In company, he couldn't ask for help getting to his feet, nor be seen to struggle, but he groaned inwardly as he rose. "You have my deepest thanks, my lord."

"And you mine. More so if this does what you say."

Madoc looked around. Parlan was standing a polite distance off and not speaking yet, but he had an expression on his face that suggested a thousand questions. There was no danger of hellfire or hanging from that quarter.

"That felt odd," said Seonag. Her pale brows were drawn together under a wrinkled forehead, but her eyes were dazed. "As…as when Beitris…my nurse," she added aside to Madoc, "was first teaching me how to stand and walk as a lady. Drawing me up straight and pressing my shoulders back. Only not in my body."

"'Twas for me like the first time I donned armor," said her father, frowning slightly at Madoc.

He, who'd known the sensation of magical ties for most of his life, nodded and did his best to give a reassuring answer. "All vows bind a man's soul…or a woman's," he added, managing a smile at Seonag. "We feel these bonds more tangibly than others, for a while. The sensation passed, yes?"

"Aye," said Seonag, and the Calhoun nodded.

"You said we werena' the lone place where you'd… do this." He waved a broad hand at the land around them. "And you said we'd be in no danger from the other lords."

"True," said Madoc. "All the connections go through me. In me, they all stop."

"It'll be quite a journey for you, won't it?"

"Yes," said Madoc. "I'm sure it will."

TWELVE

REST HAD DONE THE HORSES AS MUCH GOOD AS IT HAD MADOC, and the careful attentions of Hallfield's grooms had helped too. Rhuddem looked a few years younger when they were packing than she had when they'd reached Hallfield. Madoc would usually have thought Moiread's placid gelding as stolidly unchanging as rock, but even he pricked his ears up and gazed over his stall with new energy when Madoc entered the stables.

Madoc had politely let it be known that he and "Michael" would handle the last stage of preparation on their own. He doubted that an assassin could have penetrated into the keep at Hallfield, where few travelers stopped and new faces attracted attention, but he'd gained a certain habit of caution over the past few weeks. Then too, he wanted to pack the last of his bags himself.

He secured the items carefully: two wooden chests, one the size of his hand and the other thrice as big, as well as one long pouch made of white silk and silver thread, all wrapped for travel in thick wool and then leather. He'd bound the chests with stout cords as well as locking them. The pouch was less important. The implements of his own magic might raise eyebrows or put Madoc in jeopardy if he entered a land with a truly strict priest, but they had no power of their own. He'd knotted the drawstring and left it at that.

Satisfied that the saddlebags were in place and wouldn't fall, and that the edges of the chests would cause his mare no discomfort, Madoc bent to inspect the saddle itself. The

leather seemed sound and whole, the smell of it as primi-
tively reassuring as the other smells surrounding him, those
of hay and horse, but he couldn't let himself be lulled. He
peered carefully at the straps for minute cuts, ran his fingers over the buckles to be sure they fastened tightly, and
passed a hand under the saddle itself, checking for burrs.

Rhuddem shifted beneath his hand, and Madoc heard
footsteps crunching the straw.

"Good man," said Moiread from behind him. "Nothing
amiss?"

"Nothing to my sight," he said, straightening up and turning to face her. Light from the door fell slantwise across her
face, so that one eye peered bright out of shadow, while the
other reflected sunlight. "I'd not expected you here so soon."

"I'd get questions if I left all of this to you," she pointed
out, gesturing to the horses. "It should all properly be my job,
ye ken. They'll likely be thinking me incompetent as it is."

"Alas, 'tis true," Madoc said.

"I know. I'm a dreadful failure as a squire, aye?"

"Dreadful." Madoc pulled a face of exaggerated sobri-
ety. "Continue in this vein, and you'll never be a knight
yourself. Bad enough that you're given to drinking and
dicing, bad enough that you start fights—"

"For your sake, and I never *started* it. Well, not really
started it."

"—but now you can't even be trusted with our baggage." Madoc leaned on the door of the stall and shot
Moiread a reproachful look, clicking his tongue. "I could
wonder why I took you on to begin with."

"An act of charity, plainly. You took pity on a poor lad,
and you're convinced there's good stuff in me yet, if you
can bring it out. It's noble of you, and I'm sure you'll spend
fewer years in purgatory because of it."

"I shall put myself up for sainthood as soon as I get home."

Moiread laughed and rested her back against the stable wall, folding her arms across her chest. "You might check my tack, then, out of the goodness of your heart. Shadow's no' disposed to mind me on his back, but neither is he over-fond of me probing around his belly, and I'd rather not upset him more than I must."

"Out of the goodness of my heart," Madoc replied and left Rhuddem's stall for the gelding's. He glanced back over his shoulder. "You really named your horse Shadow?"

"I've got to call him *something*," Moiread said with a shrug. "*Black* is confusing, and *horse* is worse. And I can't name him like the ones I had in war, since we're going to civilized places, wi' women and children and all. It was Shadow or Fatty."

The name didn't seem to bother Shadow himself. He stood munching and drooling while Madoc checked his saddle, flicking his tail occasionally but otherwise giving no sign that he noticed the man's company.

"All is well," Madoc finally said and walked out into the main stable, looking around the large and mostly silent building. "Where do you suppose everyone is?"

"No supposing needed," said Moiread. "They're off breaking the colts today."

"Ah," said Madoc. "I'd no notion."

Moiread smiled. With her shift of position, the sunlight fell full across her face, turning her pale skin golden. "I was eating with the guards and the servants, mind, while you were charming the Calhoun and his women."

"Oh, you did your portion of that as well. Young Seonag's too well-guarded, or too much the lady, to follow you about, but I'd wager she'll picture your face when she hears a love song for the next month or two."

"Truly?" Moiread chuckled, a low, rich sound, and one full of as much compassion as amusement. "Poor lass. But most of us must fall a few times when we're young, and at least I'll vanish and be forgotten."

"Perhaps," said Madoc, "you give too little credit to your charm."

He'd been jesting, but as they spoke, he felt Moiread's closeness, and his own response was almost inevitable. The stables were silent and empty around them. Her eyes were shining with merriment, and her lips were as full and tempting in this guise as when she wore no illusion.

They curved into another smile. "Flattering," she said, "but I hope you took no insult. You've the rank, after all. Should I worry that I've thwarted a...deeper alliance?"

"No," said Madoc. "The Calhoun would never marry his daughter to a wizard. Magic, you see, is no fit work for real men."

Startled, Moiread threw back her head and laughed, her throat long and pale above the dark collar of her tunic. "Now *there's* an insult, if you wish it. Does he suppose you a eunuch, do you think, or effeminate?"

"I've not had the opportunity to ask. Or," he added, emboldened by her disguise and her way of speaking, "to prove otherwise."

Moiread shook her head. "Oh now," she teased him, eyes sparkling, "you've had *opportunity* aplenty. You've just no' bothered taking the chance, unless the kitchen maids have kept their silence better than they tend to do."

"The better part of diplomacy is not seducing the household. Speaking generally."

"Wise advice. I'll have to write it down when I've a moment."

Flecks of hay spun through the air between them, shining

like tame sparks. The horses shifted and sighed behind them, the sole witnesses to their conversation. Madoc was sure of it. They were alone in a way they'd never been on the road, where they'd been on constant watch for armed interruptions.

"Will that be a change for you?" he asked, stepping forward.

"Oh," she said, "I've never been the envoy, have I? So it's never concerned me before." She tilted her head, mocking deep consideration, and placed a slim finger against her pursed lips for a moment. "Should I have been spreading rumors about your...capabilities? In the interest of diplomacy, that is? I'd not want to deprive you of the girl's hand by my failure at intrigue."

"No," said Madoc. "Marrying a foreign rebel's daughter would make the English too suspicious. Besides, my taste runs considerably older."

Once he'd spoken, he wondered if he should have done so. They were alone; her father had commanded her presence at his side; and he had no wish to press that advantage, or to assume that her humor truly meant she'd accept liberties. About to draw nearer to her, he hesitated.

Moiread slowly straightened up until she was no longer leaning on the wall. Hips swaying in a distinctly unmasculine fashion, she took a few steps forward until her chest and Madoc's almost touched. "How much older, would you say?"

That was enough evidence for temptation to win out over chivalry. Madoc cupped her cheek in one hand, resting his fingers on a soft patch of skin behind one of Moiread's ears. "Old enough to know what she's about."

Moiread certainly qualified. She had for more than two hundred years. She'd first kissed a boy when she was thirteen, and had not been shy about acquiring experience in the years since. Mortal maidens might need to be chaste and demure. *She'd* only had to be discreet.

Yet even as she leaned forward to press her lips to Madoc's, she felt briefly uncertain of herself. She almost held her breath, waiting on his response, and the sound in her throat when he wrapped his arms around her had relief in it as well as pleasure.

Pleasure there certainly was. Madoc kissed deftly, his mouth teasing hers, then responding to her reaction, giving her more pressure, more heat as she demanded it. His chest was firm against hers, and the arms that encircled her body were taut with wiry muscle. He splayed one hand across the small of her back and wound the fingers of the other through her short hair, tilting her head up.

She could melt into this man, Moiread thought, like iron at the forge. The heavy liquid heat of desire was already traveling through her body, as if pure lust ran in her veins instead of blood.

Running her hands down Madoc's back, she pressed lightly with her nails and felt him shudder. His hips thrust forward, pressing his swollen shaft against her sex, a weight and contact that made Moiread groan into his mouth. She dropped her hands to his arse and squeezed, pulling him more firmly toward her and relishing the feel of the hardened muscle beneath her palms.

The hand at Moiread's back clenched, fingers dragging the fabric of her tunic and shirt across her skin with a marvelous friction that rippled out into her whole body. Teasing was over now. The kiss was forceful, hungry, and almost bruising. Moiread leaned up into it, wrapped one of her legs around Madoc's thigh, and arched her hips forward.

She was too distracted to fully control her strength.

Madoc was too distracted to resist. The stable floor was not entirely even or level. Madoc shifted his weight too far back and stumbled, without letting go of Moiread, nor she of him. Moiread heard his head hit the stall door at around the same time her arse made contact with the straw on the ground.

"Damn!" Gingerly she got to her feet, rubbing her tailbone. "Are you, er, well?"

"I managed not to knock my brains out, yes," said Madoc. His head wasn't bleeding, and he was standing up as steadily as Moiread.

That was not particularly steady, but she didn't think either of their injuries had anything to do with the situation. Her lips tingled, and even the feel of her shirt against her breasts sent pangs of frustrated longing all over her. She had a good enough opinion of her charms to imagine that Madoc felt similarly, though she didn't let herself glance toward his groin.

This was not the place or the time for any further temptation.

"If you'd like," Madoc said gravely, "I'll make a pretty apology and promise to do no such thing again."

"Would you mean it?" Moiread asked. These were dangerous waters, but she couldn't resist dipping her toes. She did, however, move back to the wall she'd been leaning against before, putting distance between them.

"If you wanted, I'd hold myself to the promise," Madoc replied with a smile. "And were you to ask an apology, I should be truly sorry for making you feel the need of it."

Moiread shook her head and, reminded by the feeling of hair brushing across her cheek, ran her fingers hastily through the tangled strands. "That would be a great pity," she said, "and I'll ask no such thing. But wisdom, at least, demands it not happen again while I look like this."

She gestured to her chest, flat to appearance if not, evidently, to touch.

"Yes, there is that," Madoc said with a wry smile. He paused briefly, then added, "Do you know, I hadn't been thinking of that at all."

"That could either be very flattering or very *not*. I shall take it as the former."

"Please do."

THIRTEEN

"I WANTED TO WISH YOU A GOOD JOURNEY, MY LORD."

"I WANTED TO WISH YOU A GOOD JOURNEY, MY LORD."

Little Seonag's appearance from an alcove near her father's chambers had been more sudden than Madoc had expected of her, and her actions in meeting him more forthright, but she made him a ladylike curtsy as she spoke, and both words and voice were carefully polite. The propriety of her manner made her actions the more unexpected by contrast, and Madoc could but blink at her at first.

"Thank you," he replied. "And I'm guessing you wished to ask me a question or two while you did, isn't that so?"

For a girl so young and well versed in etiquette, the first step must have taken considerable courage. Madoc saw no need to make the next ones any more difficult for the child. Indeed, the relief on her face was a reward in itself.

"The ceremony, the vows... You know, do ye no', that my lord father would never be able to call on those in any way but the ordinary?" She glanced at the closed door down the hall behind them. "He's a worthy man, you understand, and he has many other concerns, so..." She trailed off, biting her lip.

"I know," said Madoc, "and I agree. No man can do everything. The arts he's learned have kept your land safe and prosperous for these many years, and I admire him for that. Will you come with me a while, my lady? We can speak on the way."

He offered his arm, and she took it with gravity.

"My brother is much the same," Seonag went on, "and

my lady mother is not familiar with any of this. And I think that someone ought to know, particularly now. Father Parlan says it might not be a bad thing, if I take care and keep God's will above everything I learn."

"He seems a wise man."

"Only, my great-aunt died before she could teach me much, and she was never very skilled at writing. She left a few notes, but nothing like what you did." Her small face looked up at Madoc in the dim hallway, with every inch of her gaze full of earnest determination. "I don't know how to aid you, if you need it, and I don't know how I would call on your people, if we have need. I pray neither ever comes to pass, but if they do, I want to know how."

"Of course," he said. "To lend us aid magically… That you don't need to worry about. By the way you speak, am I right in thinking you don't know how to draw power from the land?"

"No… How would I? What does it do?"

"That depends on the spell you cast. There are those who use the power of their land for oracles, or cast spells with it every year to make for a better harvest or the like, but those are complicated works, the sort that take years to construct. *Mostly*, if you're fighting another sorcerer, and you're of the right bloodline, you can use the land's strength as well as your own. It may also give you physical strength, if you need it."

"Oh. Could I learn to do that?"

"Yes," said Madoc, "but it would take more time than we have, and more than we would have had if you had asked me the moment I arrived. *If* your father would permit further instruction, I might be able to find you a tutor for a season or two. If this peace lasts that long."

"Oh, it must!" Seonag said with a smile of pure

optimism. "We've won so many battles, and the English signed a treaty. The war *must* be over now."

Madoc couldn't match her smile, but he patted her hand where it lay on his arm. "I hope so. Now, until you have more training, as I said, you need not fear me calling on your family's power. Were you to try to use the same power at the same time, or shortly after, you might find it drained, like a well in the summertime, but it would come back the same way. You'd need do nothing, nor even know."

She nodded, flaxen braids swinging against the shoulders of her pink gown. "And once I'm trained?"

"Then you'll know how the land fares, and how to put strength into it if you have need. You'll get the sense of it without much instruction once you've learned the basics, or at least I did. The spells themselves are trickier, but once you know the other world, it reveals itself to you as much as you learn about it. I think you'd do well, if your father allows."

They came out into the great hall, with servants around them sweeping the rushes and cleaning the tables, doing the day's work to make ready for the night's meal once more. Seonag slipped her hand from Madoc's arm and curtsied again. "Thank you, my lord," she said. "God be with you on your journey. And...and with your squire as well." Her face went nearly as pink as her gown.

"Thank you," said Madoc, "and I'm sure he'll be glad as well. In truth, he needs any divine aid he can get, for his mind's mostly on a lady back home."

There, disappointment on the childish face, but no sign of either surprise or hurt. A heart already given elsewhere was no slight, not even the minor one of youth. This way, she'd have no cause to hope, but no cause to think badly of herself either. "Well, I wish him happiness, my lord," she said, with a polite smile. "And you as well."

Madoc made her a courtly bow and departed for the yard. As he went, he thought how odd it was to be rejecting young women on Moiread's behalf, doubly so when his lips still felt the heat of hers against them and he could easily call the stifled noises of her desire to his ears.

The rest of the journey promised to be extremely interesting.

Moiread paced slowly around the pen, not impatient but wishing to stretch her legs out as much as she could before taking to the saddle once again. She kept a careful eye on the horses, who stood more or less patiently, pages holding their reins.

"Will you cross the border after this?" Clyde asked, walking up to her side.

"Aye. We'll have to pass through England to get my lord home, after all, and he'd as soon not risk the sea." No need to mention the stop they were making, or that their hosts wouldn't truly be English at all.

"Some might say there's no' much less risk going by land."

"Some might," Moiread said and tried for a joke. "But they'd not be the seasick kind, would they? Green isn't my lord's best color. Besides, there's a treaty now, isn't there?"

"There is," said Clyde, frowning. "But there's men as don't need a war to make devils of themselves, lad, and there's bound to be plenty among the English who take the treaty ill. Grant was bad enough after victory."

"Not so bad as that," Moiread said.

"Oh, I'll not deny you're a bonny fighter, and I'm sure you're as good with a sword as you were with your fists. But Grant was one man. He's a soldier too, without any more power than what he has in a fight or what the Calhoun gives him, which wasna' a great deal. If you come across a

local lord or a sheriff with a similar spirit, it could go hard
for you."

Moiread paused and looked down into the lined face,
saw the genuine worry there, and wondered whose face
came to his mind when he looked at her: a younger brother,
a son, or simply a comrade of prior days? Whoever it was,
she would have laid odds that the young man hadn't survived long past the age she appeared to be.

Had they been just off the battlefield late at night, or
companions in a dingy tavern with worse ale, she might
have asked and known the question welcome. Men talked
of their pasts at such times. They honored memories. Now
there was neither time nor drink nor privacy, and questions
on such a subject would be cruelty.

She asked a different one. "How would you advise
me, then?"

"Only be careful," Clyde said with a resigned shrug.
"Keep your temper about you and your sword in its scab-
bard, if you can. And I'd say talk no more than needful
either. You speak more like an Englishman than I do—
meaning no offense—but there are few English who'd mistake you for their own once you open your mouth, I'd say."

"And I'm glad of it," Moiread said with a quick smile,
"but I take your meaning. Enemy land, so give them no
cause to start anything."

"That's it exactly. And be on your guard in case they try
regardless. I hope your lord knows what he's about, lad. I
truly do."

"Between the two of us, so do I," said Moiread.

When she heard more footsteps, she didn't have to turn
around. Although their time together had been brief, her
senses were enough keener than mortals' that she could now
recognize Madoc from a combination of his pace and his

scent. The latter, so soon after they'd kissed, stirred sensations low in her body, and she shifted her weight restlessly.

"Ready?" he asked.

"For a while now, my lord," she said, playing the cheerfully cheeky squire. "Clyde, it's been a pleasure. Farewell."

"Take care, lad," he said.

Mounted, she and Madoc rode out of the castellum and down the road, into a day hazy with clouds but otherwise pleasant. The sounds and smells of human habitation fell quickly behind them, leaving them alone in the middle of the empty road.

"I told Seonag," Madoc said, "that you were pining away for a girl in my lands. I hope you don't mind."

Moiread smiled. "Best thing for her, I'd think. And no, I don't mind the rumor, and it's not as if I'm likely to be 'Michael' again there." She looked at him across the gap between their horses. "You're not seasick, by any chance, are you?"

"Not at all. I've always been a good sailor."

Madoc sounded proud of it too. *Damn*.

"Well," said Moiread, "if you come back here and the subject arises, I suppose you can always say there was a reason you cast me off."

FOURTEEN

TURNING SOUTHEAST, THEY SOON FOUND THEMSELVES APPROACH-ing the coast. The road wound through rocky hillsides, with pale ash and trembling aspens beginning to show green leaves on one side, while on the other the cliffs fell away to blue-gray waves below. Salt was strong in the air; Madoc smelled it and thought of home.

Now and again they shared the road with other travelers: mostly merchants, one minstrel, and once a small group of pilgrims bound for Saint Margaret's chapel now that war and climate alike permitted such a journey. None shared the road for more than a few hours before their own business called them away, leaving Madoc and Moiread alone again.

Madoc was more conscious of that solitude than he'd been during any of the days before Hallfield, even during the endless hours they'd spent together at the inn. As he rode south beside Moiread, both of them hale, well, and in their right minds, he found it difficult not to think of kissing her in the stables, nor of how she'd spoken afterward— not quite a promise of more, but more than a hint. Even with others nearby, he glanced sideways at her frequently, observing her seat in the saddle and the way her hair blew back from her face.

Magical vision was no help. Madoc rode with his sight in the world of auras and magic that Moiread had showed him how to invoke. The brightness of all living things, and the colored haze around many of them, was itself distract-ing. More, Moiread was herself in that sight, and while her illusion hadn't kept Madoc from wanting her, seeing her as a woman heightened his desire, while the play of lights in her aura and her dragon-shaped shadow were a constant source of fascination.

For most of the first part of the journey, he could think of nothing to say. He felt stupid for it, calflike and all of sixteen, but if Moiread resented his silence, she gave no sign of it. Madoc thought she might attribute it—and his frequent moments of staring at her—to the mystical sight itself, and he would gladly let her believe that.

Flirting had been easier in Hallfield's stables. Riding in solitude, Madoc was too aware of how much he'd enjoyed it, but also of how closely and for how long he and Moiread would be companions. Finding aught to say that took both things into consideration was far from easy.

"Was it as you remembered?" he finally asked.

Moiread looked briefly startled, then confused, then comprehending. "Hallfield? Aye... Well, as much as anywhere ever is. Uisdean was different, poor man, but I canna' say that was such a shock. Threescore and ten, or a time for every purpose, or whatever verse you'd like."

Her shadow stretched long and winged over the road behind them.

"It must be hard for you," Madoc said.

"It is," Moiread replied and sighed, shaking her head, "and then in a while it isna', and that's sad too in its way. We get accustomed. As we all do, in *our* way. It's not as though all that many *see* old age, is it? Especially of late."

War and pestilence, Madoc thought, childbed and storm, not to mention accidents. One of his childhood friends had gotten drunk and fallen in the river when he was twenty. A miller had found his body in the lake two days later. Children had grown up hearing of his ghost.

He nodded. "There's truth in that. I'm not sure these days are any more violent than others, save for this war in particular. Though there are those who insist that the world is getting worse."

Moiread laughed, amused and scornful. "Always are, aye? The year I was born, the world was due to end by Christmastide. Even the pope said as much. My sister, Agnes, was right nervous about it, she always told me. When we were fighting, she'd say having me as a sister was nigh as bad."

"Quite a tongue on her, your sister."

"Oh, she may have been right. The Kingdom of Heaven is supposed to be quite a pleasant place, ye ken, and I wasn't often pleasant as a child. You," she added, with a twitch of her lips, "will kindly refrain from any comment on that."

Madoc bowed as well as he could from the saddle. "Do you not believe in the end of the world, then?"

"Everything ends," Moiread said cheerfully enough, given the subject, "and Saint John may well be right about the way of it. But in my life, I've heard of enough antichrists to get up a decent festival dance, if not an army, and yet I sit on this horse and talk with you, so I'm no' inclined to believe in any new one to come along."

"Like splinters of the True Cross or the bones of saints, only the opposite," Madoc said, and then whistled as a notion struck him.

"Mmm?"

"Wouldn't it be terrifying if they all *were* real? One son of the devil born in each generation, all hiding away until the moment was right? Or each one having his chance and failing, but with another one coming along who might well succeed?"

Moiread gave him a long, considering look. "Should you ever decide to set up as a prophet," she said finally, "you could probably start a fair-sized riot or two."

"It does wear on us after a few hundred years," Moiread said when the silence had crept up once again and the tension grown too thick, when watchfulness couldn't occupy her enough to keep her from stealing glances at Madoc. "Seeing time pass for others, that is. None of my generation have felt it too keenly, or at least we've none of us spoken of it, but Artair has once or twice, and my grandfather did."

Madoc made a sympathetic *mmm* sound. "Have they any counsel for it?"

"Drink. God. Duty. Endurance." Moiread shrugged, chuckling wryly. "The same cure as for all else they can't solve by force or trickery."

"And so it is with all men. We all apply the same poultices to different wounds, according to our nature...and a better man than me would say that God's the most reliable of the three, in all cases."

"A better woman than me would believe it. And I'll not say no, only that He works more slowly, when he does. Sometimes you need a quicker sort of balm, and it matters not that it's no cure in the end. But my father's brother was a monk for a decade or two," she added.

"Did it help?"

"Might have, while it lasted. He said nothing of it to me one way or another, but we were never close. And he left a hundred years ago."

"Left the monastery?"

"Left the world," Moiread said, and smiled to see Madoc's eyes widen. "I don't know how, or where for... I suspect likely to a place akin to our next stop. Artair says we know how when it's time, though he's stayed longer than most of us ever do. They say the Old Ones could move back and forth like you go in and out of a house, but that was far in the past, and it's not like they ever had much to do with us."

Madoc stared at her, then broke into laughter. "In the future, if you're going to amaze me, could you do it more gradually?" he asked, shaking his head, his eyes alight with amusement and curiosity. "I'm almost struck dumb for not knowing what question to ask first."

"I'll try to contain myself," said Moiread, meaning that in more than one sense.

The memory of their kiss still filled her with warmth, especially when she watched Madoc's dark hair fall over his brow, or observed the clean lines of his body while he mounted his horse. *Satisfying* that lust, however, would take a while, and not just in a pleasurable sense. She looked like a man, and this wasn't the battlefield, where priests and commanders alike could overlook what happened in a tent. She and Madoc would have to wait until they had a private room, and God alone knew when that was likely to be.

She bit back a sigh.

Meeting her gaze, Madoc looked swiftly away and cleared his throat. "The Old Ones, then."

"Our ancestors. *Not* human, nor even partly so. They wore man's form as you'd put on a cloak. I don't know if all shapes were alike to them, or if they were dragons in truth. It'd make their tastes a bit suspect, perhaps, if they were."

"Shall I joke about carrying off virgins now?" Madoc asked, but before Moiread could answer, he stiffened, and

the humor faded from his face. "Wait. I thought I saw—"
His eyes narrowed, and he peered off to the side of the
road, into a thick clump of trees and brush.

They didn't stop then. Stopping would have let any
watchers know they knew, and Moiread was briefly glad to
see that Madoc didn't suggest it. "What does it look like?"
she asked quietly.

"An...unraveling. A blurring. A—*damn*."

On the last word, he spurred his mare forward. The
motion might have saved his life. One crossbow bolt sang
through the air right behind him. Another punched into the
flank of his mare, who screamed and reared up, beating the
air with her hooves. Madoc clung to the saddle.

The men in the brush knew a target when they saw one.
Two more bolts took the mare in the chest.

Moiread didn't even have breath to swear.

FIFTEEN

THERE WAS A MOMENT OF GRACE FOR RHUDDEM AND MADOC both, a moment before she knew she was dying, before the wicked bolts piercing her organs made them fail entirely and her body with them. Screaming, she stayed upright for that instant, and that was long enough. Madoc kicked free of his stirrups and threw himself from the saddle with all the desperate strength he'd used to grip it earlier.

He hit the ground hard. One whole side of his body took the impact, and it jarred through muscle and bone alike. Before he'd caught his breath or blinked his vision clear, Rhuddem pitched over on her side as well, a stroke of fortune sending her in the opposite direction from Madoc.

The world was hazy and stank of blood.

Long-practiced reflex and alien duty blended for Moiread. With hardly any more thought than she'd have used when walking, she drew her sword and leapt off Shadow. The gelding was no destrier, and Moiread had never fought well on horseback.

The bastards were likely reloading. She had a window, but a small one.

She saw Madoc bolt from the saddle and hit the ground. His mare's body blocked him from her view shortly after, and Moiread didn't know if he was hurt. She thought she should check, then realized that if she missed her opportunity, it might not matter. She settled for a quick glance in his direction as she sprinted for the tree line.

His eyes were open. He was breathing. That would have to be good enough.

Nothing hurt yet. Pain would come later, when his body realized that the danger was past—assuming he lived to see the danger past. Madoc shook his head to clear it.

The first thing he saw when his vision cleared was Moiread darting past him with the bare blade of her sword shining in the sunlight. He'd almost forgotten their practice bout, particularly how fast she'd been—not lightning, but far quicker than most mortals.

Madoc rolled up to his feet. His bones seemed intact, or intact enough to hold him, and that would suffice. He drew his own weapons, sword and dagger falling easily into his hands, and began to run as well. On his way, he dismissed the *visio dei*. The world became its normal self again, mundane and deadly.

He got close enough to Moiread that her shadow fell across him as they entered the underbrush, and she looked over her shoulder to focus her gleaming eyes on him. She jerked her head leftward, then almost immediately veered right, and he knew what she meant. The assassins had likely split up, and they should do so as well.

Madoc followed her orders, dodged around a young sapling toward where he saw movement, and ignored the impulse to look back.

Trees were a damned mixed blessing. They and their branches made running hell. Moiread had nearly tripped

over two small logs by the time she reached the first clump
of armed men, and her face was well and truly scratched.

The trees did provide some cover. She was glad of that.
Crossbowmen needed time to reload, but they might have
been clever and saved a shot for, say, an angry Scotswoman
charging at them with a sword. She ducked low and
swerved around trunks just in case. With any luck, Madoc
would do the same. She'd not had time to instruct him, any
more than she'd been able to tell him he should stay put.

A moving target was probably best, in any case.

Three of the assassins crouched on a small ridge—two
men with crossbows, hastily stuffing bolts into place, and
a big fellow with an ax to guard them. He was in a good
place for it too, right where the trail opened onto the ridge,
right in position to meet Moiread.

By God and the saints, she hated it when she had
smart enemies.

One tree had grown so large that its shade and roots choked
off all plant life beneath it. Two of the men had taken up a
position there—one fellow with a crossbow, the other with a
spear and a shield, and a long sword at his waist. From what
Madoc could see in the shade of the trees and the excitement of the moment, neither looked particularly reputable,
but both looked to have some experience in violence.

Neither saw him at first. He moved lightly, and Moiread
was making enough noise in the other direction to be a
more-than-adequate distraction, particularly when what
she did made one of her opponents bellow in pain. When
both greasy heads turned toward the noise, Madoc saw his
moment and lunged forward.

Catching the movement out of the corner of his eye,

the spearman turned and quickly raised his shield arm. Madoc's sword hit metal rather than flesh, the impact jarring up his arm to his shoulder. He was inside the man's range, though, safe from the jabbing spearhead, and he recovered quickly, letting the force of the rebound carry his sword over and downward.

Battered leather armor kept the stroke shallower than it might have been, but it pierced flesh nonetheless. The spearman snarled an oath, nostrils flaring with pain, and shifted his weight quickly backward. The outside leg of his breeches grew dark with blood.

A touch: not a fatal one, nor even crippling. The man dropped the spear and brought his shield around to block Madoc's following strike while he drew his sword.

His friend was kneeling on the ground with a crossbow in front of him. A bolt was already in place; the man was now cranking the bow back. Aiming would come next. Then the shot.

The man with the ax swung. Moiread ducked behind a tree, then around, and forced her way through the brush toward the first crossbowman. He bolted to his feet, grabbing for the dagger at his waist and letting the bow tumble to the ground.

She didn't have the chance to pursue him. His friend with the ax was quick; he turned and hacked at Moiread again, and she hastily spun to block him. She'd bought herself time, though, with at least one fewer crossbow bolt coming at her head, and that had been her immediate aim. The other fellow would find it harder to hit her with the first man in the way.

For the moment, Moiread could turn her attention

almost fully to the axman. Abruptly, she shifted her weight back, dropping her sword from the ax. Before the other man could register that and follow the opening through into her kidneys, she whirled away, snapped a leg up, and kicked him in the stomach.

Armor helped him, and her foot would ache for it later, but the man staggered. Moiread spun again, landing on the leg she'd used to kick and bringing her sword down overhand onto the joint of his elbow.

He screamed.

He didn't scream for long.

Even while his hand was falling to the ground, ax clutched in his beefy fingers, Moiread drew back, lunged, and slid her sword through armor, skin, and flesh alike—a good, clean strike between the ribs, and turned so that the bone wouldn't catch the blade.

The man died fast, with a look of puzzlement mixing with the pain on his face. Moiread had seen that often.

The woods around had gone silent. Most creatures ran when men fought one another, even those who would later make a leisurely meal of the loser. In the quiet, Madoc heard three sets of quick, panting breaths, all slightly out of rhythm. He felt sweat running down his neck—or mayhap blood, since he didn't know what injury he might have done himself in his fall or the run through the forest—and ignored it.

He circled as wide as he could, given the ground, luring his foe out and using his body as cover against the crossbowman. The other lunged and Madoc met his blade. He feinted a few times, only to find himself tapping at the man's shield. Neither moved decisively for a span of moments. No sun dappled the ground on this overcast day. Beneath the trees, it was almost as dim as twilight.

When the opening came, it was slight. The other man just missed his step, and the shift in weight dropped his guard by a fraction. In that instant, Madoc darted in and struck, carving a long line with his dagger down the shoulder of his foe's sword arm. The next moment Madoc was leaping sideways, away from a return slash at his neck.

As he dodged, he also threw the dagger with a quick overhand motion that had served him well in contests and hunting. It took the crossbowman in the throat. He didn't make a sound, but fell backward, blood pooling onto the dark earth.

Madoc turned back to face the swordsman, blade ready. His enemy had other ideas, knowing himself to be alone and doubly wounded against a hale opponent who might shortly have an ally.

"Quarter, sir!" He stepped swiftly back, almost stumbling onto the corpse of his ally, with his sword and shield both raised protectively. "Gimme mercy, in God's name!"

"Fine words from a murderer," said Madoc. "Throw down your weapons."

Both men fighting Moiread had armed themselves for close combat while she was dispatching their friend. One had a short sword, the other a cudgel, with which he made a decent attempt at braining her as she drew her sword from the first man's rib cage. Ducking hastily, she took the blow on her shoulder, where it hurt like the devil but didn't break any bones.

Moiread rose, slashed, and caught the son of a whore across the neck. The spine was a sturdy piece of work;

she didn't quite take his head. It was a near thing, though, and she turned from him confident that there'd be no more trouble from *that* quarter any time soon.

A crouching strike to the thigh did for the third man. It wasn't as immediately fatal, but he dropped his sword and fell to the ground, clutching at the wound and calling on the saints. Moiread stepped back and eyed him.

She'd caught him above the knee, a shade too far forward for the large veins that could let a man's blood out in moments. He'd live. He wouldn't be a threat, and he damned well wouldn't be going anywhere for the next few minutes.

"Be quiet," she said, "or I'll gut you right now."

The man clamped his teeth down on his lip. Moiread could hear the sounds of movement from down the ridge, and then words, though she couldn't catch the sense of them.

She left the wounded man with the corpses and began moving through the woods as quietly as she could manage in haste.

With neither rope nor a second pair of hands, and not inclined to let his advantage slip nor to wait while Moiread fought the other brigands, Madoc settled matters the only way he could see.

"Kneel," he told the assassin, "hands up."

When the man complied, Madoc hit him neatly at the back of the head with the hilt of his sword. Such an injury could kill, he knew, but it was as much mercy as he could offer under the circumstances.

He heard footsteps from behind him and spun, suddenly glad he'd opted for the quick method. He was immensely relieved to see a tall, slim, familiar figure pushing her way through the undergrowth.

"I see I'm no' needed," Moiread said, her eyes running up and down Madoc's frame. "You look well."

"You look—" He peered at her. Blood stained her wrists and spattered across her armor. Still, she moved as she always did, and he could see no injuries. "None of that's yours, is it?"

"Only by right of conquest." A killer's smile flickered across her narrow face. "Let's pick up and grab the living, aye? I've a few dozen questions in mind."

SIXTEEN

Since they had no rope, Moiread slashed the sleeves off her good tunic and used them to bind each of their captives' hands together, then cut strips off the tunic itself for their feet. She shrugged at Madoc's surprised expression. "We'd have to leave it behind in any case," she said. "Only the one horse. Or none, if Shadow doesn't come back."

The mare had died during the fight, probably soon after it started. Two bolts to the chest killed quickly. Moiread was glad of it for Madoc's sake. She thought it would have pained him if he'd had to slit the beast's throat.

Indeed, as she spoke of the horses, he sighed, then squared his shoulders. "If you can spare me, I'll see if I can find him. If there were any more of these"—he cast a contemptuous eye on their attackers—"about, they'd likely have come to help their fellows, so I should be safe for a while yet."

"Aye," said Moiread, "but don't go too far, and take care."

She stood over the bound men, cleaning first her sword and then herself. In war, she'd gotten used to the feel of blood and the smell of death. She'd never grown to like it. The sooner they could mount up and get away from the corpses, the happier Moiread would be.

Granted, the proximity wasn't helping the assassins either.

Moiread examined the men. One had lank blond hair coming down to his shoulders and a sparse beard. The other, shorter and thinner, was bald as an egg and missing three teeth. Another section of Moiread's tunic bandaged his thigh, and the final scrap bound the blond man's shoulder. Neither looked wealthy, clean, or reliable. Moiread had, in her time, known mercenaries one could trust, and Cathal had spoken of them as well. These weren't that sort of men.

They wore the kind of clothing she'd expect of men in their position, nothing close to a uniform, but as Moiread watched them, she noticed one common point. Each man had a leather thong around his neck, his tunic covering the object it held.

"What's this?" Moiread bent forward and grabbed the thong off Blondie, ignoring his yell of protest. Jerking it up, she saw a small yellow-green stone in a crude tin setting dangling from the end. "You don't seem the sort for jewelry. Let me see."

When Baldy's necklace proved to be the same, she jerked it off his neck, snapping the leather cord. *He* stayed silent. Getting stabbed in the leg didn't leave a man much energy for protest.

"Huh," Moiread said, and when Madoc came back leading Shadow, she held the pendant up. "What do you make of this?"

"Very little. I'm not a jeweler." His smile was quick, but it set her at ease. In their travels, she hadn't thought to ask if he'd killed men before, or to wonder until recently how he'd react to it. Either he'd more experience than she'd thought or he was resilient, and either way Moiread thanked God. "The man who poisoned you had a chain around his neck. Should we check the bodies?"

"Fair thought. These won't go far."

Crows took off at their approach. Scavengers moved in quickly, once the fight was over. Moiread hummed a few bars of "Twa Corbies" as she knelt and examined the men. The fellow with the crossbow had an amulet like the others, as well as two shillings, three pence, and a grimy rosary. The other, the one with the ax, had a chain around his neck. His stone was larger, and the setting, also tin, was better crafted.

"The leader, I'd think," said Madoc. "He fits the description I had from the girl at the inn, though many men would."

"And these?"

"I don't recognize them, but keep watch and I'll see what I can find. *Visio dei*."

Death stained the land—shades of red and gray and black, shadows that were too thick, but all of it part of the world, all a thread in the greater whole as it was, if perhaps not as it should be. Madoc found he could look squarely around him, and even at the bodies themselves.

The amulets were a different matter. Before the attack, Madoc had briefly seen them as blurred spots on the edge of his vision. Closer, with more time, they still were blurry—and so was everything immediately around them, as if Madoc was seeing it from under not-very-clear water. Moiread's hand on the chain was a beige sort of blob, her face hazy and indistinct.

"I've not seen anything similar," said Madoc. "I would think they're for concealment, that a man could wear them and blend into his surroundings, perhaps make little sound and give little scent as well, but they're new to me. Shall we trade off?"

"May as well," Moiread said, and invoked the vision while Madoc dismissed his.

She came out a moment later, cross-eyed and shaking her

head. "Never seen the like myself. Could be the men will tell us more."

Before they left, she bent and closed the dead axman's eyes, putting a penny from her own pouch onto each lid. Once Madoc knew what she was about, he followed suit and did the same with the crossbowman he'd killed, a man who wore the same rough amulet as the others. He offered a quick prayer for their souls as well. All men fell in the end. Even if he'd not been feeling compassionate, he wanted no ghosts on his trail.

"You want yours or mine?" Moiread asked as they headed back to the road. "Best split them up for questioning, I think."

"Ah, yes," said Madoc, "and I may as well take the one who fought me. Familiarity may count for something, mayhap."

"Couldn't hurt," said Moiread.

It didn't, but Madoc wasn't sure in the end that much *could* have hurt. The blond man was ready enough to talk, having neither fear of nor loyalty to his employer, but that was because his employer, as far as he knew, was dead.

"John picked us up back in Perth," he said, his accent marking him as Scots. "Said he'd a job needed doing, paid decent. Didna' say anything of why, but he never did. Better not to ask, I always thought."

"And the amulets?"

"The what? Oh, the stones?" When Madoc held up one of the pendants, the mercenary shrugged his uninjured shoulder. "He had four of 'em, plus the one he wore himself. Said they'd make us harder to spot. And they may have worked, though we'd only caught up to you a day back, and it took us this long to find a good spot."

"I'm sorry it was such effort," Madoc said dryly. "Had you known John before?"

"A bit. Killer for pay. Usually he worked alone, but now

and then he'd have need of men, and he'd come to me if I was around. Wandered."

"Could he have made these? Was he a scholar, or did he have any sort of powers?"

"Him?" The man snorted. "If he could read the name on a tavern sign, 'twas as much as he could manage. As for powers, he'd a good right arm and a nose for a paying customer, but this was the first time I ever saw anything as might be uncanny. Perhaps he shouldna' have meddled with it, considering."

"Perhaps not," Madoc agreed.

"Unless they got their story straight between them," Moiread said, talking to Madoc after a quarter hour's questioning, "they're telling the truth. And they're neither of them helpful about it. Yours at least knew the leader. Mine just followed the sound of coin, from what he says."

"It's a pity, but it's true. You've killed the one man who might have told us more…not that I blame you for it, you understand."

"Well, there's a weight off my mind." Moiread smiled back at him. "Should this happen again, I'll be sure to ask how much a man knows before I run him through. I've got an arm and a leg to spare, you know."

Madoc held up a hand. "No, no, I think the loss of information is by far the best of the possibilities. They wouldn't grow back, then?"

"No. Killing us takes some doing, and we heal fast, but once a bit's gone, it's gone…at least in all the generations I know. My grandfather said his father could reattach most limbs if he could find them quickly enough, but I never knew the man."

Madoc took in this information, blinked, and then shook himself back to the task at hand. He glanced past Moiread to where the bound men sat several yards away. "What shall we do about them?"

"Could slit their throats," Moiread said. She didn't like killing men in cold blood, especially without last rites, but she'd never heard she had to *like* a thing to do it. "Saves the hangman's wages and the cost of the rope."

Madoc shook his head. "Mine asked for mercy, and I told him he'd have it. Or I implied as much."

"Not one to split the difference, are you?" Moiread said and gave him another smile, all the more so because she knew Artair and Douglas both would have used exactly such an opening. "Well, 'tis a large road, and it could be the next travelers will take pity on them. Meanwhile, they can repent or the like."

"There is always that hope," Madoc said with an unhopeful little laugh. "And what of us, now?" He glanced over toward where his mare lay, and his face tightened.

Moiread put a hand on his shoulder. Not a horsewoman herself, she remembered the hound she'd had as a child, faithful and eager and killed, in the end, when they were hunting boar. The loss of beasts hit harder than that of people, at times. "We can try to bury her, if you'd like."

"We've no time, and I doubt the ground here would bear it," Madoc said and placed his hand briefly over hers. "But it's a kind thought."

"In that case, we'll ride double for a while. Shadow's a sturdy beast, and we should be able to buy another before too much longer. We'd best leave plenty behind, if we can."

They kept themselves to two saddlebags. One held Madoc's treasures. In the other, they kept a spare shirt and a set of hose. Rain was common, and Moiread had found nothing like riding long hours in wet clothing to wreck a man's health. She, who didn't get sick, abandoned hers and resolved to grit her teeth and bear the discomfort if she had to. That left room for a small loaf of bread, a skin of wine, and a few carrots.

Madoc's formal clothes—as well as those of Moiread's that hadn't gone toward bonds and bandages—made a small and sadly bright heap by the roadside. "With luck," she said, "we can buy more when we get the second horse. Our next hosts must forgive our circumstances if we're not as fashionable as they'd like."

"I'm sure they'll understand," said Madoc. He sounded confident, or was putting on a good show of it.

At last, Moiread settled the packs on Shadow and climbed back up into the saddle. Madoc mounted easily behind her. Suddenly the smell of him was strong around her, drowning out the stench of blood and death. The fronts of his legs settled lightly against the backs of hers, though he sat far back enough for the rest to be decorous—disappointingly so, if better for her concentration on the road.

"If you feel the need to hold on, do," she said and added, "but you'd best use my shoulders if anyone's about to see."

She felt his laughter behind her.

SEVENTEEN

If riding beside Moiread had been tempting, riding behind her was an extremely pleasant form of torture. Madoc kept his hands to himself—it was easy enough to stay mounted with legs alone when the horse didn't go any faster than a quick walk—yet their bodies brushed against each other at every turn in the road. The slim strength of Moiread's frame was only a whisper away; the heat of her body radiated through her clothing and Madoc's; and every vibration of speech or breath sent corresponding sensation through Madoc.

Before they'd been riding for an hour, he was uncomfortably aroused, swollen tight against his braies and thankful that his tunic was loose, long, and heavy. He tried to keep his breathing regular—no call to go panting in the lady's ear like a drunken lout with a tavern maid, even if she was right there and lovely and, at least theoretically, willing.

He looked off to either side of them, forcing himself to focus on any signs of danger, any of the underwater blurring that had marked the assassins before. The process helped with his self-control. Madoc couldn't be *glad* that men with magical talismans were trying to kill him, but they did say that every cloud had a silver lining. This one was that he was less likely to be found by the side of the road ravaging his apparent squire, which probably would go some way toward preserving him from an unpleasant death.

"We'll be crossing the border soon," Moiread said, "if we havena' done it already. The lines shift in this part of the country."

Indeed, in the *visio dei*, the land they were crossing appeared looser, the lines and shapes a shade less clearly defined. Madoc said so and got a startled, thoughtful *huh* from Moiread in response. "Do you think the country's that way because we're so unsettled about it, then," she asked, "or the other way 'round?"

"I'm not sure," Madoc replied, glad in equal parts of the uncertainty, the chance to discuss it with another who had at least a passing familiarity with magic, and the chance to further turn his mind somewhere other than his loins. "It could be either. One thing oft partakes of the nature of another, if they're in long association, and I have noticed that the connection is especially strong when human beings are a part of it."

"We do leave our marks, don't we?"

Madoc looked ahead of them at the road, built in the days of the Romans and still cutting a wide and clear swath through what would have been coastal forest. "That we do," he said, and was about to ask if she considered herself part of humanity, when an idea struck him. "If we come upon a town tonight," he said, "I might be able to find out more about the men who attacked us."

"The amulets?" Moiread asked.

"Just so." Madoc smiled at the quickness with which she caught on. He ought to have expected it, but it was still a pleasant surprise. "I'll need privacy, of course, but I'd also like you to guard me while I cast the spell. It's not likely I'll provoke an attack, especially not an immediate one, but it's always best to be safe."

"That it is," she said with feeling, and then her voice took on a lighter tone, even as it dropped in pitch. "And I'm verra much inclined toward privacy as well, if we can manage that."

With those words, low and sensual, and a quick look over her shoulder, she undid all the good that an intellectual conversation had done.

Assassins kept making life difficult, even after one had killed most of them.

In the ordinary way of things, Moiread thought that she and Madoc would have reached a town before nightfall. Mayhap it wouldn't have been a large one, but it would at least have had an inn where they could purchase the use of their own room. With the ritual to add to her own sensual urges, she could easily have justified pushing themselves a fraction later than they otherwise might have.

But they'd stopped to fight. They'd spent more time cleaning up, questioning their prisoners, and getting their belongings packed onto Shadow. Shadow himself, burdened with two people and their baggage, wasn't walking as quickly as he had been. Sunset fell without any sign of civilization greater than the occasional woodcutter's cottage, and ere much longer it was getting too dark to keep traveling safely, especially when they had only the one horse.

When Moiread realized that, she could have gone back to the men they'd left bound and kicked them in the ribs a few times.

Instead, she cursed inwardly, did her best with the heat that had been growing between her legs all day and the way Madoc's breath ghosted along the skin of her neck, and made for the next lit house they saw. By the time they'd dismounted, she'd forced herself to a philosophical acceptance, one that let her negotiate cheerfully with the woman who owned the house and smile at her three children, then listen to the stories Madoc told them over dinner.

They were good stories, like those he'd told when she was delirious with poison: Welsh myths and the local tales he'd grown up with. Through dinner and after, they made a decent distraction…but when they lay down in front of the fire that night, Moiread heard every breath Madoc took, felt every hand's-width that separated them, and wished everyone else in the house on the other side of the world.

The next day brought no relief from her tension. The woman owned no animal larger than a goat, certainly nothing a man could ride, and so she and Madoc rode together again. He sat in front this time, shifting the balance of their weight to give Shadow a change. Moiread, not the horseman he was, held on to his shoulders, felt firm, lean muscle shifting beneath armor and clothing, and swore again in the privacy of her mind.

If she offered *this* up, she was owed a considerable number of years out of purgatory—perhaps even enough to make up for the rest of her life, both as she'd lived before and as she planned to go on. Had she been a better woman, that idea would have brought her joy. She'd been no such thing for three centuries, and she doubted she'd improve any time soon.

At least they'd only another day to go. Surely they'd find their needed privacy in that day! If not, Moiread thought she might build the damn inn herself.

The town they reached the next evening was the largest Madoc had yet seen. Salt and fish joined the other odors of human habitation, while seagulls circled the market along with the ever-present sparrows and pigeons. Here in the south, on less rocky terrain, the houses were largely wood, rather than earth or stone as they'd been in Scotland.

They were properly in England now. The voices of those around them rose and fell differently, and the coins Madoc got in change when he paid for their food and lodging bore Edward's face rather than Robert's or Alexander's. The young king stared up at Madoc from the silver, his hair falling around his shoulders and his gaze sharp. Despite his words to Moiread about kings and the English in general, Madoc shook his head and swept the coins into his pouch as quickly as he could.

They had plenty of England yet to travel through before they reached the gateway to their next destination. He had best get used to it and simply be glad that they'd come upon a town large enough to have an inn. He *was* glad for the sturdy walls, for it was raining again, and for the fresh bread that was all he could eat for supper.

"Bread and water?" Moiread asked quietly, herself spearing a chunk of fish on the end of her knife. "Are you feeling ill, devout, or mistrustful?"

"None of them, in truth. For what I do tonight, I must spend the day on the simplest fare." It was a pity, for the fish smelled most tempting, and their meal the previous night had not been either elaborate or ample. "Anything else can muddle the senses in this kind of work."

"Ah," she said. "There's a reason, then, to get that work done first. Other than a decent sense of what's important, that is," she added and grinned.

Riding in the spring sunlight had darkened her face, which had already been too swarthy for fashion. The contrast made her teeth very white when she smiled and her eyes a very bright blue: a shade that brought to Madoc's mind the way they'd glowed when she'd been poisoned, but which stirred no comparable fear in him. Sitting across from him that night, she was thoroughly in control of herself and all human.

Watching her, Madoc yearned to test that control—not to the point of transformation, nor as remotely close to it as she had been in Erskine, but to make that tall, strong body writhe and to hear the teasing in her voice change to the most pleasant sort of begging. He put a hand on hers briefly, as if he were making a point, and said, "In the larger way of things, you're right, but the rest of the evening feels very important to me."

There was not much room in their room, but it would suffice for both their purposes. Immediately, Moiread made more by shoving the nightstand against the window. The nightstand was barely tall enough to be an obstacle, but she doubted they'd get intruders climbing two stories. Similarly, when she barred the door and stood with her back against it, she did so more out of a sense of thoroughness. Outside did not hold the real danger tonight.

Madoc, barefoot and with sleeves rolled to his elbows, set small silver candlesticks on the floor, then placed a pure white candle within each. Between them, he spread a white cloth and a square of fine parchment on top of it. He set several vials of ink to his side and a raven quill on top of them.

"Are you ready?" he asked, looking up at Moiread. The shadows fell across his face, blurring his features.

"Aye," she said and loosened her sword in its sheath. Reprisal usually wasn't physical, but Moiread remembered her sister-in-law's tales of an angry wizard sending demons through thin air to strike at her. One never knew in these matters.

She watched Madoc light the candles and sniffed the sweet, light aroma of beeswax. Resin and cloves soon mingled with it as he un-stoppered the first vial of ink and, with quick, neat gestures, drew the first lines of a penta-gram on the parchment. He began to chant too. Moiread's magical knowledge left out many of the words he used. Some were Latin, but others were not, and she didn't think Cathal would recognize them either, familiar as he was with Arabic.

Blue ink came next, then silver. The scratching of the pen fell into rhythm with the chanting. Power tingled along Moiread's spine, and her hand tightened on her sword.

Madoc sat back finally and laid down his pen. Slowly, carefully, he took the most ornate of the amulets from the pouch at his belt, placed it squarely in the center of the parchment, and uttered one final long word.

With that, his eyes rolled back in his head, and he slumped to the ground.

Hanging in blackness, weightless and bodiless, he watched images form and dissolve in front of him. None were clear; dense fog seemed to surround everything, and the shapes were stretched and distorted, seen through the medium of Beings not used to fitting their sight to human limitations.

John, killer for pay, handed out the replicas to the men who were mostly dead now. They joked, slapped backs, and talked about what they'd buy with their payment. A few looked leery of the talismans, and the others mocked them for it.

A man passed the lot of cheaper amulets to John. The fog didn't let Madoc see his face clearly, but his tone and gesture both were impatient. "Hire whoever you need. This should be adequate," he added and set a pouch of money on the table between them.

In Erskine, John poured poison into two glasses, then

slipped out the kitchen door, shucked the robe, and bolted for the edge of town.

The world began to draw Madoc back to it, and he fought against the pull, holding on to the darkness with all his strength. There were more answers here, if he had the will to find them.

The patron held up the original amulet. Now Madoc glimpsed dark eyes and hair, as well as thin lips. "You'll need to follow them. Take this token... 'Twill make it a simpler task."

Then the patron stood at a workbench. Candles blazed in the pentagram surrounding him, and blood flowed into its lines. The headless black rooster lying outside the shape eased Madoc's momentary horrified suspicion. Still the man's face was blurry, but he wore a sleeveless white robe, such as rites often required, with a low neckline, baring a wide ring of scarred flesh that circled his throat. The outlines were unclear there too, but the scar itself was definite.

The man held up his work and smiled.

Perhaps there was more, but Madoc knew he couldn't see it. With the last of his energy, he spoke the words that dispersed the spell harmlessly, thanked and dismissed the forces aiding him, and they cast him back onto the inn floor.

The first things he saw were Moiread's eyes. She knelt next to him, but made no move to touch him at first. "Back?"

"So I believe," Madoc said, trying to stand and finding his body heavy as lead.

Moiread's arm was at his back then, and he was not too proud to lean on it. "You look wretched."

"And you've the sweetest tongue of any girl I've met," Madoc replied, laughing weakly. "In truth, I'd not tried that with stone before, nor with anything that was itself magic. It cost more than I had expected."

"Aye," said Moiread. "I'd like to think you'd have warned me if you'd *expected* this. Into bed with you now, before my arm gives out."

He was only too happy to comply and sank into the deep straw mattress with only one regret. "I'll not be any good to you tonight, I fear."

"Over my life," she said, "I like to think I've learned a wee bit of patience."

She stretched herself out next to him, and her presence was almost as welcome as the bed itself.

EIGHTEEN

"Smells like dye, even from this distance," Moiread whispered, her breath sliding over Madoc's ear like warm silk. A thrill went through him at the sensation, despite his persistent weariness and the deeply unromantic nature of their surroundings.

Those surroundings, alas, demanded attention. Madoc nodded and stepped away from the fence where Moiread leaned, back into the ring with the horse trader and the gelding he was showing. The horse was taller than Rhuddem had been, and a bit leaner than Madoc would have liked, but not obviously swaybacked or knock-kneed. Until a moment ago, he'd thought that the gelding's glossy black coat was a sign of decent health.

He ran a hand along the horse's neck. The gelding stood calmly for the touch. His temperament at least seemed reliable, a more important matter than usual when Madoc would be riding alongside Moiread. Under Madoc's fingers, though, the hair did feel a touch stiffer than he might have expected.

"You can pet him after you buy him," said the dealer, a lanky man with enormous eyebrows and almost no nose.

"Let me trot him around," said Madoc.

The dealer rolled his eyes, but put a battered saddle on the gelding's back and an equally worn bridle in his mouth. "Tack's extra," he added, to Madoc's complete lack of surprise.

Trotting wasn't bad. The gelding didn't have the most

comfortable gait Madoc had ever felt, but he didn't stumble, and his wind seemed sound enough. It helped that the ground in the pen was flat, but it was packed dirt, without the soft bark some men put down to disguise lameness. Perhaps the dealer hadn't heard of that trick; perhaps he didn't want to risk too much. Being the only horse trader in town would make a man conspicuous as well as give him advantages, and good citizens could be quite vengeful to a dishonest merchant.

Madoc dismounted, listened again to the horse's chest, and took a step back to eye his stance. The beast was doubtless older than the dyed coat would suggest and would win no races, but he would serve well enough. "Ten shillings," Madoc said.

"Where *you're* from, could be," the dealer replied with a snort. "Twenty-five."

"Twelve."

"Twenty-two."

"Thirteen," said Madoc, rapidly losing patience, "*including* the tack, and I'll not take soap and water to the poor painted beast until we've left."

The eyebrows drew down, as did the mouth. "That's a damned lie."

"And would the constables say as much?"

"They'd more likely want to know where *you* came by the money," said the other man, casting a scornful eye over Madoc. There was a fair amount to scorn. Madoc's clothing had once been good, but after two days of riding, a night sleeping rough, and a battle in the woods, it was more ragged than not. "I might take an interest myself, Taffy, if you don't take a better tone with me."

The slur almost put Madoc's temper over the edge, almost provoked him to test the truth of the dealer's statement; yet the man spoke with confidence, and he knew the town. Out of the corner of his eye, Madoc saw Moiread draw herself up, but she made no motion or sound as his eyes locked with the horse dealer's.

"Nineteen," the trader finally said. "With tack. And that's final."

Winning mattered less than being gone in that moment. Madoc dug his purse out of his belt pouch, counted out nineteen shillings, and dropped them into the trader's outstretched hand, trying to avoid touching the man any more than he could help. He took hold of the horse's reins and began to lead him toward the gate.

Falsely jocular, the dealer called from behind him: "Now remember, you *ride* that beast. You don't eat it or swive it!" He cackled at his own joke.

Moiread met Madoc at the gate. She didn't walk too closely, lest she frighten their new acquisition, but Madoc could hear her plainly when she spoke. "Aye, well, I'm sure he knows the latter from painful experience."

"You can keep your temper, then," Madoc teased as he and Moiread re-saddled the horses by the bridge leading out of town. "No buildings afire or noses broken. I call that a small miracle."

She laughed back at him, glad that he was in a jesting mood again, and comparatively soon. "I manage well enough when I have to, and it wasn't me he was insulting, was it?"

"You made no such distinction at Hallfield."

"Ah, but we were there for days. I couldn't have lifted my head among the other men if I'd not fought." Moiread swung up onto Shadow's back. She briefly felt odd, and cold, without Madoc pressed against her, but she knew that would pass. Certainly one rider apiece was easier on the horses. "And I wasn't likely to lose our only chance to buy a horse today thereby."

"Among other things," said Madoc. He caught Moiread's eye as he mounted, and she knew they both had the same thoughts—that the local lord could be as unsympathetic as his tenant, that they wanted to waste no time explaining themselves to even a fair-minded man, and that they *definitely* wished nobody to go through the saddlebags. "I confess I'd have been tempted to violence myself, had I been free to follow my own whims."

As they rode over the bridge, the horses' hooves ringing steadily on the stone, Moiread laughed again, but thoughtfully. "Save when I was at war, I nearly always have been," she said, omitting her childhood and a few of the tasks Artair had set her. "And then I led men, though under higher orders."

"Spoiled, some might say," Madoc said with the same joking lilt as before and the same gleam in his eye when he looked at her.

"Oh, aye. My nurses should have beaten me far more, and you'll not find any to say otherwise. If I'd not had Douglas and Agnes to squash me from time to time, I should have turned out far worse, I daresay."

"God forbid."

Moiread chuckled, but she wondered. She'd come to England as a soldier and a commander. In times of peace, she'd come as a lady, well-mounted and well-clothed, with her father's coin at her belt and the knowledge that mortal men, unprepared, could do little to her. At the worst, she could always play dead, or transform and fly away. It had never come to that.

Constraint, in most of its forms, was new to her. She thought briefly of what it might be like to spend every day bowing to it, to know she had as little or less recourse than they'd had with the horse dealer, and to deal with worse than slurs.

"Weighty matters?" Madoc asked.

"A bit. Endurance. Rebellion. They're both easy for me, in the end. Easier."

She wasn't really surprised when he nodded and filled in the rest. "Somewhat easier for you than for me, perhaps. Likely easier for both of us than for them." Madoc waved a hand toward the town behind them. "That may be one of the reasons for lordship. We've time and ability to see further, and decide with those on our side."

"That could be," she said, but she thought it was a question to which she'd return.

As if the horse trader had been a mortal and unpleasant version of the *visio dei*, Madoc began to notice other similar reactions. Not all the English they met were hostile, and none of those approached the dealer's crudity, but notes of suspicion and bitterness did crop up, and it was usually Moiread who bore the brunt of them.

When they met with other travelers, her voice would often draw surly looks from one of the party. At the inn where they spent the night, where little accommodation and many guests forced them to unwilling celibacy in the midst of the general crowd, one of the other patrons picked up his drink and moved across the room once she spoke.

On such occasions, Moiread's face was unreadable, and too many eyes on them kept Madoc from speaking a word of sympathy or offering what comfort she might find in his touch. She fell silent more and more in company, and he felt the guilt of it as he had when she'd drunk the poison—that he had taken her from her home and into lands of hostile strangers.

When they were alone the next day, he managed an awkward apology and was surprised when she smiled easily at him. It was a rueful smile, but one with no great pain in it, as far as he could tell. "I'm the foeman, aren't I? Kindness would be more of an insult, in its way. We fought well enough to be worth the hating."

"And it bothers you not to ride into enemy territory? Or what was, recently?"

She laughed, shaking her head so that her hair shone in the sun. "I've done the same many a time, and nobody's trying to kill me now. Or, not as an army. *And*, I think, the further we go into England, the further we'll get from the master of those assassins, if John hired them at Perth and his master gave him the means."

"From his voice, John wasn't Scottish," Madoc said. The man hadn't had any clear accent that Madoc could place. He wished he could have shared his vision, so that Moiread might have been able to weigh in.

"Not by birth or breeding, perhaps. But if the master got word of our survival after Erskine and then met John in Perth, he couldna' easily be quartered anywhere else. At least, I've heard of no magic that could let a man travel so fast."

"Nor have I," said Madoc. "But I don't know all the spells there are."

"They say, back home, that witches fly in sieves," Moiread said with a laughing sort of contemplation. "That sounds damned uncomfortable to me. But you make a good argument. Yet it seems more likely that I'm right and we've seen the last of these killers, or at least that you have."

"*Yet*," Madoc continued, quirking an eyebrow at her, "if you do have the right of it, that wizard I saw will still be lurking in Scotland. I doubt he'll have died or turned from his wicked ways while we're out of the country."

"As do I. And I'll say as much when I send messages home." Her smile turned to a wolf's bared teeth. "We'll need to clean our own house, and if my father or Agnes cannot do it with letters or meetings, then Douglas or I will manage it in other ways. We'll not let such things fester for long, have no fear. But you won't have to concern yourself. You'll have gone back home and likely further out of his reach."

"We can hope," said Madoc.

The prospect of being wrong, and of therefore still being in danger, worried him as it would have done any man in his senses. However, Madoc found he could think of that with more equanimity than he could that one sentence, so clearly meant to reassure: *You'll not have to concern yourself.*

He didn't like the idea of parting ways, of Moiread arriving home and going about her father's business while he took up his duties half of Britain away. That such a situation was the best he could hope for, the ideal result of his mission, did not make the idea sit any more comfortably.

Well, and you can meet every few years, he told himself. *Travel is far easier for her than most others, remember.*

Yet he would miss the freedom of the road and the straightforward mission before him, and he thought he would miss Moiread's company more than either.

NINETEEN

IN TIME, AFTER MADOC HAD PULLED OUT A WELL-FOLDED MAP and consulted it, they left the main road for another, and then that for a winding path into the hills. As the day was dying, they came to a small meadow with a mound rising in the middle of it, covered with pale new grass.

"Here?" Moiread asked, not entirely easily. Her father dealt with the true nonhumans, those whose blood bore no taint of mortality. He hadn't done so often, and those Moiread had met hadn't held high rank among their kind. She'd never entered their domain. To cover her nerves, she cleared her throat. "Should we tie the horses?"

"No, they'll pass through safely enough."

Indeed, viewed close at hand, the mound did reach a little above Madoc's head as he sat his horse, and it was more than wide enough to let both of them pass riding abreast. Still, Moiread's experience with horses and her own inhuman nature left her eyeing both their mounts with caution as she watched Madoc dismount.

If the nature of the place bothered the horses, they didn't show it. The new gelding—revealed by a rainstorm to be a singularly ugly yellow-brown color—put his head down and sniffed at the grass. A few feet away, Madoc approached the side of the mound, bowed, and then traced a pattern on the earthen side with his forefinger.

No gradual build-up of power followed. There was no real sense of magic at all, as Moiread was accustomed to sensing it. The wall of the mound glowed violet in the shape

Madoc had drawn—a star with many rays—then violet altogether, and then vanished. In its place, a wide metal bridge gleamed under strange light, leading off into a formless mist.

Moiread crossed herself before she thought about it.

Either Madoc saw the gesture or he noticed the tension in her face, for he laid a hand on her booted calf as he came back to the horses. "Have no fear," he said, and his voice made it clear that he thought no less of her for her uneasiness. "It's safer than many a bridge in our world, though I was more suspicious than you the first time I crossed it."

"Oh? You've been here before, have you?" She nudged Shadow forward as she spoke. Hesitation wouldn't help. Talking might distract her somewhat from the bridge, the mist, and the fact that they were entering not only another kingdom but another world, where she had neither allies nor an escape route.

"Fostered," he replied, "from ten to sixteen. And wintered here a few times after. The gate can open between Easter and Midsummer, and then between All Souls' Night and Epiphany, so…" He smiled. "It made a good place for a restless young man."

"I'd think," said Moiread.

They rode out onto the bridge. The ringing of hooves on metal was like church bells. Moiread glanced behind them and saw only mist: no trace of the mound, the meadow, or the real world. She shivered and turned her gaze forward.

Only mist lay around them for a while. Only mist lay below them as well, and that did nothing to make Moiread more comfortable. *She* might possibly be able to transform mid-fall and fly away, and a hard landing wasn't likely to kill her. Being able to transform, grab Madoc, and fly would be considerably harder. She told herself that a steel bridge was even less likely to fail than a stone one. She took heart in the good cheer she saw in Madoc's face, and even in the whistling that might have otherwise irked her while she was in such a tense mood.

Halfway across the bridge, Moiread began to see shapes on the other side. They grew clearer as she rode—not as normal fog would disperse to reveal what hid within it, but rather as if the fog itself sorted, solidified, and became earth and sky, trees and rocks.

None were familiar. A cloudless sky the soft violet of summer twilight stretched overhead, but it was full of far more stars than Moiread would ever have expected to see before full darkness. They were closer than normal stars and brighter, and they shone in many colors. She looked up at them and sought a familiar constellation, but found none. Not even the moon appeared.

A broad silver-white road wound its way between rows of orderly trees. The trunks of those trees were also pale and glimmered like pearl, and their leaves were shades of blue and violet, like the grass that grew beneath them. As Moiread passed under the first of the trees, a slim body unwound from one of the branches, and a long face peered out at her. Then the creature snapped open a pair of dragon-fly wings and fluttered off. She got only a passing glimpse of it: many-legged, with spotted fur.

"Carathin," said Madoc, awash with nostalgic amusement. "Harmless, but a bit of a nuisance, like when you're hunting. I tried to tame them a few times as a boy, but they never really took to it."

The image of young Madoc patiently offering food to one of the little beasts was almost engaging enough to distract Moiread from her surroundings for a moment, and she couldn't deny either its charm or theirs. "It's a fair evening," she said, and didn't have to force her smile.

"Fair, but not evening. There's no true day or night here. They don't sleep as we do." When Moiread didn't bother to hide her dismay, Madoc chuckled. "Worry not. They're generous to mortal needs."

"Do they mark time at all?"

"Of a sort." He gestured upward, to a cluster of three stars: one blue, two silver. "When that cluster moves all the way across the sky and back, it marks the end of one day and the beginning of the next. It was," he added, "not easy to accustom myself, by any means, and not easy to go back when I did return."

"Christ's blood, I'd think so," said Moiread, looking dizzily up at the sky again. "After six years of this?"

"Oh, I did visit my family once in a while. Nor do the people of this realm always stay here. There are rides, and hunts, and dances. Many of them are fond of our world and were willing to take a lad along if he proved himself quiet and useful."

That raised another question, one Moiread had been wondering about for a little while. "Who exactly are *they*?"

"Tylwyth Teg, my people would call them. Among themselves, the word is Caduirathi, which either means 'the people who craft' or 'the people who are formed.' I've never quite been able to determine which."

Around the next bend, a town came in view. It rose above the violet hilltops like the dawn sun, and Moiread fell silent in wonder when she saw it. The buildings were not many, nor were they large, but each was made of metal or colored glass, twisted into fluid spires and graceful domes. The largest, in the center, flashed blue and gold in the starlight, and softer lights shone back from what Moiread could only guess were its windows.

She could think of neither oath nor prayer to express

the beauty of the sight. A poet might have done it—a very good one.

"Lirened," said Madoc, sounding less surprised than she felt but almost as reverent. Then, more lightly, he added, "And our welcome. Fair wind to you, kinsmen, I hope."

He looked up as he spoke, and Moiread followed his gaze to see six figures coming toward them from out of the sky.

All six were tall and slender, armored in shining mail that they looked to wear as lightly as cloth and carrying spears and shields. Their skin gleamed golden or silver, but their eyes and their tightly braided hair were as varied as the stars or the buildings, and so were the vast feathery wings that stretched out from each of their backs.

He saw Moiread's eyes widen and knew something of what she must be feeling. Even with what Madoc had told her, even with her own experience to inform her, it was hard to look at the Caduirathi, especially the feathered ones, and not think *angels*. For Moiread to simply stand quiet and amazed spoke of both her self-control and her experience. On Madoc's first meeting with them, with far more preparation, he'd sunk to one knee and prayed.

Thirty-odd years later, he saw several familiar faces in the troop and raised a hand in greeting, just as the leader, a warrior with sky-blue hair and eyes, smiled broadly. "Madoc? You come in company, brother. And you look as though the road has been a hard one indeed," he added, eyeing Madoc's clothes and horse both with friendly disdain.

"No, in truth it was easy. Only a few people sought my life. Haryin, this is Michael, my squire. Michael, this is Haryin, Captain of the Queen's Borders."

Moiread bowed as well as one could from horseback, and yet Madoc caught an uneasy expression crossing Haryin's face. Even so, the Caduirathi smiled and bowed in return. "A guest of Madoc's will always be welcome within our lands. We must remain on the borders for this next cycle, but pray ride on and find hospitality. You will still know the way," he said to Madoc.

"Of course," Madoc said, seeing the silent request. "But I would speak with you first, to make certain nothing's changed. Rest here," he added to Moiread, "while I take counsel."

He could read her face clearly too. Dubious about the wisdom of his plan and ill at ease in this strange place, she nonetheless nodded and sat quietly as Haryin flew a short distance off and Madoc rode along.

Just out of earshot, Madoc asked, "What troubles you? I'd not bring distress to your land, yet I believed I was expected, and others have brought companions."

"Oh yes," said Haryin, and waved both of those objections aside with a slender hand. "I only find myself unsure what you know of your...*squire*, is it? For while her womanhood is no great matter, her other form—"

"Is a dragon," said Madoc, laughing in relief. "No, it's kind of you to worry, Haryin, but I knew before we ever ventured forth together. The illusion is for mortal men, though I'd no idea you'd see so clearly."

"There are few things that can block our true sight here," Haryin replied, and the invisible weight came off his shoulders. He flipped his wings, a sign of amusement. "I'll tell Her Majesty of these matters, that she may not be as alarmed as I almost was...and that your friend may not suffer as a result."

"My thanks," said Madoc.

They rejoined the patrol, whose members were making slightly awkward, wary conversation with Moiread. At Haryin's nod, they at least lost the wariness, and Moiread sent Madoc a questioning glance.

"There'll be no hiding here," he said. "I should have thought to tell you sooner, but I'd never seen illusion tried in this world. Forgive me," he said, and then addressed the rest of the patrol. "My companion is Moiread MacAlasdair, and no squire."

"Ah," said Moiread, reaching for the pendant and twisting it so that the illusion fell away. "Well, I hope this revelation causes no trouble."

"Curiosity, I should think," said Haryin, "especially at court. Your lineage is not unknown to us, but it has been many long years since we met one of your blood. Long years for us, and that is long indeed!"

TWENTY

THEY LEFT THE PATROL BEHIND THEM AND FOLLOWED THE ROAD toward the queen's city. While Moiread tried to maintain a bodyguard's calm alertness, she visibly stared to either side as they continued. Madoc watched her from time to time, seeing the land anew through her eyes and glad that he could show it to her.

For him, it was close to homecoming. He'd ridden out along this road many a time, and hunted through the forest as well. He recalled narrow paths leading to hidden lakes, broad meadows on distant hills, and long stretches of talking or singing or simply lying in the grass and watching the stars, for the queen had been an easy mistress in her way, and the land was gentle.

"No farms?" Moiread asked as they drew near to the city walls and passed nothing but more rows of trees.

"No, they grow no food that way. There are orchards in the city, and wild fruit or nuts in the forest. They get all their meat by hunting."

"Must be great beasts about, or few of the...ah..."

"Caduirathi. And both are true. There are creatures in the deep forest bigger than any in our world, and the people are not many and rarely bear children." He smiled in memory. "I think that, as much as any ties and politics, was why they welcomed their arrangement with my family."

"Did you?" Moiread asked. "Ten's not too young for a page, but there's quite a step between your neighbor's household and another world, is there no'?"

"I'd no objection when I was told. It all sounded like a great adventure, and so it was when I went away. The thought got me through more than one night that could have been bad otherwise," he said, casting his memory far back. "But then, I might have been more homesick without the novelty of it to distract me. Very little here reminded me of what I'd left, and I can imagine that as much a blessing as otherwise. Were you sent away as a girl?"

"No. We don't leave Loch Arach until we've mastered the shifting of form, not to mention our tempers...enough not to change when vexed," Moiread added, rolling her eyes cheerfully at Madoc's teasing glance. "And the first change usually comes about thirteen or fourteen. So my father and our men-at-arms trained us themselves. It's an odd custom, but it's well known that we're an odd people."

"Oh, and the world is full of such. Worlds, perhaps." Madoc gestured to the landscape around them, violet and white, with the city's golden gates drawing nearer. "The better for it, I'd say, and very dull else."

Two more of the Caduirathi stood at the gates, these of the same feather-winged sort as Haryin and his patrol but in elaborate blue-and-gold lacquered armor and carrying slim golden swords. Both were more ornamental than the patrol's equipment, but neither were entirely so. As with all their people, the gate guards looked slightly familiar to Madoc, but he couldn't place them, nor they him. They stopped him and Moiread with upraised hands and tilted heads.

"Madoc Firanon," he said, making his bow, "and companion. I'm expected."

The pair nodded silently and moved aside, letting the gates swing smoothly open.

When they'd passed out of the guards' earshot, Moiread

asked, "What good are gates when everyone flies? Pretty things, I'll grant you."

"Not much in themselves. They're only the visible part of the city's defenses, and the key to the others. Any who attempted to fly over without leave would be badly surprised." Madoc remembered the time when a sakhan had gotten too close, and the burns along its vast catlike body when he and Haryin and the others had gone to end its misery. "Yet it's true that they're less cautious here."

"No war?"

"Nothing significant. Though I saw little of them, there are other places and other peoples, but all far from each other. It would take a grave insult or a dire threat to make the journey worth the fighting."

She chuckled. "Were men to think that way, my brother Cathal would have had to stay home a century longer than he did, or at least to pick a foe closer than Jerusalem. I'm not sure how either of us would have liked that."

"Ah, well," Madoc said, "for those who need to depart for a time, there *is* travel. And there is always your world."

"Aye, there's that," Moiread said and then fell silent, watching in wonder as they made their way down the city's central street.

Madoc stayed quiet too, content to watch her and the city alike, to take joy both in the familiarity of homecoming and in the novelty of her presence. The two went together surprisingly well, he was finding.

The city was a wheel of color and light. Shining multicolored buildings rose graceful to either side, as bright and fascinating as they'd been from a distance. Up close, they showed polished doors of white wood, carved with flowers and beasts, and crescent-shaped windows without shutters. In between, the street was smooth indigo stone, wide and even and surprisingly clean. Shadow and the new gelding weren't the only horses, but there weren't many.

There weren't many people, for that matter. Moiread saw Caduirathi on the streets as she rode, and going into or coming out of buildings, but there were perhaps five or ten for each block, far fewer than what she would have expected in a town of such a size. Indeed, there was more space between even the smallest buildings than would have been common elsewhere. Miniature forests often filled those gaps. Moiread also noticed hedged-in gardens and, once, a fountain of fire. The buildings rose upward rather than spreading out, but even so, most of their inhabitants stayed within, or each of them had a good deal of room.

Those who were on the street largely shared the metallic skin and bright hair of the patrollers, but the wings varied. Some were as leathery as Moiread's own when she transformed, in colors that matched the person's hair. Some were insect-like and shimmering, while others were almost mist-like, and she couldn't see how they supported the full weight of even those as slim as the Caduirathi.

Men and women both wore loose-wrapped garments, like togas, woven carefully around their wings, and many wore open sandals. Most carried no weapons, though guards like those at the gate did pass through the streets, watching everyone around them carefully.

The blue-and-gold building was in the center of the circle. As Moiread and Madoc neared it, the other structures also got larger and more ornate, and the number of guards increased, until they came to another smaller pair of golden gates and a half-dozen Caduirathi met them.

"Her Majesty waits for you," said the leader, once Madoc had given his name. "We shall care for your mounts."

"I thank you," said Madoc. He didn't look entirely easy as one of the guards led away their horses with their saddlebags, and Moiread wasn't overjoyed about it either. Still, when royalty summoned, there was no delaying.

Side by side, they followed their escorts through a lush garden, up a set of golden stairs and through sapphire doors, and then through many gold-and-white stone halls and up winding staircases until they came to the throne room.

That room was a long oval, the walls unornamented save for wide curving windows. A circle of glowing wisps on the ceiling lit it without torches or candles. A small crowd of Caduirathi within looked Madoc and Moiread over curiously, then parted and let them proceed toward the front of the room. There, a deep-violet carpet covered a short set of stairs, and a lovely woman sat on a delicate golden throne.

Moiread needed no prompting from Madoc. She went to one knee and bent her head, waiting for the queen to speak.

"Do rise," she said, her voice sweet but metallic, like the strings of a gittern. "Son of our hall, we rejoice at your return."

"My lady Gilrion," Madoc said in a courtier's voice that glided like warm silk. "It soothes my heart to be here once again. As my kind counts such things, it's been too long since my last visit to your lands, and I have sore missed them, and you. I beg that you allow me to present my most noble and skilled friend, Lady Moiread MacAlasdair."

Moiread rose and curtsied, awkward as that was in male attire. "Your Majesty," she said, knowing that her skills in this area would be a poor shadow of Madoc's and so not trying to compete. "Your hospitality is a great honor, and your kingdom amazes me."

Queen Gilrion herself would have been amazement enough. Ridged golden wings fanned out behind her, matching the pure gold of her eyes and hair, while her skin shimmered silver. If the white gown she wore was the silk it appeared, then the fabric alone could have bought a small kingdom, though there was far less of it than in most gowns Moiread had seen. The price of the golden circlet on her head, studded with square purple gems the size of Moiread's thumbnail, could have probably purchased *England*.

The queen surveyed Moiread calmly, smiled with full, pale lips, and said, "We have no doubt of your ability, lady of the MacAlasdairs. Madoc is a man of excellent judgment. He has our regard and our loyalty both, as few merit and fewer among mortals."

Ah. Although not Artair or Douglas's equal in intrigue, Moiread nonetheless had trained with them, and she was a woman of the world. Gilrion wasn't doing anything so vulgar as making a threat, even a veiled one. She was only letting Moiread know how matters stood, should Madoc's description of her turn out to be less than accurate.

"Our acquaintance has been brief, Your Majesty," Moiread said, weighing her words carefully. "But from it, I would say that he deserves the regard and loyalty of any who know him. I'm not surprised that a woman of your wisdom sees so clearly."

She didn't look at Madoc to see how she was doing, no matter how much she wanted to. Moiread kept her eyes on Gilrion's face, waited, and saw the queen's smile widen fractionally. She felt that she had passed one test, though there were likely more ahead.

"Tomorrow we will feast and make merry in your honor," said Gilrion, "and discuss all that is needful. But it is a long way to the world of man, and I think you have both come a long way in it." She clapped her hands, and two of the courtiers detached themselves to come forward. "See to our guests' comfort."

Both of the courtiers who took them up the stairs had known Madoc in his boyhood: Erulhieth, who'd been full-grown then and, like the queen and the rest of her subjects, looked no older now, and Celened, who had been a child himself and thus one of Madoc's partners in mischief and idleness when they could manage it. Quick of speech and laughter, Celened lost no time in recounting old stories as the four of them made their way to the living quarters, nor in asking questions.

"And what have you done, roof brother, that so many unpleasant men should seek you with so many instruments of death? Stolen the jewels from a crown, or the wife from a prince?"

"You esteem me too highly." Madoc laughed.

"Then could it be what you know? Celened's red-orange eyes danced like flames in a hearth. "Did you over-hear dire secrets? See rites of a mystic and fell cult?"

"Insulted the ale in the wrong tavern," Moiread suggested with an amused twitch of her lips.

Erulhieth witnessed it all in calm silence, as she had done as long as Madoc had known her. She had never been a woman of many words, nor had her moods ever been public. Once at Moiread's room, she gave Madoc their version of a bow between equals, a brief lowering of the head with her hands flat at her sides. "I rejoice to see you well, Madoc Firanon, and I wish you a pleasant evening."

"And I you," he said. "Both of you."

In company, he couldn't let himself linger and watch

Moiread depart. Instead, he had to follow Celened up
another flight of stairs and through a short hall. His old
friend fell oddly silent in the process, and Madoc was wondering how to inquire what was amiss when they came to
a door.

"Your quarters," said Celened. "But stay a moment and
tell me true: is the dragon woman with you by your own
wish? If you were silent earlier out of threat to yourself,
or because you would not endanger Haryin and his troops
in battle, then be assured that Her Majesty has more than
enough strength here to address any such danger."

"Did she tell you to ask me that?"

"She did give such an order, but I ask also as your
friend, and for myself. The lady seems amiable, but so do
many hazards."

"It is true," said Madoc, and he couldn't be angry. In
Gilrion's place, he might well have done the same. "And
I thank you for your concern, but need it not. Moiread has
proven her loyalty, and her friendship, more than once, and
she has never threatened me or mine."

"As much as one could wish," said Celened, his usual
smile reappearing, "particularly in one so comely. To bed,
then, and rest. I warn you, you'll need it tomorrow!"

He departed, and Madoc slipped into a low-ceilinged
square chamber whose walls were pale gold, where thick
rugs covered the floor and a wide bed hung with dark-
green canopies filled nearly the length of one wall. A vast,
white marble tub sat in front of it, with pine-scented steam
rising from the water. A small table nearby held bread,
fruit, and wine.

The magic-borne luxury of Gilrion's realm had always
been a wonderful change. After weeks of riding and sleeping in dubious inns, not to mention the pitched battles,

it was close to heaven itself. Madoc ate his fill, quickly undressed, and slid into the hot water, letting it cover him to his neck.

He didn't turn at the knock on the door, but called, "Come in." Even in the mortal world, a man expected to have the occasional conversation in the bath, and the Caduirathi had no squeamishness about such things.

The voice he heard, when the door had closed behind his guest, had no squeamishness in it either—only low, rich appreciation. "That's quite the view," said Moiread.

TWENTY-ONE

As Moiread's escort had told her they would, the walls had lit up when she spoke a name, showing her the path to take. Still, she stood for a tense heartbeat before she knocked, and knew vast relief when she heard Madoc's voice and knew she hadn't wandered into some stranger's quarters.

She was more nervous, truth be told, than she'd been with any of her previous lovers. Most of those had been spur-of-the-moment affairs, hasty fumblings in the heated aftermath of battle or the tipsy conviviality of celebrations. It had been a long time since she'd planned a tryst, and she'd never journeyed there through such unfamiliar surroundings as she had that night.

Moving forward was the best cure for nerves. She stepped further inside and closed the door behind her. Water splashed as Madoc turned to face her. Wet and taut with muscle, his arms and chest gleamed pale in the light, and water matted the thick, dark hair on his chest.

"No," she said, raising a hand before he could leave the tub. "I wouldn't dream of cutting your bath short."

She'd had one herself, and her hair now fell damply against the collar of her short white tunic. The palace was warm enough that she needed no more, and the closer she came to Madoc, the more she knew that warmth was unlikely to be a problem any time in the near future.

"No?" he asked, recovering enough to tease her with a knowing smile. "I should indeed think you'd know I need one, but what then do you come to do?"

Moiread trailed her fingers from his elbow to his shoulder, relishing the way his arm tensed beneath her touch, then plucked a soft cloth from a nearby stand. "I'd a number of ideas on the way here. Finding you as I do, I'm now thinking you might wish an attendant, aye?"

"Oh, aye," he said. His voice was still teasing, but lower and huskier, and Moiread saw his eyes darken. "That's most generous of you."

"I take my duties very seriously," she replied. Dipping the cloth into the hot bathwater, she slowly set to work.

Up his lean, corded arms she went again, from fingers to shoulders, then down the length of his spine as far as she could reach and up again to the back of his neck, rubbing not with her full strength but firmly enough that Madoc groaned in satisfaction and leaned back into her hands. Knotted muscles from long days on the road eased under her touch, and when she reached the top of his head, he was practically purring, his eyes closed.

"If you fall asleep now," she said, soaping his hair, "I may stab you."

"I'd not be so ungentle, I promise. Even if I didn't fear your threats."

"The which you do." His hair was thick and silky between her fingers.

"I like to think I have that much wisdom," he said. Before she could reach for the pitcher, he caught her wrist, turned it over, and brushed his lips across the vein just below her hand. "Among other attributes."

After Moiread rinsed out Madoc's hair, she leaned forward, the angle now pressing her breasts against his wet back. The thin fabric of her tunic quickly grew damp, and the friction quickened her breath and made her bite her lip to keep her concentration on the task at hand. Slowly she circled the cloth down Madoc's neck and over the hard planes of his chest, washing his sides and trailing down toward his flat stomach, until a new and far more pleasant tension entered his body and the sounds he made spoke more of urgency than relaxation.

By the time she'd reached the limit of her arms' length, Moiread could see the tip of Madoc's erection sticking up through the water, flushed red and rising tight against his stomach. The sight drew a quiet hum of arousal from her throat and sent a pulse of longing through her sex, already damper than the tunic she wore. Still she made no move toward Madoc's groin, but drew her hands back up to his shoulders, stepped back, and made her way to the other end of the tub, making sure Madoc had a clear view of her breasts in their almost-transparent covering as she walked.

"My lady MacAlasdair," he said huskily, "you're the most dreadful tease."

"Aye?" She started to wash his legs, trailing lightly up over shin and calf. "I'd say I'm a very good one."

Yet she moved a touch more quickly up one muscular thigh and then the other, her will to torment and prolong not as powerful as the growing need in her body. Each gasp she heard from Madoc, each low moan, fired her blood more, and when she finally closed her hand loosely around his cock and he thrust up into her touch, she mingled her groan with his. He was both long and thick in her grasp, and felt as hard as the marble of the tub and almost as hot as the water.

After a few lingering strokes with the cloth, each a little firmer than the last, Moiread cast it aside and took him into her bare hand, fingers playing over the length of his shaft. The tip was wet with more than water then, and Madoc had once more thrown his head back against the rim of the tub. His hands clenched on the sides, knuckles white.

Deceived by his posture, Moiread blinked in surprise when he suddenly closed a hand around her wrist—and then actually yelped as he sat up swiftly and, with his other arm, pulled her into the tub on top of him.

There was a moment of laughing confusion while they sorted out limbs and angles. Considerable water splashed onto the floor, but it was mostly pleasant, though Moiread grazed her elbow against the tub and swore. "I don't think this is built for two people," she said, raising her lips from Madoc's shoulder, "or not two of our size."

"Likely not," he said against her neck, hands tracing heated patterns along her spine, "but we're surely used to thinking on our feet, no?"

"We're neither of us on our feet."

"Ah, if you start bringing logic into this, you'll spoil everything. Besides, I'd never resist you for long like this." He shifted them, with more sloshing of water, so that she straddled his lap and he could cup her breasts through the wet cloth. "No man could, no matter the space at hand, not with such a clear view of these so lovely and stiff." He took one of Moiread's nipples in his mouth through the thin, wet silk of her tunic, and she cried out, rubbing her sex against his cock where it throbbed between her thighs.

Her tunic was in the way of a full joining, and the angle wasn't quite right, but when Moiread moved to rectify that, she found Madoc's hands on her thighs, holding her firmly in place while the pressure of his fingers stoked her desire further. Still kissing her breasts, he chuckled at her sound of frustration and swept his hand under the hem of her tunic.

"Oh," she said, breathing the word out, and could

manage nothing more coherent. The water lapped around them, caressing Moiread's skin in a gentle counterpoint to the more insistent pressure of Madoc's body. It paradoxically stripped some of the slickness from her, but the slow intrusion of one finger and then a second quickly remedied that, and when Madoc began to rub the outside of her sex as well, she was reduced to desperate whimpering.

Only then did he change their positions once more, guiding the head of his erection to the cleft between her legs and letting her sink onto him. The tub made her move slowly, despite her eagerness, and keep briefly very still when he was all the way inside her, both caught in the moment of pleasure and working out how best to proceed. Madoc, perhaps in the same state of mind, was patient, but she felt small pulses and jerks that said he wouldn't be for long, and those movements wore away at her own endurance.

Experimenting, Moiread gradually settled on a slow, subtle rocking that kept their bodies close together, brushing against each other with every slight rise and fall of her hips. She was already breathing fast, already closer than she'd been much further into matters with other lovers. Slow and subtle sped up as she found balance and rhythm, as Madoc's hips arched below her and his hands roamed feverishly over her breasts, as his ragged moans echoed in her ears. Back arching, thighs clenching around Madoc's hips, she built quickly and inevitably toward a climax that drew a scream from her throat and sent colors exploding behind her closed eyes.

Madoc wasn't far behind. A deep thrust upward sent half the water out of the tub—his hands digging hard into her thighs as he muttered an awed oath in Welsh—and a rush of warmth within to match the heat without. Then he collapsed, a stringless puppet, and Moiread let herself fall against his chest.

"Stay." It was the first thing he said.

"Hmm?"

"Stay. If you want…like. They'll think nothing less of us here."

His shoulder fit her head nicely. "Good," she said, not disposed to argue. "That just leaves the one problem then, aye?"

"Oh?" He brushed wet hair away from her neck with one hand. "Problem?"

"Getting to the bed before my legs give out."

TWENTY-TWO

THE CADUIRATHI HAD BELLS AND HOURGLASSES TO MARK TIME, but in the dark silence of his room, Madoc had no way of knowing how long he'd slept. He knew that his weariness from the journey was gone, though it would take a few days of rest to truly build up his reserves again. For the moment, it was enough to open his eyes easily and take in the beautiful woman dozing at his side.

Moiread slept on her back, one arm thrown across her chest as if even in sleep she guarded her neck. She'd managed to strip her wet tunic off before tumbling into bed, and her naked skin glowed in the dim light. A faint scar ran down the outside of that arm: an uneven line, probably from a blade. The arm was muscular, the hand long-fingered and callused from blade and rein. As Madoc watched her, she glanced up at him through her dark lashes and turned so that she could run a finger down his bicep.

"I didn't want to wake you," he said, though he was turning to her as he spoke, sliding his arm around her waist and pulling her toward him.

She shook her head, her hair brushing lightly against his bare shoulders. "Didna' do any such thing," she said, her voice low and slurred with drowsy contentment. "Can only sleep so long."

Madoc made a wordless sound of agreement, running a hand down the smooth tightness of her side. There was another scar there, faintly raised to his fingers, this one a rough semicircle: a spear point, mayhap. He passed it, making her shiver, and went onward to the rise of her hip.

"Ah," she said and nibbled on his neck, at the same time throwing a leg across his hips and wriggling against his already-hard cock. "I could fancy this way of waking." She flicked her tongue across his earlobe and added, pretending apology, "But I'd not wish to keep you, if you're wanting to be out of bed."

"No." He cupped her arse, stroking and squeezing. "Not at all."

"Not…" Her breath caught. "Restless, then, or hungry?"

"Both, in a way," Madoc said and threw back the covers.

The Caduirathi kept their dwellings warm. He'd often appreciated it, but never so greatly as when he and Moiread both lay bare to the world, when he could spread her thighs with his hands and leisurely bring his mouth to the cleft between them, until she swore and begged and tugged at his hair and finally peaked with a long, rapturous sigh.

Only then did Madoc slide up and enter her, savoring the ongoing tremors around his member as long as he could before he had to give way to the strongest of impulses, burying himself in Moiread again and again until his moment of crisis came. She was as eager for it as him, wrapping her legs around him, urging him on with voice and body alike, and finally holding him tightly through the final throes.

It was the best morning he'd had in a good while.

Afterward, Moiread put on her now-dry tunic and went back down the hall and up the stairs to her room, sneaking at first and then moving with more confidence when she saw nobody. Gilrion's people seemed to get by without

servants even more than the MacAlasdairs did at Loch
Arach, and Moiread wouldn't have begun to know where
the courtiers were, especially as she'd no idea what time
of day it was.

Satisfied as she was with the morning and the previous
night, and much as she liked the luxury and security, the
palace was damned disorienting. Moiread felt no connection to anything real. The world beyond the hall might have
been the same formless mists they'd come through, and the
world beyond that only a dream. Cathal had spoken of sailing in similar terms, but there he'd had the sun and moon,
light and dark to go by. She put out a hand and touched the
marble wall to feel its solidity, and then grimaced at her
own thoughts.

Food would help.

Despite her hunger, she bathed again when she got back
to her room, as much for the indulgence of it as to get clean.
Soft towels sat by the tub, fresh and dry after the night
before. When she went back to the wardrobe afterward, she
found a small array of robes such as the Caduirathi wore,
all brightly colored, and a pair of Roman-style sandals. She
chose a deep-rose-colored robe and found that it and the
sandals both fit her perfectly.

Well, magic.

Like the others she'd seen, Moiread's robe came down
to her knees and pinned behind her neck as the tunic had
the night before, leaving her back and shoulders bare, her
breasts and thighs covered only by a thin layer of silk. She'd
never fussed over modesty, but she thought of going into
the hall so attired and cringed. It'd be akin to those dreams
where she stood naked at mass, with everyone watching her.

But they won't be, she told herself, *or not for your
clothes. Everyone wears such things here.*

Nobody except the guards had worn weapons in the hall, so she left her sword and its belt behind. *That* wouldn't save anyone from an attack here. It was by no means worth angering the queen. The belt of fine gold mesh for her eating knife did little to salve Moiread's feeling of exposure, but nobody—as her mother had often said about other matters—had promised her life would be a walk in a garden.

She did the best she could with her hair, finding neither wimple nor cords for plaiting it but only a wide gold fillet, which she tied around her head. If her hair had been longer, Moiread reflected, she'd have looked about twelve.

Then, dressed as best she could manage, she headed out into the hallway and said, "The great hall, please."

On the wall, a strand of pale-blue light appeared, stretching out along the course she was to take.

Moiread followed, down stairs and through hallways, past large doors that led off to unknown parts of the palace and wide crescent windows that looked out over the city, and finally into the queen's hall.

She smelled food as she drew nearer, and entering indeed showed her that many of the Caduirathi sat at long oval tables full of dishes, which Moiread hadn't seen the night before and which looked far too large and solid for anyone to have carried into the room. Now that she wasn't so tired, she also noticed that the floor was clean and polished, without any rushes to be found.

Magic was a wonderful thing.

Most of those assembled didn't bother looking at her, and of those who did, most noted her with brief curiosity. A few glanced toward the dais and the small table there—where Queen Gilrion sat with a few of her people and Madoc—then, reassured by their queen's calm, turned back to their meal or their conversation.

As Moiread hesitated, Gilrion's eyes lit on her, and the queen smiled with far more warmth than she had the night before. "Lady MacAlasdair," she said, and stretched out a slim, glittering hand. "Come and eat with us."

Bowing, Moiread ascended the stairs to the dais, relieved at the invitation. For one, though she'd never minded taking her meals with the men-at-arms, she'd no idea who those *were* in this hall, nor where to find them, nor how to speak to them. For another, it was always better to have royalty friendly than not, particularly when the royalty in question ruled a magical realm and she had no easy means to escape it.

She was careful about her curtsy and her smile, and thanked Gilrion again for her hospitality before she sat. She neither looked too long at Madoc, who sat on the queen's right hand, flanked by one of her men, nor avoided doing so. She gave him the same smiling nod she would have had they passed the previous night in separate beds. Even she had learned discretion over a few centuries, and this was not the first time she'd used it, though she wished she could have spoken a few words to Madoc. Familiar company would have been good, and the dark-green robe he wore suited him well.

"I'm pleased that I could provide comfort," said the queen. She'd changed her gown for one of pale blue that shone less, and she wore a thin gold circlet in her hair rather than her crown. Moiread guessed daytime, or whatever this was, was informal. "I hope you found it to your liking."

"Very much," Moiread said, and laughed quietly. "You may be fortunate in having gotten me, Your Majesty. A few of my family would have driven themselves mad by now, trying to discern how all is done here, and quite probably would have pestered your people to madness as well."

"Oh?" Gilrion asked, surprised but, praise God, amused with it. "Craftsmen, are they?"

"Scholars, more like. My sister in particular."

"Is she the one who fashioned the illusion necklace?" Gilrion glanced to Moiread's neck, which was now bare. "My border captain told me of it, and it sounds like a work cleverly done."

Being a queen, and good at such things, she had no trace in her voice of either *for a mortal* or *but of course it didn't fool us for a moment*. She might not have thought it. Moiread would have, in her place, but she knew herself to be a nasty superior sort from time to time.

"That one was my brother's work," she said, "but it was Agnes who discovered the way of it."

A sound of trumpets from outside cut off Gilrion's reply and sent her mind to other matters: namely, to the maiden who floated into the hall, almost a copy of the queen save that her eyes and hair were deep violet. She wore no circlet, but small white stones glinted in her braids, and her robe was long and deep blue. A dark-haired man walked at her side and barely took his eyes off her to see the court, while at one of the higher tables, a richly dressed silver-haired man rose as soon as the maiden entered the room.

Two other women followed her, but although Moiread hadn't seen any of their people looking less than breathtaking, the violet-haired lady's presence made them seem dimmer, and the intensity with which she and the two men regarded one another made it clear that they were the primary players in whatever scene would next take the stage.

Madoc smiled with both recognition and pleasure, and Gilrion positively beamed.

"Namwynne," she said, "my youngest daughter. She's been briefly abroad, to meet and bring back the son of my old friend and ally, the Sea King. It is fortunate indeed that you've arrived. Now she'll truly have her choice."

"Her choice, Your Majesty?" Madoc asked.

"Why, yes," Gilrion said with an affectionate look at her daughter as she came toward them. "We have no pressing need of alliance now. She is of age and inclination, and I will be indulgent, as I can. She may choose a husband as she pleases, for I have faith in her judgment—within reason, of course."

"Of course," said Madoc. He didn't sound nearly as poleaxed as Moiread would have under such circumstances.

Then again, he knew more of this place and its royalty than Moiread did. Perhaps he'd expected some such announcement. Perhaps he'd even been looking forward to it.

TWENTY-THREE

IN RETROSPECT, MADOC COULDN'T BE ENTIRELY SURPRISED. HE was a fairly young man, and an eligible one as his father's heir, even if Rhys had been shy about arranging matches in the last few years. Now that Madoc came to think about it, his father might well have broken his reticence and sent a few messages when he'd heard of the journey—though his mother was the most likely coconspirator with Gilrion, if such existed.

Yet he hadn't thought of the matter, particularly not in Gilrion's realm, and he was conscious of Moiread's presence as he rose to greet Namwynne.

"You've aged, hall brother," she said cheerfully as he rose from bending over her hand. "It suits you well."

"You've not, and it suits you better," Madoc replied, only half forcing his courtly good humor. He'd always liked Namwynne. Under normal circumstances, this would be a joyous meeting indeed. "It's been too long since we've met. I bless the luck that sent me here so close to your arrival. May I present Lady Moiread MacAlasdair, who has kindly accompanied me and saved my life several times by so doing."

"The lady of the dragon-folk?" Namwynne turned to Moiread with an eager smile and a graceful curtsy, her silver wings fluttering as she rose. "You are most deeply welcome here, and I am so glad to meet you. I've heard tales of your kind, but never thought to meet one."

"Daughter," said Gilrion, lifting a jeweled hand and a golden brow at once.

"Oh, forgive me. My tongue often runs away."

"Not at all," said Moiread. She smiled, and it looked as though she meant it. "I could say the same thing, but I think my stories are probably a wee bit less accurate than yours. We should trade a few, perhaps, and see if we can't get at the truth of things."

"I'd like that very much," said Namwynne. "And this is Lord Arbelath"—she gestured to the dark-haired man—"another guest, for it seems my mother is set on welcoming many visitors indeed."

"Say rather that it seems the time for such," said Gilrion, "and I am not one to stand in the path of what wants to be."

The new arrivals sat, and the meal went on. There was roast boar and sliced fruit, nuts and the strangely flavored bread made from them, good mead and sharp cheese. As Madoc watched, Moiread ate well, joined easily in the conversations or listened with interest, and looked neither sad nor angry, neither awkward nor reproachful.

He hoped she was sincere in that. It was a pleasure and a relief, though not a surprise, to find that she wouldn't make a scene. Yet she was her father's daughter and had centuries of practice in keeping her countenance, and he would be riding on with her after a few days. He watched carefully, therefore, and not without worry.

Later, as the court danced to welcome its youngest princess home, Madoc finally had the chance to speak with Moiread.

The Caduirathi's dancing usually happened on the wing. In the palace, such festivities took place in a large square surrounded by slender trees and artfully crafted crystal spires. The patterns of the dances held layers on layers, with partners trading above and below as well as down lines or across circles as humans did. In some, one partner would trail ribbons for the other to catch, or drop flowers onto the ranks below.

In kindness to their guests, they'd included a few sets where one could remain on the ground. Madoc knew what was expected and partnered with Namwynne for the first of those, while Moiread danced with Sir Cauldir, the silver-haired Caduirathi who'd been *very* attentive to the princess's entrance. During the second, Moiread and Madoc found each other.

The court's wardrobe masters had dressed Moiread in a soft velvet gown the color of amber, pinned at one shoulder, and had fastened her short hair up with small star-shaped blue stones. She resembled a statue of some ancient goddess, with all the color and vitality of a living woman. A man could have taken the sight of her to his grave and been content, Madoc thought, but he could have wished she'd been less lovely at that moment. Words stuck in his throat at first.

"Congratulations?" she asked, as they touched hands and stepped together. "Or good hunting, is it?"

He should have expected no less, not from her. There was no trace of anger about her, nor any wish to see him uncomfortable, but she wasn't a woman to shrink from matters at hand. "Neither, had I my own will in matters," Madoc said honestly.

"Oh, come now. *I'd* be happy enough for such a match, in your shoes."

The figures of the dance spun them away from each other and sent them processing with other partners through a curtain of multicolored ribbons from above. Moiread danced as she fought, with less elegance than precision, but she kept up well and followed the beat of the woodwinds and harps well enough.

When they took hands again, Madoc continued. "I'll not say it's any hardship. If I could insult Her Majesty by refusing, I'd be unwise to do so. The alliance would be a fair one, and the two of us are friends from my childhood. But it's nothing I came seeking, or knew of until the moment the queen said it. I vow I'd have told you otherwise, before—"

Moiread chuckled and squeezed his hand. "Chivalry becomes you," she said, "but dinna' worry yourself. You made me no promises, nor would I want any. I'm no betrayed maiden in a song. 'Twas a pleasant night. I'm glad for what it was, and I'll no' ask more."

Her bluntness gave Madoc his breath back and took it away in the same instant. He was glad of the dance, which took them spinning away once more and joined him briefly to Erulhieth, who danced in silent and calm joy and lent a little of that serenity to all her partners. By the time Madoc came back to take Moiread's hands and dance in a circle, he'd worked out what to say next.

Moiread knew the substance of Madoc's words before he spoke. There could be no other, however she wished it as she watched him come toward her, dark hair tousled and pale face glowing above a deep-red robe.

"I would gladly give you another night, or many such nights," he said, "and count myself fortunate indeed. But here and now, with the queen herself suggesting the courtship—"

"Aye, the last thing we want to do is offend her," Moiread said, and meant it. Even had she not wanted Madoc to succeed in his quest, they were two mortal guests in Gilrion's court. The woman could probably make life difficult—literally impossible—if she wished, and with no earthly authority there to intervene.

The night before had been good indeed, in a way that sent shivers of pleasure through Moiread when she remembered it. It was not, however, good enough to risk death for.

She smiled to see the relief on Madoc's face. "I could almost be insulted myself," she joked, "for you thinking I'd have little enough sense to be angry."

"I'd thought better of you, yes, but…well, best to be sure." He sighed as the dance wound down, and he started to lead her toward the side of the square. "It'd be easier if you weren't a lady in your own right, you know."

"I do," said Moiread.

Any man could dally with a lowborn girl, and only the most foolish or pious of prospective brides would take any notice of such things. Taking one's leman to travel would have raised eyebrows, but wasn't unheard of. At least, that was the way of the mortal world. The Caduirathi might have taken matters differently, but one set of manners seemed to translate well enough.

But Moiread came of nonhuman and noble blood. Had she and Madoc obviously been lovers, once the queen had suggested him as a suitor, it could have been a not-very-veiled refusal at best, and a slap in the face in all probability.

Matters went that way betimes. Not all desires saw fruition. Moiread was long grown and long experienced in the world. She smiled at Madoc and parted amiably, joined one of the Caduirathi for a goblet of mead, and spent the rest of the night in dancing, feasting, and conversation. She enjoyed herself, at that. The court was new and fascinating, the people pleasant, and the food just short of divine.

If her bed felt cold that night, it was still soft and wide and well furnished with thick blankets. If her room seemed a touch too silent, a shade emptier than she'd have liked, it was still a room of her own, soft carpeted and well appointed, with luxury she hadn't even known at home. She could have been in the field, trying to find a few hours' sleep on rocks and mud beneath her bedroll, or on the floor of an inn where they changed the rushes once a year if that.

She'd learned long since to take the good of a moment and ignore the bad. It wasn't easy, but life often wasn't.

TWENTY-FOUR

"And do you truly breathe fire?" Namwynne asked, her violet eyes bird-bright with curiosity. "Doesn't it hurt?"

"Aye, and no," said Moiread cheerfully. The air was cool enough to walk comfortably, the forest smelled of slightly more metallic soil and slightly sweeter pine, and Namwynne was proving congenial company.

For hunting, the princess had dressed practically like the rest of them: long breeches of drab green tucked into boots, a gray robe pinned up around her waist, and brown leather gauntlets that laced up her arms to the shoulder, keeping her arms safe while giving her wings freedom. She'd pinned back her hair into a tight knot on top of her head, and although she hung sensibly back behind the men, she carried a bow as if she knew how to use it. She walked beside Moiread without seeming to begrudge her guest the necessity.

If she did lose Madoc's company to someone, Moiread reflected, at least this woman seemed to be worth him. "We can," she went on, "but only in dragon's shape—I couldn't do it to toast my bread, which I've sorely regretted on a few evenings in the wild—and it feels a bit as if you could make yourself sneeze, only more so. Fire other than our own doesn't hurt us at all, as a general matter. One of my great-aunts swears by it for cleaning herself after a long day. She'll not go near a bath, only steps into the fireplace for a while."

"Stars and sky," said Namwynne, her tone making it

clear that the phrase was an oath. "Should we have given you a larger hearth, perhaps, and no bath?"

Moiread laughed. "Not me. I find the water soothing, and it's always done well enough for me. You can't always be minding what your ancestors say, aye? Though my father would doubtless wish I did more of that."

"And your mother?"

"She died a good while back," said Moiread.

Namwynne blinked. "Ah. I…I'm sorry."

She said it with the air of one being polite about a matter she'd only encountered in books or tales.

"Thank you," said Moiread, "but she's been in heaven—or so I like to think, with all the masses we bought for her soul—a good hundred years or so, and these things do happen. At least to us. Do they," she ventured, watching the princess for any sign of discomfort or offense, "to you?"

Namwynne hesitated before speaking. "In a way, yes. We go onward. We lose this form when our time here has passed and we wish to be—" She used a word that didn't translate to Moiread, frowned, and said, "…to be another thing. And we can die, and that's often unpleasant. Though some find the waiting to return restful, it's only seemed boring to me, like having to spend days abed. Mother says that's a sign of my youth."

It was Moiread's turn to blink. She looked up ahead to where Madoc walked and chatted with a few of the other hunters as they flew close to the ground. She didn't wish to interrupt his reunion with friends of his youth, but she would have appreciated a guide. These were strange waters she was entering.

Again, carefully, she asked, "Waiting to return?"

"Oh yes," the princess said in a matter-of-fact tone. "We come back the next morning. Here, that is. It's harder if we're in your world. We lose our wings there too." She smiled wistfully. "It's a lovely world, or it was the few times when I saw it, and I would dearly love to view it from the air. Greatly do I envy you that."

"If you can find me when next you come, I'd gladly show you about," Moiread said. She made the offer almost absently, her mind adjusting to what Namwynne had said.

She'd heard stories, of course. Madoc had told her one or two, but those had mostly been about *pigs*, not people. The Norsemen's heaven, or their equivalent for warriors, was a place where they fought all day and their wounds healed by mealtime, but Moiread had never heard that those wounds included death.

Granted, she'd been on enough battlefields to know that a day full of warriors fighting one another probably would end, in the normal course of things, with at least one fatality. She'd never thought about it, nor thought past it to what that implied. It had never been important. It had never been real.

"I must have worn the same face, often and often, when I was first here," Madoc said, falling back to walk beside them.

Namwynne laughed. "And not so rarely after that, you know! I liked you fosterlings for all the questions you asked, that I might overhear and learn what otherwise I considered it beneath my own dignity to inquire about."

"You had a great deal of dignity in those days," said Cauldir, joining them with a smile that Moiread thought seemed a trifle forced. Still, he talked lightly enough, and God knew she wasn't familiar with his people. She couldn't trust her judgment as completely as she could have done with a human.

"Say rather that I *thought* of it more," Namwynne replied. "As a young maiden may seek to seem more maiden and less *young*. Lady MacAlasdair, I know not if you fell into such folly too, or if perhaps you've seen it in your attendants."

"Both," said Moiread, grinning. "My youngest brother and my cousin Erik could speak well on how high my nose got, and how vastly above them I held myself for a while… or tried, aye?"

"Oh, Her Highness seemed above us indeed when I was a child." Madoc smiled, rueful and admiring at once. "And not as though she had to try for it. To us she was full-grown, and that she spent any time in our company seemed like the very stars coming to land."

"You've learned elegant speech indeed, hall brother," said Namwynne. She laughed again, and a strand of violet hair slipped out of its imprisonment and trailed down her neck. "But I've not forgotten the pranks you once pulled. You and Celened had no notion of *stars* then."

"His ideas, I swear it." Madoc put his hand to his heart.

A soft chuckle ran through the group, but stopped as one of the hunt's leaders turned back, putting a long finger to her lips. All fell quiet, and up ahead Moiread could hear rustling in the brush: the sounds of a great beast. Namwynne lifted herself up from the ground with a few graceful, near-silent wingbeats, but made no motion forward. Madoc hung back as well and, curious as Moiread was, she did likewise. Footsteps on the ground might well scare away the game.

In talking to the other hunters, Moiread had gained some idea of the type of prey they might find, but her jaw dropped when their quarry burst from its cover. Like a wild boar in its shape and the wickedly sharp tusks jutting from its mouth, it was near the size of a bear, almost man height at the shoulder and solid enough to crush branches in its wake. Short, leathery wings beat the air at its back, raising it half a foot off the ground as it pawed the air with razor-edged hooves.

"Christ's bones," Moiread muttered, drawing her sword just in case.

Boar hunting was chancy sport even in the mortal world, where the boars were generally smaller. She'd seen more than one man killed or crippled that way, and dozens of dogs injured—and the Caduirathi didn't hunt with hounds. The hunters darted in and out instead, jabbing with spear and sword, then dancing out of the way of the lashing hooves or the deadly tusks.

"They'll tire it out," Madoc said at her side, "and make it safer for one of them to give the killing blow."

"Never entirely safe. They're vicious beasts," said Namwynne. "Meat-eaters, when they can get it, and eaters of men as well. I remember—"

A high squeal from behind them interrupted her, followed by another branch-cracking rush of movement. Two more of the creatures rushed from the underbrush. Perhaps they were a touch smaller than the one the hunters had surrounded, but they were vast, and while they had no tusks, their teeth were pointed like those of sharks. They charged toward the princess and the two humans, wings giving them greater speed.

Namwynne screamed. A shout of alarm went up from the main party. Moiread couldn't turn to see if any of them were coming to their aid, and she doubted they could get there in time. She doubted that the three of them could hold off the sows, and while she could heal and Namwynne could come back from the dead, Madoc had neither protection.

There was only one thing for it.

"Get behind me," she shouted to both her companions, then dropped her sword and transformed.

In times of peace, the shift felt like a good stretch, one that didn't quite hurt but that made her feel the pull on her muscles. Done suddenly, it was more painful, but most times when she'd had to change quickly Moiread had other things on her mind. That was true now as well.

To Madoc's eyes, the air around Moiread shimmered, then twisted, and then the immense form of a silver-white dragon crouched between him and the wild sows. Her scales flashed in the light; her wings snapped out with a sound like a thunderclap; and the sows shrieked in terror.

Madoc himself let out a muttered oath and involuntarily stepped back, putting a hand to his sword hilt. He knew Moiread wouldn't hurt him, nor any of the Caduirathi, knew that she'd transformed to protect them—but instincts died hard, and she was intimidating in this form. To one who didn't know her, she would have been terrifying.

She whipped her sinuous neck down and closed her jaws most of the way around a sow's throat. The beast reared and struck at her with its hooves, drawing blood in a few places, but Moiread didn't appear to notice. Her teeth closed tighter, and then she wrenched her head sideways with another swift motion. Madoc could hear the sow's spine crack, and the life quickly went out of it.

The other beast squealed and ran, galloping off into the woods with no thought of its pack mate. Moiread seemed content to watch it go. She lowered the other body carefully to the ground, then turned to face Madoc and Namwynne.

Her eyes fairly glowed, like they had in the inn when she'd been poisoned. Now Madoc saw what she'd been fighting against and fully understood her fear. Even knowing that she was in full possession of human wit and human consciousness, it was hard to overlook how vast she was, and how sharp her teeth and talons were. The sight of her made him uneasy on a primal level, one he had to fight to ignore. Imagining her taken out of her senses by injury and bloodlust, in the middle of a populated town...

She would have taken shuddering the wrong way, so Madoc squelched the impulse.

"My thanks, lady," he said, and bowed. "Are you all right?"

He gestured to the bleeding scratches on Moiread's chest. She regarded them for a moment, then managed a recognizable shrug: *Nothing to worry over*.

"And mine as well. That was magnificently done, and well-timed indeed." Namwynne smiled. A few of the hunters were rushing back toward them now, Cauldir and Arbelath foremost among them. She turned to give them a reassuring smile. "All is well, I promise! Lady MacAlasdair has kept the danger from us."

"We'll have all the more meat on our table too," said Arbelath. "For the price of a few bad moments, much as I wish they'd not happened. It's early for their breeding."

"Nature doesn't often ask our blessing," said Namwynne. "We can only be glad when we survive."

TWENTY-FIVE

At the top of Gilrion's palace, up a winding staircase made entirely and alarmingly of transparent blue glass, a pearl-white door opened into a small circular room, one which Moiread found familiar in many ways. No matter what the world, some principles seemed to apply. Whether a room for magical work should be up high to be closer to the stars or simply harder for anyone without business there to reach, the height was almost always there.

Unlike her father's workroom, there were no candles on the walls and no pentagrams on the floor. Five windows let in light, each from a different direction. Five fist-sized gems, one set below each of the windows, shone red and green, blue and gold and diamond-clear. The air smelled of roses and cedar.

Moiread hadn't expected to be there. When Gilrion had turned to her the previous night and said, "You will find clothing for the rite in your wardrobe. Bring no weapons," as if she were offering another slice of roast boar, Moiread had nearly choked on her mead.

"I hadn't expected it, but I should have," Madoc had said later as they walked the corridors. "You yourself are from a powerful family. You don't lack for magical skill—"

"Not *entirely*," Moiread had said with a snort. "There's a good few who'd say differently."

"You know at least the rudiments, and you've power to back that knowledge. More, you put yourself between her daughter and danger. She's pleased with you."

"Ah," said Moiread, and didn't touch on any of the

things she could have said. Temporarily alone with Madoc in the hall, having spent the evening watching his legs beneath his dark-red tunic and his forearms when his sleeves fell back, watching his lips and his eyes now, she knew it was best to keep the conversation as impersonal as she could. "And I suppose there's no illusion to maintain. That is, if you've no objection."

"None. Your presence would only help, and so would a closer tie…to your people." He'd stuttered a little over the last few words.

A day later, Moiread bathed thoroughly in herb-scented water, clothed herself in dark-blue silk with a white sash at her waist, and walked barefoot up many stairs, all of which were colder than she'd have liked to tread without shoes. Did those who came this way usually fly, she wondered, or was this a matter of mortifying the flesh before the ritual?

Gilrion, Madoc, and Namwynne already stood in the room, in silk robes like Moiread's. Gilrion and Namwynne both wore their hair loose, and it tumbled down their backs to their waists. Neither wore crown or circlet.

On the floor, outside where a circle would have run between the four outside gems, two shining dark chests sat at Madoc's feet. One was small, the other slightly larger, and the locks on both were silver. The soldier in Moiread, who'd sacked a few castles in her day, quickly estimated their value and whistled silently.

She bowed. "I'm honored to be here," she said, looking back and forth between the others. "How is it that we proceed, exactly?"

"Join hands," said Gilrion, and held out her own, the fingers shining of themselves but bare for once of rings.

Namwynne took one, Moiread the other, and Madoc stood between them: symbolic, he supposed, in a way.

If Gilrion marked it or minded, still her face remained serene. Her eyes were like polished sovereigns when they met his. When she spoke, every word was carefully shaped, and every syllable at the right volume to fill the chamber. "Madoc, son of Rhys, what do you seek?"

"Friendship and favor," he replied, trying to be as careful and knowing he'd never quite manage the resonant precision of her speech. "Between you and me. Between our children and our children's children. Between your land and the land of my fathers."

"Madoc Firanon," Gilrion said, "what do you seek?"

"Safekeeping for the treasures I bring, so that none may use them against my people. Refuge for my folk who may need to flee our conquerors."

Namwynne's hand was cool and smooth in Madoc's left. In his right, Moiread's was rough and warmer than any human's would have been. Power ran between them in a ring through him. There was no seeking and directing here, as there would be in the mortal world, or at least not when Gilrion was in charge of the rite.

She called, and the land answered. Her daughter was a part of that, and Madoc and Moiread rougher threads in the same tapestry, borne along by their surroundings even as they lent their strength to the weave.

"Madoc, son of my hall, what do you offer in return?"

"My strength, if you would have it." That strength, or the mystical part of it, began to flow from him in earnest as he spoke the words, as naturally as water ran downstream. "My skill with a sword and a spell, should you have need. The hospitality of my land, that you and yours may ride freely and without harm."

Wingless and closer to mortal in Madoc's world, the Caduirathi still found little that truly endangered them, but silver weapons could kill them, or cold iron. Madoc suspected that creatures like Moiread in dragon shape could manage it as well. Wounds that didn't kill could hurt or vex, and there were mortals enough who would wish to do so, for a growing assortment of reasons. What Madoc pledged had taken some haggling with the sterner of the priests at his father's court.

"What more do you offer?" Gilrion asked.

The magic was twisting between them, an unseen braid with two strands.

"New blood," said Madoc. "A child of my line in each generation, as fosterling and apprentice, and fostering in turn for those of your line who wish it."

With six siblings living, that would be easy enough to ensure—save for an enemy managing to wipe them out root and branch, in which case the other obligations of the oath would most assuredly come into play.

Gilrion took a breath, then dropped Namwynne and Moiread's hands and held hers out. Madoc stepped forward and took them. The invisible braid knotted itself twice, once at each set of clasped fingers, and became a stable, solid cord, then vanished. Madoc felt one end of it in his soul, as he did his other ties of alliance, and knew he would soon cease to notice it as he did them, unless dire events indeed called on it.

Out of the corner of his eye, he saw Moiread standing straight and composed, her hands now folded in front of her. A faint flush stained her cheeks, and her eyes were bright. That was no surprise—effort was effort, magical or physical, and Moiread was neither a wizard by inclination nor in her own land—but it reminded Madoc of the last time he'd seen her flushed and excited, and he had to fight the memory back lest he become distracted.

The robes didn't conceal much, another reason for self-control.

To all appearances unaware of the struggle within Madoc's head and loins, Gilrion let go of Madoc's hands. "Show me what you would give into my keeping."

It had been a long time since Moiread had taken part in any major spell casting. Whether unfamiliarity made the difference, or being in a foreign land, or simply having exhausted herself on the hunt the day before, she was far wearier than she'd ever remembered being. By the time the spell stopped calling on her power, it was a fight not to lean back against the wall and close her eyes.

Interest as much as willpower kept her awake. Magic might not have been her primary skill, nor was she the scholar that others in her family were, but the novel means of spell casting were interesting, and the items in the locked chests more so. She watched as Madoc lifted the first chest, unlocked it with a small golden key, and lifted out an object wrapped in white silk, one that turned out to be a small and delicately wrought chalice: dull iron and set with garnets around the rim.

As when she'd first seen the wings of the Caduirathi, Moiread's thoughts immediately launched themselves along one path. Speech at such times, unless it was part of the ritual, was often dangerous, so she bridled her tongue, but she stared gape-mouthed until Madoc met her eyes and shook his head with a faint smile.

"The Chalice of Emellyr," he said, holding it out to Gilrion with both hands. "Whatsoever any traitor drinks from it will turn to fire in his throat. I give it to you, for your safekeeping and use, until I or one of my kin comes to claim it."

"I do so accept." Gilrion wrapped her hands around the bowl. "I will relinquish it to none but you or your blood."

She stared at the chalice intently, her eyes shining. Under that calm metallic gaze, the relic swiftly and suddenly disappeared. It was as if she'd made the air itself a cloak and cast it over the chalice. When Gilrion opened her hands again, nothing fell to the floor.

Agnes or Douglas would kill to be there. Moiread wasn't turning her nose up herself. New experiences had become rare for her, but she'd had many in the last few days, and this was becoming the strangest of all. She would have been alarmed, save that Madoc looked pleased by this turn of events.

After a short time, whether to let the flux of the energies settle or simply to be properly ceremonial, he turned and opened the larger chest. This one held a large chessboard made entirely of gold, the squares either white or rose and the border pure yellow gold. A silk bag went with it, and after Madoc handed the board to Gilrion, he opened it to withdraw a rook made of glimmering topaz, veined with silver.

"The Chessboard of Gwenddoleu ap Ceidio. Assemble the pieces, and they'll play by themselves. Assemble them and think of a battle to come, and they'll show what will happen, if you can read the signs rightly. I give it to you for your safekeeping and use, until I or one of my kin comes to claim it."

Again Gilrion spoke the words of acceptance. As with the chalice, the chessboard and its men disappeared beneath her gaze, and she slowly lowered her hands to her sides. "Is that all we do here?"

"It is, and it is enough," Madoc replied. The phrase had a liturgical sound from his mouth.

"Then it is done," said Gilrion, and she stepped back beyond the edge of the invisible circle they'd created.

It broke instantly, but with no feeling of violence—rather, as an apple plucked from the tree, a separation whose time had come. The magic lifted quickly and naturally, and Gilrion laughed. "I can see why, son of my hall, you had no wish to leave such treasures near those who rule your people."

"Who rule them for now, Your Majesty," Madoc said, and smiled. "You have my thanks a thousand times for your aid in this, if I hadn't mentioned it before."

"Not quite so many times as there are stars in the sky, but it will serve. I'll go far from unrewarded too." She glanced over at Moiread and made a gesture of acknowledgment with one hand—a bow, from anyone less majestic. "And I thank you for your strength, Lady MacAlasdair. I hadn't known the feel of your people in such endeavors. It will serve better than otherwise, I suspect."

"I'm honored to help, Your Majesty," Moiread said, though getting her tongue around the words was difficult.

"And now that we've thanked each other sufficiently," Namwynne put in, "food and rest would sit far better than words, no matter how sweet."

Moiread chuckled. "I like you, lass," she said, and tried not to gauge how Madoc looked when he laughed as well.

TWENTY-SIX

GILRION WOULD HAVE WELCOMED THEM LONGER, MOIREAD knew, and despite missing Madoc's presence in her bed, she might well have been happy to stay. Good food and good rest went a long way, even without an entirely new world to explore. Yet their quest was only partway done, and as Madoc said, they needed to make their way onward before either weather or politics turned dangerous in their own lands.

The last feast was festive indeed. Moiread ate her fill of silvery fish and sweet fruit, drank as deeply of the mead as she dared when on duty in a strange land, and sat afterward listening half drowsily to minstrels and conversation alike.

"A word, my lady?"

It was Sir Cauldir who spoke, silver hair bound back into a complex arrangement of braids. Up close, Moiread saw that his eyes were reddish-gold, like amber. Like all his people, he pleased the eye. Were she less wary of insulting either the princess or Madoc, Moiread might have chosen to dwell on that in more depth. An empty bed didn't have to stay that way.

Ah well. Fortune laughed at all men—or women—from time to time. "Of course," Moiread said and kept her voice strictly polite.

"I hope you've taken pleasure in your time with us."

"A great deal, and I thank you."

"Such news gladdens me"—Cauldir elaborated with a graceful wave of jeweled hands—"for I know that you have no childhood attachment to my queen's lands, such as Madoc does."

He glanced over toward the benches where Madoc sat, laughing with the guard from the borders and Namwynne and even dark, quiet Arbelath. Moiread knew she could go and join them. She knew also that her presence would be foreign, a boulder in the stream of the conversation. They would adjust and flow around her, but better they not have to, particularly on this last night. Better to let them speak of old memories and not force them to explain jokes.

"Aye, well," Moiread said with a shrug. "Perhaps 'tis better, in a way, that I see with fresh eyes. It's clear that Her Majesty has been good to him, and that he remembers her court fondly. As well might anyone," she added.

"And yet, in truth, he is no real part of it. He must feel that isolation, that distinction, from time to time."

Cauldir spoke pleasantly, and his face showed only concern. Inwardly, Moiread cursed. She was the wrong member of her family for the task at hand. "Depends on your point of view, no? Plenty of men make foreign lands their own, with the time and the will for it."

"Mortals," said Cauldir, "and other mortal lands. We are not the same, not in blood or even in flesh." His wings flapped once, perhaps in emphasis. "And while I welcome visitors and pilgrimages, I can see nothing but hardship for both parties coming from a more permanent connection."

He didn't look back at Madoc and Namwynne, but he didn't need to.

"Aye?" Moiread reached for another bit of fruit. It was a little like a pear, but red and dipped in honey. Did Cauldir not know her lineage, she wondered, or did he see that differently? "It could well be," she said neutrally. "There are tales enough of such in my own family."

Cathal aside, it was rare for the dragon-blooded to marry full mortals, but even those with their own magical lineage had occasionally found the alliance trying. One of Moircad's aunts had decamped to her own family, and a great-great-uncle on her mother's side had simply vanished. Chiefly, Moiread remembered her father frowning over the possibility of broken alliances, and a number of elaborate and tense visits of state.

"Yes," said Cauldir. "I thought such a one as you would understand."

"In a way." Moiread spread her hands. "Most marriage is a hardship of one sort or another, my lord. Your princess has a choice in hers, which is a great deal more than most get in my world, and certainly more than royalty do."

The musicians played on in the background. The melody was slow and unobtrusive, unlike the music Moiread had danced to a few days before. One strain of it swirled high like bagpipes, but with a more metallic note to it, while a steady drumbeat kept up a darker undertone.

"He'll perish well before she does," said Cauldir, no longer pretending to talk at all abstractly.

"Likely," said Moiread. "It often happens that way."

"Among your people, or among mortals?"

"Both. There's been many a lass whose husband was her father's age—or the other way around, especially when matters of alliance are concerned—and if childbirth doesn't carry her off, she'll likely have a pleasant widowhood before long. Even a young man can perish easily enough of plague or war or misadventure. Dust we are, and to dust we shall return, and all that."

"That isn't our way."

"So I hear." Moiread chuckled. "I'd envy you if I thought there was any profit in it."

"Then there's naught about this"—he gestured to the table—"that troubles you?"

"It's not mine to find troubling or not, my lord," Moiread replied. "In truth, I wouldn't be quick to take a mortal to husband, but matters between my people and humans are not as they are with yours, and I doubt *husband* means quite the same in your world as mine, and it's of no matter regardless. This is a matter for my lord and your princess, and for their kin. I'm none of those and have no stake."

She stopped. Ordinarily such a pause in the conversation would have called for another drink of mead, but Moiread wanted all her wits about her. This was taking a turn, and she knew not where it would lead.

Silent for a little while, Cauldir sat back on his bench, silver brows drawn together, fingers resting motionless on the tabletop.

A new song began, this one a duet of two female singers, with a harp playing in the background. Another woman's laugh rang out over the whole proceeding, clear and almost as musical as the song itself. The magical lights shone down from the walls, never flickering or flaring as torches in Artair's hall would have done.

"And if I were to give you a…stake?" Cauldir finally asked. "A reason to take an interest?"

Careful.

Moiread slowly slipped a curious smile onto her face. "What would you offer, and for what sort of an interest? Your queen has already granted us considerable aid."

"Aid to Madoc, yes. And I would by no means betray her, or deny him those favors, but there is some power in my own grasp as well, both of arms and of magic." The red-gold eyes watched her for reaction. "I could aid your land, if need be, or I could do a service for you yourself."

War had not been so long ago. Famine ruled in many parts of the country, and the MacAlasdairs' magic could only keep Loch Arach from the worst of it, not guarantee comfort. Moiread herself was a warrior, and she had her enemies. Fey magic could be helpful—perhaps lifesaving—and there was always guest right, the chance to spend more time in this lovely new world.

"If?" she asked. "What do you imagine I could do, if I were so inclined?"

Cauldir smiled. "I wouldn't ask you to harm the mortal lord, mind—"

"*Good.*"

Her voice was a growl. One or two of the courtiers turned their heads, and Moiread gave them the best innocent smile she could manage, given that her mouth wanted to grow fangs just then.

That hit, if only for a moment. Cauldir sat back, one hand dropping to his waist but not *quite* to the hilt of his sword. In the next breath he was smiling again, though more thinly than before. "Indeed, your loyalty is to be admired. Yet it would hardly be disloyal for a friend to persuade, would it?"

"You'd promise me favors just for a word in his ear?"

"More than one word, surely. Whatever he decides, he'll go back to your world until the end of his quest. All know that much. You'll be traveling together. There would be time to convince him." Cauldir tapped a long finger on the table. "And journeys, especially those in mortal lands, oft take longer than the travelers expect."

"Ah," said Moiread. "Long enough for her to believe herself abandoned and turn to you, you mean? It's a shabby sort of a trick, my lord."

Color flared in Cauldir's shining pale cheeks, and his

lips went thin. Anger—and guilt—looked the same in both races, it seemed. "I use the arts that I can, madam, nor do I scruple when the welfare of my princess and my kingdom is concerned."

"And both mean her marrying you? Regardless of her own mind, or her mother's will?" Moiread shook her head and sighed. "Were I a cynical woman, I'd say that was awfully convenient for you."

"Neither," said Cauldir, and Moiread had to admit that even in anger his voice was melodious, "permit elevating a mortal lord's son to my queen's family, nor letting the ruling bloodline of our land so debase itself."

The voice from behind them was quiet and, on the surface, amused, but it was a cold humor. "Should I ask my cousin, sir, whether he considers himself debased? Or my mother whether our land has fallen into ruin in the generations since that marriage?"

By the guilty start he gave, Cauldir hadn't heard Namwynne approach. Moiread would have felt smug about that, but she hadn't either. The princess had perhaps been floating, and the hall was far from quiet, but mostly Moiread had been distracted. She kicked herself for it, mentally.

"Your Highness, I—" Cauldir began.

"In future schemes of this sort, you would do well to study your history beforehand. It would save you embarrassment, and what I suspect will shortly be a great deal of inconvenience."

A look passed between them, and steel shone beneath the violet of Namwynne's eyes. She hadn't moved, nor spoken further, when Cauldir bowed his head. "I'll depart tomorrow. Please believe that I had your interests at heart."

"Would that either of us could command belief so easily," said Namwynne. She stood watching as he departed, then sat down by Moiread in the place he'd vacated. "I extend you my mother's apologies, though she knows nothing of this, and I would rather it remain so. While I would never say her wrath is *unjust*, it can often be intemperate, and I care not for such scenes. Cauldir will go, and he will not act against you or yours. I give you my word on it. But I'll not stop you bearing this tale to higher ears, if that is your wish."

"No," said Moiread. "I've met his like among mortals. It's mostly more trouble than it's worth to seek vengeance, even when they stay dead." She shifted uneasily, crossing her ankles over each other. "How much did you hear, my lady?"

"Enough to thank you."

"You're welcome, Your Highness, but I didn't refuse for your sake, not mostly."

"No." Namwynne smiled. "But refuse you did, and you kept him speaking long enough to reveal his true nature. That is not without worth. Then too, I am myself fond of Madoc Firanon and disposed to thank any who keep his interests in mind."

"Ah, well, I did promise as much. He's a good man too. I'm not of the mind that marrying a mortal is certain disaster, though I've also not given it much consideration. If it's your will…" Moiread hesitated. *I can vouch for his skill in the bedchamber* was not politic, and she felt strangely cold as she went on speaking. "Well, I'll back you, if you want, and I'll try to bring him back safe this way when his quest's done."

Namwynne laughed quietly, shaking her head. "No, lady. No, though I thank you again for the kindness. I spoke truth when I named Madoc the brother of my hall. In my heart, he could be another of my mother's children. I truly made my choice long ago." She looked back over her shoulder at Lord Arbelath, and now Moiread saw a glimmer in her eyes that she'd missed before.

"Oh," said Moiread, not giving voice to any of her thoughts.

The princess might have guessed a few anyway, but her smile remained. "He is restfully quiet and knows when to pursue his own devices and leave me to mine, and he rides most well. And I have loved him, and he me, since before my hall brother left us."

"Your mother will be relieved, I expect."

"Not her. She's known almost as long, but she wouldn't have the Sea King or his son too certain of their chances. It always suits her ill to be taken for granted, be it by her oldest friends." The violet eyes actually rolled a little. "Were she otherwise, we might have all spared ourselves trouble, but I cannot wish her different than she is."

"I know that feeling well," said Moiread, remembering Artair. She let out her breath and the tension in her back, and leaned against the table. "By the way, what does 'Firanon' mean? He's got another name in my world."

"Oh!" said Namwynne, surprised but glad to be able to share knowledge. "It's the line of the cousin I spoke of. He wed a mortal woman and went to her world, and came back when she died, though he himself has been in the mountains of late, far from this hall. She was one of Madoc's ancestors. I could not count how many generations back... far enough that the marriage would not mingle close kin, else my mother would not have suggested it. They've all *looked* mortal for years."

TWENTY-SEVEN

"I DO NOT, I TRUST, SEND YOU AWAY HEARTBROKEN," SAID Namwynne, as Madoc and Moiread left her party at the border of the city. She'd leaned in to give him a sisterly embrace and kiss, so her words reached his ears alone.

Madoc shook his head. "It will beat a while yet, I promise you."

Sharply as his thirteen-year-old self would have remonstrated with him... Well, he was thirteen no longer, and no longer infatuated with the fairy princess. The deepening of the alliance might have been as inconvenient as it was helpful, in its way. The Caduirathi had their own quarrels, and Madoc would not have liked to leave the mortal world for years at a time, nor did he think that Namwynne would have been happy staying by him in Wales. Leaving, he was well content.

"Take care that it does," she said. "Your world has far worse dangers in it than women, from all I hear. I wish to see you whole at my wedding." She spoke that sentence more loudly, and addressed it to Moiread as well.

"I'll be sure of it, Your Highness," Moiread replied, and a quick smile passed between the two tall, dark women.

Namwynne had reported little of their conversation the night before, or of the reason for Sir Cauldir's departure. Well after she'd announced her choice, and Madoc had congratulated Lord Arbelath, she'd mentioned that Cauldir had asked Moiread to dishonorably help advance his suit, and that Moiread had refused him in scathing terms. "And she is very loyal," Namwynne had said.

"She takes her duties seriously," Madoc had replied. "Including those her family gives her." He hoped that his company made Moiread's task more pleasant. It could only be better than a muddy campaign against the English, at any rate, and the surroundings were certainly more novel.

They rode back along the roads by which they'd come, watching a landscape of silvers and violets that held nostalgia for Madoc and fascinated Moiread. She gestured to a large white form as it flew over the forest once and asked, "Does everything here fly?"

"All the beasts and people, yes. The scholars I knew said that this was a world of air, where ours was one of earth."

"Perhaps my ancestor comes from a place of fire, then."

"It's a sensible explanation. I'd not like to try to find out myself." Madoc smiled. "You might have to leave me behind for that, fragile mortal flesh that I am."

"Not from what Namwynne says…or not entirely."

"Ah, that. Her Highness does me too much honor. We age slowly, but we're far more capable than you of injury. It may have been different in the beginning, but we know little of that, though it was the start of my family's dealings with hers. A many-times-great-aunt on my father's side. He's none too comfortable speaking of her. He wasn't the child they fostered in his generation, but my aunt Joanna took the veil after her time here and had no children."

"Aye, well," Moiread said. "I can see how being here would make a woman want to be closer to the divine."

"Or how the men here would make human suitors look like shaved bears," Madoc replied, the memory of their coupling too fresh for him to feel any qualms when she laughed and didn't deny it.

When they passed the transition this time, Moiread no longer looked nervous, and she peered around the other side with a new wonder in her gaze, one Madoc remembered well. "There's a shift," he said, "or there was for me. I always expect the sky here to be blue or gray, but at the back of my mind I always know there's a place where it isn't."

"Aye, that," Moiread said. "Leaving home is always that way when you come back. But this is on a far greater scale." Her smile flashed out. "I could say a thing or two next time Cathal starts holding the Holy Land over my head. Or France."

The road stretched lonely and pine-flanked ahead of them, the sky overcast above. "Glad to have been of service," said Madoc. "And my thanks for yours. Namwynne told me of that last evening."

"Nothing to it," said Moiread, shrugging. She was wearing armor again, and Madoc was beginning to accustom himself once more to the clink of chain as she moved, not to mention seeing a young man in her place. "A man who'd try such tricks would try to get out of paying for them, no doubt. I confess I'd not expected that to be part of my duties, but—" Another shrug.

"Neither had I, I swear."

She made a *hunh* sound in her throat, then asked, "Do you mind a rather intimate question?"

"From you?" Madoc let memories fill his gaze, smiled slowly, and watched with satisfaction as her eyes darkened in response. "Never."

Flushing, likely with remembered heat rather than modesty, Moiread laughed and then cleared her throat. "Why've you not been married already? Eldest son of a lord and all... No matter your inclination, I'd have thought your father would take a hand, aye?"

"He did, once. When I'd finished my fostering with

Queen Gilrion, I was to wed the middle daughter of a wealthy man. The month before I was to come home, she perished of a fever."

"I'm sorry," Moiread said, crossing herself.

"Doubtless it's a sad matter, but it's no wound to me. I never knew her. I hear tell she was a pleasant girl, and her portrait was comely enough. That's all." They turned around a bend in the road, and Madoc turned his head to shield his eyes from the sun. "By the time she died, my father had married and had more sons, and my next-eldest brother had gotten a local girl with child."

"But you're the eldest, and surely your brother wouldn't have married the woman."

"Either matters less for us. Clydai claimed the boy as his, and so the lad's an heir, maybe. A man's land is split among his heirs. I'll have more than my brothers, should none of them choose to fight the matter. Father remembers Llywelyn and his sons, and how maybe we'd not be a subject people now if that had gone differently." Madoc sighed. "To put it shortly, in Wales a man can have too many heirs."

"Aye, that's true anywhere in its fashion, though not so dramatically for us. The Church is helpful for that, or war." Moiread chuckled. "Cathal and Douglas do best when there's half a continent between them. And too many daughters are by no means convenient for a man, as I'm sure my father could tell you. Especially for us, as we're no' good breeding stock for mortals."

"We've never had that problem," Madoc said dryly.

"Different blood mixes differently. My sister's husband turns into a seal when the fancy strikes him, and she's practically littered. Well-formed bairns, at that, and healthy and well-behaved last I saw. The eldest will be changing soon, one way or the other," Moiread went on, with the faint sound of surprise common to mortal and immortal alike on realizing that a babe in arms had somehow become old enough for his first horse. "There aren't many noblemen with inhuman blood. Fewer these days…fewer of any of us. And I'd not have done well as a nun."

"No." Madoc hadn't meant to sound either as forceful or as sensual as he did. He caught an appreciative smile from Moiread. "I'd have made a poor monk myself. But I don't believe I've ever given my father more to concern him."

"No," Moiread said in her turn, catching the question he hadn't asked. "When we can, it's a matter of will. Which, as my family's not the only dragon-blooded one about, says either that our full-blooded ancestors were different in that regard or that Roman women were interesting creatures. My father took in a bastard once—not his, but a dragon-blooded girl who didna' know *her* sire. Said it raised a good many questions, but he's no' yet gotten answers."

"I'd not heard of others. I'd barely heard of your family, in truth."

"We try to keep private," said Moiread, "and we're the most known to the mortal world. The others wander, as my great-grandfather did, and many of their children dinna' bear their names. There are few, even so."

"Mayhap *you* should have tried to wed your family to the Caduirathi."

"Aye, could be." Moiread smiled impishly. "I could turn back and ask Cauldir for his hand now." She made as if to turn her horse.

Without thinking, even knowing that they'd both been jesting, Madoc put out a hand and caught her reins. Both of them froze in that moment and stared at each other. Faint drops of fog clung to Moiread's hair and her eyelashes. Madoc leaned forward.

The gelding, displeased by his proximity to Moiread, snorted and stamped.

"You couldn't get through again without me," Madoc explained feebly. He drew back his hand and urged his horse forward, turning to watch the road.

TWENTY-EIGHT

THEY DREW NEAR TO THE WELSH BORDER. THE ACCENTS SOFTened. If they were still largely English and southerly, Madoc could nonetheless hear traces in them of the voices he'd known in boyhood. From the road, he could see mountains in the distance and sheep nearer by, grazing placidly on the hills. The air felt like home, smelled like it.

That familiarity flowed into his veins with every breath, loosening the muscles in his back and at the same time letting him sit on his horse with more alertness than before. Being on alien ground had taken effort Madoc hadn't known he'd spent. Now he had that strength back.

He knew any security he felt was an illusion. The land he rode through was still England. Wales was yet under English rule and likely would be for as far as he could see into the future, and even home could have plenty of enemies. Madoc knew all of that well. His spine and his gut disagreed, and he was willing to indulge them, particularly when he could watch Moiread as well as the land.

As in the Caduirathi's world, she watched their surroundings with more interest than mere caution. There, she had evidently been caught up in wonder, half disbelieving what she saw and not knowing what to expect. As they journeyed through England and approached Wales, her expression was different: less awe, but more comfortable admiration.

"I feel better near the mountains," she said as evening fell and they neared a small town. "Being up high lets me think clearer, mayhap." A smile tugged the corners of her mouth upward. "And if any of my siblings were here, they'd have a pert answer to that. One of many reasons I prefer your company."

"And it's glad I am to hear it," Madoc said. He spoke lightly but knew she probably sensed the thoughts that exchange led to, and the heaviness in his groin that made him shift in his saddle. He doubted Moiread had any idea of the less-physical warmth he felt at her words, nor did he think he wanted to tell her—not on the road and in the middle of their quest, at any rate. "A trait of your people, do you think? Or is it just what you're used to?"

Moiread thought about it, dark brows slanting slightly. "Bit of both, I should think. We're at our best in the air, that's certain, but being raised up high would help there. I've known men who didna' feel right unless they lived by the sea, so it could be that."

"It could." From the village, the road wound back upward into hills and then the mountains. "This feels right to you?"

"I'd like a bit more height, but aye. I could spend a while here and not get restless…or no more than I'd get anywhere," she added, and her eyes met Madoc's briefly. This time, she was the one who looked away.

She hadn't meant anything. Truly. She'd been talking idly, making conversation on the road. Of course Moiread hadn't seriously considered living in Wales, any more than Madoc had been seriously asking her if she could.

If she did really think about it—if, perchance, their exchange had made her turn the possibility over until she caught herself—there were of course reasons why it wouldn't work. Not that Moiread had never thought to leave Loch Arach. She probably wouldn't find it wise to do so before Douglas brought home a bride and confused matters regarding the ranking woman in the household, but she'd always thought she'd travel then, or go to a foreign war as Cathal had done.

There weren't that many foreign wars anymore, or at least not that Moiread had heard of. The last real Crusade had been more than thirty years ago. Humanity being what it was, she was sure another war would break out somewhere if she waited a year or two. Failing that, she could always travel.

It would likely be no *hardship* to live in Wales—from what she'd heard and what she saw as she neared the border—but she wasn't sure she could keep her temper long in any land under English rule. It didn't matter. The issue was unlikely to seriously arise.

All the same, Moiread was glad when they reached a town near sunset, and she could shake off her thoughts. She was happier still, and for other reasons entirely, to find that she and Madoc could secure a room for themselves on the second floor. It had been a long few days since they'd bedded, and she'd spent the ride aware of his proximity, of the breadth of his shoulders and the clean male scent of his body. From the light in Madoc's eyes when he looked at her, and his smile when she told him of the room, she believed him to be equally enthusiastic.

So he proved a little later on. They'd gotten through dinner without appearing to be more than man and squire, sitting well apart and paying most of their attention to the food, but once they reached their room, matters changed quickly. Madoc shut and bolted the door behind them with a decisive series of heavy thumps, then crossed the room and, without hesitation or even speaking, took Moiread in his arms.

Armor hindered the preliminaries somewhat. Even the light chain and leather that they wore for traveling was a barrier. When Madoc pressed Moiread to him, the metal links dug into both of their chests. In the first heated moments of the kiss, when his tongue claimed her mouth and her lips were desperate against his, it didn't matter. But then Madoc tried to slide a hand up to Moiread's breast, and she attempted to trail her fingers down his neck.

"Bugger," she said.

"Damn," Madoc said at the same moment.

Laughing, Moiread stepped back. "Might be something to be said for self-control, at that. Swiving in armor's a madman's act, if there's any other way handy."

If she spoke as one who knew from experience, Madoc didn't care. Whatever Moiread might have done before him, for that evening she was with him: her body lean and strong against his, her dawn-blue eyes shining for him, her laughter low and sensual in his ears. Nothing else mattered.

She helped him off with his armor and boots with as much skill as the squire she seemed outside their room, and Madoc stripped hers off with faint memories of his own service. Both lingered more, and let their fingers stray further, than most actual squires probably did with their masters—rumors about the last English king notwithstanding. When they finally stood free of metal and leather, both were flushed and panting, and the air around them was warm and thick with lust.

Moiread shook out her hair, smiling. "And I'm glad anew that I keep this short. Though I do hear men prefer otherwise," she added with a teasing glance at Madoc.

"It couldn't look lovelier on my pillow," he said,

running his fingers through the short dark locks in question, "if it grew to your waist." Madoc closed his hand gently, tugging Moiread's head back a little, and bent to kiss her once more.

This time there was no barrier between them but cloth, and Moiread rendered that ineffective as quickly as possible. Madoc had half expected the way she snaked her hands under his tunic, caressing the bare skin of his back and sides. He did *not* anticipate the moment when she suddenly tightened her grip and wrapped her legs around his hips, letting him lift her off the floor, but he had no objections. For all her strength and height, she wasn't a heavy woman, and the pressure of her sex against his cock brought a groan from his throat and his hands to her arse, keeping her right where she was while she wriggled in pleasure and nibbled on his neck.

All the desire that had built over their time in Gilrion's land, not to mention all that had come before and only partly been quenched by their night together, took hold of Madoc then. He bore Moiread backward onto the bed, hurriedly pushing up her shirt to bare the full ivory softness of her breasts, the pale-rose nipples already taut and pointing up toward him. Taking one into his mouth, he lashed his tongue over it, making Moiread curse in Gaelic and writhe beneath him, while his hands found the juncture of her legs.

Even the cloth was damp. At the pressure of his hand, Moiread let out a boiling-water hiss through her teeth. She'd thrown her head back against the pillow, and the dark cloud of her hair was, as Madoc had said, lovely. In the throes of passion, she was an image a man could treasure for a lifetime. Indeed, the memory of her had made the last days at Gilrion's court a torment, for then he'd known precisely what he was missing.

Now, with not just memory but Moiread herself at hand, he was practically bursting.

When she tried to sit up, reaching for him, Madoc pushed her back down to the bed. "No," he said against her breast as he raised his head to speak more distinctly and began peeling down her hose and breeches. "I'd not trade last time for the world, but I'd not make it through now. Not even begin."

Moiread smiled smugly. One long stroke of Madoc's fingers banished the satisfaction from her face, though. Her eyes widened and her mouth fell open, signs of passion he could have easily read, even if her thighs hadn't clenched around his wrist. "You think"—she panted—"I can?"

"Oh, but it matters less, in my"—he skirted the stiff pearl at the top of her sex with his thumb—"limited experience of women." He chuckled when she growled another oath at him. He thought that one was Gaelic, and badly pronounced at that. "If I were a stronger man, I'd see how many times I could break you, *cariad*, but I'm a very weak vessel just now."

And he almost immediately proved as much by snapping his laces in an attempt to undo them one-handed. He cursed halfheartedly, but in truth couldn't have cared less. A heartbeat later, he was sliding into the slick heat of Moiread's body, feeling her gasp and then hearing the little *nn*-sound of pleasure she made in his ear.

Passionate as she was and had been, Madoc didn't want to make assumptions that might leave her unsated, not with his breaking point so near. He took his weight on one hand, letting the distraction tame his lust an atom or two, and slid the other hand between their bodies, resuming his task of earlier with a more distinct goal in mind.

Before long, Moiread was bowstring tense, her head

tossing back and forth as her hips thrust upward. A little longer, a few more circles of Madoc's fingers, and the spasms of her climax rippled through her. She turned her head to the side in time to bury her scream in the pillow, and clung to Madoc as he groaned her name and finally let go.

TWENTY-NINE

MOIREAD WOKE AND DIDN'T KNOW WHY.

Around her, the room was quiet and dark, the shutters closed against the night air. Madoc slept next to her, turned on his side with one arm thrown over her waist. His lashes were long and dark against his cheek, his hair tumbled over his forehead. The sight was one to remember and cherish, but Moiread was on too sharp an edge to appreciate it fully.

She was a sound sleeper. A day of travel and a good seeing-to doubled that. No bodily need had woken her, so she thought of those senses that were more than human, even when she slept. Had she heard a noise from outside? Breathed an unfamiliar odor? Seen a flash of light? Waking, she could perceive none of those.

They were indoors, and high up. The door was barred. Anyone trying to open it would make more than enough noise to wake her and Madoc both. Moiread had thought them well guarded, or she would have kept watch—and yet, her instincts had brought her back to waking.

The first thing was not to move. If no attack was visible and incoming, then she shouldn't let an enemy know she'd sensed him. Moiread breathed deeply and slowly, like a woman asleep, and watched the room from under her eyelashes.

There: outside the shutter, a sound. It was quiet enough not to wake a normal person, but whatever had made it was larger than a stray owl or rat.

Moiread centered herself, pressed her hands against the mattress, and breathed out *visio dei* as quietly as she could.

The world took on its overlay of auras. Madoc's red-and-silver nimbus was fainter as he slept, and the room, not being living, looked mostly as it usually did. Without other distractions, it was easy for Moiread to see the glow beyond the shutters. It was silver-white, like hazy moonlight, but it flickered weaker and flared stronger as she watched. The creature giving off that aura was moving.

As subtly as she could, Moiread put a hand over Madoc's mouth, then nudged him in the ribs. He opened his eyes and, although he looked dazed at first, asked no questions. If they lived, Moiread thought, she'd buy him a drink for that.

"There's a thing outside the window," she whispered. "Magic."

Then she dismissed the vision and rolled off the bed toward the side where she'd laid her sword. She'd just hit the floor when the first of the shapes came through the wall.

The last set of assassins had been murderers for pay, sneaking bastards, and generally unpleasant men. They'd attacked Madoc in daytime, however, not dragged him from a pleasant sleep to face them without armor, weapons, boots, or, for the love of Christ, *breeches*. Nor had they gotten themselves to the second story and then stepped through stone.

He could find himself missing those men.

By the side of the bed, Moiread landed cat-light in a crouch and came up in one smooth movement, sword shining like a beam of moonlight in front of her. "Come on then," she snarled, and Madoc, grabbing for his own sword and dagger, thought he saw long fangs in her open mouth.

Four men, or man-shaped beings, faced them, two coming in from each of the outer walls. In the darkness, Madoc couldn't see much of them, but he got the impression that their arms were too long and their faces too short, and their eyes shone flatly red. Faint moonlight through the shutters glinted off edges and points, showing they were armed.

They were also quick. Moiread blocked the two nearest her, but the other two shot across the room toward Madoc. He ducked behind the clothes chest and shoved it toward them, catching one in the legs, then desperately rolled sideways to avoid the point of the other assassin's sword. The blade sank deep into the mattress, and a drift of tiny feathers flew upward.

Madoc brought his weapons up and blocked the next blow. The man in front of him fought with long knives: ideal for a small room, in the way that neither his nor Moiread's swords were. He pushed in close, forcing Madoc back against the bed frame. Pained breathing from the side said that the other assassin was solid enough to hurt when he got several pounds of wood in the leg, but Madoc didn't have time to be glad about that.

One blade came around snake-quick toward Madoc's neck. He caught it clumsily with the edge of his sword and ducked under, avoiding the partnered strike to his ribs and spinning himself around the attacker so that Madoc now pinned *him* against the bed. As he passed close to the other man, he felt a chill despite the exertion. His laboring breath brought him the scent of cold metal, too strong to be the blades.

The wounded man was on his right now, sounding in better shape with every breath. The other was in front of him, not quite able to react yet. Madoc leapt backward, sweeping sword and dagger in arcs from the outside in, until he stood on his guard with space to fight. He could hear Moiread's breath on the other side of the room. The scuffle of feet and ring of blade on blade mirrored his, but he lacked the leisure to find out more. He was simply glad to be in a better position.

With that in mind, Madoc began to press his advantage, only to see the air ripple in front of him. The assassin stepped *through* the corner of the bed and emerged on Madoc's left. His friend moved in again, a spiked length of metal heavy in one hand.

A small room, surrounded by humans, and foes who were quicker than mortal men: if the assassins' master had set out to create the worst circumstances for Moiread to fight, he could scarcely have done better. That could mean all kinds of troubling things, but she didn't have the luxury of pausing to consider them. The blades coming at her were far more urgent concerns.

She cut high. One of the men dodged the blade, while the other came in for her kidneys. Moiread rolled backward away from them and sliced upward as she rose, blocking a sword aimed at her throat. The men didn't have her strength. Her assailant's arm gave under the blow, and she forced him back. He swerved sideways before she could follow through, though, quick as the flick of a snake's tongue.

Downstairs, voices were rising. Moiread couldn't spare the time to listen, but she knew they'd be alarmed. Humans might or might not be able to hear the sounds of steel on steel from the floor above, but the scuffling and thumping would not sound normal. Before long they'd be running up the stairs. If they were wise, they'd have their own weapons, and they'd most likely do nothing except maybe die if one of the assassins could get free of Madoc and Moiread long enough.

She was glad she'd barred the door.

Both of the not-entirely men came back toward her. Patches of mangy fur dotted their faces and the backs of their hands, and Moiread thought she saw a flash of pointed teeth. They lunged and struck, collecting themselves as she dodged, and then one pivoted out of the way in time to dodge her return slash.

Moiread let her sword arm fall, delayed long enough for the other assassin to get behind her, and then reversed the motion. Her sword itself was too large and too heavy to turn around in time, but her elbow moved well enough. It struck the man-thing in the face with a *crack* of bone that did her heart good to hear.

The creature snarled. High, chittering, the sound brought to mind the titters of a monkey she'd seen in court some years back, all evil mischief and thwarted rage. Moiread hoped there was pain in the mix too.

Stepping back, she swept her sword up in front of her again. This time it cut deep into an outstretched arm, drawing both blood and another shriek—but the creature she'd elbowed recovered more quickly than it should have. Moiread threw herself backward, away from its oncoming stroke, and felt her back hit the wall. One elbow crashed through a window; she felt blood and splintering wood, and knew pain would come later.

Try something new.

She opened her hand and let go of her sword. As she'd thought it would, the motion got the creature's attention. It moved in as Moiread snapped her weight backward. The assassin's blade passed within inches of her torso, but she caught its arm with both hands. With a flick of her hip, she threw the creature forward, breaking its arm and sending its head through another shutter.

Shards of wood lodged in its throat. Enough blood went up for it to be a fatal wound. Moiread wouldn't trust in that, but she had hold of the creature's sword arm, which meant that she had a shorter sword.

Grab. Lunge. *Stab*.

It even rhymed.

The point of the knife should have hit Madoc in the arm, even ducking away as he was. He saw its outline collide with his arm, felt nothing, and at first thought he'd been wounded and not yet realized it. That happened betimes, or so he'd heard. As he pulled himself back and around to the assassin's side, though, he realized that there was no blood, and the fabric of his tunic was as yet intact.

It seemed the creatures needed to be substantial to strike. He would be thankful for small blessings, if he survived.

A shift of position put him in front of both assassins again, though Madoc didn't know how long that would last. He feinted backward, tried to put more desperation in his face than he felt—that wasn't saying much—and watched as one of the men advanced, swinging a morning star. Then he ducked low, practically going to his knees, and slashed low, forward, and *in*.

Whatever the beasts were, they bled. And they had hamstrings, although one of them was now considerably lacking in that regard. He squirmed on the floor, letting out inhuman cries mixed, disturbingly, with good English blasphemy.

His friend might have taken notice but didn't pause,

just moved in on Madoc in a whirlwind of blades. One hit the nightstand as Madoc ducked behind it, knocking pitcher and basin sideways to the floor in a crash of porcelain shards. If Madoc hadn't already regretted fighting half naked, he would have then, though for a mercy, the broken bits missed him.

The nightstand itself was too large and solid to shove as he'd done the chest. Indeed, hitting the oak made the assassin's blades shiver. From the grimace on the man's face, Madoc suspected he'd felt the impact right up his arm and into his shoulder.

Madoc saw his moment and took it. One step forward gathered his weight. A spring up and over brought him to the top of the nightstand: a precarious perch, but one from which he had the twin advantages of height and surprise. Madoc's attacker had been circling sideways to get at him. Now he gaped and tried to raise one of his knives.

It didn't work. Madoc swept his sword around and down, taking a knee to add further to the force of the impact. Flesh parted. Bone snapped. The assassin's head tumbled from his shoulders in a gout of blood.

Thumping filled the room, coming from the door. "What in Christ's name are you playing at?" the innkeeper yelled. "Open up, or I'll have the law on you!"

"That," Moiread said from the other side of the room, "could really only improve matters."

THIRTY

"Talk to him," Moiread whispered. "You're better at it, and I'd rather he didn't see me right now."

Madoc wasn't entirely thrilled about facing the innkeeper in his condition either. His tunic covered everything essential, though, and he needed no illusion to seem masculine. He wondered why Moiread couldn't invoke hers, but had no time for debate, nor any real interest. As she'd said, he'd likely handle the encounter better.

He unbarred the door and opened it a crack. The burly middle-aged man on the other side stared at him and then past him to see one headless body on the floor, quite a bit of blood, and another figure cursing and shrieking while it clutched its leg. He might have seen, even in the half-darkness, that neither looked entirely human. He couldn't fail to realize that neither had come in through any human means.

"I... You... Those—" the innkeeper stammered and raised a suddenly shaking hand to cross himself. His face, florid when he'd taken their money and served them dinner, was parchment-colored.

"I know, yes. It took me by surprise too," Madoc said, using his most calming voice and hoping that it cut through the assassin's howling. That was growing fainter as the pool of blood spread.

He heard footsteps and then Moiread cursing. "Stay still, ye wee bastard." With luck, his body, distance, and the creature would block all she didn't want the innkeeper to see.

Madoc patted the other man on the shoulder, redirecting

his stunned gaze. "My good man," he went on, sliding into the most courtly and condescending tones he knew. The conversation would almost be a nastier bit of business than the fight, but there was likely no getting around it. "Don't think that I'll hold you at all responsible for the attack. You'd no way of knowing. Who could?"

"Well, yes," the innkeeper said. "But what—"

"Best not to ask, I'd say. Best not to know. There are foul things in this world, and an honest man should trouble his mind about them no more than he has to, yes?"

"Yes, m'lord."

"We're all right. We've dealt with the matter, and I'm certain it won't happen again. And, of course, we'll pay well for the damage to the room. There's no point in you suffering for this night's work, is there?"

"Thank you, m'lord," said the innkeeper. "Will you be, ah, staying the rest of the night?"

"We will." Madoc hadn't known before he answered, but it made sense in retrospect. Wandering out into the night was probably more dangerous than lingering. "And we'll need water and soap as soon as you can manage them. After that, I suggest you get some sleep, good man. We'll settle up come the morning."

As he watched the man's retreat, Madoc reconsidered. Now that the fight was over, the smell of blood and death in the room was nauseating. It was impractical to leave— and likely too late. Madoc sighed, shut the door, and lit the candle by the bed. Light revealed a scene less pleasant than the smell had been.

"Dead," said Moiread, standing up from the hamstrung creature. "Damn. I'd hoped we could ha' made the thing talk. Now we'll need to get rid of the bodies, but first I'll ask for your aid."

"Of course," Madoc began, but when she held out her arm, he stopped and stared in as horrified surprise as the innkeeper had done.

The flesh around Moiread's elbow bristled with wood. The points had stuck right through the cloth of her tunic, and the once-brown fabric was a dark, dripping red.

Had she been able to tend her wound one-handed, Moiread would have done so before her body realized what had happened. The wooden shards had started hurting like the devil before Madoc had gone to the door. Only the importance of him placating the innkeeper—and then her desire to get information out of the assassin beast—had let her put off her request.

As it was, she bit her lip and looked away as Madoc drew out each sliver. Her other hand clenched at her side. If she'd been on the battlefield, and he a page who knew nothing of her, she would likely have been yelling and swearing. She did swear, under her breath, with the next-to-last piece. It was lodged sideways and required turning to get it out, and for a little while, all she saw was white.

"My thanks," she said afterward, drawing her ruined tunic over her head. That hurt too. Everything would for a while. Best to concentrate on other matters. "Not sure what to do with the bodies. Mayhap if we throw them out the window, I can go drag them off and bury them."

"To hell with the bodies," said Madoc, reaching for her arm again. "You'll need a dressing on that, or…good God."

He gaped. Moiread followed his gaze. The sight that met her eyes was, to her, nothing remarkable. She'd known it almost from birth. The wounds were closing up, their edges drawing slowly together as she watched. Vessels knit, then muscle, then skin. Bones would have taken longer, but she'd been lucky.

"Aye, well," she said with a shrug. "Good of you to think of it."

She didn't want to look too closely at Madoc's expression. When he gave her a smile, she wanted to remember that instead, however faint it was, and she cursed herself inwardly for her doubts. Madoc knew what she was. He'd seen her transform. He'd gone to bed with her regardless, and surely that was as much as she could want.

There was knowledge and knowledge.

A clean transformation could be majestic. Watching her flesh move as it healed wasn't.

None of that made any real difference. There were tasks at hand. She reached for her clothing, tattered and blood-stained as it now was. "Let's have done with this. And you should come with me. Best you not be alone here."

Dragging inhuman corpses out a window in the dead of night went about as well as it possibly could have. The innkeeper and his guests had evidently decided to turn a blind eye for the rest of the evening. Madoc heard no sounds of alarm and saw no lights go on, throughout the whole endeavor. The village was small enough to have plenty of space around the inn, so he doubted neighbors would raise the alarm.

Thank God for small mercies, he supposed.

After the bodies were gone, the room did smell a touch better. The innkeeper brought two basins of water and some strong lye soap. Madoc and Moiread washed the room as best they could, then did the same to themselves. The sting of the soap and the cold water felt right to Madoc.

The process also occupied his mind, which he needed, lest he descend too far into guilt, worry, or both.

True, Moiread was his bodyguard, and being injured on his behalf was her duty. True, she'd accepted that duty freely, and Madoc had given her a chance to back out earlier. And true, she healed more easily than he would. She'd almost certainly suffered worse.

He couldn't forget the blood-soaked sleeve of her tunic, nor her expression as he dug wood slivers from her arm. Nor could he stop hearing her voice in his mind, saying that it was best he not be alone.

Being an ally, even a mortal and breakable one, was fine. Sneaking back to the inn with Moiread, Madoc had felt himself a burden instead.

Moiread added another entry to her mental list of wrongs to hold against the English: making her spend the rest of the night in a room that stank of inhuman blood. At least the bed was clean enough, for all the damage they'd managed to do to the mattress. She'd slept on worse.

She wasn't likely to sleep at any rate, not for a while. Moiread sighed again. "Y'know," she began, wringing bloody water out of the cloth and into one of the basins, "tonight means we'll need to start treating inns as we do the wilderness."

"Set watches," said Madoc, none too cheerful but at least resigned. "Likely even when we're not in private rooms. I doubt these things would have had trouble killing a half-dozen other travelers if they'd needed to."

"Or simply setting fire to the building. It'd be less sure to kill us, maybe showier than their master would like, but—" Moiread dragged her mind away from unpleasant speculations and back to unpleasant reality. "Aye, watches. And even when we're not asleep... Well, we should stay on our guard. More so than we were. Bed sport's quite a distraction, done right."

"I wish I could argue that," Madoc said with a rueful smile that was damned distracting itself. "But I'd never lie well enough to say you *don't* hold all my attention at such moments."

"Charmer," said Moiread.

"Yes, for all the good it does me now. It's not that I was overjoyed with whoever's trying to kill me *before* this, understand, but now I could manage to hold quite a grudge." Running a hand through his wet hair, he grimaced. "Not to say that I'm feeling amorous right *now*, mind."

"Aye." Cold water and rags only went so far. "We'd best find a bathhouse tomorrow, or a river, before we leave. We'll never keep the horses calm else." She didn't want to say that she had trouble enough as it was. Pointing out her nature felt like a bad idea. "Try and get some sleep. I'll wake you when it's your turn."

Both of them knew how hard sleep would be in that room, but Madoc, like Moiread, clearly knew well enough to try without protesting. He lay down on the less-damaged side of the mattress, his weight sending another drift of feathers flying out into the air, pulled the slashed blankets up to his chest, and closed his eyes.

Moiread stood up and blew out the candle. Then she sat down at the foot of the bed, holding the assassin's naked sword across her thighs. Beyond the broken shutters, the stars glinted down at her. After the colors of the Caduirathi's land, they seemed very pale, and the night around them very dark.

It was beautiful in its way. It was vast. That was all

right. Just then, it was comforting to think of a great, wide world that would go on around, and without, and despite her. Just then, Moiread needed to know as much.

THIRTY-ONE

IN THE FIRST BLEARY LIGHT OF MORNING, THEY LEFT FOR THE town bathhouse, a squat stone building that might have been left over from when the Romans ruled and the English themselves had been a subject people. Townsfolk rose later than farmers, so there were few to stare, and Moiread thought they'd gotten the visible blood off at the inn. Still she was glad of her cloak, and the morning chill to justify it.

"We should take turns," she said at the entrance. "Stand guard."

"It seems a common theme of late, but yes. A pity."

"Aye." Men and women washed together in all but the wealthier towns. While neither of them would have been able to act on what they saw, Moiread wouldn't have been above a bit of teasing. It was a long, chilly ride ahead.

They both hesitated, the moment grown clumsy, before Madoc gestured toward the door. "You took the first watch," he said, "and besides, I'm not entirely lost to chivalry."

Moiread wasn't about to object. Her sense of smell was keener than a human's, and the reek of dried blood lingered on her skin. Half of her found it sickening. She worried about the other half. As she was soaping her hair, she wondered if Madoc had thought of that too—and how much that consideration had been behind his offer.

Sensible of him, if he had thought of it. Certainly it was no cause for Moiread to feel uneasy. Madoc had seen her poisoned, half out of her mind and losing control, long before he'd ever gone to bed with her, and it hadn't dampened his lust. He'd seen her transform and kill and been just as eager in the inn. Danger didn't put a man off.

That night, awake on a farmer's floor after a watchful and mostly silent ride, she thought *Danger doesn't put a man off in the first rush of desire*. She was not the sole woman around—there had been women in plenty at Gilrion's court, and Moiread had no doubt that Madoc could have found a willing barmaid at the inn—but she was there steadily, she was young and clean and in good health, and she'd offered herself to him.

Men took what was convenient. She'd done it herself. That meant little about the person in question.

In the morning, Moiread dismissed those thoughts. She knew herself to be comely enough. Men had truly desired her before. One or two had known what she was.

The next night, she thought that those men hadn't been human. She thought that a man who'd been half raised by his father's priest, wherever he might have spent the next few years, might easily come to have words like *demon* and *monster* at the back of his mind when he looked at her, even if he never did anything so ungenteel as speaking them, even if he didn't let himself think them directly.

She sharpened her sword and stared at the dark sky.

The hours past midnight bred such notions as meat bred maggots. Moiread knew that. Every enemy loomed like Goliath between matins and lauds. Every corner held a dagger, or worse. She'd drunk herself back to sleep in the field during such hours. At Loch Arach, she'd changed shape and hunted.

On the road, she stared into fields and waited for the next, more menacing set of assassins: men who spat lightning or had six arms, probably. She considered the doubtless dark and unstoppable power of their master, and all the horrific fates that seemed almost certain. And she came up with reason upon reason that Madoc's desire for her couldn't have been true and wouldn't last.

It occurred to her during one of those endless hours that she almost welcomed that last set of thoughts. They were a plague in the dark hours, a wearying, endless wheel spinning in her mind—but in another way, she realized, they also felt like a shield.

Because, she said silently to herself, *why does it matter if he wants you, and for how long? You've gone without men before. Why is it so damned important whether or not this one came to your bed eagerly?*

Why are you suddenly so set on thinking he didn't?

They rode silently now for the most part, wary from the danger they knew to be both uncanny and persistent, too short on sleep to have energy for idle conversation. By the third day, words were elusive. When Madoc did speak, he often found himself stopping and seeking the right phrase, even a common one.

He felt pared down to the essentials, with no cushion between him and the world, nor any reserve to draw on for aught save emergencies. He trusted himself in fight or fire, but he couldn't have thought up a witty sentence for any reward. It was as well that other matters demanded both his and Moiread's attention.

On the third day, riding past the ruins of a Roman fort, Madoc thought *other matters* might well be part of the drain, and not just because they meant silent watchfulness during the day and half a night of sleep. When he *did* think, rather than reacting to his surroundings or the task at hand, it was always along the same lines: his enemy was still set on his death. He'd still managed to find Madoc, and he possessed enough power to either summon demons or reshape men. Madoc couldn't tell which.

"I've never heard of the like," he said during one of the rare moments of conversation he and Moiread had managed since the attack. They were eating bread and dried meat by the side of the road, while their horses rested and drank. "Not in any book, nor from any magician I've known."

"No," Moiread agreed. "My father may know, or Agnes—they're both more familiar wi' magic—but I'd need candles to send them messages that they could actually get and reply to in time. Not to mention pen and paper and ink."

They hadn't ridden through any real towns since the inn, so Madoc had another reason to rejoice when he saw the signs for an abbey. "We can pass the night there," he said. "I can't imagine killers would enter *those* walls."

"No' likely." Moiread's accent had grown stronger over the last few days. "Even the most evil mortals wouldna' want that sort of price on their heads, and the others... Well, the saints have their power, and I'll no' deny it. Though—" She frowned. "Best to be safe. I'll need to stop for a bit, and I don't suppose you've any lengths of cloth on you?"

"The wrappings," said Madoc after a moment's thought. "From the treasure. But why—"

As they crested a hill, he could see the abbey in the valley below. It was a homely, solid place, a nest of thick gray walls and modest spires surrounded by the peace of fresh-plowed fields and budding orchards. To normal sight, it would have been lovely. In *vislo del*, the new growth was a riot of color, and silver lines of magic laced through the walls like a spider's web on a dewy morning.

"I dinna' think they'll see through my illusion like Gilrion's folk did," Moiread said, correctly interpreting Madoc's sudden pause and knowing the conclusions he'd draw. "But I dinna' know that they *won't*, aye?"

Madoc looked back at her, and his gaze automatically fell to her chest, a sight almost as disconcerting as the view of the abbey below.

Breasts painfully flattened with silk, tunic bloused out over her belt as much as she could manage, Moiread rode by Madoc's side through the abbey gates and, as far as she could tell, didn't get a skeptical glance. Either her illusion held, the physical disguise was good, or there was some advantage to their hosts' not being supposed to deal often with women.

Yet she was nervous as they went on, and not merely because of her guise. For the first time since the war, Moiread was in a stronghold of the English. It and its residents belonged to God and in theory had nothing to do with war, and the figures coming back from the gardens and fields looked not in the least intimidating, but England was England, and the English were the English. Moiread braced herself at least for the need to keep her temper once they heard her accent or Madoc's.

The monk who greeted them, once their horses had been stabled, didn't inspire ease on that score at first. He was tall and thin, with silver hair around his tonsure and an aristocratic appearance to his face. He spoke like a nobleman too. "God give you good evening, and welcome. I'm Prior Michael. I hear you seek lodgings for the night."

"If you would be so kind, yes," said Madoc. To Moiread, he seemed to be visibly making an effort to use his normal charm. Could the prior see Madoc's exhaustion as she could? Or did her awareness come from feeling the same—or from knowing Madoc too well?

Regardless, the monk smiled. If he felt anything but pleasure at Madoc's accent, he concealed it well. Granted, they'd arrived mounted and armed, which spoke of men it would be best to please. Not all possessed the sense to see that. At least the prior was smart. "We've beds aplenty in our dormitory, and I would welcome the company at mealtimes, not to mention the news from abroad."

"Thank you most kindly," said Madoc. "As for news—"

Prior Michael held up a hand. "No, no. Refresh yourself first. We'll have time enough at dinner, and I'd not keep a weary man from a bit of rest. Nor am I free from my duties yet," he added with a wry smile. "I like to believe I've learned patience by now, though the Lord is fond of showing me my folly in such matters. But I do what I can."

Moiread hadn't expected to find herself liking him. Of course, she knew the English didn't all have horns and tails—bad as *that* figure of speech was for one of her kind. She'd dealt with their captive soldiers well enough during the war. They *had* been captive, though. They'd been in her power and had known it. She'd grown used to thinking of the English as folk who wore their power heavily.

Some had. Some still did. Prior Michael could well be one, as gracious as he was to rich noblemen. But as Moiread made her way to the dormitory, she felt no urge to watch her back, nor any sense of unfriendly eyes watching her and begrudging her presence there. That alone was an unexpected gift.

"Of course," Prior Michael said with a small self-deprecating smile, "we're far from the court here, almost at the border. We've little to do with the king and his councilors. For myself"—he shrugged—"I'm happiest that way. In truth, our Lord knew what he was about when he made me a third son. But such doings do make for interesting stories, little as I wish a part in them."

"Alas," said Madoc. "I've been abroad for a year or two myself. You may know more than I do of my home. But—"

He told the man what he'd heard on the road: new colleges at the universities, the young king of Aragon, a book about hell from an Italian which he'd heard was quite good. He tactfully didn't mention the antipope, and he avoided, with a sideways glance at Moiread, talking in any detail about Scotland.

Prior Michael broached the subject himself, though not directly. "It's to be hoped that we'll get some rest from war for a time," he said. "Not that every boy in the village isn't sad to have missed his chance. But their elder brothers are generally wiser, or the ones who came back are."

He looked around the small guest hall: comfortable and homely, with a fire flickering on the hearth and small stained-glass windows keeping out the darkness. "But then, we've had the luxury of *sending* them. I shouldn't complain that they go. Rather, I give thanks that their foes won't come to us."

"Aye," said Moiread. Far from the grudging tone Madoc had feared he'd hear from her, she spoke with great understanding.

All the same, Prior Michael raised a hand. "I mean no insult to your people, sir, of course. The Scots are only the most recent of England's enemies, and of themselves they're good men."

"Some of us," Moiread said. "But all men are terrible in war, Prior."

THIRTY-TWO

THE STORM HIT SHORTLY BEFORE SUNSET. MADOC HAD BEEN expecting it. The day had been hot for spring, and though it had started clear, clouds had piled up in the sky all afternoon, then grown dark and lumpy. He and Moiread had hoped to keep going until full nightfall and a town. They'd tried to hurry accordingly, but the road was yet uneven from the winter thaw.

Still they pressed on as the wind picked up and they felt the first few drops. They were just across the border from Wales, and both would feel more comfortable once they were over it. In addition, the more distance they covered quickly, the better chance they stood of losing any assassins who'd taken up the chase after their colleagues' deaths.

Then a wall of water fell on them from above.

The rain came down so fast and so heavily that Madoc could barely hear Moiread's cursing. Through a veil of water he did see her pulling on her reins, controlling the gelding who wanted to bolt for cover.

"Come on, then, boy," he said, leaning forward and patting the gelding's head. "We'll find a place away from this mess. We've only to keep to the road for a while. We've got to stop soon," he called to Moiread, as they got the horses moving again. "They're as likely to break a leg in this as not."

"Or our necks," she called back grimly. "Aye. I—"

Lightning turned the sky blue-white. A heartbeat later, thunder cracked across the valley. Madoc's horse screamed and reared, hooves lashing at the hostile sky. Madoc had kept his seat in worse conditions, but it was briefly a chancy thing. He pressed his legs tight against the gelding's sides and hung on to the reins.

"*Verra* soon," Moiread yelled through the rain.

Few people, including assassins, would brave such weather, and the rain would most likely wash out any physical tracks they left. Madoc tried to keep those small blessings in mind as he urged his horse onward. Looking to either side showed him no shelter, only the forbidding rise of the hills. The trees alongside were too short to provide any sort of cover. He wiped water out of his eyes, pushed sopping hair out of his face, and squinted ahead, but he could see no more than a foot in front of his face.

The next stroke of lightning forked down into the ground not far off. Stories of hail and whirlwinds came to Madoc's mind. He prayed hastily and silently that such catastrophes would stay away. In the immediate aftermath, his prayer seemed to have reached sympathetic ears, for nothing worse happened than the continued sheets of rain and the occasional thunder.

He saw the shape to his left before he heard the voice, or at any rate before his mind could assemble the sounds into words.

"Lord bless us, man. You can't stay out in this!"

The speaker was a tall man with dark hair and a full beard. More Madoc couldn't say, for the rain blurred his face and plastered his hair and clothing to his body. At his feet, a large dog drooped its head, looking equally miserable.

"The two of you come with me," the man went on. "It's but a short way to my house, and my wife will set us right soon enough."

"Thank you," Madoc said, and those were the last words he managed until they were under a roof.

Foul weather had a silver lining. Once Moiread was out of it, she was too relieved for brooding. Life shrank to the simple things. A fire crackled on the hearth. A heavy cauldron of potage bubbled above it. Beside it, three pairs of wet boots steamed, while Moiread curled her bare toes against the dry floor. John's wife had provided rags to dry her hair and hung up her cloak. For the rest of her clothing, she stood near the fire and waited.

Contentment of this sort was a purely animal pleasure, the passive side of the almost mindless joy of the hunt and the kill. Moiread would take that and be glad.

John and Matilda hadn't spoken about themselves, being too busy getting dry in the first case and seeing to guests in the second. Their house was big, with two rooms on the first floor and a second story beneath the thatch. A byre stood on one side. "Your horses can go in with our mule," John had said offhandedly. "Be good company for the old bugger, I shouldn't wonder." Judging by that, the sides of meat hanging above the fire where they'd catch the smoke, and the rich smell of the potage, Moiread thought the couple was likely prosperous and probably free, not serfs, from what little she knew about such things among the English.

In their persons, they were healthy but middle-aged, bordering on old. Both had silver streaks in their dark hair and wrinkles around the eyes. They dressed plainly, talked amiably, and watched their visitors with no lack of curiosity.

"Are you soldiers, then?" Matilda asked, settling down

by the fire with a spindle and yarn. She'd stared at Madoc and Moiread when they'd removed their cloaks, revealing their swords and armor, though she'd remembered herself soon enough and looked away.

"Simply travelers, mistress," said Madoc. His voice sounded close to theirs, but his accent was a shade deeper, more musical. "But there's plenty of danger on the roads, I fear, and our journey is a long one."

Moiread saw the couple exchange glances. A sword was a rich man's weapon—or a brigand's, perhaps. Her and Madoc's horses were of no particular quality. Their clothes *had* been good, once, but rain made many men equal.

"Blades are cumbersome things in a hospitable house such as this, I will say," Madoc went on, "and I'd not want them in your way. Is there a place we can lay them?"

"Stand 'em by the door," said John after a brief silence and another marital glance, this one more relaxed. "Thank you."

"It's you we have to thank, good sir." Madoc smiled and, once Moiread had taken his sword, reached for his purse. "And I'd be glad to do as much materially."

"No need."

"The need of my conscience, not to drip on a man's floor without recompense. Nor to partake of his wife's excellent food and not show my appreciation."

"Thank you, then," said Matilda, taking the offered coins. "For the praise as well."

She got to work setting out the food: bread with butter, the potage in dark clay bowls, and a jug of a similar clay, full of rich ale. Moiread ate heartily and quickly, letting Madoc do the lion's share of the talking. The dog curled in front of the fire, snoring steadily.

"We had soldiers coming through for a while," Matilda

said when the subject of roads and visitors came up. Dinner was half done then, and the patter of rain on thatch had slowed. Moiread hadn't heard thunder for a good quarter hour. "When there was that revolt against the old king, two years back or so. The year the great tree fell down in the churchyard." She shook her head. "A shame, that."

"The revolt, or the tree?"

Matilda shrugged. "The tree. Took three men to shift it, and they had to rebuild the chapel after. The other's a matter for great lords, not us. God will guide them as He wishes."

"We can but hope they listen," Madoc said, a touch of dryness in his voice.

"Well, and if they don't, we'll live on, most like," said John, reaching for the jug of ale. "So far, the cow gives as much milk under the son as she did the father, and the oats come in as well. I'll not trouble myself about such matters until they come to my doorstep."

The knock on the door couldn't have come at a better moment—or a worse one.

If Madoc had been inclined to think the timing of the new arrival any sort of omen, the voice that called through the door would have convinced him otherwise. It was young, male, and as rural as those of their hosts. "Da? Mum? Are y'well?"

"We are," John shouted back, and started to get up, but Moiread was closest to the door and knew the duties of a good guest.

Finding her on the other side of the door, the young man on the threshold peered suspiciously at her from under thick black brows. "Sir?"

"Michael," said John, "and Madoc. They're travelers.

Have yourself a seat, Adam, as you're here. Gwen and the babe well?"

"They are," Adam said and came in slowly, shutting the door behind him. He seated himself on the bench between his mother and Madoc. "I was worried the storm had caught you out or knocked a branch down on the house."

"Kind of you to be worried, but we're well. Though it did catch me out, and our guests too, as you see." John waved a hand toward the row of wet boots.

"Soldiers?" Adam, like his mother, asked.

"Only travelers," said Madoc. "Do you get many knights on the road?"

"Not lately and not knights. Though there might be some men coming back."

"That'll take time," said John. He glanced at Madoc. "And you'd know better, perhaps. Is there truly a treaty with the Scots? Ralf Atmill heard there was, when he was sowing beans up at the manor, but tales get lost in the telling."

Across the table, Moiread reached for her spoon. The motion wouldn't have seemed deliberate to any of the others, but Madoc could read the hint. "There is. As of May Day."

Adam snorted. "Trust a stripling and a woman to eat out of the savages' hands. His grandfather would have known better."

"You were barely walking then," said Matilda, shaking her head, "and none of us is to know what a king would have known, or done."

"We'll light a candle for thanksgiving," said John, "and pray for the returning and the lost. The levy took a few village men," he explained to Madoc and Moiread, "mostly for archers. Adam was far too young, and our other sons not yet born. 'Tis strange, to think of it… There'll be men returning to grown sons and daughters they never met as babes."

"The way of the world, at times," said Madoc. He tried to get a view of Moiread's face, but Adam was leaning forward, blocking his line of sight.

"When the realm is threatened, aye, of course," Adam said. "I wish I *had* been old enough to go."

"God disposed that too. And rather to our joy," John said, which softened Adam's face. "Gwen's too, I'd think. How fares my namesake?"

"Plaguing the life out of the dogs, the goat, and his mother at once. And eating enough for an army. Gwen swears he's taller every dawn than he was the previous night."

The young man laughed with paternal pride and leaned back. With a clear sight of Moiread, Madoc searched her face for anger, ready to try to calm her by a look or to take her aside if that failed.

To his relief, but his surprise as well, there was no need. Moiread sat silent and thoughtful, to all appearances not just calm but amused. It seemed no act, either. The slight smile on her lips touched her eyes.

Madoc would have paid gold to know what she was thinking then.

THIRTY-THREE

AFTER THE BORDER CAME THE MARCHES, THE BORDERLANDS OF Wales that English lords had held for Moiread's lifetime. Grim gray castles lined the hills they rode through, squatting atop mottes like enormous grave mounds. Moiread and Madoc stopped at none. They stopped as little as possible, in general.

"Are the English so cruel here already?" Moiread asked once.

"Not worse than any other lord of any other place, I believe. Not yet. Each of the lords is a king himself, in many ways, and many have Welsh blood and hold to our laws. But"—he shrugged—"they've more to do with England, by necessity. And we're too close to the border here. I'd not risk tales getting out."

"Ah. Wise."

"It would be a bitter thing to meet with trouble so near the end, though logic would say I should comfort myself, in that case, with what I did accomplish."

"Which is plenty." She heard *the end* mostly without pain, even with gladness. Who wouldn't look forward to an end to roaming, to roadsides and flea-infested inns and, foremost, to the hunters who had dogged their steps with supernatural persistence? She did. It had been pure chance that the journey had as much good in it as it had.

She would miss the good. She missed things at times, but the world spun onward.

Besides, it would have taken a harder woman than her

to feel sorrow in the face of Madoc's obvious joy. He was quiet about it, and he'd not been melancholy elsewhere, but a light had come into his eyes when he crossed the border that Moiread hadn't seen before. She'd caught him whistling that morning.

She knew the feeling. Her home was far away, but she remembered her own joyful return and was glad to be out of England. Knowing the English ruled in Wales weighed more lightly than she'd thought it would, just as it had been easier than she'd thought to cope with the farmer's son's slights on her people.

And it was a beautiful land.

Meadows and trees spread out on either side of them, liquid emerald in the early-summer sun, with gray stones here and there. White sheep and black cows dotted the hillsides, with men and boys and dogs occasionally taking an interest in them. Even the dull gray of cottages and the brown of plowed fields blended well, grounding notes among the brighter colors.

The shape of the buildings, the dress of the people, and the voices she heard were all different from those in Scotland. She supposed that the plants weren't quite the same either, to those who cared about such things, and the hills weren't as high or as steep. Compared to many places, though, and particularly to England, her surroundings were very much like home.

"It's a pretty place," she said, gesturing around with one hand as they were riding one afternoon.

"Loveliest the world over, I'd say," Madoc replied, his returning smile tilting the edges of his eyes, "but then, I'll never pass as impartial."

"That'll likely make you a good lord."

"If I'm careful," he said and then shook his head at

her frown. "I've not grown morbid about our chances of coming through this, no, nor my likelihood of inheriting. It's only that there's a balance needed, yes? Between loving your own land and seeing it clearly, the rotten parts as well as the sweet. Or between tending to your land, your people, and seeing the wider world and your place in it. A lord might grow unwise, else."

"Aye, that's so."

Madoc smiled, more abashed than he'd ever looked while naked. "I didn't mean to give you a lecture."

"You didn't," said Moiread, who'd mostly been thinking about how easily he'd read her face—wondering how she felt about that, and how she should try to feel. She considered what he'd said, felt the weight of it balance in her mind, then nodded slowly. "Being a man as well as a dragon. So to speak. I'd agree, but mind, I've had few lessons, not being the heir or even the second."

The conversation brought back memories: herself, Cathal, Agnes, and her cousin Erik, answering questions under Artair's gimlet eye or learning from Douglas the knowledge he'd devoured far earlier. She recalled books edged with gold leaf, wet days in front of the fire, the restlessness of pent-up youth. Douglas had been and was the young laird, but misfortune happened to MacAlasdairs as well as human men—and besides, Agnes and mayhap Moiread would need an eye on their husbands' estates.

That line of argument had been singularly unconvincing when she was ten.

Ten had been a *very* long time ago.

"I've had too many, I sometimes think," said Madoc, "and few of them formal. Books, mostly, and watching my father or Gilrion...and spending a great deal of time going over the matter, so that I may be best prepared when it comes my turn."

"Is that why the magic?"

He tilted his head minutely from side to side. "I like that for itself. There's a pattern to it and a richness, like a good poem or a song. But then, I also like magic for what it can do to aid us in this world. And there are patterns in lordship too. I was young when I began to learn of them both," Madoc added. "They may have spun themselves together in my mind."

"Young, hmm?" Moiread asked. "You're not far from it now. But then, you're not as mortal as you first let us think. Does your bloodline make aging as slow as ours does?"

"A terribly personal question, that," Madoc teased, lips quirking at the corners. "But I think to a lesser extent. I didn't look fifty, last I had a mirror to hand, but nobody with sight would think me eighteen either. My father's coming to the end of his days"—he crossed himself, though he spoke with acceptance rather than grief—"but he's more than twice my age, and hale enough to be lord in truth as well as name."

Visio dei had its disadvantages, but it did show quite plainly that all of those Madoc and Moiread encountered on the road were human. Madoc thought that he was learning to read it. He had a vague notion that the colors around a person glowed brighter when they were upset or excited, that violence would darken them and evil acts warp them.

There was one man they passed, middle-aged and harmless to all appearances, who rode in a grayish cloud that might have once had violet patches. Madoc kept his hand on his sword, and when the man passed without any move toward them, Madoc tried not to wonder what the stranger had done—or might yet do. If he'd known the auras better, been more certain of the meanings, Madoc might have pursued him, but he couldn't kill a man on such scarce evidence, and he was on his own quest. Another would have to intervene down the road, if intervention became necessary.

On the other hand, the vision did let him relax around the group of pilgrims they encountered. Six men, one of their wives, and her maid were making the journey to Holywell. All seemed to be enjoying the journey and the chance-met company as well. They were quick to offer food, conversation, and particularly wine, of which Madoc drank only enough to be polite, as it was barely watered.

The colors around the pilgrims ran clear as light through stained glass, a few faint shadows signifying perhaps a tendency toward temper or a hint of business done sharper than conscience could wish. They were simple folk, and merry. Madoc easily turned the few questions they asked back toward them, so that they talked of the pilgrimage and the wool trade, told stories and sang.

He joined in the songs, and to his mild surprise, so did Moiread. Her voice was strong and sweet, though she stumbled a little over a few words and only hummed along when the verses were in Welsh. The pilgrim with the lute eyed her after one song.

"You're lucky to have broken so, boy," he said and added with a sly grin, "and luckier that you weren't in the East a few years younger." He made a snipping gesture with his free hand. The other men, Madoc included, winced.

"Do they really?" asked one of the younger men. "They couldn't."

"The Crusaders said it," said the lute player. "Men

who were at Constantinople when it fell. Would you doubt them?"

"Perhaps 'tis I should be making a pilgrimage," Moiread replied. As it had from the beginning, her accent drew a few sideways looks, but nobody commented.

"At least light a candle or two in thanks," Madoc offered, with a shudder that he didn't have to exaggerate much.

He was glad of their company, glad of the vision that let him accept it with an open heart, and glad to be seeing his homeland through magical eyes as well as mortal ones. As they went on, the faint glow of the trees and meadows seemed to be calling to him, welcoming him back. He saw the vibrant shades of new life in the springtime and the darker solidity of the earth that had always been there, the brighter glow of beasts and the varied colors of the people. All was familiar from using the *visio dei* before, but all seemed different here and now.

When they'd left the main road and the pilgrims behind, Moiread glanced over toward him. "The country's the best place for it."

"That it is." Cities and castles made using the *visio dei* difficult. With large numbers of people about, Madoc had found that he might spot someone if he was particularly looking for them, but otherwise people tended to blur, and it was hard to look directly at them. Nor could he sustain such vision for nearly as long. "Here in particular."

"That partiality again?"

"Yes. I wish I could show you…or that you could see for yourself, were we not worried about attacks. I can only imagine what it'll be like at home. You should see the lands there, even normally."

When Moiread smiled, Madoc realized that he'd come close to babbling. He truly did need to leave the vision aside when he was in exalted company, but Moiread didn't seem to mind. Her voice was warm when she answered: "I expect that I will. I'm with you to the end, remember?"

THIRTY-FOUR

By NOW, ARRIVING AT A CASTLE FELT ALMOST ROUTINE. Llanasef Fechan was only the third keep Moiread and Madoc had specifically journeyed to, but the prickly uneasiness Moiread had felt at Hallfield had diminished greatly during their journey. She could watch levelly as servants led Madoc off to meet with the lord his kin, while others took Moiread toward the barracks. Any danger that awaited Madoc within the castle's walls was not one Moiread could prevent by being at his side.

She prayed for his safety. She had a vague idea, one she'd no wish to examine closely, of how it would hurt were anything to happen to him. Yet the die was cast. She could do nothing. With any luck, she wouldn't need to. The lord was of Madoc's blood, and though that didn't always count for much, he'd agreed long ago to the alliance.

Moiread surrendered their horses to the grooms gladly—there were no longer treasures in their saddlebags, another weight off her mind—and then ventured out into the courtyard.

Llanasef Fechan sprawled low and long across the hilltop, the gray stone walls letting more sun across them than Moiread was used to. Each of the four towers had statues carved into the stone at its corner: graceful maidens in robes to the east and west, warriors with spears to the north and south. The work was impressive, though she was no artist to judge.

Otherwise, the keep was like others: well, chapel,

stables, buttery, smithy, stores, and a good population of people occupying it. Some hurried on errands. Others, like the men her guide was leading her toward, stood leaning against one wall, enjoying the sunlight and chatting.

Introductions came next: Alan, Tomos, and Luc, the man who'd led Moiread over. All were middling young and healthy-looking. All wore swords at their waists and armor on their backs. Tomos had a broken nose, which Alan quickly explained was the result of a fight over a horse, and not to be mistaken for any heroic scar.

They welcomed Moiread easily, called her "boyo" and treated her as a slightly younger brother, speaking to her the way she remembered addressing the raw recruits when she'd been at war.

The memory made her blink. Those days seemed a long time ago, and further away than the length of England and Wales would have sensibly explained.

"All right, then?" asked Alan. "Not wearing you out, are we?"

Moiread laughed. "Only trying to get my bearings. After so long on horseback, part of me still thinks the ground should be moving, aye?"

"Boats are worse," Luc said and talked for a while about his cousin who'd sailed to Italy with his lord. They passed around a skin of wine, very weak—none of them were on duty then, but it would be their turn in a few hours, and the commander ran things tightly—and compared stories, most of them exaggerated, until a new arrival made them straighten up.

The boy was perhaps fourteen, with a youth's spidery arms and legs. His straw-colored hair fell in a page's cut, a neater version of the sort Moiread herself had, and the rich blue-and-yellow color of his clothes, as well as the jeweled dagger at his waist, spoke of rank. He stood on no ceremony, though; his face was all eager openness.

"Hallo!" he said, his voice in the wavery in-between stage. "Are you Lord Madoc's man?"

"Aye, m'lord," Moiread said and bowed. "I'm Michael."

"And this is Iestyn," said Tomos. "My lord's eldest son and heir."

"I hope," said Iestyn, painful with memorized dignity no matter how much he clearly wanted to skip the preliminaries, "that you and your master find our hospitality to your liking."

"I'm sure we will. You've been quite kind to us already, m'lord."

"I'm glad to hear it." Iestyn hesitated, while his father's arms men deliberately did not look amused, and then came out with "You're a Scot, yes?"

"That I am." It seemed pointless to try to hide it. Nobody would ever mistake Moiread for Welsh once they heard her—nor, thank God, for English.

Iestyn looked her over, trying to be subtle, clearly a shade disappointed in her apparent youth. "Were you a soldier? Did you fight the English?"

"Oh, a bit. I'm older than I look, but I was too young to fight until the last few years of it."

Iestyn's dark eyes widened. Even the men-at-arms looked impressed. "I'd heard it was hard fighting, that," Alan said.

"Hard as any I've had. I've not a great deal of comparison, y'ken."

She honestly hadn't. There'd been raids in her youth. She'd gone on a few. But that had been theft and brawling—and once in a while a killing when events got truly bitter or out of control. War had been different. She hadn't expected how different it would be.

"What was it like?" Iestyn asked. "Where did you fight? Did you kill many Englishmen? Was it all with a sword, or did you have a lance too?"

"We *are* English subjects, boyo," Tomos said dryly. "You should perhaps sound a little less gleeful."

For the moment, said Iestyn's snort. At twelve, he was already too wise to speak those words aloud. "I'm only curious. I've never seen a battle."

Moiread's first thought was that he was too young for it—but there'd been plenty of boys his age fighting at her side, or carrying arrows and water to those who did fight. Besides, they were all young. "Messy things. They serve their purpose at times. And I was mostly a swordsman. Horses dinna' care for me."

"Oh, that's a pity. I've a white mare of my own—my lord my father gave her to me on my birthday—and she canters as sound as anything."

"You and Lord Madoc should get on well, then."

Iestyn smiled with a boy's good cheer. "Good! He'll likely be my brother, after all."

Bronwyn was sixteen years old, short, slender, and pale, with dark hair drawn up into smooth, round cauls on either side of her long, oval face, and big, dark eyes that regarded Madoc with calm politeness. She'd made her curtsy well when they met, the dark-blue folds of her gown falling in graceful lines, and smiled at him with a well-born maiden's proper demureness.

"My eldest," Lord Elian had said. "My treasure."

Walking alongside them in the castle gardens, with Elian's wife, Teleri, on his right hand, Madoc was aware of how the four of them fell into pairs. Young Iestyn had run off after making his greeting—as quickly as manners and his father's rule would allow. Guests from afar might be interesting, but the ceremony of the first meeting generally was not, at twelve.

The fifth among them did nothing to disrupt the pattern. Signor Antonio was a scholar but no priest. He was older than Madoc but in healthy, well-fleshed middle age, with no trace of gray in his thick black hair. In a saturnine way, he was handsome. Yet as he walked the gardens with them, a tall, solid figure in his dark, high-collared robes, there was nothing about him that suggested romance. Indeed, he seemed set apart from the other four and from Llanasef Fechan itself. Perhaps his faint accent gave that impression, or his studies had lent him a cosmopolitan air.

Madoc was glad for the scholar's presence, as another outsider to the family, and glad for what he heard shortly after the women took themselves off to a bench in the corner of the garden and left him, Elian, and Antonio to speak. "Antonio will be aiding us," Elian said. "I have some knowledge of the art, but no gift, much to my sadness."

Unlike Calhoun, he sounded truly regretful. His line was mortal, but many of them had at least dabbled in sorcery over the years. It was one reason why they'd long been friends with Rhys and his forefathers. Such shared gifts tended to produce either love or hate—or often both, varying with time and tide. Madoc could only be thankful that the alliance with Elian had been steady, and now that he had a skilled man on hand to help.

Llanasef Fechan was close in feeling to Madoc's land, but it was not his. Subtle differences could do more to trip up a magician—particularly in such significant rites—than vast gaps that a man could easily see and avoid. Madoc had been tempted to keep the *visio dei* in effect, that he might better learn the land that way, but his first view of the castle in that sight had nearly crossed his eyes with the confusion of motion and color. He also wished no distraction around folk who would not understand it and could well take offense.

"Then you have my most heartfelt thanks," he said, with a small bow in the scholar's direction. "And I'll try to keep myself from asking too many questions. It isn't often I have a chance to compare learning in these matters."

"Ah," Antonio said with a careless flick of his hand, "my lord flatters me by asking my aid, and I will do what I can, but my learning is small. A few books here and there, a master met by chance in my life... I expect I would have as many questions for you as you for me. But in working together, we will assuredly each learn a great deal."

"Oh, of that I'm certain," said Madoc.

"And perhaps we may all talk at our leisure," Elian suggested. "I've some wine from France, a decent vintage. After we dine, there may be time for two men of learning and one eager listener to enjoy it and to speak of many things."

"I would by no means impose on your time more than I've done already, my lord," said Madoc, smiling, "but that sounds like more than a pleasant way to pass an evening. Though I would not take you from your family."

Mother and daughter were talking quietly. Green branches dipped over them, almost touching the white linen top of Teleri's headdress. Sunlight speckled the scene with flecks of gold. Looking at the pair, Elian smiled fondly. "Were it more than an evening, I would be most loath to go. But we can all spare each other for so short a time. You will be here for several days, yes?"

"If you're gracious enough to harbor me so long."

"Then we can both pass a great deal of time in the ladies' company." His smile took on a significance, though a sincere and wholesome one, that made Madoc once more aware of how they were paired with the women. "And my son will have a chance to plague your serving man. He *is* Scottish, yes?"

"Oh yes," said Madoc.

"Don't worry." Elian clapped him on the shoulder. "I know well that any ideas Iestyn gets into his brain are likely his own fault. My boy was a shade bloodthirsty before you ever approached my gates. God willing, the stories will sate him for a few years yet."

"Such are the ways of boys," Madoc agreed with a laugh. He had to force it, though, and he wondered at Elian's sudden reassurance.

Truly, the reminder that Moiread was to all appearances a man now, and the hindrances that created, were uncomfortable. Still, Madoc had passed more than a few nights celibate before, and the world went on. As for Iestyn or the other men, surely Moiread could look after herself.

Even so, Madoc glanced off toward the main castle when he could, seeking a woman he knew he wouldn't see, and wondered what she was about.

THIRTY-FIVE

AT DINNER, MADOC STILL WONDERED. MOIREAD SAT A SHORT distance away at one of the lower tables, but too far for him to speak to her or overhear what she said to her companions. She looked in good humor. She smiled and laughed with her companions and talked easily, making lively gestures with her hands.

They'd bought good clothing on the road, replacing both that which they'd ruined at the inn and that which they'd had to leave behind on Rhuddem's death. Moiread wore a cream-colored linen tunic trimmed with green, along with green hose. Her hair, grown out of its crop over their journey, was neatly tied back.

Even though her illusion of masculinity was firmly in place, Madoc felt desire stir as he watched her. The gestures were hers: the flash of her eyes, the way she turned her head, the outward flick of a hand to dismiss a point. The rich darkness of her hair was unchanged, and the brilliance of her eyes. He knew her true form—both of them—and seeing her as a man now, he realized, held the additional thrill of secrecy, of knowing what those around her couldn't guess.

"Lord Madoc?" Teleri spoke gently, calling his attention back to the table.

"Ah, I'm sorry. I just…wanted to be sure Michael was having no trouble. Not that your men would give any, I'm sure."

"I'd like to think not," said Elian. "The pair of you must

have had a hard time of it, though, if you came through England. Bitter feelings there, I'd think."

"Some, yes," said Madoc. "We kept to ourselves as much as we could. Michael tried to speak rarely."

"Did they offer you insult?" Iestyn asked. "Did you fight?"

"Some, but nothing dire," said Madoc. "On both counts. Michael broke a man's nose, I believe, but that was hard to avoid."

"Didn't you want to?" Before Iestyn could say more, he caught a quelling glance from his father and fell silent.

"Wanting's no part of it," Madoc replied. "We had to get ourselves here, didn't we now? Besides, the wars are done for both our countries. Two men on their own would have been fools to try to start them up again."

"I should like to think," said Bronwyn, speaking for the first time during the meal other than pleasantries, "that no man would be fool enough to begin another war. Not in our lifetime, I pray, and not after."

"Would you have the English foot on our necks for all time?" Iestyn blazed up, whether out of patriotism or the chance to needle his sister Madoc wasn't entirely sure.

"It's been there all my lifetime, and it doesn't weigh so heavily to be worth the hardship of lifting it. The trouble with you," Bronwyn added, "is that you're too young to believe anything but the most romantic of stories."

"Oh? Well, the trouble with you—"

"Enough," said Elian. "Disgrace our house in front of a guest any more, and it'll go badly for you both. Madoc, I ask your pardon for my children."

"Not at all," Madoc said. "I've heard worse arguments from men three times their age."

"Ah, you've been at a court or two in your day," said

Signor Antonio, getting a general laugh from the table. "What *would* you counsel, Lord Madoc? Prudence or boldness?"

"I am, thank God, not likely to be the one deciding," he replied. "Lives and land both hang on such choices. I would not spend them lightly, but neither would I hoard them when spending can gain a people's freedom. What say you, sir?"

"Ah." Antonio spread ringed hands, his smile deferential. "But I am a foreigner, and my own people more the conquerors than the conquered. My views mean little. Man is born to submit. It is only a matter of knowing the right master. That's as much as I would dare to say."

Later he said more, but not of politics. In Elian's solar, drinking good red wine, they spoke of angels, spirits, and demons. Madoc argued for the French translation of *Liber Sacer*, the grimoire from which he'd learned much of what Gilrion's court had not taught him. Antonio held firm for the Latin and mentioned something called the *Secret Book of Raquiel*, which he'd read in Greek but sadly not brought with him.

From there, they moved to the details of the ritual proper, working out the day and hour, who should stand where, and how far away the guards should be. "I would have Lady Bronwyn as our fourth," Antonio said. "I know Iestyn's your heir, my lord, but a boy his age is young to be given such a weighty task."

Elian nodded. "Time enough for such things when he has a cooler head on his shoulders. Bronwyn will do well. Besides," he added with a smile at Madoc, "the last I spoke with your father, he believes it might be best for us both if she had some part in binding our lands."

"Truly?" Madoc asked, hearing the blatant second meaning to Elian's words. The patterns he'd sensed that afternoon were real, then. As in Gilrion's court, he was not particularly surprised. Courtesy and duty drew a smile from him, and he was saying, "It is an honor for you to consider such a request, sir," before he'd even thought the words.

"We can speak about it more after the rite," Elian said. "Best to complete one task at a time, when God gives us such luxury."

Sleep should have been easy. Long practice had left Moiread far from picky about her bed, and this one was likely to have clean bedding, warm blankets, and a whole roof overhead. She'd done considerably worse. She'd been on the road all day. By rights, she should have been dozing in her plate at the meal, as she'd almost done on the night when she'd met Madoc.

After an evening of trying not to watch him, of smiling, laughing, and not turning her head to note when he left the room with Lord Elian, of responding with polite interest to comments about his likely marriage, she knew she'd only spend hours tossing restlessly.

Taking sword and whetstone, she left the hall and found herself a bench up against the castle wall, just beneath one of the towers. She was far from the only person in the courtyard. Servants went back and forth, extinguishing fires and sweeping rushes, and carrying plates of food back to the kitchens. Men-at-arms went up to their duty on the walls, or came back for their own meal and bed. A few glanced at Moiread. She nodded greetings, and they raised no alarm.

Pools of yellow light dotted the dark courtyard, shining out of open windows and doors. People with candles or lanterns made smaller, moving sparks. Around them all, the castle loomed, a collection of great dark shapes, and the stars shone impassively above. A crescent moon cut a slim slice out of the blackness.

Madoc would, of course, marry the girl. Bronwyn was no fairy princess with two other suitors, playing out a game for her mother's pride. Nor was she a child whose father distrusted magic. She was a lady of Madoc's own people: beautiful, young, virtuous, and a possible link in a wise alliance. Moiread could see nothing to impede the match.

It was none of her affair.

She scraped the stone up one side of her blade. It was a good sword. It took an edge well, balanced nicely, had a fine grip. She'd trusted it for years. It had served her well, save when it was too large for the fight at hand, as it had been in the inn.

As I am, she thought. *As we all may be soon*. On the battlefield, the MacAlasdairs in true form were creatures of awe and terror. That had served well when the world was a wilder place. It was useful still in some battles, when their side didn't need horses or could work around them. Those fights were getting rarer.

Ah, yes, Moiread mocked herself. *The time may come when all I'll be is stronger than most men and much harder to kill. Such sad days are at hand.*

All the same, she felt a pang at the idea of her other form being useless, dwindling to an interesting relic like the Roman ruins and the burial mounds of the old Celts. It was a night for pangs. It was a night for self-pity.

Moiread tried to shake off the feeling the way she'd often done with melancholy—by turning her attention to her task and her senses. She concentrated on the regular scraping whisk of metal on stone, on the footsteps of those crossing the courtyard and the low barking of the castle dogs as they fought over scraps, and then on the singing of night birds in the distance.

Then she heard the voices from the window above her.

They were quiet. She didn't think any human would have heard them coherently, and she hadn't done so until she began to listen. One was young, female, and noble— most likely Bronwyn, unless Teleri sounded young for her years.

"I like him. I hadn't expected that."

"That isn't wholly a misfortune, signorina," came the second voice, low and male, with a hint of Italy in the softness of his final vowels and the fluidity of the words themselves. "As he is here, and the marriage looks likely. A bride should like her groom when she can."

"But I still have my fears."

Under the window, Moiread wondered if she was overhearing a nervous girl's talk with her confessor. She hesitated, stone idle in her hand, thinking that she should perhaps go, when she heard the man's reply.

"I share them. But if it is to be marriage, that opens other doors. Many a man has taken his wife's counsel to heart. Many a man and his land have done better thereby."

That did not sound like worries about the wedding night. Moiread slowly and quietly re-sheathed her sword, but didn't stand up yet. If Bronwyn hoped to sway Madoc, it would be best if Moiread—and perhaps Madoc and Artair—knew what she wanted.

She waited and heard in time a faint, accepting sigh. "And he doesn't seem unreasonable, thank God, nor like a man who delights in war. It's only that I never believed matters would truly get so far."

"Alas, child," the man replied, responding to the faint note of accusation in Bronwyn's voice. "It is only the

Almighty who sees all, or can do all. Whatever we may have hoped, he is now here. A wise carpenter uses the branch he has and does not lament the tree he imagined. If you are to deal in power, and I believe you will, you must learn such lessons."

"Yes, I see that."

"Trust in God. Trust in your father. And trust in me, hmm? You may like the man and marry him. All will be well."

"Thank you," said Bronwyn.

"It is my duty and my pleasure, signorina. Now...to your chambers. You've a guest to delight tomorrow."

Moiread also made for her bed, thinking all the while. The conversation was *probably* harmless, or at least not urgent. Bronwyn feared war, or that Madoc was preparing for it, but he was cautious about the whole matter himself. They might work well together in that respect.

They might work well together in general.

As Moiread walked the last few steps to her bed, she was tired indeed.

THIRTY-SIX

IN THE ABSENCE OF OTHER GUESTS OF RANK, MADOC SHARED A chamber with Iestyn. The boy's two younger brothers were babes in cradles, sleeping but a few steps from their mother, so his quarters had the most room and the least noise. The bed was a comfortable one. The lad slept soundly, barely turning over as Madoc slipped into the room and stole over to stand beside the window.

It had been a long day and a late night. Madoc's very bones felt heavy. Still, there was more work for him to do. A wise man learned his surroundings as soon as possible, in every possible way. Moiread, sleeping in the hall below, would have agreed. The thought of her let Madoc summon the will to stay awake a little while longer.

Vislo del, he whispered into the quiet night air. The spirits came at once, changing his sight of the world around him. Neither walls nor furnishings showed any color, but Iestyn's small form slumbered inside an orange-and-gold aura of surpassing vibrancy. The boy's personality might have played a part in that, or the general vigor of youth. Either way, he practically lit the room like a fire. Smaller, duller sparks studded the walls and bedding: insects, rats, and other creatures best not thought about too closely. Elian's servants clearly changed the rushes often—and kept anything biting out of the bedclothes, as far as Madoc could tell—but nature was generally inescapable.

Llanasef Fechan was built low, so the room was not far above the ground. Outside the window, Madoc could see the faint but healthy green glow of grass and fields, the deeper and more enduring color of the trees, and as with the vermin in the castle, the dim presence of animal life. None of the brighter auras of humankind entered his view, which was natural so late at night. Anyone awake, save the guards on the wall above him, was likely to be inside.

That was sight taken care of.

Madoc put his hands flat on the windowsill, curling his fingers around the ridges and gaps of the stone. With a deep breath, he called up the simplest of his power and sent it out into the land—not trying to bind or mark, simply to become familiar, as a new lord might ride out to see the fields and forests in his charge.

It was familiar, this land, even if it wasn't his home. Madoc knew the feel of it: milder and wetter than Scotland had been, and more welcoming to men, or at least more used to them. Magically, it gave more easily on the surface, clay rather than rock, but a deeper layer budged only reluctantly. A wise magician also learned that the initial give was deceptive. The power in the land closed back in quickly, resuming its former shape with a slow, persistent strength.

Always, with magic as with men, it was better to persuade than to force. In Hallfield and at Loch Arach, that persuasion had been an almost businesslike matter: simple offers, negotiation, and final acceptance. At Llanasef Fechan, the exchange would be more akin to the playing of a song. As a ballad could move men's hearts to valor or sorrow, Madoc would make the native power feel that he and his were worthy of loyalty—even of friendship, if a nonhuman force could reason in such terms.

The land's power was only half of the matter, of course. Elian and his bloodline were another matter, one for which Madoc had less idea of the best tactics. They would be deliberately meeting his will with theirs, which would make things easier, but Madoc knew that magic could also respond to what a man felt, even if he wouldn't admit it.

Or a woman, he thought. Bronwyn had made her views clear. They were wise enough, and Madoc agreed somewhat, but he couldn't promise her that there would be no war. His quest was in part a preparation against any such eventuality, after all, and there seemed at least one among the English who took defense as aggression. If her doubts were strong enough when she entered the ritual, they could cause problems.

Courting her might help. He'd already agreed to the marriage, or not disagreed with it. If he played the ardent suitor, affection could overcome Bronwyn's worries.

He'd have little time to do that. And it seemed dishonest to try to sway the girl by the heart, particularly when—

—when he had no such feelings for her. Oh, she was lovely, well-mannered, and intelligent, as far as he could tell. If their fathers were both in assent, Madoc would be foolish as well as insolent to act like the stripling hero of a bad song. As a wife, Bronwyn was all a man could reasonably wish for.

He wished for Moiread, which was not reasonable.

The prospect wasn't *unthinkable*. Madoc had been considering that on their approach to Llanasef Fechan. Her father was a wealthy lord, and one of his father's allies. His nonhuman blood might make children possible between them. Indeed, such children might have abilities neither line had yet shown. As a match, it might be wise.

Yet Moiread had lived three times his age. She'd been to war; she'd roamed as she pleased; and she'd soared on high in a shape that put all humans to shame for power and majesty. Asking her to bind herself to him—and to the life of a lady in a mortal castle far from her family, however loose he could make those bonds—seemed almost an act of hubris.

Before talking to Elian, Madoc might have found the courage to speak with her before the end of their journey. But if he incurred Rhys's displeasure and endangered the alliance—no. Offering Moiread a marriage that would please both their families was one thing; begging for her to join him as a wife his father would scorn was another.

Madoc sighed.

He could see no way out. Best to concentrate on what he could do. He turned back to the land, learning its moods and secrets, spending his last energy that way until he was too tired to think.

Moiread had forgotten it was Sunday. Traveling did that. When one of the servants gently nudged her and said that she might want to wash and dress for mass, she had half a mind to grunt and turn back over. Respectability called, though, and it *had* been a while.

Once she'd taken her seat in the castle's chapel, she was glad she'd come. What she could hear of the priest's Latin, slightly muffled by the rood screen and the fact that he faced the altar, bordered on painful at times, but it didn't matter. Moiread knew the words as well as he did and could make up the difference in her mind. The colored light slanting in from the stained-glass windows, the smell of incense, and the chanting songs were all familiar, touchstones in the middle of the alien land and her own mind's confusion.

Her last confession had been in London. She hadn't been nearly as remorseful for most of what she'd done as she probably should have been, and she couldn't summon sorrow over either fornication with Madoc or such murder as defending them from assassins had involved. She trusted that God would understand—and she'd bought enough indulgences in her life to help Him do so. Besides, hell couldn't hold everyone who'd committed such sins. She took communion with a glad, untroubled heart, aware as usual at such moments of a larger pattern beyond even the worlds and forces the MacAlasdairs knew.

After, Moiread felt cleansed and renewed. If the sight of Madoc walking with Lord Elian's family brought a pang or two, well, even the Divine could only do so much with her undoubtedly flawed soul. She smiled, let them go, and followed the general crowd out of the church.

It had been her intention to go up on the walls and look around. Doubtless there was a good view from that height, and the presence of the guardsmen meant there'd also be decent company. She'd turned toward the outer stairs when she heard footsteps approaching her from behind, but conscious of the need to seem human, she waited until she heard her alias before turning.

A dark man in dark robes stood before her. "Your pardon for the interruption, young sir," he said in the same Italian-accented voice that Moiread had heard the night before. "I am Signor Antonio, late of Sicily, now adviser to my lord Elian."

"Michael MacDouglas," Moiread said and bowed.

She'd heard of Antonio in passing, though none of the castle's men had thought him noteworthy enough to comment in any detail. Perhaps, being regulars, they'd not faced the scrutiny of his gaze. His nostrils practically flared as he peered at her. Had she opened her mouth wider, he might have counted her teeth.

"Manservant to Lord Madoc, yes? I hope the two of you have had a pleasant journey."

"Pleasant enough, good sir, especially now that we're enjoying your hospitality. It was passing long, I'll say."

"So I would think. You come from Scotland? Master Iestyn was quite enthusiastic on the subject."

"And bless him for it, for it's the land of my heart."

"You must be quite a warrior, then."

"I do well enough, I like to think." Surreptitiously, she sniffed the air, but if she smelled off, she couldn't tell it underneath the general mixture of courtyard odors. Was it Scotland that drew Antonio's attention? "I hope my lord has had no cause to complain."

"Only the deepest praise has reached my ears, I assure you."

"That would probably be Iestyn," Moiread joked. She'd shared a few of her stories with the boy—the ones that didn't come close to revealing her identity. "Still, it does my heart good to hear what you say...signor, is it?"

Deliberately, she mispronounced the title, letting her accent deepen as well. She doubted that the man had heard of the MacAlasdairs, or that he'd mean them any ill if he did, but he *was* a learned man. Cathal's wife had figured them out from rumors and books.

Politely, Antonio nodded. "Indeed. A scholar, though a minor and specific one. How did you find our mass?"

"A privilege to attend. The chapel is beautiful, and the singers in excellent voice. My Latin's not good enough to follow much wi' the difference in our tongues, I fear, but your priest has a most holy manner to him."

"He does carry himself well, does he not? I've seen few with more bearing, even when I spent time in Rome itself." Antonio glanced over his shoulder, then bowed. "And now

I must be away. My thanks for your conversation, Master Michael, and God give you good day."

"And you, signor."

Moiread headed for the wall and didn't watch him walk away. She wished she could have, but she suspected that he would turn back at some point to watch *her*.

THIRTY-SEVEN

"A MOMENT OF YOUR TIME, MY LORD?"

Moiread paused outside Elian's solar. Within, Madoc lifted his head from his writing. The gladness in his eyes and the genuine warmth of his smile were so welcome that Moiread was almost sure she was imagining them. "Any one you'd like," he said. "Come in."

She did, and closed the door behind her. She'd had a stroke of luck: Elian was hearing a case from one of his tenants; Bronwyn and Teleri were sewing in the garden; and Iestyn had surrendered himself to Antonio's instruction until at least noon. Even the servants were elsewhere.

Mindful both that luck could turn and that sound could carry, Moiread kept her voice low. Quickly she laid out the conversation she'd overheard. When she came to the end, she shrugged. "I can't say there's anything truly sinister in it," she added. She half wished there had been. Knowing as much made her add, "Many a girl goes into marriage thinking to change a man. Girls of rank particularly."

"And it would be no great change." Madoc looked back down at the parchment on his desk. His hair, grown overlong on their journey, fell into his eyes. He absently pushed it back. "As I told you, I'll fight if it seems for the best, and I'll prepare for the day it does, but I'll not rush into spending men's lives."

"Yes," said Moiread, forcing out more words because they hurt, as in practice she'd pushed the sore muscles of the day before. "She's a touch more reticent than you. I don't blame her, with that brother of hers. She may grow to think differently. Or the matter may never arise."

"Yes," Madoc said.

Shadows fell across his face. Outside, one of the servants yelled correction to an underling. Moiread didn't think any but she would have heard it. To a mortal, all would have been silence.

And after all, there was nothing to say.

They were both full grown, neither naive. What Madoc might have felt, what Moiread might have wished he felt, would be of no great matter.

She pressed her palms flat against her sides. He would notice if she clenched her hands.

"And Antonio?" Madoc eventually asked.

"Was only saying what my father would have told me… or what I would have told the girl, for that matter. A bit suspicious of me, I think," she said and briefly outlined their conversation. "But then, I am from Scotland, and if he has no desire to see war, perhaps he fears I'll influence you too greatly. Or perhaps Bronwyn does."

"Odd that Bronwyn would confide in him, isn't it?"

"He seems to be her brother's tutor. He could have been hers. Or he could have been an outsider, and so easy to take her fears to, with less worry that she'd sound disloyal."

"Her fears," Madoc repeated, and frowned. "From what you say, it sounds as though she was hoping the marriage wouldn't come to pass. I'd not marry a woman unwilling."

Moiread's face was hot and cold at the same time. She forced it to calmness, her voice to dispassion, and hoped that she was fooling Madoc. "Unwilling when you hear of an alliance isn't unwilling once you meet the man. She likes you, remember? She said so. Many a couple have started worse."

"I suppose," he said, "there is that."

"Aye. I'd best go. It can't take me long to tell you the state of the horses."

"Have you gone near the horses?" he asked, flashing a smile that hurt worst of all.

No, worse was that he made her laugh, even at that moment. "As close as I have to, to keep up appearances."

She opened the door and stepped out into the hall. There was no place to run, much less hide. She kept her steps even, the sound of her boots on the stone regular and untroubled, as she walked away.

After the footsteps in the hallway had faded away, Madoc leaned back in his chair and closed his eyes. His dinner sat like lead in his stomach; his hands felt too unsteady to hold a pen.

Moiread was right. Protest was useless, and it would be cruel to demand it merely to prove she cared—if she did. They would each survive. They each had their work to do.

Pain was of no particular significance. He took a long breath and slowly let it out.

"Lord Madoc?" Antonio's voice came from the door. "Are you well?"

"Ah," he said, startling a little. "Tired, I fear, though I can't justify it. My lord's hospitality has been most generous. I cannot complain of my rest, and yet—" He raised his hands and let them drop into his lap, illustrating his weariness.

In response, Antonio chuckled sympathetically. Madoc heard footsteps and the *shh* of robes against stone as the other man entered and took a seat. "I think that the calculating of such intricate matters is as tiring in its way as a day's ride. Though perhaps I only wish to think so, since I am more capable of one than of the other."

"I'd be inclined to agree." Madoc opened his eyes and threw himself into conversation. "I hadn't expected you back so soon. Not that I'd complain of the company, but I thought you were valiantly attempting to install a few more words of Latin in Master Iestyn's head."

"Ah, but a wise man chooses his battles, does he not? Or perhaps I see myself confronted with too formidable a foe. After all, none of the trivium can compare with the allure of the training ground on such a day—or perhaps with a real Scotsman and his tales."

"My apologies?"

"The fault is hardly yours. To a martial young mind, Master Michael could only be more intriguing if he had a scar or perhaps an eye patch. And he does in truth seem a valiant young warrior. I hope he had no need to prove as much on the way here."

Moiread was the last person that Madoc wanted to discuss. Still, the scholar was being not only polite but flattering. "A time or two. No serious injury to either of us, thank the saints for that. I did lose a horse, which was a great pity. My current one is no replacement."

Briefly, Madoc considered telling Antonio about the assassins, but held off. He'd told Elian a rough outline, leaving out the demonic elements and the magic. If Antonio's lord wanted him to know, he knew already.

"Then let me extend my admiration to your skills as well," said Antonio. "And how fare your calculations? I confess I'd hoped to come back and find you'd done the greater part of the work, lazy wretch that I am."

"Lazy? No, I'd not say that," Madoc replied. "It's hardly any of your fight, is it? So it's quite generous of you to lend your aid, both here and at the ritual itself. I fear that I'm as yet undecided as to the timing. From what you've been able to tell me, and what I remember, there are no adverse conjunctions in the near future." The stars weren't dramatically favorable either, but a man could wait a year for *that*. Neutral would suffice. "Thursday would be the best for alliance, governed as it is by Jupiter, but that's the better part of a week from now. If need be, Tuesday would suffice, with Mars for protection from foes."

"I'd say you'd be better to make it Thursday." Antonio smiled. "As I am certain that a longer visit would please my lord and his family well."

"You quite set my heart at ease, good sir."

She likes you… Many a couple have started worse.

Madoc shut his eyes briefly, shaking off Moiread's voice in his memory, and then picked up the parchment he'd been working on. "If the day is settled, then we should begin work on the hours. I've started in on the table here. It shouldn't take much longer, I hope."

"You must look forward to being done with all of this," Antonio said.

"Oh…" Madoc shrugged. "I'd not mind staying off a horse for a month or two. But the trip has had rewards other than the obvious. Even if I could have accomplished as much by staying home, I'd not have missed the journey."

"Have a seat, boyo," said Tomos. "It's not so much that you've run *us* ragged, mind, but the body's got a way of deceiving you when you're young, you know. If you don't put up your blade and have a drink, you'll be barely moving by nightfall."

He was right. Moiread had said similar things herself.

Still, she put away the wooden sword with reluctance. For a blessed hour or so, she hadn't thought beyond the next block or thrust. She knew she'd miss that state of mind quickly. There was no getting away to hunt in this castle.

Physically, the rest and shade were welcome. Sweat plastered Moiread's tunic and shirt to her back, stuck her hair to the sides of her neck in straggling bits, and ran down from her forehead to sting her eyes. They'd not practiced in armor, saints be praised.

"What'd you leave behind?" asked one of her previous opponents, a middle-aged man with a large beard.

"What?" Moiread was too tired for politeness, or really for coherent words. She got out half a mumble, half a breath, but the man seemed to understand.

"A man fights like you do when his life's not on the line… He's likely trying to forget something. Either behind or ahead."

He handed her a skin of chilled wine and water, which both quenched Moiread's thirst and bought her time to think. "I'd a girl back home," she said, settling on that first lie Madoc had told about her, back at Hallfield when she'd thought the trip was going to be just another task for her father. "You're right. It's not a matter I like to think on."

"Women," Tomos said sympathetically. "'Tis true they're the source of all evil, and now of my stiff arms tomorrow. But…" he added, seeing a female figure coming toward them from the kitchens, "nothing is as good a cure as a bit of the sickness, you know. Jenny, girl, is that for us?"

The kitchen maid, dark-eyed and buxom, held out a dish of plums. "As you're working so hard in our defense," she said, "and in honor of our guests." She aimed a sideways smile at Moiread, not to mention a significant look from under her long eyelashes.

"Pretty boys that they are," said Tomos, rolling his eyes amiably.

"Both the gift and the company are welcome," Moiread said and made a small courtly bow. "Though I fear we're none of us fair company for a delicate lass right now."

Jenny wrinkled her nose playfully. "You do all seem fair warm. There's a little lake a short way off, you know. It would be easy enough to find, I'm sure."

"If my master needs me for nothing, I may seek it out. I'd not want to distress any of my hosts, aye?"

"Aye," said Jenny, and turned with a sway of her hips.

"As I was saying," said Tomos.

"The lure of the foreign," the man with the mustache said.

Moiread stifled a sigh. The girl was comely. A bit of a kiss and a cuddle might be nice, and there were enough women glad to stop there, with no risk of discovery for Moiread and none of a nine-month burden for them. It might take her mind off Madoc.

It might get *back* to Madoc. She wasn't sure how either of them would feel about that.

She shook her head, mostly to herself, and offered the dish to Tomos. "Have a plum."

THIRTY-EIGHT

As it happened, Moiread went to see the lake after all, but as a guard for Madoc's ritual, and Jenny was nowhere nearby. Tomos noted that fact on the way down and shook his head in mock pity.

"It's likely for the best," Moiread replied. "Keeps my mind on the business at hand, aye?"

They were two of the four guards, all mounted and armed, who would keep watch. That duty included containing Iestyn. While the boy wouldn't take part in the ritual, Elian had said it would be good for him to listen and know the oaths that bound his people. He would wait with the guards, near enough to hear Elian and Madoc's voices when they raised them to take vows. Wide-eyed, he rode with straight back and an evident desire to impress all men and gods who might be watching. Antonio had made clear to him the importance of not interrupting the ceremony. Moiread hoped the warning would hold.

She had to grant that Iestyn, energetic as he was, had been well-behaved enough so far, and also that he rode almost as well as she did, which fell short of Madoc's skill but was better than any member of his father's house other than the guards. Antonio didn't ride at all—four servants carried him on a litter—while Elian and Bronwyn sat on their horses as if they were animate chairs.

Generations before them, most with more worldly aims, had worn the dirt smooth and bare on the broad road they traveled. Elder trees flanked them, flowers white against glossy green leaves, mingled with the solid green of hazel. The sky above was clear, the sun bright. It was going to be hot before the day was out. Whatever hours Madoc and Antonio had calculated, Moiread was glad they meant starting at terce, before the sun was yet high.

"Were there stories about this place before?" she asked Tomos.

"A few. Come bathe at the dawn of the new year, and you'll be healthy all year through. If you don't die of the chill. I think girls see their husband if they look in the water at Midsummer. They may have to be naked."

Iestyn stifled a snicker. Fourteen was like that. Moiread suspected he'd try and hide by the lake in a week or two, possibly bringing a few friends, and all of them probably getting their ears boxed if the stories were true and the girls caught them.

At the end of the trail, the small valley widened. A meadow of high grass, mingled with white clover and yellow buttercup, spread out around a pool no wider than Moiread was tall, but mirror-clear in a way that suggested depth. Butterflies took flight at their approach, shining blue and yellow in the sun.

The guards at the head of the procession fell back to join Moiread, Tomos, and Iestyn, while the ritual party stopped.

"Remember," Elian said to his son, "do as you're told. This is solemn work we're about."

"Yes, my lord," Iestyn said, sounding sincere.

"Good luck," Moiread said.

Madoc smiled. "Thank you," he replied, and briefly it was as if they were the only two present.

Then he turned his horse, Bronwyn at his side, and followed Elian and Antonio up to the lake.

Thoughts of Moiread would be a distraction, as would thoughts of anything but the ritual. Madoc was glad that he'd spent so long learning to concentrate. It had been harder to put Moiread out of his head than it had been anything else in his life as a magician.

He tied his horse to a tree and heard Antonio rising from the litter nearby and giving instructions to his servants. "An hour, no less. Bring wine and food for all of us too."

The scholar spoke wisely. The ritual was not likely to be as taxing as scrying on the assassin's amulet had been, but magic was effort. Madoc almost wished he could have asked for a litter as well, but he possessed no scholar's title to soothe his pride.

He stood in the west: ending, receiving. Elian took his position across from him, with Antonio as the aged north and Bronwyn as the younger, vital south. The pieces began to snap into place: sword into sheath, foot into stirrup, the feel of a thing going where it should to do the job at hand.

Elian stepped forward to the edge of the pool. "Let Earth and Sky, Fire and Water, and all Creation witness what we pledge now. With these holy waters do we swear."

He plunged a golden chalice into the pool and withdrew it, holding it up with water streaming down its sides. The man had some sense of a performance. Madoc also strode forward, and the two met on the edge of the lake, the cup now held between them.

"I, Madoc, heir of Avondos, son of Rhys, son of Aberthol," he began in Latin. The words were the same as he'd used at Hallfield. The power started feeling the same too, but then it went awry—subtly, like a wrong note or a snag in cloth.

Keeping his face blank, Madoc paused as if to take another breath. The flaw was definitely there. It was to do with the binding nature of the oath; he couldn't yet tell precisely what. He did know, though, that he didn't want to risk going further unless he knew more.

"Are they really doing magic?" Iestyn peered over at the four by the lake, their figures shrunken by distance. Their voices traveled as indistinct murmurs, with a few words surfacing here and there. The moment of the actual vows must yet have been in the future. "Like Merlin?"

One of the guards shifted uneasily, not willing either to deny events by the lake or to condemn his lord for hosting them, but clearly uncomfortable discussing it. Moiread thought that the others' hesitation had less to do with the rite itself than with Iestyn. How much had the boy's father told him, and how much did Elian want him knowing at his age?

Her pay didn't depend on Elian's favor, so she answered forthrightly. "Aye. Though I think they're all too sharp to get stuck in a tree for the sake of a woman."

"Yuugh, no." Iestyn's upper lip curled. "Father and Signor Antonio are far too old."

"So was Merlin," Moiread said dryly. A few of the guards snickered at Iestyn's further grimace of disgust.

The horses cropped grass, staining their bits with green slime. Shadow flicked his tail at flies. Returning to a less-disturbing subject, Iestyn asked, "How do they do it?"

"I think they call on the saints, and the archangels, and so on."

"But Father Evan does *that*. And people go on pilgrimages to call on saints when they're sick. And that's not magic."

"No," Moiread replied, mindful that the guards were watching her and also that Iestyn wasn't the most discreet of students. "I think it's in how you do it. A common man begs a saint for a favor. A priest talks with a friend he knows well, and a magician… Well, for him it's like knowing a man at court."

Iestyn worked that out, twisting his fingers in his horse's yellow mane. The guards looked curiously at Moiread. She thought it was only curiosity, but it would do no harm to reinforce her role. "But I'm far from an expert, aye? You could ask Lord Madoc to explain more of it, or Signor Antonio."

"*He* only explains tedious things," Iestyn said, much put-upon as only a stripling expected to learn Latin verbs could be.

"Does he, now? Might it be that you've never asked after the ones that aren't tedious?"

"No." Iestyn made a face. "I asked about the scar on his neck once, and he just said it happened a long time ago and wasn't a fit subject for a young gentleman."

The world paused. Moiread chose her words carefully, sounding as casual as she could. "Scar on his neck, you say?"

"Oh yes. About here." Iestyn tapped his collarbone. "A whole ring. The robes mostly hide it, but I talk with the pages, and Alan—not the guard, but the boy who brings water for baths—has seen it plenty. That's how I know. But Signor Antonio won't tell me."

Any man could have a scar on his neck. But Moiread recalled the questions Antonio had asked and the conversation she'd overheard, and she felt her other shape flex and roar within her. Still she hesitated, not knowing the truth and afraid to disrupt the rite—until a surge of power twisted itself on the hill. One of the human outlines there started to blur and twist.

"What in God's name?" Tomos asked, seeing it too.

"Nothing in God's." Moiread kicked out of her stirrups and leapt off Shadow. "Get the boy to safety. The castle, if you can make it. If not, find distance and cover from the air. *Now*."

She slapped the gelding's rump hard, and he bolted away. The slap was almost unnecessary, since the horse was already nervous. He scented the transformation to come.

Madoc didn't have long. Even having started the ritual so recently, he'd invoked power. A stone falling downhill became harder to stop with each passing second, and so it was with a spell that had not reached its end. More than that, the other three participants would notice his hesitation before too much time had passed. If they doubted him, their concentration could waver, making the whole endeavor harder.

Quickly he reached out. The power tied into the land. He'd grown familiar with the land over his evenings at the castle, so navigation was a simple enough matter. *There*, near him, was a loop when there should be a straight line, so to speak. Madoc tugged gently, but the entanglement didn't budge.

On closer inspection, it felt as if the flaw in the magic would also catch Antonio, standing next to him. The exact structure, and thus the way through, remained unclear. Antonio's face was blank with focus, and Madoc didn't want to alarm him.

He needed better vision. He could manage that.

"*Visio dei*," he breathed.

As his vision changed, he felt a sudden rush of power toward him. A snag at one end had come loose. Warmth rushed through the land and out of the pool, spreading out around the four of them. Outlines shivered. Grass, trees, and sky all took on sharper edges, more brilliant colors.

Antonio staggered. Catching the motion, Madoc turned, only to stand aghast at what the spirits revealed.

A red line twined through the earth and around Madoc's foot, growing up his leg like a vine. The other end lay just out of Antonio's reach.

It lay, indeed, in the dark, glittering shadow that surrounded him, the same sort that hovered over Moiread: wings, tail, serpent's neck. *Dragon.*

The shadow writhed. The neck twisted, sending the head open-jawed toward the sky. Antonio bared his teeth and hissed at the air, ignoring the three faces gaping at him in alarm.

Then his shadow flexed, rippled, and flowed like oil over his body.

THIRTY-NINE

As it had with Moiread, the change happened fast. Antonio vanished into his shadow. Madoc had a moment to see his outline flicker, and there was a dragon in his place, a vast blood-red beast larger than Madoc remembered Moiread being. Crouched, it snarled again.

"Oh, God in heaven defend us," Elian said, his voice barely louder than a whisper.

God was providing neither defense nor information, leaving Madoc unsure what to do. Draconic form didn't necessarily mean malice, as he knew well, and as suspicious as the red strand between them had looked, there might be an innocent explanation. "Antonio," he began, raising a hand.

He barely had enough warning to duck. Claws like short swords slashed by a hair's width above his head. The dragon hissed in frustration, then drew its head back. Madoc glimpsed a huge coal-black eye, shining with predatory rage, and saw the chest beneath the crimson scales swell.

Fire.

Darting sideways, grabbing his sword from its sheath and knowing it would do little good against the monster, Madoc knew quickly and too late that he'd been wrong—not about the fire, but about the target. Antonio's long neck pivoted with a speed no man used to natural creatures could have expected. Opening his immense jaws, he spat a stream of white-hot flame toward Elian.

The air singed around the fire. Madoc could smell it, just as he could hear Bronwyn's shriek of anguish. He spun, sword in hand, sure that he couldn't help and that he would see his host's death shortly before his own, but not knowing any better path to take. Elian wouldn't believe himself abandoned; perhaps that would matter.

Crossing over the edge of the lake, the fire sent up a cloud of steam, though it was higher than the water. Madoc couldn't make it out clearly, but for a moment it looked like the flame had to push its way through an invisible barrier. It gathered and slowed, and in that was Elian's salvation.

The lord couldn't dodge the flame entirely, but he'd already been in motion at the moment Antonio had attacked him. The delay carried him to the edge of the fire, which only licked at his trailing leg. Had he not been by the pool, that would have been small mercy indeed, for his clothing caught instantly, but he flung himself into the water, screaming but alive.

"Follow him!" Madoc yelled. He couldn't see Bronwyn, nor did he have time to turn and look. He could only trust that she'd take his advice, and hope he could buy her enough time to manage it.

He threw his dagger, aiming for the dragon's eye, and almost hit it. Antonio swung his head back around toward Madoc, though, and the blade bounced off the scales of his jaw, not even scratching them as far as Madoc could see.

A quick leap sideways saved Madoc from another pass of the claws. He stabbed in their wake. This time, steel did carve through scales to flesh, and Antonio's blood spilled to smoke on the grass. The dragon roared with what Madoc wished he could believe was serious pain, but he knew from his memory of Moiread's healing that the sound was more likely to be wrath.

For certain, the wound didn't stop Antonio. He lunged, and the tree Madoc sheltered behind swayed under the force of the attack. The gashes in its bark went almost to the center; it would not hold much longer. Neither, Madoc was sure, would he.

The change was swifter and more painful than Moiread had thought it would be. She'd pushed herself to what she'd thought was her limit, but the magic she'd felt spread outward and got behind her will, shoving her into her dragon shape. Thus aided, it hurt like the devil. In a few heartbeats, Moiread could have sworn she felt every claw rip through flesh, every muscle surge and expand.

Her bones lengthened and hollowed.

Her body expanded, taking on matter from *elsewhere* and weaving it into her shape.

Skin became scales. Teeth lengthened and sharpened within a long mouth, around a forked tongue. Spines and wings tore themselves out of Moiread's back. She screamed in pain. In dragon form, it became a roar that shook the trees around her.

If Iestyn and his guards hadn't gotten themselves away, that would surely have sent them running. Moiread couldn't move to check. Pain held her captive. Then instinct brought her up on her hind legs, slashing at the air and roaring.

Fire burned deep in her belly. When the smell of smoke filled her nostrils, Moiread first thought that it was coming from her. Then she saw the cloud rise over the pool, the flame flickering under it, and the great, dark shape from which it spread. The smaller figures outside the pool ran back and forth as the other dragon moved. One of them screamed.

Madoc.

The fire was nothing to the rage. It started in Moiread's chest and kindled across her body. Pain vanished in its wake. Thought nearly followed. She was in the air before she was conscious of either leaping or spreading her wings, arrowing up out of the meadow and over toward the ring around the pool.

Wind streamed past her. Her wings beat like thunder. Flocks of birds fled screaming from her path.

The shape had its own will. When the air grew thick around her, slowing her progress, Moiread's first impulse was to snap at it. Her teeth closed painfully on empty space. This was no solid barrier, nor a natural one.

She strained against it, using every muscle in her shape to its fullest, but the air grew thicker as she got closer. Before long, she needed all her strength to stay aloft.

Magic. The ritual had begun. Doubtless it had its own protections, and the land would have responded. Whether Madoc had intended it or not, anyone not part of the original four would find it hard to enter the circle.

She would have hoped betrayal and attempted murder would break that circle on its own, but she didn't have God's car. Hissing in frustration, Moiread hovered in place and bent her mind to reasoning quickly.

One thing oft partakes of the nature of another, she remembered Madoc saying, *particularly if they're in long association*.

Even by human standards, Moiread didn't have *long* on her side. Hopefully *close* would do instead.

She thought of Madoc: the taste of his lips and the feel of his hands, the flash of his smile and the glint of his eyes. She remembered the feel of his cock inside her and the sounds he made at the moment of climax. She thought of sweat and seed and even blood, for she was sure she'd scratched his shoulders once or twice in the course of events.

Slowly, the air parted before her. She gathered herself and dove.

Another roaring breath from Antonio, another dodge sideways and down, and a clump of trees behind where Madoc had been standing began to smolder.

It was spring, and a wet spring at that, even for Wales. The leaves burned slowly. Later it would be a worry. If Antonio set anything else aflame, matters would grow worse, but Madoc couldn't spare time to think about that. Nor could he give attention to the splashing in the pool behind him, except for a brief prayer that Elian and Bronwyn were both keeping themselves afloat.

He wove a serpentine pattern between trees and hillside, finding the turns the dragon was too large to take swiftly and the openings too small for him to reach into quickly. Legs aching, lungs burning, Madoc leapt out of the way of a bite that would have taken off half his torso, rolled forward, and spun around toward Antonio's tremendous blood clot of a body before the dragon had time to react.

Antonio was coiling around to face him when Madoc drove his sword into the dragon's side. It was a deeper wound than the one to the hand, and wider too. Madoc ripped downward as he pulled the blade out, spilling more hot blood onto the ground and sending up a smell like a blacksmith's forge. Yet scales and skin were both tough, and Madoc didn't dare to put his whole weight behind the blow. With no sure way to kill the beast, he couldn't risk committing himself so fully to any one strike.

Accordingly, he was throwing himself backward almost

as soon as he struck, yanking his sword down and out to the sound of Antonio's snarl. That one *was* pain as well as anger, Madoc thought, but he couldn't be sure that he'd hit anything vital. He wasn't certain what that would be in a dragon.

Madoc turned. A small rise in the meadow, between him and the pool, was his next source of cover. He started to make for that, saw the motion of Antonio's long, barbed tail, and threw himself sideways at the last second. Against an opponent of human speed, he would have been out of danger, but Antonio was quicker. The tail knocked Madoc off his feet and threw him forward, over half again his height of ground. Madoc crashed into the earth with one leg bleeding, and the impact jarred through his whole body.

That was it, he thought, as he rolled desperately onto his back and clumsily brought his sword around in front of him. The dragon was springing, eyes glowing black. Madoc might be able to get to his feet in time, but he'd never get out of the way. The teeth in its huge mouth were yellowed like old ivory but looked razor-sharp.

A shining golden missile flew through the air, meeting Antonio halfway through his descent. It struck the dragon right between the eyes, with a splash of water and a flash no sword blow had produced. Nor had any of Madoc's cuts made Antonio hiss as that blow did. To his amazement, the dragon actually cringed back, interrupting his deadly arc and falling to earth with less grace than Madoc had yet seen from the monster.

It was the chalice, he recognized, while instinct drove him scrambling to his feet: the chalice and the water of the pool. At that moment, a small, wet hand caught his upper arm and pulled him backward.

"Get *in*." Bronwyn sobbed as she spoke, rendering the words barely comprehensible. "I'm sorry, I'm *sorry*, I didn't know, but get into the pool, it may help, it helped Father a little, I think, please, I'm sorry."

Well, if she'd gone mad or was confessing her sins, Madoc could understand both impulses, and her thinking wasn't bad. He stepped backward, keeping an eye on the dragon, until he could lower himself into the pool feetfirst, holding on to the shore with one hand. The water was cold and he could feel no bottom, but it did seem to ease the pain in his leg.

And, to his amazement, Antonio gave one final hiss, then spread huge wings and launched himself upward, out of the grove.

All was silence, save for the subdued crackle of dying flames in the trees. Madoc looked behind him and saw Bronwyn clinging to her father, each of them with one hand on the lake's edge. Both of their legs moved, paddling at the water and keeping them afloat. Elian was alive, then.

"Is he...is he gone?" Bronwyn asked.

Madoc looked upward, saw red like a wound in the blue summer sky, and shook his head. "Going, perhaps...no." The red shape was circling the grove and picking up speed. "On my word, both of you hold your breath and duck."

He saw in Bronwyn's face and Elian's alike the same knowledge he had: even that, risky as it was, might not save them. The water hurt Antonio, but a man could ignore pain and even wounds if he needed to. What protection it did grant would be temporary... They couldn't tread water forever.

It was the best that any of them could do.

Madoc watched the shape grow closer. "*Pater noster qui es in caelis, sanctificetur nomen tuum...*" he began. The prayer brought back memories of Moiread now, rather than thoughts of heaven, but he couldn't regret that. If he was to die, that was how he would like it. God would understand.

Antonio stopped circling and began to dive. One more word, Madoc thought, and then their fate would be whatever it was. He drew a breath, filling his lungs as full as he could manage.

Then a silver-blue spear of a dragon streaked across the sky and clamped her jaws around Antonio's neck.

FORTY

FIGHTS BETWEEN DRAGONS WERE RARE. MOIREAD'S ONLY EXPE-
rience had been in play with her siblings. From that, she'd
expected the red dragon to pull back and claw at her chest.
She'd guarded herself accordingly, as best she could.

She hadn't expected it to writhe its head around until it
could fix its black eyes on hers. Neither had she anticipated
the blast that hit her in her mind: distilled pain, absent any
wound. Moiread opened her jaws without thought, instinct
prompting her only to get away from the source of her
agony, and around the pain she heard a voice.

Begone, hatchling. This is my land. My stock.

Confused, she could only roar and shake her head. The
red dragon sighed. Its blood dripped from its neck and
burned on her teeth, but it spoke with a tone akin to patience.

You cannot win against me. You... Laughter echoed
through her mind, sounding almost gently surprised. Were
it not for the edge of utter ruthlessness that came with it,
she could almost have believed it was friendly. *You even
smell like them. I was born of a goddess. Leave now, leave
me to what is mine, and I will let you go. Your courage is
worth that, and the world is wide.*

Even if Moiread could have spoken back, she wouldn't
have. The time for talking was far away. Under the pretext of listening, she filled her lungs and summoned fire,
breathing it right into the other dragon's face. Nor did she
wait to see the results, but threw herself at her foe, sinking
claws and teeth alike into its body.

It was ready for her. The fire washed over its face, burning scales off its jaw and neck, but its eye remained as clear and glittering as before. The red dragon met her charge, slamming its shoulder into her chest and twisting to rake its claws toward her underbelly. Moiread backwinged hurriedly, just missing the strike.

The hell of it was that the other could well be right. Its voice in her head was *old*, despite its strength. The images that arose when it spoke were of ancient temples and warriors in togas, people and places that had been ruins in Artair's day. The act of mind-speaking was one Moiread had only heard of in stories—a mark of the oldest blood, the most direct descendants of the true dragons.

She might well lose this one.

The two of them circled each other, rising and falling. Moiread watched the other's patterns for openings, knew it did the same with her, and knew she couldn't spare a glance below her to the figures she'd briefly seen in the pool.

Mine, the other dragon had said. She found herself thinking the same word. Had she possessed the other's ability, Moiread would have thrown it at him like a spear: *Mine. Mine, damn you.*

But the other had meant *my stock*. Moiread knew she didn't mean that. Nor did she mean *my people* as her father did: his responsibilities, his charges, his subjects.

She meant it as she might have said *my home*. In that moment, she knew that Madoc would always be hers in that sense, whether or not he wed Bronwyn—or any other woman. A part of her would always be in his keeping, and his presence would always, even if she never saw him again, be where she belonged, where she felt right and herself and at ease.

If she didn't come out alive, it would be enough to know

that he went on, and not just because she'd have died fulfilling her duty or keeping her father's bargains. A part of her would as well, and the rest of her would be easier for it, whether in heaven or lower.

Home was a good cause to die for, if she had to die. Moiread had known that for years. So, she now realized, was love.

The next pass showed an opening, a gap in the red dragon's defenses. Moiread feinted upward, wings buffeting the air behind her. The other shot up to intercept her. She switched direction and came in along its side, claws extended.

They pierced deep, digging into a still-healing earlier wound. Injury from their own kind healed more slowly; the other dragon shrieked.

Your mum might've been divine. I'm sure all the soldiers say so, Moiread thought at her opponent, in case he could hear her. *But you bleed like one of us.*

She had barely time to think it. Then the red pivoted midair, a move fast enough to completely belie its size. Moiread had no time to get out of the way before it grappled her. The weight of it bore her backward. As she lashed her head, trying to get her neck out of the way, she felt its fangs graze her throat and seek purchase.

Her wings fanned the air frantically, pushing her back against the other dragon's grip. She almost escaped, only to have the red tail wrap around her torso and pull her back, digging in with a barbed grip.

It was her turn to scream her pain to the heavens. Though she did so with another gout of fire, the red's grasp was strong.

Whatever she felt worth dying for, she thought with bleak humor, she was likely to prove it soon.

Breathe.

Cold water lapped around Madoc, soaking his clothes and his boots. They didn't feel as heavy as he'd have expected. Indeed, it was far easier to support himself in the pool than he'd realized. Perhaps it was magic, or perhaps terror lending strength to his muscles.

Neither Bronwyn nor Elian looked to have trouble staying afloat either, for a mercy. Elian's eyes were open and half focused, and his legs kicked regularly. The water made it impossible to see his wounds, but perhaps they weren't so severe as Madoc had first thought.

"Can you run?" he asked.

Elian's lips moved soundlessly before he managed a sound. "Wha—running? Maybe." His words came out slurred, which didn't surprise Madoc. Elian's face was whiter than paper, his lips vaguely tinged with blue. Madoc thought injury was more to blame for that than water.

"I can help him," said Bronwyn. Tears were still pouring down her face, and she spoke unsteadily.

Madoc could make out few details of the battle above him. The red dragon and the white twined in the sky, like the old legend come to life.

"Make for the tree line as soon as you can. Take cover. Find a place under a tree or a rock where he can't see you from the air. Hide. Then don't move until I say, or unless the forest catches fire. Understand?"

"Yes," said Bronwyn.

With one eye on the circling dragons above, Madoc helped Elian climb out of the pool and get an arm around his daughter's neck. The lord's glazed eyes turned toward him for a moment. "You?"

"I'll run if I must," Madoc said. "But I'm armed and unwounded. I'll fight if I can."

Elian nodded, raised his good hand, and squeezed Madoc's shoulder. Then he and his weeping daughter made for the trees, moving in a painful hobbling run that had Madoc watching the sky even more anxiously.

Magic for offense took time. He had that now, and a place of power, if he could tap into it. He couldn't fight in the sky beside Moiread, but he didn't have to leave her to battle alone.

The first thing was to get the lay of the land. *Visio dei*, he called, summoning back the spirits that he'd banished to fight Antonio, and what they revealed made him wince.

In magical sight, the dragons looked as though they fought in the middle of the night sky, or were two colliding thunderstorms, a flashing field of darkness surrounded each, overlapping as they clashed. Although they'd looked physically about the same size, the shadow around Antonio was far larger. Whatever that meant for dragons, Madoc was certain it didn't bode well for Moiread.

She screamed in pain. Madoc couldn't have said how he knew it was her, but he did, and his whole body turned to ice. Almost instinctively, he drew his sword and thrust it above him with one hand.

The pool shone opalescent around him. It held power— mostly for Elian's line, but Madoc had gotten far enough into the ritual that at least a little came to his call. The sword was a conduit, linking him with the sky and both the water and the magic it held.

The powers were already there.

Madoc wanted to cry out incoherently: *Help her, save her, please*, knowing only a blind and desperate rush of emotion, but he knew that wouldn't work. Magic demanded precision. The spirits, or angels, or whatever the beings he called on, were extremely literal creatures, and he would be sloppy with their power at his own risk—and Moiread's.

He mastered his feelings in a moment of savagely applied will, clamping down hard on everything but perception and intention. If his body had been icy with fear, so too did his mind become cold: a spear of stark, chill facts, with all of his heart gone to fuel the spell itself.

"Go to the aid of Moiread MacAlasdair," he said in Latin. As he spoke, he watched Moiread struggle above and pictured her as well in her other form: naked beneath him, armored and fighting at his side, laughing and thumping the table across from him, dancing with him in Gilrion's court. The dragon was only one of her faces, and he knew in that second that he loved them all. "Help her defeat Antonio and stay alive. Go."

Power spiraled up from the water, twisting around him and climbing up the sword to spread into the sky like reversed lightning. Shapes followed it, beings of light that Madoc, even in *visio dei*, could only half make out. He felt his own strength being drawn with them.

That was well.

A glimmer of light at the sides of her vision was all the warning Moiread got. Nor did she heed it at the time. She was fighting desperately, lashing her neck away from the red dragon's seeking jaws, trying to pull herself free of its grip before its claws found her guts.

Then light hit them, bright enough to dazzle her, but from the sound of it worse for the red, for Moiread found herself abruptly out of its grasp. She couldn't see what assaulted the other, but it roared and flamed and slashed, precision. The spirits, or angels, or whatever the beings he called on, were extremely literal creatures, and he would be sloppy with their power at his own risk—and Moiread's.

He mastered his feelings in a moment of savagely applied will, clamping down hard on everything but perception and intention. If his body had been icy with fear, so too did his mind become cold: a spear of stark, chill facts, with all of his heart gone to fuel the spell itself.

"Go to the aid of Moiread MacAlasdair," he said in Latin. As he spoke, he watched Moiread struggle above and pictured her as well in her other form: naked beneath him, armored and fighting at his side, laughing and thumping the table across from him, dancing with him in Gilrion's court. The dragon was only one of her faces, and he knew in that second that he loved them all. "Help her defeat Antonio and stay alive. Go."

Power spiraled up from the water, twisting around him and climbing up the sword to spread into the sky like reversed lightning. Shapes followed it, beings of light that Madoc, even in *visio dei*, could only half make out. He felt his own strength being drawn with them.

That was well.

A glimmer of light at the sides of her vision was all the warning Moiread got. Nor did she heed it at the time. She was fighting desperately, lashing her neck away from the red dragon's seeking jaws, trying to pull herself free of its grip before its claws found her guts.

Then light hit them, bright enough to dazzle her, but from the sound of it worse for the red, for Moiread found herself abruptly out of its grasp. She couldn't see what assaulted the other, but it roared and flamed and slashed, not at her but at enemies she couldn't see, ones that paid seemingly no attention to her.

Whatever they were doing to the red, she saw no wounds, nor did she know how long their attack would last.

She thought, for the first time, about giving the red a chance to surrender, or to fly away.

But she'd seen a little bit inside its head when it spoke. She knew the feel of it, the cold hunger for power, the view of humanity as animals for the slaughter. If she let the red go, it could fly away to shape another land to its selfish whims—or it could come back in fifty years, all that callousness turned to vengeance.

Moiread spread her wings and flew upward, letting a thermal lend her strength. Before the red could break free of the shapes attacking it, she folded her wings and dove.

This time, her jaws closed around its spine. This time, the angle was right. She heard the cracking sound she'd wanted.

All the same, she bit down hard as she bore the red to the ground and tore her jaws away bloody.

It was always best to be sure.

FORTY-ONE

HOWEVER LONG HE LIVED, MADOC DIDN'T THINK HE'D EVER forget the moment when the two dragons landed: Antonio a still-bleeding corpse that shook the ground with his final impact and, far more important, Moiread bearing him to earth and then circling to land a shade less heavily. Her sides were heaving, her wings beating slowly, but she was alive.

Madoc pulled himself from the water and ran toward her with a strength he wouldn't have dreamed he possessed a moment before.

When he reached Moiread, she was a woman again, though her eyes were glowing and there was a line of scales along each of her cheeks. Neither mattered. Madoc was only glad that she was human-sized-and-shaped again, that he might the more easily throw his arms about her and pull her against him.

She embraced him just as enthusiastically, before both of them pulled back at the same moment.

"Are you well?" Moiread asked.

At the same time, the words mingling, Madoc said, "I'm sorry... Are you injured?"

"No," she said, and kissed him. If she minded the condition of his clothing, Moiread gave no sign, any more than it occurred to Madoc to mind the blood spattering her body. So long as none of it was hers, he was happy.

Their condition, not to mention the setting, *was* enough to keep them from doing more than kiss, and that was as well. As they parted, Madoc heard a quick intake of breath from behind them.

"Hello, lass," Moiread said calmly, stepping away from Madoc to face Bronwyn, then shifting her gaze to Elian, leaning on his daughter's arm. "Best we get your father back to the keep, aye? The guards'll have gotten your brother there long ago, and he'll be wanting to know we've all come through in one piece."

"I... Yes." The immediate task kept Bronwyn from asking questions for as long as it took to transfer Elian into Moiread's arms.

In the process, they got a glimpse of his flesh where the fire had seared him. From Elian's ankle to his heel, his skin was an angry red, blisters rising in many places. "You should be all right, my lord...with care, if nothing festers," Madoc said cautiously. "The sort of burns that kill are...darker."

"Aye. It could have been worse," said Moiread. "Though this willna' be any pleasure trip, and I'm sorry for it."

"You're a woman," said the lord, looking up into Moiread's face. "Madoc's servant Michael, but...a woman."

"Aye, my lord. Seemed more practical, for the road and all."

"And a—"

"Dragon. Aye. Long story, I'm afraid."

Moiread started walking as they spoke, and Madoc, following behind them and Bronwyn, noticed how smooth her pace was, how Elian's weight barely slowed her at all, and yet how carefully she held the injured man.

There were so many pieces to her: the strength and the care, the creature who'd broken Antonio's spine and the woman who gently bore the wounded. Before Madoc had known her, such different elements might have seemed an odd combination. Now they blended into one another, grew out of each other like solid trees sprouting from the yielding earth.

Lost in thought, he almost missed Bronwyn's question. "And Signor Antonio? He was a...a dragon too."

"Aye," Moiread said again. "There are a few of us, here and there. I couldna' tell you how many."

Bronwyn looked back over her shoulder, past Madoc, to where the red dragon's corpse had become a man's robed form, neck bent at an angle that none could survive. She said nothing.

"Did you know?" Elian asked.

"No, not until he changed." Madoc could only see the back of Moiread's head, but he thought it shook slightly back and forth. "Nor did he know what I was. He was... verra old, my lord, even as we measure age, and his blood ran not nearly as mortal as mine. If he'd not transformed, we might have passed each other by completely. I wonder why he did, in the end."

"My fault, I think," Madoc said and described briefly the spell and his invocation of *visio dei*. "When the spell and the place and the vision combined, I suppose anything within that circle had to assume its true shape. He was more dragon than man, you said."

"Certainly that's how he thought," said Moiread. "I know he was your adviser, my lord, and I'm sorry for the loss of the man you think he was, but if he valued you at all, it was as a farmer prizes his best pig."

"Ah," said Elian, and sighed.

Bronwyn sobbed—once, and then again, standing still and making broken little sounds.

They both turned toward her, but it was Madoc who spoke first. "Did *you* know?"

"Not what he was. I swear. But...I... He said it was the only way..." They waited, silent, and then she looked at Madoc and wailed. "I didn't want you dead once I met you!"

The next few minutes were awkward, to say the least.

Because God was either merciful or ironic, the need to get Elian back to the castle at least kept them from standing around staring for long. Rather, it kept *Moiread* from standing around staring, and all the others followed when she started walking.

In her arms, Elian was rigid from more than shock. Madoc was silent. Bronwyn wept quietly as she followed. And Moiread—

—she was too tired to know exactly what she felt. She knew the aftermath of battle well, and this was the same, even if they'd all come through alive. Tasks lay ahead of her. She could feel once she'd gotten them done.

They walked up the road, a strange and somber procession. The keep was none too far away. Doubtless, men were arming themselves and preparing to ride to their rescue. The whole fight had really not taken much time at all. That was how they went, generally.

"Tell me everything," Madoc said calmly. "From the start of it."

Bronwyn did, in a tear-choked voice but more coherently than Moiread might have expected from a girl her age. "I never wanted the alliance. If we had it, I thought we would be that much more likely to go to war, and it never seemed worth it. And I didn't understand the spell, but the English have magic too, I've heard, and wouldn't it just provoke them? I was very...outspoken about that. Signor Antonio found me after an argument. He agreed with me in every particular. He was sympathetic. He said he'd take care of the matter."

"And did he say how he'd do that?" Madoc asked.

"No. But—" A great sniffling breath. "I knew. I *knew*. Especially when he began disappearing, or when he'd shut himself in his workroom and not want to be disturbed. I knew he meant to kill you, or I'd have asked."

"Likely he was the man you saw in your vision," Moiread put in. "Iestyn mentioned the scar on his neck, just before Antonio changed." She made as much of an apologetic gesture as she could with her head alone. "I've been a wee bit distracted since then."

Madoc laughed, though the mirth in it was sharp and dark. "So you might say, yes."

"I didn't want to kill anyone," Bronwyn said, "but I didn't want a stupid war either. And he kept asking if I still wanted him to 'see to things,' and I said—"

"'Who will rid me of this troublesome priest?'" Madoc quoted. "Only rather the other way around, yes?"

"I... Yes. I'm sorry. I thought it was one man, one that I didn't know, against my people. My brother. I thought *Antonio* was a man, and not... I'm sorry," she said and began to cry again.

That was when the first outriders reached them, their faces pale and their eyes wide under their helmets. Staring followed, and questions. They had the wits to send back for two men and a litter to carry their lord, and for the messenger to take Bronwyn with him.

"*Michael?*" asked Alan, one of those who stayed behind. He was gaping at Moiread, his gaze shifting from the blood on her clothing to the curves beneath it.

"More or less," she said, and then the giddy humor of a battle's aftermath sprang up in her, and she tipped him a tavern maid's sly grin. "More *and* less, aye, depending on where you look."

The group of them was laughing—carefully in Moiread and Elian's cases, near-hysterically in all of them—when the litter bearers came.

From the time they entered the castle, Moiread stuck close to Madoc's side. Those who weren't taking care of their lord stared at her, but she gave every appearance of not noticing. She flatly, albeit politely, refused the offers of clothing more suited to her status or a place to lie down. She did take the sword Tomos offered, a replacement for the one she'd left in the meadow when she transformed.

"There's some chance," she said, during one of the rare moments when she and Madoc were alone, "that we should make a run for it now."

Madoc knew what she meant. The two of them were the only witnesses to Bronwyn's confession. They were also in Elian's keep, surrounded by his guards. A dishonorable man would use the latter to solve the former problem. Madoc had enough faith in Elian to shake his head at the suggestion, but it yet worried him.

Thus Moiread stood behind a screen while Madoc changed into dry clothing. He pretended to avert his eyes while she stripped, washed off Antonio's blood, and put on a hastily scrounged gown, and they both ignored the maid's subtle sounds of disapproval. Both ate, but Moiread took food first and waited, and each stood guard while the other got a few hours of sleep.

The castle was like a roadside camp, but with enough witnesses that, even if they had the energy to speak at length, they couldn't have talked about anything important.

When the page came the next morning, calling them to Elian's chambers, Madoc blessed the hour.

Elian lay on his stomach, looking weary but better than he had the day before. At one side of his canopied bed stood Father Evan and Bronwyn, the latter with her head lowered and her hands clasped in front of her.

Nobody knew what to say at first. Nobody knew where to look. Between Bronwyn's shame, Elian's injury, and the minor but present incongruity of Moiread, standing like a half-wrapped statue in badly fitting brown wool, awkward glances ruled the moment.

"I am glad to see you so well, my lord," Madoc finally said.

"I thank you." Elian cleared his throat. "Best to settle matters between us as soon as we can, yes? My household has committed great wrongs against you. What atonement would you ask of us?"

The man's face was firmly set, but Madoc could read fear in his eyes, and no wonder. By rights, Madoc could have asked for Bronwyn's execution, at the least. He sighed. "We all live. Antonio is dead. Let it be an end."

"Your generosity shames me."

"You have always been my father's friend," Madoc said, searching his weary brain for the right words, "and I hope you will be mine as well. Perhaps in time we may discuss your son's marriage to one of my nieces, if you wish. I fear I cannot now countenance the one you and my father had planned."

"No," said Elian, "of course not. Bronwyn will be leaving in a month. She will spend five years in France, serving the sisters of Abbaye-aux-Bois. With God's grace, she will learn from that." He cast an eye at his daughter, who flinched.

Madoc might have pitied her, had he not remembered

the tavern in Erskine and Moiread's delirious gaze. "She did save me at the last," he said, finding refuge in facts. "For which I am thankful."

"There is that. And now—" Elian beckoned the priest forward. The man held out a small chest, carved of fine wood and inlaid with gold. "I know I cannot be part of the rite until my body is whole again. Let me swear friendship as I can. In this chest is the jawbone of Saint Eluned." He placed a hand on the lid and took a breath. Madoc felt the subtle rise of power around them. "On it and before God I pledge my friendship to Madoc ap Rhys and Moiread MacAlasdair. Let God's wrath fall upon me should I, or any of my house, cause them harm by action or inaction, by word, deed, or thought. Amen."

The feeling of binding, of a spell completed, accompanied his last word. Madoc knew that he'd given them at least a night's sleep, and he stepped forward to perform his half of the oath with a good heart. With that alliance, and the remnants of the rite, he could raise the shield from his own home, and perhaps it was best that way.

"Then it is done," said Elian, "and I may rest easy. I bid you both farewell, as I doubt I'll see you before you take your leave."

Doubt, he said, but Madoc heard the command beneath the words.

FORTY-TWO

MORNING MEANT LEAVING. MOIREAD HAD BARELY NEEDED TO exchange two words with Madoc to settle that. He knew what she did: safe they might be, and she gave Elian credit for the oath, but welcome was another matter.

She was glad to have slept before they left, and to eat one last meal that wasn't tavern food, but Moiread was also glad to know that the road was in front of her. Soon the castle walls would no longer confine her, nor would she have to ignore stares from all quarters.

Many of the guards had been quite decent. Iestyn had clearly had trouble getting his head around the notion of a *girl* who fought, but enthusiasm had quickly won out. Madoc took more than equal place in his regard now, and that was fine. With luck, Moiread's example—and a few stories of Scathach and Boudica that she'd related—would leave the boy more flexible than most of his generation.

Still, she was a woman. She fought. She'd been involved with a strange matter out by the pool, one that had left Antonio dead. A few people had seen great winged shapes in the sky. At least one had talked. The main story held that Antonio had turned into a dragon, but only that Moiread, Madoc, and Elian had defeated him. Other rumors, and speculation about what power one had to have to kill a dragon, ran rampant.

The maids flinched whenever Moiread looked displeased. When she went to lead Shadow out, the groom stood well back from her.

Yes, she'd be glad to get away.

Shadow himself was disposed to be nervous. Moiread couldn't be too surprised; she'd practically transformed on his back. She kept a tight hand on the leading rein and watched him warily as she checked her saddle.

"It's going to be a long ride for you, isn't it?" Madoc asked, his shadow falling over her while she was bent to adjust straps.

"He'll calm down. I hope."

Hearing footsteps crossing the packed dirt of the courtyard, Moiread straightened up, then paused as she saw Bronwyn.

Elian's daughter wore dull brown, long-sleeved and almost shapeless. She stood with her hands clasped in front of her. Both the garment and her pose made her look years younger than her age. The dark figure of Father Evan, a short distance away, added to the impression of a truant child.

"My lord, my lady," she said quietly and bowed. "I wanted to apologize again. I should never have trusted Signor Antonio, nor should I have given in to my own fears. I thank God that my folly and sin resulted in no worse than what did happen, and I most humbly ask your pardon."

"You have it," Madoc said with little of his usual courtly manner. "I hope your time in France aids you."

Bronwyn bowed her head.

She really was very young. Antonio had been incredibly old. What chance would any lord's naive daughter have against a mind formed in the intrigues of Rome? Moiread stepped forward and put a finger under the girl's chin, lifting it upward. "Lass," she said, "I'll not say you did right. But you did, in the end, no worse than a score of kings and a pope or two." Evan, who'd heard that, flinched in a rather amusing way. "I dare say hell doesn't quite gape before you, if you don't make a habit of this."

"Thank you, my lady."

"That said," Moiread continued, letting her arm fall back to her side, "you tried to kill someone I love. Had you succeeded, I would have sworn my life to your torment. And I live a very long time. Nor am I the only one." She allowed her eyes to glow a shade brighter than the girl could mistake for mortal. "Bear that in mind, should temptation whisper again in your ear."

Without waiting to see Bronwyn's reaction, she turned, swung herself up into the saddle, and nudged Shadow toward the castle gates.

"So, then," Madoc said once they'd left the castle behind and were on the road again. "You put the fear of God into her, rather."

"She had that already, or she'd not have confessed. Finding that you've been consorting wi' a demon is a bit unsettling for a girl her age, aye?" She smiled grimly. "But I find that fear of this world lasts where concern for the next might not."

"Your people aren't demons. She knows that."

"Her father does, and her mind might. Otherwise? It's not as though she's seen much to compare with us, aye?"

"Neither have I," said Madoc. The sky was overcast, the air chilly and damp. Rain was likely coming. He felt no cold, particularly when he looked over fiercely to meet Moiread's eyes. "I've never glimpsed a demon outside of some probably inaccurate books, and I would never have thought you one."

Moiread had never in their acquaintance been one for blushing, but her tanned skin burned rose-copper at that statement. "You weren't raised like most," she said.

Although she shrugged in a very matter-of-fact manner, she didn't sound able to disguise the pleasure in her voice.

For the sake of diplomacy, and not giving away too many secrets, she'd left Llanasef Fechan in female attire, without any illusion to shield her. She would change at the first inn and ride the rest of the way as a man, yet Madoc knew he'd always have her true appearance in his mind—both true appearances, at that, and he couldn't imagine her without either.

Nobody approached to overhear or interrupt. Madoc nerved himself to speak the words that had been in his mind ever since they'd left the castle gates, the ones he'd felt unable to simply spring on Moiread out of the blue. He'd led up as far as he could manage; now he must make the leap.

"Did you mean what you told her?"

"Every word of it. But I'll grant the bit about the popes was mostly rumor." A sly, teasing smile widened, lighting her face like the dawn itself. "But particularly what I said about you. Though if I've read aught wrongly and you feel nothing for me, I'll bite my tongue about it for the rest of our journey."

"No," he said, the joy in his heart joined by a sense of great honor. "I suspect I'll love you as long as I live and, if God is willing, as long as you do."

"Aye. Well." Moiread tried to move closer, but the tan gelding snorted and shied. She and Madoc both laughed ruefully. "Demonstrations later, then, when the damn horses are na' involved. We've a few days left to us yet."

"On this journey, yes. And I've been thinking."

"A young man needs a hobby, I hear," she said, her voice full of giddy mirth.

"I'll not be marrying Bronwyn for an alliance," Madoc

went on, after pulling a face at her, "but another lord's daughter may sit well with my father. One whose family is in Scotland, for instance. One whose blood could mingle favorably with ours. One who'd saved my life a few times."

"It is generally the reward, I hear." Moiread's pale-blue eyes shone. "Do you think you could bring him around, then, to this woman?"

"It's likely. If, of course, she were willing to come to a foreign land and tie herself to the lord of its people."

Given Moiread's face, Madoc didn't quite have to hold his breath as he waited for an answer. Still, when she said, "I think a land would be a deal less foreign with you there," he beamed with happy relief. When she added, "And a tie or two will do me good," he sent a wordless prayer of thanksgiving heavenward.

"Then it's all settled but the talking," he said, "and I'm good at that."

And the road in front of them was as magical as any shining path in the otherworld.

*Keep reading for a sneak peek of the next book in the
Dawn of the Highland Dragon series by Isabel Cooper*

HIGHLAND DRAGON MASTER

PROLOGUE

THE TENT SMELLED OF TALLOW AND SMOKE AND BLOOD. MORTAL
men said they got used to the reek after war had gone on
long enough. Erik doubted he ever would.

At least the blood was mostly old by now. Dragons
weren't carrion-eaters: the inhuman part of him stayed
quiet. It was the human side that wanted to howl with
fury, a longing that had become familiar in the days since
Balliol's treachery and only intensified now, with the
moans of dying men only a few paces outside.

In the face of Erik's rage, Artair MacAlasdair's calm
stillness would have been offensive, had Erik expected any
other reaction. He'd rarely seen his uncle roused to any

emotion, and never to passion. In Erik's youth, it had been
a joke between him and Artair's younger children that the
MacAlasdair patriarch wouldn't have done more than lift
his eyebrows if someone had cut his head off.

Now Artair sat in Erik's tent, drinking bad wine and
picking weevils out of bread with the same air he'd used
when presiding over holiday feasts in his own castle. He'd
seen as much fighting and death that day as Erik, but his
white hair and beard were neat, his blue eyes as impassive
as the glaciers they echoed in color. Under their scrutiny,
Erik could give voice to but a bare fraction of what he felt.

"I'd thought," he said, his own wine cup neglected,
"that we'd *done* with this. Years ago. Will they not stop
until the Day of Judgment itself?"

"Likely not," said Artair. "I don't know that stopping's
in their nature."

The devil of it was that Erik didn't know if the older
man meant Englishmen or mortals. Like Artair's daughter
Moiread—now married to a Welshman and unable to take
an active part in the war, lest other lands be drawn into
the conflict—Erik would have ardently voiced the former
view. Artair himself had argued for the latter on more than
one occasion.

We've never tried to take London, Douglas, the
MacAlasdair heir, had said once.

Artair had tilted his head, dragon-like, and peered at his
son. *Because we wouldn't, or because we can't?*

There'd been no good answer then, there wasn't one
now, and it mattered little. Four years of fighting already,
nearly twenty before the treaty the English had broken,
and many days it seemed as though the wars would go
on until there was no man left able to lift a sword—or
until the vindictive bastard who'd taken the crown at

Westminster felt his father's honor satisfied, whenever that would be.

"Your eyes changed," Artair observed with neither fear nor admonition. "Maintaining your form becomes harder?"

Not wanting to voice the words, Erik nodded, once. For the most part, the MacAlasdairs kept firm control over their shapes once they'd passed through the trials of youth. Dire sickness or wounds could make the matter more difficult, though, as could great strain on the mind or heart. Spending the days killing didn't help either.

Artair finished his wine. "I'm sending you away from the front. Douglas and I can take command for a time—and after this, there's likely to be a lull, for the winter if no longer."

"My lord—"

"Soon you'll begin to see them all as prey." The single sentence, delivered with only fact and no feeling, cut Erik's voice off entirely. Artair crossed the room and put a hand on his nephew's shoulder. "Be at ease. It comes to us all in time, and you've not failed me. Indeed, I need you for another duty just now."

Erik bent his head in acquiescence. "I'm at your service, my lord."

"I've had a message from Cathal's wife," said Artair. "You wished a way to make the invasions end? She may have found one."

ONE

BORDEAUX WAS FAR EMPTIER THAN IT HAD EVER BEEN IN ERIK'S long life. In the past two centuries, he'd been accustomed to seeing the cities of men grow greater and more crowded, pushing out their borders every time he visited and building new houses almost atop the old.

Now many of the houses sat empty, their windows black as the empty eyes of a skull. The noises of the street were almost a whisper compared to what they had been. Sellers of fruit and fish, meat and leather still plied their trades in the markets, but there were far fewer, and their voices sounded muted, afraid. The rumbling of carts easily drowned them out, and while most of those carts held goods for the market, still there were many with a cargo of the dead, open eyes oft staring up to an unseeing heaven.

Man was a fragile creature. Never had Erik seen that more clearly than in the last ten years.

He walked without fear down the pitted cobblestone streets. The dragon-blooded took no harm from mortal plagues, save perhaps to their mind and soul. That horseman might ride after him and the other MacAlasdairs in vain—or perhaps simply leave the duty to his brothers. Certainly they were War's creatures often enough.

War was the root of Erik's mission, after all.

Although far fewer ships sat in the harbor, there were yet enough that their masts made a bare-branched forest against the blue summer sky. Men crossed the docks with their burdens: barrels of goods, pails of tar, even the occasional horse or cow. Other men stood or sat in more idleness, fishing off the docks or talking over mugs of ale.

Some such idlers stopped Erik, as men in their position always had done with a well-dressed man who carried a nobleman's arms. They asked him to join them in drinking—and doubtless stand them a round later—which he declined; asked if he'd found himself lodging and care for his horse, which he had; and asked if he'd need of fresh fish, which he didn't. He did accept one offer from a young towheaded man for directions.

"I look to hire a ship," Erik said. "And men. I wish to make a voyage westward."

"Hmm," said the young man, and put his head to one side like a spaniel seeking a bone. He had great brown eyes that only heightened the impression. Those eyes scanned the ships in the harbor with alertness, though, and he gave answer promptly enough. "The *Hawk* might do it, m'lord. She's small, but she's been known to take human bundles from time to time, and she's not beholden so far as I know."

It sounded promising. "And where might I find her captain?"

"Aboard, most likely. They made port but two days ago. She'll be looking at every board, if the past's any measure."

"She?" Erik asked. It was no shock—among his line, the women fought nearly as much as the men, and such had been more common even among mortals in his parents' day— but it was a surprise to hear as much from modern lips.

The young man rolled his eyes. "Not that there hasn't been a bit to say about it. But her husband's dead, and they'd no children, so…" He shrugged. "The world's not over-blessed with men these days, no?"

He crossed himself as he said it, and Erik joined him. "The *Hawk*," he said.

"Down at the end," said the young man, and waited expectantly until Erik handed him two pennies.

The docks creaked beneath Erik as he walked toward his destination. That sound, and water lapping against wood, brought back memories from his youth: fishing out in boats on the loch with his cousins, with more joking than actual fishing being done in the end. Cathal and he had been of about an age, or close enough to make little difference among the MacAlasdair youths. Together they'd hidden from tutors, run races, and later planned to court kitchen maids.

Cathal had been the one to explain Erik's current mission—or, rather, his wife had. A charming woman, unnervingly intelligent and more unnervingly familiar with the magic that Erik had only half learned in his youth, she'd been the one to unearth the relevant legends. Their two daughters had served the evening meal while Sophia told stories, their eyes as grave and brown as their mother's, but with a dragonish gleam in their depths.

Such an evening left a man brooding, apt to consider his own past and perchance the future to come.

Such a man, Erik told himself, would do well to concentrate on the task at hand, ere he fell into the harbor and earned himself an unpleasant evening. He turned his attention to the ship he was approaching.

The *Hawk* was a flat-bottomed cog, its oak boards weathered smooth by the ocean but to all appearances solid and sturdy. As it lay in harbor, the single sail was furled against the mast. Above it, a blue flag displayed a single yellow silhouette that might have been a hawk, an eagle, or indeed a giant bat. For certain it had a head and wings, but that was all Erik could make out from a distance. The ship looked to be a good length, eighty feet or so, and sat well in the water.

Two figures stood on the deck. At such a distance, a mortal man might not have known that one of them was female. The dragon-blooded had better eyes, but save for her sex, her height—greater than that of most women—and the gleaming copper-red of her hair, Erik could make out no more of her.

Approaching, he hailed the ship. The captain set her hands on her hips, considering, and then nodded. "Wait there," she called, gesturing to the docks, "and I'll come ashore."

Erik heard a familiar note in her voice, but he couldn't place it. Not until she reached the docks and he looked into a tanned face with wide, almost-black eyes, in which gleamed small specks of golden fire, did he know her. Then, laughing in amazement, he saw the joke of the flag.

If the man before her hadn't gaped and then broken out laughing, Toinette would have thought herself wrong about his identity. The world had big men in plenty, and blond men—whole countries full of big, blond men. There might even have been a few big, blond men with the same shimmering blue-green eyes as the one in front of Toinette had.

His expression convinced her.

"Erik MacAlasdair? What are the odds?"

Not so great as all that, come to think of it. The world could be small, and it was growing smaller of late. In truth, there'd been times when Toinette had wondered if her blood would be all that was left.

Best not to brood on death. Better to step forward and let Erik embrace her. His lips brushed lightly over hers: a quick kiss of greeting, as between any friend and another, quite unlike the rather messier and more daring one that she remembered receiving behind the forester's cottage at

Loch Arach so many years ago. His arms were stronger, though, and Toinette stepped back feeling a tingling echo of the same thrill she'd had at sixteen.

"A pleasant surprise," he said, and the accent of Scotland in his voice called back memories of hunting and hawking, of stone halls and the triumph of controlling her heritage for the first time. "Captain Toinette?"

"Captain Deschamps, rightly."

"I heard," he said, and bowed his head. "I'm sorry for your loss."

"Thank you. It was ten years ago now, so—" She spread her hands, smoothing the air as time did pain.

Erik looked slightly surprised. "Ah. Not the plague, then?"

"Only mortality—though you might say the plague counts. He was middle-aged when I met him. A very kind man, and not a very curious one."

"God rest his soul."

"Yes," said Toinette. "Quite likely. And how many times have you wed since we last met?"

"Two." He made sure that none of the crowd were likely to be listening, and then added, "Both longer past than your man."

"Quite a crowd in heaven, I'm sure. Children?"

"No."

"I'm sorry." He didn't ask in return. Toinette would not bear to a mortal; the blood didn't cross that way. Men could crossbreed, with difficulty and rituals. The older ones, like Toinette's father, didn't even need those. Whether mortal or magical, though, bearing the child of a man with dragon's blood had certain risks unless you yourself had it to begin with. To Toinette's mind, it was a bad deal either way.

To her relief, she saw no great pain in Erik's face, nor heard any in his voice when he spoke again. "It happens. You look to have done well."

"I have." She smoothed her hands down the crimson wool of her skirts. "Amber and wax from Muscovy this trip. Lighter than furs, and less likely to leave the crew scratching."

"Only half frozen, I'd think." Erik laughed.

"As long as it's the right half, gold does a lot to thaw a man again." The setting sun glinted red-gold off the water, catching Toinette's eye. "Here, you didn't come all this way just to compare our lives or ask for a rematch at archery, did you?"

"No, no more than I did to let you redeem yourself with a falcon. I need to hire myself a ship."

"Welcome words. There's a tavern down that way"— Toinette jerked a thumb to indicate where—"that's half-decent if you watch the landlord while he's pouring the wine. I've a mind to talk over meat and drink."

The tavern was small and reasonably clean. The table wasn't sticky, and the rushes had been changed within the last fortnight. Toinette had been right about the wine too, and the pottage, though mostly cabbage, tasted as if the bits of meat might truly have been rabbit.

Such qualities drew a number of guests, mostly the quieter sort of man from the docks by the look of them. None sat very close to Toinette or Erik, and all seemed absorbed in their own affairs. Still, Erik switched into Gaelic as he put down his spoon and asked, "You've perhaps heard of the Templars?"

Toinette thought for the time it took her to sip wine and put the cup back down. "Crusader knights, weren't they?

And maybe devil worshippers?" A hundred-odd years since their parting had left her accent rusty, but Erik could understand her well enough.

"Aye, so the king said at the time, I hear." He hadn't bothered about it much on that occasion. Moiread MacAlasdair had said she didn't care if they'd each kissed Satan's cold arse in person; the men didn't matter, only their artifacts. "They had a great deal of treasure."

"Had?"

"Philip claimed most of it." Indeed, those who felt safe speaking of such matters suggested that greed had been the fuel for those pyres. Erik wouldn't have been surprised. "But there are those who say he didn't find all—that a small company of the knights smuggled some out and brought it to an island west of England. Of those tales, a few say that it wasn't only gold. They speak of magic enough to reshape the world, or a part of it."

Toinette's crimson lips pursed. "Ah," she said, amused. "And I daresay you've no wish to hire an English captain. The war progresses?"

"It does. That's the reason I'm going." Erik said. "It's a small chance, but I'll take it for my people's sake."

"How very loyal of you."

As it had always done, her gaze grew remote when speaking of such matters, and the humor in her voice was lofty: *These affairs have so little to interest me*. When Erik was fifteen, he'd blushed and stammered and grown angry. When he was eighteen, he'd blushed and stammered for different reasons, and the anger had taken a distant place.

Toinette had been his first kiss. He'd never asked, but he was dead certain he hadn't been hers.

Older, he drank wine and composed an answer. "There's not so much fighting these days. We're preparing for David to return. I've been told I can be most helpful in this manner." When Toinette's dark eyes didn't waver, he added, "And I'd like a reason to be away just now."

War grew weary for most men. For the dragon-blooded, it could be dangerous. Too much death without a respite could lead to bloodlust, or to enough distance from mortals that their lives became playthings. Artair MacAlasdair was very careful about such tendencies in his kin, even in the cadet branches.

"I'd imagine many people would," said Toinette. "For all there are fewer men about, we'll likely find a crew easily enough. But first," she added, raising a slim sun-browned hand, "let us talk payment."

TWO

"And half the treasure," said Toinette, pulling off her second boot and propping her feet up on the end of the bed.

"If treasure there be." Marcus, already as horizontal as it was possible for a man to be, gave her a skeptical look from the depths of his pillow. "He's chasing legends. Will you start too?"

"I *am* a legend."

"Captaining one merchant ship doesn't make you an Amazon."

"A girl can dream." Toinette didn't correct him. While Marcus knew a great deal about her, his knowledge did not extend to her other form, and she was content to leave it that way. "Besides, that's why I'm having him pay in advance, and pay well too. I've not gone soft in the head just because we made land."

"Oh, I was just crediting it to old age."

"Bear in mind," Toinette said, giving him a baleful look, "that you sleep sounder than I do, young man."

Marcus laughed. "You'd not kill me. What other man would you trust to share a bed and not to turn you out for better company half the nights?"

Desire, whether for men or women, had never burdened Marcus overmuch. If he'd been a more faithful man, or a less adventurous one, he would have made an excellent priest—which would have been a great loss to Toinette, as he was a damned good first mate. "And I suppose most of them would snore worse than you do, at that. Smell worse, almost definitely."

"I can live, then?"

"Oh, for now. It's late, and I'd as soon not go to the trouble of cleaning your blood off the mattress. And innkeepers make an unholy fuss about corpses in their rooms."

Toinette stretched herself out, luxuriating in the length of the bed and the softness of the straw mattress. She'd chosen shipboard life freely and had yet to regret it, but all the same, it was lovely to have her back truly straight for a night or two. She wiggled her toes.

"Speaking of better company," said Marcus, "will *you* be needing the room to yourself while we're here?"

"Doubtful."

On the occasion that Toinette took a lover, she generally either went back to the man's accommodations, hired a room herself, or—at times—found a stable loft or similar convenience for an hour's privacy. When none of those options presented themselves, Marcus took himself out to find his own amusements for a while. It was never very long. The last man Toinette had let stay afterward had been Jehan. After he'd died, it had seemed a slight to his memory for others to remain.

Marcus was different. Wherever Jehan was, Toinette was sure he understood.

"Ill-favored city, is it?" Marcus asked.

"When I was young, it might have seemed otherwise. Now?" She shrugged. "The more men I've had in my bed, the more they all seem the same—and the less worth the trouble of getting them there."

That might have been true after ten years, it was certainly true after more than a century. The exception who came to mind... Well, he was paying her, and they'd be on a ship full of her men for months. Best not to even think about that one, much as she might like to.

From the street outside came off-key singing: men drunk enough to take their chances in the darkness.

"They left out a line there, I think," Marcus observed.

"D'you want to go out and correct them?"

"I might, if they don't stop soon."

"It always is a shock," Toinette agreed, retrieving her share of the blankets, "how noisy cities are after the sea. Though the beds make up for it. And the food. I can't say I'm looking forward to biscuit and fish again."

"You're the one who took the man up on his offer. And how does he intend to *find* this island, come to that?"

"He managed to get his hands on a map. He says it's a long story. I'll have it out of him by the third day at sea, I'll wager—but meanwhile, I've seen the map, and it does look real. Besides, MacAlasdair's not the sort to chase nursery tales without any solid sign. Never was."

Punctuating her sentence, she blew out the candle and settled down into the bed. Marcus, a foot away, was a comfortably warm presence. Even summer nights in Bordeaux almost never got very hot.

His voice came out of the darkness, half drowned in a yawn. "How do you know this fellow, then?"

"Oh," said Toinette, her own voice slurred as her eyelids grew heavy. "Long time ago. You might say we grew up together."

In a way, she thought as she slid down under the waves of sleep, it was true. Only growing up meant more to the dragon-blooded than it did to mortals—and she, looking back, could never have said when it had happened to her. Adulthood had come in fits and starts, blood and pain and madness.

Toinette supposed that much was common enough even for mortals.

Loch Arach had long been familiar to Erik. As great a distance as it was from the island that he called home, it was still close enough for frequent travel in dragon form. Lamorak MacAlasdair held the island with his brother's backing, and both knew it. A year or two sometimes passed between visits, but never more.

When Erik was fifteen, he'd gone to Artair MacAlasdair's castle. To mortals, that had been the fostering common with most young men. For Erik, as for the others in his line, it had been more: his transformations had begun. Unlike the island, Loch Arach had room to keep changing and hunting a secret. Moreover, Castle MacAlasdair had *rooms* with magic woven into the walls that could hold a dragon if one's nature broke free of control.

However many branches the family had, the youth came to Loch Arach. Erik came to suspect that Artair was fond of the arrangement. He was as canny as he was old, and no stranger to the advantages of strengthening blood ties with a bit of mingling.

Young Erik had welcomed the journey. He'd had a glorious few months at first: training both of his forms, playing games with his cousins, hunting in the forest, and swimming in the lake.

Shortly after harvest, a small band of traders had come through. With them had come a girl.

Erik still remembered his first look at her. She'd been thirteen and spider spindly, her hair a roughly cut shock of carrot-orange and her face all outthrust chin. Her clothing had been patched and too large; her hand had lingered near the dagger at her waist too long for any sort of courtesy. Standing in the tower room at Castle MacAlasdair, she'd watched the assembled MacAlasdairs with barely disguised skepticism.

The girl was named Antoinette. She had no last name; Fitzdraca would do if one was needed. She was dragon-blooded. She would stay with them until she learned to control her abilities. They would treat her as one of the family. Artair had explained those facts briefly, and to say that his tone had brooked no disagreement would have been untrue only in implying that any tone of his had ever allowed for argument about anything. Antoinette was staying. It was a fact, from that moment as unchangeable as the hills around them.

Later Erik had discovered that Toinette had marched up to Artair, told him of her situation, and offered to demonstrate her powers. He and Cathal had speculated about whether she'd *started* by sticking her hand in the hearth fire just to get Artair's attention. It had seemed like the sort of thing she'd do.

Poor relations, especially illegitimate ones, were supposed to conduct themselves with a certain humble gratitude, and while Toinette had never seemed ungrateful, she'd been far from humble. From the first, she'd kept up with the MacAlasdairs, refusing to be left behind or to keep her questions to herself. Erik, fifteen and very conscious of his dignity as a young man, had thought more than once about throwing her into the loch. His own status as a guest had tied his hands, though, and he'd never managed to persuade Cathal to do it, not even when Toinette had won both of their pocket money at dice.

He outdid her in hunting, in both forms, and he was far better with dogs and falcons. Those were his consolations.

Over three years, he'd found out very little about her past. Her father had been a scholar calling himself Antonio. He'd not bothered marrying her mother, which explained some of Artair's interest in her. Since the MacAlasdairs had settled Scotland, if not before, no man of their line had accidentally sired a child on a mortal woman. Toinette's father, by inference, must have been only a generation or two removed from the Old Ones, the true and immortal dragons. Toinette didn't talk about her mother.

She'd grown up in London, not quite a child of the streets but not far from it either. At twelve, on the cusp of womanhood, she'd started changing in more ways than one. She'd managed to make it out to the countryside before her first full transformation, she said, and since Erik had never heard stories of a dragon rampaging in London, he was inclined to believe her.

He'd never heard exactly what rumors she'd followed to find the MacAlasdairs. Toinette didn't talk much about that either.

Not that she'd been silent, by any means. As a girl, Toinette had been full of questions and opinions, songs and stories and challenges. At fourteen, she'd broken her arm trying to outdo the others in flight, and even the quick healing of their blood hadn't spared her a week of miserable boredom. At fifteen, she'd taken to writing bad poetry. Erik and Cathal had found some and read it aloud, and Erik had gotten a water pitcher to the head for his pains.

By the time he'd been eighteen and Toinette sixteen, she'd been tall and willowy, finally graceful in skirts. Her hair had grown. Braided about her head, it had looked to Erik like a flaming halo, though she'd never achieved any kind of sainthood.

He'd more than reconciled himself to her company.

Their fights had continued, but with an undertone that had left him with a spinning head and embarrassing dreams.

Then Artair had sent her away. He'd been kind about it, letting her choose her path. She'd ended up leaving with the traders who'd brought her, with enough money to give her a good start regardless of her sex.

"I could go to a convent, too," she'd said as they'd sat behind the forester's cottage on her last day at Loch Arach, enjoying an adolescent refuge for the final time. "But I couldn't see myself among nuns."

Neither could Erik, but he didn't consider it the better part of chivalry to say so. "I can't see why you have to go in the first place," he said. "To go back on hospitality after so many years—"

Toinette had rolled her eyes. "Don't be a fool if you can help it. You and Cathal are old enough to wed now. Any lord who's thinking you over for his daughter will go sour on the whole idea if Artair has a ward around old enough to warm your beds. He cares more about land and arms than blood, so I'm a hindrance right now. Sensible man."

"Heartless, you mean." Erik said, trying to pretend his face was red from outrage.

"Hearts don't do anyone much good. He's been nicer than I'd a right to expect. Besides"—she shrugged—"it's about time I saw more of the world. But before I go—"

She'd leaned forward, awkwardly since they were both sitting, grasped his shoulders, and pressed her open mouth to his.

Girls hadn't been *rare* in Loch Arach, but Erik had never gotten the nerve to approach one. They were servants, or villagers, and he was a guest at the castle. He'd no wish to risk Artair's wrath. He'd looked, and dreamed, and thought things might be different when he went home.

At the touch of Toinette's lips, his body had lit up with internal flame. He'd kissed her back clumsily but intensely, their tongues sliding against each other, and wound his fingers into the red silk of her hair. He was leaning toward her, trying to figure out how to get closer without falling over on her, when a voice called her name from a short distance away: Agnes, Cathal's older sister.

Instantly they broke apart, and Toinette sprang to her feet. "I'll be there directly!"

Erik—not inclined to stand up just then and unsure he'd be able to any time before sunset—had stared up at her. "What... Why did you do that?"

"I wanted to know," she'd said, "if it'd be better now I'm older. And it was. Thank you."

Then, skirts whirling as she turned, she'd left him to his confusion and lust.

THREE

CREW VANISHED AT EVERY PORT. SOME FOUND NEW SHIPS, SOME tired of life at sea and headed off to seek a farm, and a few met a more final end, whether by tavern fights or spoiled food. Toinette was only thankful to be seeing fewer deaths from the plague.

Erik's mission meant losing more than usual. Men who'd been quite content to sail from France to Muscovy, or London to Spain, heard *mysterious island west of England* and shook their heads. Sailing was dangerous enough on the routes men knew practically by heart. They sailed on respectable merchant ships, not as pirates or explorers. The whole venture sounded foolhardy.

Knowing that very well, Toinette didn't bother trying to convince them. It wouldn't have done any good, and she had a conscience, shriveled and shrunken though it might be. Risking her life and those of willing men was as far as she would go.

Thus she drew more heavily than usual from the taverns. The *Hawk* would sail decently with ten men. Counting herself and Marcus, that left eight. Erik would likely be useful if they met with pirates, but she didn't want to count on him for running up the sail or manning the wheel.

"And you don't *have* to come," she told Marcus as she made her plans, the notion having occurred to her while she slept. "I'll not hold it against you."

He made a *pfah* sound through his beard. "And will I live forever if I stay?"

"I don't know," said Toinette. "Make friends with an alchemist, and you might manage it yet."

"I'll take my chances. If this island *does* exist, I want to see it. If it doesn't... Well, you're a woman of some sense. I'll wager you'll turn back before we run through our supplies."

"That I will," said Toinette. They both knew that the matter wasn't so simple. Storms and calms interfered with a captain's best will, often to the cost of lives.

But Marcus knew that, and he was a grown man. Toinette made certain that the rest of the men she hired knew it too. Five were from her old crew, loyal enough to stay with her no matter how dubious the voyage, or young and adventurous enough to welcome the risk for its own sake.

Of the other three, Roul was a branded poacher, Sence a dark and morose man who spoke little, and Emrich a scarecrow who looked around constantly and sat with his back to the wall at all times. Toinette was doubtful of their company, but they all spoke knowledgeably about their time on ships. If nothing else, they were reasonably young, strong of back, and whole of body.

Taking no chances, she had a shipbuilder come aboard and tour the *Hawk*, keeping an eye out for any gaps in the boards or unsoundness in the wood.

She didn't think of speaking again to Erik. The preparation was hers to handle. She'd taken passengers before. When she was ready, she would send a message to his inn. Until then, she had no time for nostalgia.

"'Ware the barrel, there!" Toinette shouted as Erik approached the *Hawk*.

He sidestepped quickly out of the way as two men

carried an immense tun up to the ship's gangplank. Their fellows were rolling or lifting barrels of a similar size, as well as vast boxes and sacks. The docks near the ship were as busy as an anthill on a sunny day.

Toinette took her sharp eyes off the activity to walk down and meet him. "Rather chafes to know the two of us could have all of this done in an afternoon," she said.

"We could put our shoulders to the wheel even in this form. It'd make your reputation," Erik joked, looking at her. She wore a light-blue gown of thin wool with green and white embroidery, and her hair was pulled simply back into a white net. There was nothing ornate about her, but she looked every inch the well-to-do merchant's widow, and while she was tall and tanned, nobody seeing her would have credited her strength.

Toinette laughed. Her eyes thinned a trifle, though, and there was sharpness in her voice when she first spoke. "I don't doubt it. That's the problem." The mood lifted, or seemed to, and she gave him a freer smile. "Come for inspection?"

"Gawking, you might say. I don't know what *should* be going aboard."

"Biscuits, wine, cheese, salted pork, turnips, and peas, enough for three months." Toinette gave him a flat look. "If we've not found the place when we're six weeks out, we're turning back, and I'll hear no argument on it. Understood?"

"Completely."

"Good." She turned back to look at the ship. "Also fishing nets and lines, soap and brushes for the ship, sailcloth and wood for repairs, which God willing we won't need to make at sea. Medicines."

Erik glanced at the ship. "Do you have a physician?"

"Not as such. I know a few things, and Marcus and I are

both decent with a needle, should it come to that." She gestured to a tall, bearded man in black who stood supervising the loading. "Marcus. He's my second-in-command. You'll treat what he says like it comes from me—and you'll treat what *I* say as law, at least until we hit land."

"Of course," said Erik, affronted. "Do you think I wouldn't?"

"I don't think you'd be a fool about it," Toinette said, and her expression added *unlike most men*, "but if aught goes amiss, there'll likely be no time for debate. I know the *Hawk* better than you do, and unless you'll truly surprise me with your recent history, I know the sea better than you do."

Erik nodded assent. "I helped my cousins on my mother's side build a *drekkar*—one of their ships—once, but it was only fit for a few boys to row about in and pretend. Other than that, I've only been a passenger, and that rarely."

"We'll not hold it against you," she said with another grin. "You're a well-paying passenger, and it's an interesting journey you've got for us."

"Is that why you agreed?"

In his own voice, he heard the echo of his eighteen-year-old self asking *why*. If Toinette thought of the kiss, she didn't show it, but her smile was that of the brash, sharp girl she'd been. "I agreed because you offered me money," she replied, "but I'll say it's a more exciting job than I've had in a few dozen years. And you're a better employer."

"True," said a lanky and dark-haired young man coming off the gangplank.

"You've never met the man before in your life, Gervase," Toinette said, shaking her head at him.

"No, but he's not having us ship goats anywhere, nor swine, and that's a high virtue already." Gervase's words sounded of Paris. He'd a gold earring in one ear and a non-chalant look. "Sir, I'm most sincerely at your service."

"Even if I'm taking you into uncharted waters?"

"Ah, but I know in my heart that the captain will bring us back safe. And if my heart's wrong, my nose rejoices still that I'll have only a dozen men in high summer to endure."

"We're all likely to be bad enough, by the end," Toinette warned him and Erik both. "Water's for drinking, not bathing, unless you fancy a dip in the ocean, and quarters are close."

Erik shrugged. "I've been on battlefields. It can't be worse." He remembered the stench of blood and offal at midday and grimaced. "We'll have the sea around us. That can only help, aye?"

"That's the spirit," Gervase chimed in. "And men, unlike beasts, clean up after themselves."

"They do on the *Hawk*. That reminds me: if Marcus hasn't yet given the new hands the word about drunkenness, see that he does. And—" Toinette turned back to Erik as Gervase bowed and ran off. "How's your stomach for the ocean?"

"Decent, or I'd not be doing this." That wasn't entirely true. Loyalty and the force of Artair's command could probably have gotten Erik onto a ship even if he knew he'd keep nothing down for a month. As fortune had it, he was a fair sailor, but Artair hadn't bothered asking.

Toinette's thin lips quirked up at the right corner. A suspicious man might have thought she knew damned well what Erik wasn't saying. "Good. Buy ginger, in case. The sea's rougher where we'll be going. And I'll tell you the same as Marcus will tell the men: if you disgrace yourself, whether from motion or drink, you'll be cleaning it up. I don't have the hands to spare."

"Quite a tone to take with a customer," he said.

"You hired a ship, my lord, and sailors." The title wasn't *quite* sarcastic. "If you want a nursemaid, you'll have to find one separate."

Erik made a slight bow. "In truth, Captain, I can't imagine you nursing anyone."

"Nor can I. Oh, and if you fight with the men or otherwise get in the way of our tasks, I'll have you in chains until the journey's end."

"And what…" Erik took a step toward her, so that Toinette had to tilt her head back a little to meet his eyes. Although it hadn't been his intent, the gesture made him notice the slender length of her neck and the shadowed hollows behind her ears. He smiled. "What would you do with me then?"

"You couldn't break free of irons in human form." Mindful of the crowd, Toinette spoke softly. The words hit Erik's ears in small puffs of air. "And even a dragon couldn't fly all the way to your destination. I'd assume you'd be reasonable."

"I could be *very* reasonable," he said, his voice low and his body tightening both at her presence and at the images in his mind. "I'd hate to disappoint you, Captain."

She flashed him another grin, even as she stepped back. "Then I trust you'll behave. I've a ship to run, after all, and a duty to my men."

FOUR

THEY CAST OFF ON A CLEAR DAWN, WITH THE SUN RISING GOLD in the west and the sea stretching out clear and shining before the *Hawk*'s prow. As many times as Toinette had made the slow journey out of Bordeaux harbor, as many more times as she'd left other ports, she never ceased to feel a thrill in those first moments. She could pretend to forget the danger and boredom that were both nearly certain to lie ahead. For a little while, the world was new and she could go anywhere.

"A fair wind," she said to Marcus, watching the sail snap briskly above them, "and a good tide."

"Yes, for so long as it lasts."

"Your constant cheer is one of the things I cherish most about you."

"I'm surprised. You have such a wide assortment to choose from."

"I try to vary my preferences from time to time. Keeps things fresh." She leaned on the railing and sighed with contentment. "How are the new hands?"

"Shaping up. The rest of the men have a wager on about what Emrich's fleeing. I only pray he settles once we get further from land," Marcus said, shaking his head with the air of an exasperated tutor.

"What are the current favorites?"

"Theft's well ahead, though none's so sure as to specify what. Next is that he's a serf who's run from his lord. Murder's half and half. Longest odds against an angry father or a jealous husband, given his looks."

Toinette laughed, finding double pleasure from the way the open air caught the sound and sent it back to her ears. "Oh, have they not heard? You never can tell with women. And he might've been quite comely back when he ate more."

"How generous of you," said Marcus. "How fares our passenger?"

"Asleep, or so he declared his intentions when he came aboard. As I've not seen a hair of him since we cast off, I can only guess he slumbers like a babe." She shook her head.

"The privilege of rank, or at least of wealth."

"Aye," said Toinette, leaning against the rail. The deck rose and fell steadily beneath her feet, a gentle rocking motion that could easily have eased her into sleep herself, no matter how hard the berth. "He's welcome to such luxuries."

"For now," Marcus said, giving her a knowing look.

"Everything is for now, isn't it?"

Marcus snorted. "I've no objection to you turning philosopher on us, Captain, as long as you don't abandon the ship for a convent before we get paid, but in this case I think we can both see the future without the help of any stars."

"You could go to bed yourself," Toinette suggested, falling into a pattern the two of them had danced many times. "I can keep order, whether you believe it or no."

"I'll have to eventually." Marcus turned to look behind them, where buildings were becoming indistinct and hills were rapidly receding. "But I've a mind to enjoy what might be my last sight of land."

"Before what, this time?"

"'Eaten by serpents' is the favorite," said Marcus, speaking not only for himself, as Toinette knew, but for prevailing opinion among the men.

"Well," said Erik from behind them, "I'd be inclined to pity the serpents in that case."

The years had taught Erik to get up at dawn when the need arose, but they'd never taught him to like it. He'd come onto the *Hawk*, found his quarters, and stretched out. The pallet and blankets in the corner of the hold were no bed, not even such a one as he'd had at bad inns, but he'd had worse in war and managed.

For that matter, he remembered his last voyage, seventy-five years before. That ship had been older, without the shelter of a sealed deck and a separate hold. The men, Erik included, had slept in what little shelter the sides of the ship could provide, with hard planks beneath them and leather bags lined with fur for warmth. From what he'd seen as he picked his way back to his not-too-private quarters, the crew had the same bags and little cushioning beneath, but not being at the mercy of the rain and the waves was a pleasant change.

Waking, he'd come up to the deck to discover that he'd not slept very long. The sun was still low in the sky, but they were well on their way, perhaps three hours into the journey. He'd spotted Toinette leaning on the forward rail and gone to join the conversation.

The looks of shock he got from both her and Marcus were not surprising, though not particularly flattering either. He'd met Marcus briefly the night before, and the man had struck him as experienced enough to be jaded about the habits of the wealthy. Toinette's cynicism he knew very well.

"I don't *think* that was an insult," she said, turning to face him. "Or I choose not to take it as one."

Marcus chuckled. "I like the idea of not being a pleasant meal. Suggests we'd fight too hard, even from the inside."

"You take my meaning well then, sir," said Erik, with a small bow.

That had indeed been part of what he'd meant. The other part was a joke between him and Toinette, one which would have betrayed their other shapes to explain. From her slight, skeptical smile, he thought she'd heard it.

"The captain was just saying I'm a man inclined to look on the bright side," said Marcus solemnly. "Even going to the ends of the earth."

"Not quite so far as that, I believe — and hope."

"If I see an edge, we're turning around," said Toinette, shaking her head. She was facing into the wind now, but it didn't budge a strand of her bright hair, tightly coiled as it was into its net. It did ruffle the crimson folds of her gown, showing her slim curves more clearly.

Erik allowed himself a moment of indulgence before returning his gaze to her face and laughing. "Nonsense. You've read Aquinas. I know, as I was there when you had to recite."

"How did she manage that?" Marcus asked with enough interest to make Toinette glare in his direction.

"Badly. I'm surprised she's gotten the use of her hand back."

"Remind me to have you both thrown overboard when I can spare the men." Toinette made a pretense of turning back to the rail, only to reverse course and add, "And my Latin wasn't half so bad as your figuring."

"A very cogent argument."

"Hmph." She looked at Marcus, who was standing in silent but obvious amusement. "Don't you have supplies to check, or men to flog?"

"Or sharks to be eaten by? I take your point, though I don't know how you'll send *him* away."

"I can't," said Toinette, mock-groaning. "He's paying."

"How long has he been with you?" Erik asked as Marcus strode away over the deck.

Toinette hesitated a moment, searching his voice for prying or possessiveness, the sort of quality that would demand a sharp answer. She heard none, only a friendly question. It was a pleasant surprise from a man. "With me alone, these ten years. He sailed with my husband for five years before he died."

"And he thinks you're…"

"An adventurous young woman who married an older man. Hardly a creature of myth. He also doesn't ask inconvenient questions."

"A good quality in a companion."

"That it is." Toinette clasped her hands at the small of her back, lacing her fingers together, and stretched. The surrendering crack of her spine felt good. So did Erik's eyes on her outthrust breasts.

She'd never been able to be very dishonest with herself. As a boy, Erik had been handsome in a gawky kind of way. He'd grown into himself in the last century, into a long nose and a square jaw, arms that rippled with muscle and thighs that filled his hose nicely. Jaded as Toinette was, she couldn't stand near him and not feel desire ripple through her.

After Jehan's death, she'd never taken lovers on board the *Hawk*, be they crew or customer. Men were too unpredictable, too apt to resent each other's access to any woman's bed or to think that their presence there gave them authority. Erik was *possibly* less dangerous in the second case, but the crew were no less prone to the first.

"What sort of birds are those?" Erik asked, sensing and then breaking the silence before it could become too awkward.

Toinette looked up and out. She spotted white wings, black heads, and a profile she knew well. "Terns. They'll follow us for a little while, but they don't go very far from land. Once we get further out into the ocean, we might see porpoises."

"Do you catch them?"

"No. The men think it's bad luck. For all I know, they might be right. No sense tempting fate on a voyage like this, is there?"

"Not in the least." Erik grinned. "I've a fair idea of how daft the whole venture makes me sound."

Toinette glanced back from the water to meet his eyes. "Do you think it's daft?"

"I don't know," he said. "Artair doesn't, and it's seldom that he's far wrong."

"I'll take that as a compliment too."

"You're very quick to seize those."

Toinette shrugged. "I've an eye for a good thing, and I'll take what I can get." She turned back to the waves, watching them rise and fall. White foam broke around the *Hawk*'s prow, and the boat rocked steadily onward. She could feel the wind as if she were the sail herself.

"Almost as good as flying, in its way," said Erik.

"Oh," Toinette laughed, "better to my mind. Much of the time, anyway."

"Truly?" Perhaps remembering how quickly she'd taken to the air at Loch Arach, Erik sounded completely surprised.

"Mm hmm." Toinette turned around again, facing into the wind and taking a deep, salt-scented breath. "Flying, you're above everything. You see it from a distance. It's you and the stars and the clouds. The birds if you're staying low enough. Don't mistake me, there's a glorious sort of freedom in all of that."

"But…"

"But on the sea, you're a part of things. You smell the air, you see the way the water changes from place to place, the difference in what you catch for dinner or the whales in the distance. You get to know the ship too." She smiled. "I wager I could tell the *Hawk* beneath my feet even if I were blind. It's a place to come back to, a thing you make and maintain—and I'd say *that's* the mark of souled creatures, though I'm no priest. Craft."

"Earth and water, not air," Erik said thoughtfully.

"And not fire, God willing. Rather the opposite of your line."

"Yours too—or rather your blood," he amended the statement quickly.

"Ah, well, perhaps it's the mortal in me. Drawn to what will outlast short-lived men and so forth." Toinette waved a hand in the air.

"That could be on both counts," said Erik, looking out to the water. The wind played with his golden hair. He had less to disturb than Toinette did, yet it still ruffled in the breeze, and strands clung to his neck. "The Norsemen carve dragons' heads on their boats, you know."

"They might just want to frighten their enemies."

"We are often things to be feared," Erik agreed, and his smile was devilish.

Toinette returned it. "Some of us more than others," she said, "and perhaps for different reasons. Depending on who it is we're frightening, of course."

For just a moment, before she went to check on Marcus, she let Erik see the veiled challenge in her eyes.

It would be a long voyage. With no privacy, there was also no danger that either of them would get carried away. And few people were more qualified than Toinette to play with fire.

ABOUT THE AUTHOR

Isabel Cooper lives in Boston in an apartment with two houseplants, a silver sword, and a basket of sequined fruit. By day, she works as a theoretically mild-mannered legal editor; by night, she tries to sleep. She has a house in the country, but hopes she doesn't encounter mysterious and handsome strangers nearby, as vacation generally involves a lot of fuzzy bathrobes.

ALSO BY ISABEL COOPER

Dark Powers
No Proper Lady
Lessons After Dark

Highland Dragons
Legend of the Highland Dragon
The Highland Dragon's Lady
Night of the Highland Dragon

Dawn of the Highland Dragon
Highland Dragon Warrior
Highland Dragon Rebel

21982031733821